The Other Side of Forever

"...but whatever came, she had resolved never again to belong to another than herself."

—**Kate Chopin,** ***The Awakening***

Also by Norah Pritchard

The Northfield Series

The Other Side of Forever

Maybe Someday With You

If You Were Mine - Coming Soon

Be Your Everything - Coming Soon

Cookbook

Dinnertime: Fast and Fresh Family Meals for Every Night of the Week

The Other Side of Forever

A Northfield Novel

Norah Pritchard

W L
Willowcrest Lane

For my mom, Linda Scalzo, who shared her love of reading and writing, and encouraged her daughters to read books voraciously, especially the banned ones.

And for my husband, Tom, my forever happily ever after.

Chapter One

*T*OTALLY FAKING IT.

That was the first thought, however inappropriate, that flashed through Allie Hart's mind when she walked into the bedroom and found her husband with his pants around his knees, banging their neighbor silly.

But think it she did, as she observed the truly impressive writhing and moaning. As the one who had been married to Corbin for the last eight years, she had done her fair share of pretending in bed, and she knew the tells of someone faking it.

As this pretty woman would soon find out, Corbin was always out for number one, in life, in business, and, tragically, in orgasms.

She leaned against the doorframe and took in the scene, strangely dispassionate for someone catching their husband with his pants down. Literally.

Corbin's white thighs quivered behind the woman, whose long blond hair hung in her face, but Allie knew who it was right away. Dahlia had been babysitting for them for at least a year. Sammy said she was the best cuddler ever. Apparently, his daddy agreed.

"Honey, I'm home."

"Jesus Christ!"

Like cockroaches, they scattered. Corbin grabbed for his pants first, and Dahlia pulled a sheet over her cuddly self. "Ohmygod, Allie," she whimpered. "I'm so sorry."

"Hi, Dahlia," Allie said kindly.

After all, she could afford to be magnanimous now. She had taken a decision Allie had wrestled with for far too long entirely out of her hands. After eight years of marriage, Allie had learned she could forgive almost anything of her husband if it meant keeping their family together. Apparently, infidelity was a hard limit.

While Corbin and Dahlia scrambled to get dressed, Allie mentally inspected her heart as if it were a bruise she was poking around for any twinges of pain. To her relief, none of those emotions surfaced. Just a bone-deep tiredness. If she prodded harder, maybe she felt even a little bit of relief.

She scanned Corbin's bedroom, noting the cold, modern pieces of furniture. Metal and iron, black and gray. Sharp, steel pieces that masqueraded as art yet looked like weapons. None of it was hers. Her bedroom was down the hall next to Sammy's. She had begun sleeping there over a year ago when things started to fall apart between them.

Her room and Sammy's were the only spaces filled with color in the apartment. The throw pillows and plants, heaps of books, and Sammy's toys formed their sanctuary in a place that otherwise felt foreign.

Allie turned to leave.

"Dammit, Allie. *Fuck! Wait!* Can you give me a minute?" Corbin was hopping around on one foot, still struggling with his pant leg. She took a second to notice uncharitably how awkward he looked. It was a rarity for him. Her husband was an attractive man if you liked that removed, sophisticated vibe.

She didn't anymore.

Corbin had the look of wealth and leisure about him. He was aging well, and his various memberships at clubs kept him in good shape. Soft, elegant hands, subtly highlighted hair, although he would never admit it, and perfectly hydrated skin that only monthly facials could achieve.

Once upon a time, Allie had found him wildly attractive. He was somewhat of a fairy tale come true; a rich young prince courting the naive, wide-eyed girl from the wrong side of the tracks, whisking her off to his penthouse in the city. Unlike Prince Charming, however, Corbin wasn't committed to the happily ever after part.

Dahlia probably thought she was lucky to have his attention. *Good luck with that.*

"Take all the time you need," she said, twisting the heavy diamond and platinum wedding ring off her finger. She set it down gently on the dresser. "I'm leaving."

Welcome to Northfield Village
"Where Life is Worth Living"
Mayor Theodore Clairmont

FOUR MONTHS LATER...

Allie Hart was raised by a family of strong females with strong opinions and even stronger superstitions.

Her three aunts, her mother's sisters, were almost as close to her as her mother. That would have been a lot of female perspectives to begin with, but add in her three sisters, a host of female cousins and second cousins, and the Hart family had a distinct matriarchal bent.

Her eyes caught on her son's ruffled, honey-colored hair

asleep in the back seat. Her own son, Sammy, was the exception.

As the only boy in a family of women, he was understandably doted on. The little prince. Their darling boy. He had only to ask, and the Hart women were all too happy to give. Allie might have worried he would be spoiled, but Sammy was an old soul. In his seven short years, he had been dealt hardships that earned him an uncommon empathy, making him all the more lovable.

The Hart women were somewhat notorious in the tiny upstate New York town where they lived. Since there were so many of them, you didn't have to look far to find one. Aunt Rosa owned a floral shop on Main Street. Aunt Giulia worked at the local bank, and Aunt Sophia was on the school board of the Northfield School District. Allie's mother, Annette, owned a successful interior design studio in the village.

The Hart women were known for being professional. Dedicated. Driven. And unlucky in love.

Some said it was a curse. Others were more pragmatic and attributed it to a rash of bad luck that had simply lasted for generations. With bad breakups, cheating spouses, early death (God rest Uncle Pete's soul), or just plain abandonment like Allie's dad, each of the women had had their happily-ever-after cut short.

This made it particularly hard for Allie to roll back into her hometown eight years after she had left, with divorce papers stuffed in a moving box in the trunk.

So much for breaking the curse.

Allie didn't really believe they were cursed. She was a firm believer people created their destinies. Corbin had always told her she was too naive, but she didn't care. She preferred to look at the bright side of life.

She pulled up to the single stoplight on Main Street and looked around. Northfield Village, on the banks of the Erie Canal, was only a six-hour drive from Corbin's apartment in New York City, but she hadn't been back to visit very often after she moved. Not much had changed.

Main Street was still charming and nostalgic with the lampposts and red-brick buildings. It felt like old Mayberry if you didn't notice the modern luxury cars parked along the street. The carefully preserved old-world feel of the village made it a mecca for the most wealthy and affluent.

As she waited for the light to change, she spied a group of women in expensive spandex sitting around an umbrella-covered table outside of a yoga studio. Their yoga mats were slung on the back of their chairs, bobbing like pastel buoys in the water while they drank a small fortune in masticated vegetables.

Northfield had always felt like another planet to her.

She drove past the clock tower and the village green where the annual fall Harvest Festival and Holiday Candlelight Night were held. The businesses and shops thinned out, giving way to the surrounding neighborhoods. She passed a mix of historic Victorian and Craftsman homes with immaculately landscaped lawns.

The Hart girls hadn't started off on this side of the canal.

Even back then, she had known there were two sides to Northfield. An old familiar chill sprang up in her chest, taking her by surprise. It had been long since she felt that way, thanks to Corbin scrubbing away every vestige of her "government-subsidized upbringing," as he called it. She shrugged it off and pulled into a driveway a few streets away from the village, wincing when the low-slung Mercedes bottomed out with a noisy scrape.

She had argued with Corbin about getting the car, especially living in a city where they rarely drove. It was much too small for a car seat. Impractical. Ostentatious. She had said as much when Corbin insisted on purchasing it, but like most things in her marriage, it hadn't been about what she wanted. Corbin liked the image it gave them.

She couldn't wait to get rid of it.

"Come on, honey bear. Time to wake up." Allie leaned into the backseat and stroked the back of her fingers over Sammy's cheek.

This kid. He was so adorable with his freckled nose. He never sat still long, so full of mischief and energy. She admired him for a minute before reaching in and disentangling him from the seatbelt straps. Careful not to dislodge the pump attached to his side, Allie helped him out and leaned him against her, bumping the door closed with her hip. She turned around to look at their new house.

It was even cuter in person. The cozy cedar-shingled house had been painted white, making it glow slightly in the lavender evening sky. It was just light enough to see the wide front steps leading up to the covered porch. Already she pictured ferns hanging from the porch ceiling. Was that a porch swing? Adorable. Oh, yes, she would be putting that to good use.

In the four months since Allie had walked in on Corbin and Dahlia, her sister and mom had stepped up in a big way to help smooth their move back home. Amber found them this house they were renting from a friend of hers. It was in the end stages of a remodel, but the owner was a friend and had agreed to let them move in early. Eventually, Allie would purchase a house in Northfield, but she was in no hurry. If anything, her marriage had taught her not to settle.

Thankfully, Corbin hadn't contested the divorce. He had even been more than generous with the settlement. Probably more to do with his guilt than anything else.

"We're home." She bent down to kiss Sammy's forehead. He smelled warm and sweet, a little bit sweaty, and all boy. "Let's go see our new house."

In the way only little kids could summon, his body went from deep sleep to a wriggly, excited boy in the space of a few seconds. "Whoa! Let's go in!"

"Okay, okay, hold on!" She laughed, catching his hand and leading him around a big silver truck with a ladder in the back. One of the contractors must be working late. "It's all ours, bud. Look at that big yard!"

"For our dog!" He shrieked in excitement.

She stopped. "Ah, no, I was thinking more about playing catch and camping," she hedged.

Sammy's biggest wish since he was old enough to request presents from Santa was for a dog of his own. Corbin had not been the dog type, but maybe she could swing a pet now that they were on their own.

The front door was propped open with a small wedge of wood. She pushed the door open further and gave a little knock.

"Hello?" Her voice echoed in the empty entryway.

The smell of fresh paint and turpentine stung her nose as soon as she stepped over the threshold. Blue painter's tape still edged the trim in the foyer and up the stairs to the right of the door. The sound of a classic rock song admiring big-bottomed girls drifted down from one of the rooms upstairs. Quickly, she glanced through the other three rooms that went straight to the back of the house. The living room, dining room, and kitchen were four neat squares visible from the entryway.

Bright and open and smelling of fresh paint and fresh starts.

"Come on, Mama! I want to see my room!" Sammy's excited voice was already halfway up the stairs.

She followed him up the wooden stairs and paused at the top to glance at the three new, unstained doors off the landing.

Two of the doors in the hall were closed, and the third was a bathroom with a charming round captain's window. The door at the end of the landing was partially open, letting the sound of the radio float into the rest of the house.

"Is this one mine?" Sammy tugged her into the room with the open door. The room was small but bright and airy. A sloped ceiling and three tall windows on the back wall framed a queen-sized bed. A soft grunt came from behind her, and she jumped.

Allie paused for a minute at the sight before her. The closet's double doors were open with a ladder set inside. Two long, powerful-looking jean-clad legs stood facing her on the ladder's bottom rung. A man's head and torso were hidden inside the closet, his arms raised and busy working on something in the ceiling.

Her gaze drifted up and caught for a long minute. A leather toolbelt hung low from narrow hips, tugging down his waistband and revealing that intriguing V-shape between a man's hip bones. The man's navy-blue t-shirt lifted as his arms moved above his head. Each rise and fall danced the bottom edge of his shirt up to reveal a strip of his taut, tanned abdomen. A drill whirred in the closet and, moving closer, she heard him whistling softly along with the music.

"Hey, who's that?" Sammy tugged away from her before she could stop him and ran to the closet. A coil of electric wire on the ground next to the ladder tangled up his legs and he tripped, grabbing the ladder as he went down. The ladder jerked and a loud crack sounded as the man startled, lost his balance, and teetered on the rung. On its heels came a roar from one loud, angry man.

"What the —! "A dark-haired head emerged from the top of the closet with an angry jerk, his hand covering his forehead.

The drill bounced hard and broke against the hardwood floor. Allie jerked Sammy away before it hit him and looked up.

Dark eyes. Square jaw. Broad shoulders.

One pissed-off man looked right at her.

Chapter Two

SHIT. Davis Henderson's head throbbed enough to make his vision blurry around the edges, and his best drill was now in pieces. Automatically, he bent down to collect them and looked up, his temper flaring along with the pain in his head.

"Goddammit!" he roared, rubbing his head where he knew soon would be a lump.

"Hey, don't yell at my mama!" *Oof.* A small body slammed into him, and he fell back to the floor while dodging the kid's flailing fists.

"Sammy! Stop! Stop! It's okay." The woman grabbed the boy around the waist and pulled him back. Davis shook his head slightly and caught the boy's fists in his hand. Dammit. The kid was little, but he had good aim.

He put his hand on the boy's head and held him at arm's length. "Hey, it's okay. Your mom is fine," he said gruffly.

The woman nudged the boy behind her. "Sorry we startled you. I called out, but you must not have heard me."

The kid was still behind her, but one eye peeked at him suspiciously from beside her hip. Davis sized him up against Ben, his seven-year-old. Sammy must be around the same age, although he was smaller than Ben. Some of his irritation melted away.

Some, but not all. Didn't this woman know someone could get hurt barging in like that?

"Good job taking care of your mom, kid." He rubbed his head and came away with a smear of blood. "You've got some tackle there."

"Yup. I'm real strong." The boy poked out his arm and pointed it at Davis. "See? Feel that."

Davis pinched the miniature bicep dutifully. "Massive."

The kid nodded and took another step out from behind the woman. "I'm the man of the house now." He puffed up his chest proudly. "I can stay up later, and we're getting a dog, and I'm going into second grade!"

The woman put her hands on her hips. "Sammy, I didn't say we were getting a puppy." She sounded exasperated. She turned back to Davis with a friendly smile. "You must be the contractor. I'm Allie Hart. We're renting this place."

As he rose, Davis took in her appearance. She was a bright little thing with her summer-yellow sundress and honey-colored hair. *Sunshine.* His eyes widened slightly at her rather magnificent chest visible above the dress's deep neckline. He trailed his gaze up to her hair, pulled back into a messy bun on top of her head. His perusal stopped at her face where twinkling hazel eyes met his.

"Owner," he corrected, probably more curtly than necessary. "I'm Davis Henderson. You must be Amber's sister?"

"Did you get that from the cup size?" she asked with a hint of teasing in her voice.

He scowled. He couldn't help it. It was his default expression, but he did try to ease his face a little when he felt the kid's eyes on him. His kids were always telling him to smile more.

"Sorry, I'm just teasing," she said. "Anyway, we were

supposed to move in tomorrow, but we got here a little early, as you can see." She looked around the room where they stood. "The place looks great." Her gaze returned to Davis. "I saw the porch swing and knew it would be perfect for us. Worth the drive, huh, Sammy?" She asked her son, with her hand on the boy's shoulder.

"Yeah, it's awesome," Sammy said happily, then yawned big enough that Davis could see his back teeth. "Do we have beds?"

Allie dropped a quick kiss on the boy's hair. "We'll share mine until the rest of our stuff is delivered. Bedtime can't come soon enough," she said with her own yawn.

Davis realized they were both drooping with exhaustion. He had no idea how far they'd come, but clearly it was time to clear out and let his tenants have the place.

"I'm done here for the night," he said, loading his tools into the toolbox. "I'll clean up and meet you in the living room to give you the keys."

"Okay, thank you," she said, pausing as if to say more, but Davis turned his back, methodically coiling excess wire onto the roll while listening to their footsteps go down the stairs.

So that was Amber's sister. Davis could see the physical resemblance. The Hart sisters were knockouts. He had heard there were four of them, but he had only met Amber, and now Allie. Both women were on the petite side, with the same honey hair, and were not hard on the eyes. At all.

Davis had met Amber at the Northfield Pub where she worked weekends. She was loud and fun, a damn good bartender, and a pool shark. He had lost some money to that woman. Amber was attractive as hell and a flirt to boot, but she was way too young for Davis to take seriously. That didn't stop most of the younger men on his work crew from trying to score a date week after week. Davis knew better. He had a sister, Layne, around that age. He was thirty-seven years old, for

Christ's sake. If he should forget, his own two kids made sure to remind him regularly just how ancient he was.

Thinking about Ben and his older daughter, Claire, Davis checked his watch. He needed to get home soon. It was Friday night after a long week. His sister was with the kids tonight while he had worked late to get the wiring finished.

When Amber had asked, or more like begged, Davis to rent this house to her sister and nephew, she made it clear they would be fine with a little dust and paint around while he finished the renovations.

When he agreed, Amber batted her eyes, thanked him profusely, and told him to come by the Pub for free drinks whenever he wanted. That wouldn't be necessary. With his own two young kids, he spent most of his nights at home, and he liked it that way just fine.

Davis knew he had a reputation as a grumpy asshole, but he couldn't find it in himself to care. If it wasn't his family or close friends, he didn't allow himself to care about most things. It was safer that way.

Finally, Davis set the wire in the toolbox and stretched mightily to work out the kink in his back. He felt every one of his years in the protesting muscles and joints. He had put in extra-long hours this week to make sure the rental was livable for the new tenants, even if it wasn't finished.

Now, he had a cut on his head, a nasty headache, and he was hot and tired. He couldn't get out of there fast enough.

Sammy and Allie were sitting on the only piece of furniture in the room when he came downstairs, a big, comfortable couch that had been delivered earlier. The woman's head was bent over a backpack as she rummaged around inside.

"Are you hungry, Sammy? How about some peanut butter crackers?" Allie bent over the couch to ruffle the boy's hair.

Davis snuck another quick glimpse of tanned legs and round hips before he looked away. He wasn't dead. He couldn't help but notice the Hart sisters shared not only angel faces, but also the generous curves over which lesser men might have done stupid things. A spark of attraction lit up his body, taking him by surprise. He pushed it down ruthlessly.

Allie looked up and met his eyes. "I have to grab your checker from the car, buddy," she murmured and moved toward the front door. "I'll be right back."

Davis checked his watch impatiently. *Just give her the paperwork and get the hell out.*

He turned back to the living room window and took in the sleek car parked next to his work truck. Not really what he would have expected her to drive, but expensive foreign cars were the norm in Northfield. He didn't pay much attention to that kind of thing. What drew him to Northfield hadn't been the affluence. It was the community. Small towns had a way of supporting their own. He hadn't known it when he moved here, but he would need that desperately one day.

The kid still sat on the couch and stared at Davis solemnly. His eyes were the same shade of hazel as his mom's. His hair tufted up on the side of his head, and he had a crease on his cheek as if he had just woken up.

What was their story? Where was his dad?

Ah, hell. A rogue protective instinct took Davis by surprise, and he cursed silently. He'd hang out a minute just to make sure they were okay, then he was leaving.

"Hey, kid. I'm Davis." He held out his hand. "What's your name?"

"Not 'posed to talk to strangers."

"Guess we're not strangers anymore, now that your mom introduced us," he said mildly.

The boy's nose crinkled as he thought about that. "'K," he said and looked at Davis's hand blankly.

"Like this." Davis wrapped his fingers around the boy's small hand and gave it a firm squeeze as he shook it up and down the way he had taught Ben. The way his father had taught him. He could still hear his father's voice telling him a man's handshake said a lot about him. "Nice to meet you."

The kid grinned and gave Davis's hand a pump. "Nice to meetcha. I'm Sammy." He looked around at the bare room with interest. "It's nice here."

"Glad you think so. Been working real hard on fixing it up for you and your mom." Davis walked around the room to check the molding and trim he had finished last week. His construction company handled building projects at all stages, but renovating old homes was his favorite type of project.

The old Craftsman had been in sore need of updating when he had bought it to flip, but it had potential. Besides, it didn't get much better than Northfield for prime residential real estate. The cookie-cutter houses going up now in suburban tracts weren't made like houses used to be. He loved the character of these older homes. They had a story in them that took some patience to get to, but he was good at that.

Sammy scratched idly at a scab on his knee. "My mom said I can get a dog. Maybe."

"Yeah? I have a dog. His name is Walter. I left him home today, but he's usually with me when I work."

Sammy perked up. "I love dogs. I love dinosaurs, too. I brought my whole collection. Did ya know there's a lot of lakes around here? They're called fingers." He paused and crinkled his nose. "So weird. We're going to camp out at one. Maybe. My mom's scared of bears."

"Yup," Davis said easily. "They're called the Finger Lakes. I like to camp at some of them, too." He tossed a tape measure on the couch next to the kid. "You know how to use that thing? I could use some help measuring this trim."

Sammy's eyes went wide. He bounded off the couch, tripping over his feet. "Yep. I mean, nope, but I want to."

Davis showed him how to open it and measure the windowsill. Sammy leaned his head over, completely obscuring the view from Davis. He smiled and shifted the boy slightly to the side.

"Here, like this." He pulled the tape out and handed it to him. "Hold this here against the trim to measure." Sammy's lower lip jutted out as he held the tape up to the window. Davis took out his notebook and jotted down some measurements that he'd have to go back and remeasure later.

"Dinosaurs, huh?" he asked absently, eyeing the awkward way the kid was trying to pull out the tape measure when Allie walked into the room shouldering an oversize duffle bag.

"Mama, Mr. Henderson let me help him measure! And he has a dog named Walter, and he likes to camp." Sammy's eyes widened as the thought occurred to him. "Hey, maybe we can camp together."

Allie laughed lightly and patted the couch. "Come on over here. Let's check your blood sugar."

A rising unease settled in Davis's gut as she took a small, zippered pouch out of the duffle and took out what looked like a pager. She tore open an alcohol pad, rubbed it over the boy's middle finger with a practiced movement, and pricked Sammy's finger with the device.

Ben hated needles. Davis would have had to hold him down to get him to willingly be poked. Sammy looked more interested in the tape measure he still held in his hand.

"Little pinch," she said with her head bent over the boy's

hand. They both sat there quietly until a drop of blood welled on his finger. Quickly snagging the drop on the narrow tab of paper in the device, Allie read a number on the machine and handed over a tissue for Sammy to hold on his finger. "Your blood sugar is low. How do you feel? Are you feeling shaky?"

"Nope." Sammy kicked his feet and snapped the measuring tape.

"Let's get you some juice." She dipped back into the backpack and came out with an apple juice box. "Drink this, Sammy, all of it. I'm going to talk to Mr. Henderson in the kitchen while I get you a snack. Do you want to play with your cars?"

The slurp of the straw cracked like a whip through the quiet room and the boy let out a startled laugh. It was a typical gross boy noise that Ben would have found funny, too. Allie's laugh joined in, and her eyes met Davis's over the boy's head.

The tiredness on her face melted away and her eyes lit up, softening her expression. Her pink smiling mouth shot a bolt of lust straight through Davis. Abruptly, he turned towards the kitchen.

Time to get out of here.

Chapter Three

"Do you need help unpacking your car?"

Allie turned around to see Davis in the arched doorway that separated the kitchen from the living room. He took up space the way men do, casually and unapologetically, which made her feel strangely unsettled.

Everything about him made her feel that way. He was as big as a house, first of all. His wide shoulders strained the T-shirt he had on. Her gaze caught on his biceps crossed over his broad chest and lingered on the trail of a tattoo that peeked out from beneath his shirt. He crossed one booted foot over the other and leaned his shoulder against the kitchen doorway while she gave in and studied him from under her lashes.

"We're okay. Amber's coming over tomorrow to help, and the movers will be here sometime this weekend with the rest of our stuff."

He was handsome. Not the sophisticated, suited-up, perfectly dressed, white-collar kind of handsome she was used to. Davis Henderson had the rugged look of a man who made a living with his hands. He looked like he could split a cord of wood or build the whole damn house they were standing in, by himself.

From the top of his dark, tousled hair, speared with finger tracks where he had raked it back, to his brawny arms and chest, down to his long legs covered in ancient denim, his masculinity was hard to ignore. His unsmiling eyes met hers when she made her way back up his body, studying her with just as much frank interest.

A long-forgotten warmth unfurled in her body, and she recognized the pull of attraction. Since when did men in tool belts inspire that reaction? She needed to get a handle on this pronto. The last thing she needed was the hots for her grumpy landlord. The cut on his head caught her eye. Medical stuff she knew how to handle. She went to the table and dug around in her purse for her first aid kit. "Come here."

He raised an eyebrow. "Excuse me?"

"The cut on your head." She waved at his head while still rummaging. "I'm a nurse. I'll fix you up."

Davis didn't move.

"Just come sit down for a second," she said, exasperated. Honestly, men could be such babies sometimes. "You're bleeding, and it's going to drip on the floor."

A slight exaggeration, but Davis sat down stiffly.

"Hold this." She handed him a superhero bandage and bent close to look at his forehead. She was close enough to smell the good old-fashioned manly soap he used, the cheap green kind Corbin wouldn't have touched with a ten-foot pole. She inhaled surreptitiously. It made her stomach do weird, fluttery things. "It's not a deep cut, but you have a bump already starting under it."

She tore open an antiseptic wipe and dabbed gently. They were close enough that she could feel the heat from his body, but it didn't feel strange. She was comfortable taking care of people. From the tense set of Davis's body, however, he wasn't used to being taken care of. She talked to distract him while she worked.

"I'm a pediatric nurse. Up until last week, I worked in a doctor's office where we lived in New York City. I'm looking for a new job in case you know of any openings."

"Is your son—" He stopped. A muscle tightened in his jaw. He cleared his throat. "Is he sick?"

"Sick...?" She cocked her head at the odd question, and then it dawned on her. "Oh, because of what you saw in there?" She pointed toward the living room. "No, he's not sick. He's diabetic."

"Isn't that dangerous?"

Allie eyed the tight set of his jaw curiously. She was used to answering all types of questions about Sammy's disease. She would rather people ask than stare or assume, but Davis's reaction seemed intense. "It can be, but we're very careful to manage his blood sugar."

In the two years since Sammy's initial diagnosis, they hadn't had an emergency besides the one that sent them to the hospital where he was first diagnosed. Allie's throat tightened at the memory of the most terrifying night of her life.

That morning when she had gone into his bedroom to wake him up for preschool, she found him in bed, confused and nauseous, with a strangely sweet scent on his breath. His eyes wouldn't open, and he had been mumbling, not making any sense. She called an ambulance, and they rushed him to the hospital. Doctors had diagnosed him with type 1 diabetes and told her he was in diabetic ketoacidosis. She spent four days in the hospital with Sammy, learning how to regulate his insulin and blood sugar, so she could manage it at home.

Annette and Amber had come to stay with them in the city so they could attend classes for families and learn how to care for Sammy's disease. Corbin had been away that week which, looking back on her marriage now, had been the final nail in the coffin. The hurt she felt when he abandoned her and Sammy when they needed him most wasn't easily forgotten.

Allie eased the bandage over Davis's forehead and patted his shoulder, noticing how he stiffened while she cleaned up the wrappers. "There. All done. So, you own this place?"

She smiled to reassure him, which he didn't return. *Tough crowd.*

"My brother, Shepherd, and I own Henderson Construction in the village. We do remodeling and renovations, from commercial buildings to homes like this. But this place is mine. I bought it because it had good bones."

She looked around at the kitchen, seeing it through his eyes. The kitchen was bright with natural light from the large window above the sink. The wide-plank floors looked original and had a shiny patina that gleamed despite the settling dusk. An older-style round dining table and chairs sat in front of a small bay window next to the back door. The house faced east, and she was already picturing long weekend mornings sitting in the sun at the table and drinking her coffee while Sammy ate his breakfast. Like the windows upstairs, the kitchen was charming and cozy. Not a trace of cold metal or steel in sight.

Good bones, indeed.

She looked at Davis with a new appreciation. "The kitchen is beautiful. Did you restore it yourself?"

He nodded once, a hint of red appearing high on his cheekbones. *Talented and humble.* "I'm not done with the trim in here," he said tersely, gesturing to the bay windows, where she noticed pieces of unpainted trim had been leaned against the sill. "If you don't mind a little noise and dust, everything should be done in a couple of weeks."

"I don't mind at all," she said. "Thanks again for letting us move in early. School starts on Monday for Sammy. I wanted to be settled in before that."

"The keys are on the hook by the door. Your sister took care of everything. She left a note on the table for you."

Allie crossed to the kitchen table and leaned over to read the note written in her sister's loopy handwriting. Amber had drawn a rough sketch of a brontosaurus wearing a bowtie at the bottom.

Welcome home! Mom and I picked up some groceries for the morning and there are meatballs and sauce for dinner in the fridge. I'm working tonight, but I'll see you guys in the morning for breakfast! XX Amber

Allie's mood lifted with an almost giddy relief at Amber's thoughtfulness, as well as the prospect of a hot, homemade meal. She moved around the kitchen checking the cupboards and fridge. Amber had filled the cupboards with cups, coffee mugs, plates, and bowls. The fridge revealed milk and eggs, bacon, orange juice, jam, and a foil-covered pan of meatballs. The counter was stocked with cereal, bread, and peanut butter, and a bag of her favorite ground coffee had been set next to a drip coffee maker. It was such a thoughtful gesture that her eyes stung again.

Davis's voice broke into her thoughts. "My number is in the paperwork in case you need it. I'll be finishing up inside next week, and then I plan on tearing out and replacing the back deck, so you won't be able to use the kitchen door for a while." He nodded at the table and chairs. "Amber and some guys were here earlier to drop off a load of furniture. Looks like she left dinner too."

"Meatballs and sauce. My mom's recipe." Allie grinned up at him. How could she not be happy? She had her own house, a dinner she didn't have to cook, and a big, strapping man with a tool belt, like some dirty fantasy come to life, standing in her kitchen.

By nature, she was used to making the best of any situation, a glass-half-full kind of person, but even for her, things had been dark the last few months. Suddenly, in her new home, she felt a little glow again. Impulsively, she held out the pan under Davis's nose. In her experience, food could make anyone smile, maybe even the hard-eyed man in front of her. "Doesn't this smell amazing?"

He hesitated, but when she lifted a corner of the foil on the baking pan and the scent of savory herbs and spices in the meatballs drifted out, he took a careful sniff. Allie got caught up staring at the grooves and planes that formed his face. The stubble of his five-o'clock shadow looked rough, and she found herself idly wondering what that part of his face would feel like rubbed over her own much smoother skin.

"Smells good."

"Did you eat?" she asked. Feeding people came as naturally to her as nursing. Really, they were the same. One took care of physical ailments while the other comforted everything else.

"I'm not hungry," he said abruptly, heading toward the door. "I'll get the car unpacked before I head out."

Unless you were Davis Henderson, apparently.

"Oh, that's not necessary," she called after him. "If you would just give me the key..." Her voice trailed off when she realized she was talking to an empty room. He was striding through the living room and out the front door, those heavy work boots resounding on the hardwood, before her mouth could snap shut. If he wanted to help, she wasn't going to stop him. Who was she to object to watching his porno arms lift her household goods for her? Nope, all good, buddy. Carry away. She would bank those images for later. Like, in the dark later. Maybe the shower? She reined in her imagination firmly.

She looked around for a way to heat their dinner. The appliances were all shiny and new and... hers. A smile lifted the corners of her mouth until it became a grin, and she did a twirl right there in the kitchen.

Just because she could. Just because it was hers.

"Whatcha' doing, Mama?" Sammy peeked over the porch rail at Allie. She was bent over in the garden below the front porch, poking through the garden beds, looking for God only knew what. On her hands and knees with her head buried and that perfect heart-shaped ass wiggling in the air, Davis was doing his best not to stare.

"Well, Sam-I-Am, we're having a dinner party for two in our new house, and I'm finding us some flowers." Allie's voice came out muffled as she bobbed around the wildflowers and weeds that took up most of the area.

Davis squinted. Those were definitely not flowers. He had been mowing the lawn here all summer, but flowers had not made it onto his priority list. He turned back to haul another suitcase from her car and made his way over to the porch.

"All the best dinner parties have fresh flowers on the table," Allie said, triumphantly holding up a fistful of wildflowers. Her messy bun bobbled on her head.

So she was cute. It wasn't a crime to check her out. He wasn't going to do anything about it. He absently rubbed the bandage on his forehead, still shocked he had let her put it on him. Hell, he was surprised he was still there. He should have been long gone by now. Instead, he found himself listening to her humming as she dug around in the garden beds.

He stopped next to Sammy, and they both looked at her prize doubtfully. "Aren't those weeds?" Sammy asked.

"Wildflowers, bud. And these are daisies. The most under-rated flowers out there. They can grow anywhere with just a little bit of light. Gardens, sidewalks, the side of the road. They're scrappy little things. They're a sign of new beginnings." She paused at the top step and gave Sammy's side a nudge with her elbow. "Perfect for our first night here."

"Cool," Sammy said, unimpressed. "Can I watch my show on the iPad?"

"Go, heathen boy. And make sure you wash your hands for dinner," Allie called after him as the screen door slammed. She winced and smiled crookedly at him. One of her incisors was turned slightly, adding to her charm. *Shit.* It had been a long while for Davis, but he didn't realize he was this hard up.

They were standing on the wide front steps close enough he could see the flecks of green and gold in her eyes and the dark fan of her lashes when she blinked.

"Thank you for all your help—" She reached for the box in his arms.

He held on.

She tugged.

He didn't move.

He could have sworn he heard her mutter something about big, bossy lumberjacks, but his mom had raised him right, and he could at least help her unpack the car. He jerked his chin toward the screen door curtly. *After you.*

She looked up at him another second with her perfect angel face, a furrow between her brows before her face broke into a mischievous grin that had him staring. "Oh, fine, put those muscly arms to good use, big guy," she announced and swept past him.

As he trudged back and forth with boxes, someone in the house turned on Dusty Springfield's "I Only Want to Be with You." He found himself listening to mother and son singing as they unpacked.

At one point, he walked into the kitchen to find Allie and Sammy holding their fists up to their mouths like microphones, belting out *be with youuuuu* as loudly and off-key as he'd ever heard. They didn't even flinch when they caught sight of him standing in the doorway. They just laughed and kept singing.

He headed back outside, thinking about his own home. When was the last time he had caught Claire and Ben acting silly like that? Hell, when was the last time he had done something silly *with* them? His house was always too damn quiet even with the kids home. The contrast was even starker now. It felt like a private glimpse into their lives, and he wondered about their story again. Allie didn't wear a ring on her finger, and he knew from the paperwork she was using her maiden name. *Who was Allie Hart?*

As he entered the kitchen, hefting the last box, Allie was balancing on her knees on the counter, reaching high up in the cabinet. She turned and wobbled slightly, tipping. Davis tossed aside the box and in two long strides, caught her from behind just before she fell. His arms locked tightly around her ribs. He held her still for a minute with her back plastered to his front while she regained her balance.

Allie turned around, still in the loose circle of his arms, with his hands spanning her slender waist. They were close enough he could feel the warmth of her body and see the light dusting of freckles on her nose. Her hands fluttered slightly like she was unsure of where they should go before finally resting lightly on his upper arms. They stood that way, in the tight space between the counter and his body, for a long, electrified second.

"Careful," he said huskily.

"I'm always careful," she said, seeming to not notice she was tracing her fingers over the grooves of muscle and bone of his arms. Davis stifled a groan as the scent of her filled his senses. Vanilla, warm, and distinctly feminine. Tantalizing.

"Allie."

"Yes," she breathed, blinking up at him. "I mean, what?"

A sandy-brown head popped up next to them. "Mama, are you petting Mr. Henderson? Fun!" Sammy wedged his squirmy body between theirs and stuck out his tongue like a dog. "Pet me! Pet me! I'm a doggie! Hey, wanna stay for dinner? It's big noodles. Not basketti."

Allie cleared her throat and stepped back, grabbing the Mason jar of daisies Sammy thrust at her. She met Davis's eyes, looking flushed and shy. "Yes, you're welcome to stay for dinner," she said softly. Two sets of identical hazel eyes looked at him, one pair innocent and one pair hesitant.

He felt a little like he had passed the most important test of his life, one he wasn't sure he wanted to take. He walked to the back door where he had dropped the box of pots and pans, giving himself a minute to clear his head and cool off.

"Please can you stay?" Sammy begged. "I'll show you my collection of cars, and we can find the box with my dinosaurs. I had the biggest collection in my class," he said proudly.

Before Davis could respond, he heard a gasp and the sound of glass shattering. He looked first at the daisies in a puddle on the floor, then up, as if in slow motion, to find Allie's horrified eyes staring at his ring finger.

"You-you're married?"

What the hell? Davis took in her face as hurt clouded her

eyes for a brief second before rage took over as she strode toward him.

"You asshole!" The door slammed closed in his face then opened again and slammed even harder.

So much for new beginnings.

Chapter Four

The bell on the door of Henderson Construction tinkled merrily, completely opposite Davis's mood as he entered the old pickle factory on the north end of Main Street.

The almost violent surge of lust he had felt after Allie fell into his arms in the kitchen had finally started to fade. It had felt like a Mack truck slammed into him. He had wanted to sink his teeth into her and see if she tasted as good as she smelled.

If her kid hadn't interrupted when he did, Davis wasn't sure where that would have gone. Things had felt a little too electric between them. Her lush curves and stroking fingers had him ready to lift her onto the counter and fit his hard places into her soft ones.

He looked around and breathed deeply, feeling himself calming in the familiar space. This was what he needed to be focused on. His work. The company his father had founded, and he and his brother, Shep, now owned was booming with all the reconstruction and new builds around town. Between taking care of the kids and running a busy company, there was no extra time for the kind of attraction he'd felt tonight. Even still, as he walked through the empty office, his mind replayed scenes from earlier and left him feeling unsettled.

He had known as soon as Allie's gaze caught on his ring earlier that she had the wrong impression, but he hadn't been able to bring himself to correct her. It didn't matter anyway. She was nothing more than his tenant. Not that she had given him a chance to explain. She'd find out about Mel soon enough in a town this size.

That thought was enough to make him pause. He had begun to date again only in the last year, but only very casually and quietly, no kids or family involved. That's all he was interested in. He wanted no expectations, no strings, and no chance of losing another person he loved.

Frankly, dating was a hassle he didn't need anyway. He felt like a damn relic when one of his younger, single employees showed him the apps people used now to date. Swipe right, swipe left. It all felt like being back in middle school passing notes to girls. He had never bothered with that then, and sure as hell didn't want to do so now. When he and Melody had met, it had been so easy. Attraction. Friendship. Love.

Death.

The pain of losing Mel used to hit him like a shotgun blast in his chest every few minutes when he remembered that she was gone. Gradually, the pain had become duller, though it was still there.

It liked to sneak up on him when he didn't expect it, like when he was wrapping presents on Christmas Eve by himself or making pancakes for the kids on Sundays with her recipe. Lately, whenever Claire asked him to do something girly that he was clueless about, those were the times he felt Melody's absence the most. But it was a softer sadness now. Time had seen to that.

That thought made him swear softly as he opened the door to the office he shared with Shep.

"Happy Friday to you too," Shep drawled, leaning back in the swivel chair at his desk.

"What are you doing in here?" Davis crossed to the filing cabinet to look for the blueprints for Allie's house. He wanted to go over the remaining projects and make sure he wasn't missing anything that would prolong the work there. Get in, get out was going to be his mantra for the next two weeks.

"Working on an estimate. Why are you back here so late?"

"Just left the Lincoln Street house," he muttered, rifling through the cabinets behind his desk for the blueprints.

"Amber's sister is renting it, right? When does she move in?"

"Tonight," he said curtly, in no mood to talk about the woman responsible for his foul mood.

Shep leaned back in the chair and linked his hands behind his head, looking Davis over carefully. "Does she look anything like her sister?"

Davis glared at him.

"Damn." Shep whistled. "Like that, huh? I've got to meet this woman. It only took one night for her to get under your skin."

"She's not under my skin. She's pissed off."

Shep's face went serious. "What happened? Was there something wrong with the house?"

"Nothing wrong with the house."

Shep relaxed his shoulders. "Then why was she mad?"

With an irritated sigh, Davis pushed the filing cabinet shut with more force than necessary. "She slammed the door in my face when she saw my ring."

"Jesus. There's a lot to unpack there, brother. Help me out here."

Davis swore again and half sat on the edge of the desk. He

had been up since five thirty that morning, and he still had a full night ahead with the kids and chores before he could go to bed. Why he was bothering to share this with his kid brother was beyond him, but as business partners, they had learned early to always be straight with each other.

"She showed up with her kid around seven. I was finishing up the lights in the master closet and didn't hear her come in. Her kid tripped and knocked into the ladder I was on, and I lost my balance. Broke my drill. Got this." He pointed to the bandage, and Shep started laughing.

Shep's eyebrows rose as he continued to snicker. "She kicked you out after she made you fall?"

"No," Davis said irritably. Shep wasn't going to let this go. "I was helping her unpack some boxes, and when she saw my wedding ring, she got pissed and slammed the door in my face."

Shep sat still for a full thirty seconds. Then he picked up the pencil and tapped the eraser on the desk twice with a thoughtful look on his face. "What about your ring made her mad?"

"Don't look at me like that."

"Like what?"

"Like there's something happening there. It's not," Davis said shortly.

"It's been almost three years, brother." Shep's voice was sympathetic. Melody had been well-loved by everyone in their family. They all missed her.

"I know how long it's been."

"If a pretty woman was interested enough in your ugly mug to take offense to your wedding ring, it feels like you left out an important part of the story."

"Nothing to tell."

"What's she like?"

Davis grimaced. "Young. She's not much older than Layne.

So fucking gorgeous it makes your teeth hurt," he added grudgingly.

Shep grinned slowly. "I see. So, in other words, not a member of the Casserole Brigade?"

Davis shifted uncomfortably and ran a hand through his hair. The Casserole Brigade was a sore spot. Right after Melody died and Davis was thrown suddenly into parenting two kids solo while grieving his wife and trying to keep his business afloat, he had come close to sinking. Seeing his struggle, friends had stepped in to organize meals. For weeks, while Davis navigated life as a newly widowed father, his family and friends took the responsibility of dinner off his shoulders, and he was eternally grateful.

Eventually, as time went on, and the fog of grief cleared from a daily tornado to a more manageable shitstorm, he mastered the basics. He got a lot done before the kids woke up and after they went to bed. He learned to cook a handful of healthy dinners. Nothing fancy, but green vegetables were on their plates most nights. It was somewhat of a joke that the kids didn't like his cooking, but he did his best.

Hell, he didn't enjoy food like he used to either. It just didn't hold the same appeal with Melody gone, but like most things after she died, he went through the motions.

His lack of appetite had been the least of his concerns. Ben had taken to screaming every day when he was dropped off at preschool. He started sucking his thumb again, a habit he had quit early on. What really hit him was when Claire didn't talk for a while at school. His usually bubbly, talkative little girl had gone silent.

With therapy and time, they were all doing much better now. An image of Allie and Sammy singing flashed in his head. Well, maybe not that happy, but they were surviving the best way he knew how.

As the months passed after Mel's death, the dinners made by his closest family and friends came to a natural end. But casseroles had continued to come to his door, accompanied by Northfield's most determined and solicitous single women. Many of them handed over their casserole dish along with their phone number. He was grateful at first, of course, and even flattered, but absolutely not interested in anything beyond friendship.

Northfield was too small of a town to date anyone in it casually. He had learned that lesson quickly. He would never risk making things awkward for the kids, or risk jeopardizing his friendships when things came to an inevitable end, which was always only a matter of time. He had tried to explain that they didn't need the food anymore, but some of the more persistent ones just kept showing up. After a while, he started bringing the pans of food to his work crew. The guys ate well, though he took a lot of ribbing about it.

Davis pinched the bridge of his nose. "No," he said tightly. "It's not like that."

"What's the problem? You've been dating this last year."

"Casual dating is different. We're not meeting each other's families. I've met Allie's kid already." He ran a tired hand through his hair. "The kid's got a medical condition. Diabetes."

Shep sighed. "Ah, hell. Poor kid. That freaked you out, huh?" he asked knowingly.

Shep knew more than anyone how much Davis struggled with fear after Mel died. Logically, Davis knew his family was safe. Mel's accident was just that, a freak accident. But after losing someone he thought he'd grow old with and being left to raise two young kids on his own, fear had crept in, taking much of the joy out of life. Allie and Sammy's off-key singing from earlier played in his head. His house had once been like that.

Davis rolled his shoulders and turned back to the file cabinet. "She seems like she takes good care of him. There was just a misunderstanding tonight."

"Where's the kid's dad?" Shep missed nothing.

"None of my business." He found the file and sat down to read, done with the conversation.

For a while, they were quiet as they worked. "You can't keep everyone casual in your life forever," Shep said quietly. He stood and laid a hand on Davis's shoulder. "I mean, I can, but you definitely can't," he added with a wolfish grin.

Davis thought back to the look in Allie's eyes when he had been holding her. So damn inviting, and a little shy too. Appealing as hell. He looked at the clock on the wall. "I have to get home. Layne's with the kids tonight."

"Yeah, tell them I'll be there on Sunday to crush Ben in our Fantasy Football picks."

Davis grabbed the file he came for and started out the door. "Will do."

"And Davis?"

He turned to look at his brother's sly grin.

"I can't wait to meet her."

Davis glared at Shep, well-known for his affinity for beautiful women. "She won't like you either," he growled and left the office.

Shep's mocking laughter trailed after him.

Chapter Five

"HELLO, my darlings! Welcome back! Sammy, my little love bug, you are enormous. Is that a mustache I see?"

Amber Hart leaned in close to eye the nonexistent fuzz on her nephew's upper lip. She had knocked on the door that morning with hot coffee for Allie and a smoothie for Sammy, and she and Sammy were chatting while Allie made breakfast.

"'Course not, Auntie, I'm only seven." Sam scoffed, holding still and preening under his aunt's inspection before she picked him up for a big, twirly hug. In addition to being Allie's sister, Amber was her best friend and most staunch supporter, even if they were polar opposites. Amber was flamboyant and flirty, the life of every party. Allie envied her natural confidence, even if, as she suspected, Amber sometimes hid behind that facade.

"Easy now. He just ate, Amber." Her warning was half-hearted though, as Amber and Sammy started their familiar dance-off routine.

"Oh, yeah, but can you do this?" Amber did an impressive lawnmower move, complete with pantomiming putting on goggles, and yanking the gas starter. They erupted into giggles, trying to outdance each other.

"I can! I can!" Sammy crowed with delight. "Watch me moonwalk, Auntie!" Sammy's feet slid across the floor as he showed off his latest move.

"That kid is an animal, Allie. He's gonna go pro." Amber collapsed into a chair at the breakfast table a while later when Sammy headed toward the living room to play with his cars.

Amber was all va-va-voom curves and cleavage barely contained in her cropped white tee and tiny denim shorts, though it was actually pretty tame as far as her usual. Amber took perverse pleasure in wearing the most outrageously provocative clothing. It drove the aunts nuts, which made Amber cackle and try even harder to outdo herself.

Allie loaded Amber's plate with scrambled eggs and bacon. "So, how are things? Still working for Mom?"

"Among other things." Amber lazily shrugged one tanned shoulder. "Let's talk about you." She poured a stream of maple syrup over the bacon and dug in.

Food was the Hart women's love language. Making it, eating it, thinking about it— food had always played a large part in their lives. "Tell me everything," she said around a mouthful.

"You know everything that I do, Amber. Thanks for setting up this place, by the way." Allie fiddled with the freshly filled jar of daisies in the middle of the table and then leaned over to give her sister an impulsive one-armed hug. "Love you, Am." Their childhood names— Al and Am they had called each other since they were old enough to talk. Despite moving six hours away, they were still as close as ever.

"Of course. How are you feeling?"

"Good, actually." It had felt strange when she realized that a marriage could be dissolved in an afternoon. Even more strange, she didn't miss being married at all. Had she loved Corbin? At eighteen, looking at two pink lines on a pregnancy test at her mother's house, she had thought so.

Corbin had been like a freight train when they met the summer after her high school graduation, courting her with a determination unlike anything Allie had experienced in her limited knowledge of high school boys. He had been older, sexier, and more sophisticated with his fancy car and apartment in the city, and she had fallen hard.

"God, that guy is a massive prick," Amber muttered.

Allie lowered her voice in case little ears were listening. "Corbin's a good dad, Am. We weren't in love anymore, but I was content to stay married for Sammy's sake. They adore each other." She shrugged. "Catching him cheating was about the only reason I would have ever left him, but when it was in my face like that, he made the decision easier for me."

"But did he have to be so cliché about it? I mean, other pieces of furniture are less insulting than your bed." Amber's nose crinkled with disgust.

She had a point. But then again, Corbin had never been creative in the bedroom.

Allie shrugged. "That was his bedroom. We haven't shared a room in a year."

Amber looked at her speculatively. "No sex either? How's that working out for you? Are there cobwebs down there?"

"Just fine, Am. We're not all sex goddesses like you."

"It's a tough job." Amber grinned wickedly. "But you know what they say…"

Amber had never been shy about her appetites. She ate up men the way Allie ate up her beloved Ben and Jerry's at night. In generous portions, with an extra carton or two in the freezer for backup.

A door slammed outside, and they both looked out the window. Allie recognized Davis's big silver truck parked in her driveway. The man himself was lifting a red gas can from the truck bed. He wore another T-shirt, gray this time, a backward baseball cap on his head, and shorts that did nothing to diminish his powerful thighs. A massive golden retriever leaped down from the bed of the truck after Davis and sniffed around the walkway.

Hot anger surged, topped off by embarrassment, in her chest. Davis and his brawny self could hop right on a bus and go straight to hell. Or at the least, back to his wife, as far as she was concerned. It stung that the first man she found herself attracted to postdivorce shared a glaring personality flaw with Corbin: loyalty. As in, none of it. *His poor wife.* She scrubbed harder at the syrup on the table with a washcloth.

"Sweet baby Jesus, I would eat him with a spoon." Amber let out a long whistle and fanned herself. Allie poked her. "Ow. What? Say 'thank you' to your favorite sister. Davis Henderson is a gift. God, have you seen his arms? I want to rub myself all over them." Amber's eyes closed like she was picturing it.

Allie scrubbed harder. "I have. Attached to his hand, which was wearing his wedding ring," she said tartly.

Amber straightened up with a strange look on her face. "His wedding ring?"

Allie gave a sharp nod. "He was here last night when Sammy and I got in. He's as bad as Corbin." She wrenched the washcloth back and forth violently. "All smoldering eyes and 'Can I help you unpack your car?' I think he got the message, though," she added grimly.

Amber's eyes widened. "What did you do?"

"What do you think? I kicked him out and slammed the door in his cheating face."

Amber clasped her hand over her mouth. "You didn't?"

Allie tossed the washcloth in the sink irritably. "Of course I did. Just because I'm not in love with Corbin doesn't mean I'm not a little sensitive about cheating spouses, remember?" She looked over at Amber's stricken face. "What's wrong with you?"

"Am... Davis has been widowed for almost three years."

"Wh-what?" she sputtered. "But I saw his ring. He had on a ring." She looked back outside to where Davis was talking with an elderly woman on the other side of the fence. Why would the man still be wearing a wedding ring three years after his wife died?

"Shit," Allie whispered, then she looked around guiltily for Sammy and his ever-present swear jar.

"Yeah, that's awkward," Amber murmured. "Let's worry about that later, though. I think I'm having an orgasm." She fanned her face and kept her eyes glued to the window where Davis was now bent over petting the dog.

"Amber!" she hissed. "He's going to see you!"

The thought of how she had flirted with him last night made Allie's face burn. A widower? She groaned miserably. How was she going to face him now?

"Please, I hope he does. Look at his shoulders." Amber ran her finger down the window like she was tracing his body. "And those thick thighs. I love a man with thick thighs." She looked over at Allie. "You really kicked him out?"

"Yeah," she said morosely. "Sammy invited him to stay for dinner after he unpacked most of the car for us. I thought it was a nice gesture, so I said yes. Then I saw his ring."

Amber looked even more interested. "You sure you weren't perving on the good Mr. Henderson yourself? I'd bet you're the only woman in this town that's ever slammed a door in his face. I've been watching women do stupid things to get his attention for years."

"I was being nice. He's my landlord."

"Mm-hmm. That big, cranky grizzly bear could set fire with his smolder. I've been trying to get him to take me out for ages."

Something hot flared through her chest. Must be the orange juice she had earlier. "How's that working for you?" She kept her eyes safely on the dog.

"It's not," Amber said cheerfully, continuing to ogle.

Allie peeked outside. Great. Now Davis was Weedwacking the edges of the driveway, every muscle in his tanned forearms on display. Dear Lord, another image seared forever into her brain.

"He comes into the bar with his work crew sometimes. He's pretty quiet, doesn't stay too late. Never has more than a beer or two." She leaned one shapely hip against the counter and looked at Allie, her expression thoughtful. "He's actually a really good guy. His kids are around Sammy's age."

Allie straightened up with a frown. She knew that look. "Whatever you're thinking, stop. Been there, done that. I have the divorce papers to prove it."

"I get it." Amber held her hand up. "I'm just saying that you never know. Keep your options open. Corbin already took eight years of your life. Don't let him dictate your future too."

"Ouch, Amber. Too soon."

"Sorry." Her sister grinned unrepentantly. "I know you. You've been emotionally neglected for too long. Physically neglected too. We need to take care of that, by the way." She paused suddenly, eyes wide. "Wait. Have you *ever* been with anyone besides Corbin?"

Allie ignored that last question. "We're good on our own. Besides, I'm not alone. That's why I came home."

Amber just looked at her. "Mm-hmm. I'm not saying you need to rush out and get married again." She shuddered. "Just let yourself have some fun. Time to live a little."

Allie snorted. "I don't have time for that." She held up two of Sammy's toy cars left on the counter with her eyebrows raised. "I'm momming so hard right now."

"I'm not saying you need a husband, just a nice, big..." She wiggled her eyebrows up and down and looked out the window. Allie followed her gaze and blinked at the sight of Davis wiping his face with the bottom of his T-shirt. They stood there, mesmerized, as his shirt lifted to reveal seriously lickable abs. *No dad bod there.* "... distraction," Amber finished, her tone quite satisfied when she caught Allie looking.

"Oh my God! Stop."

"You need to loosen up, Al. Do you know what you need? A snack. Being married was like having a depressing microwave meal dinner every day for years. Withered peas. Mystery meat. Time to indulge in something delicious." She tapped her fingernail on Allie's nose and whirled away toward the window again.

"I'm a single mom, Amber. All I need is a nap."

"Ooh, naked nap, yes! I love that idea."

Allie groaned. "Whatever you're thinking, stop."

Before she could blink, Amber leaned over and yanked up the window. "Hey, Davis! Are you thirsty?"

"HEY, DAVIS!" Amber Hart sashayed out onto the back deck holding a glass. "You look like a tall drink of water. Oops, I mean, you look like you could *use* a tall drink of water."

She flipped her long hair over her shoulder and thrust her hips to the side, giving Davis a prime view. Everything Amber Hart did drew attention to her assets, which were considerable. He seldom paid any attention, but watching his crew get tongue-tied when they played pool at the pub when she was working was funny.

"Hey, Amber. Thanks." He nodded gratefully at the glass she held out. The day was already warming up. His plans included getting Allie's lawn finished, heading home to do his own yard work, and then spending the rest of the afternoon swimming with Ben and Claire. Not too many more warm days were left before fall. He wanted to get another few weekends out of the pool.

Since the beginning of summer, Davis had come by the Lincoln Street house on Saturday mornings to mow the lawn. He could have paid for a lawn care service, but he liked the work, and it gave him something to do while the kids spent time with Layne.

He looked over at the neighboring yard. Mrs. Autovino was out hanging her laundry on an old-fashioned clothesline. The woman must have been close to eighty years old yet insisted on doing things the way she liked. He knew this for a fact. He had repaired her clothesline last week, and his ears were still ringing from her instructions. He usually spent a few minutes chatting with her when he came over each week and helped her take care of anything she needed. That's how Northfield worked. People looked out for one another. It was the biggest reason he'd stayed here with the kids after Mel died.

"Oh wow! A dog! Nice dog, come here!" Sammy came shooting out past Amber like a rocket. He stormed down the steps, and Davis put out a hand to steady him as he passed. The boy and the dog ran to each other like in a TV commercial. Sammy had his arms extended, and Walter's ears were flying behind him. Sammy threw his arms around the dog before they both flopped down and rolled on the ground together.

Just as quickly, the screen door banged open, and Allie's voice rang out sharply. "Sammy! You can't run up to dogs you don't know!"

"Okay, sorry. But we're best friends now. See!" Sammy and Walter stared at each other blissfully before Walter nosed a ratty tennis ball into Sam's hands. "You wanna play fetch, boy? Go get it!"

Sammy rolled the ball a few feet away, and Walter scrambled to his feet to play his favorite game.

"Come on, Walter, get your ball," Sammy called. Walter lifted his head, his ear perking up his ears at his most favorite word in the world.

Walter was a massive pain in his ass, but his kids had begged for a dog, and their therapist said it might be a good idea to facilitate their healing. Turned out, Walter was still a massive pain in the ass, but he was loyal and smart, and he had helped the kids and Davis through some tough, lonely nights. For that alone, he'd throw the damn tennis ball for him whenever he could.

The backyard of the house was surrounded by an unstained picket fence. Walter had already found a comfortable spot under a big maple tree and was rolling on his back happily while Sammy scratched his belly.

"He's gentle. Walter loves kids," Davis said.

Allie pursed her lips but acknowledged his words with a nod as she watched Sammy playing with Walter. Amber stood next to her, leaning over the old deck, also watching the two play.

The two sisters were similar in their considerable attributes, but only one of them made his eyes pop out of his head. Allie's bright-pink top and shorts caused a barely held in groan. This woman would kill him. She was all lush, soft curves this morning, with her hair down and curling around her full breasts. He remembered exactly how they had cushioned his arm when he caught her in the kitchen.

Though Amber stood next to her sister with a kid-sized shirt on, he couldn't tear his eyes off Allie. Her face was scrubbed clean, and she looked young and fresh. The thought made him scowl. He was too damn old to be lusting after his tenant like this.

Allie kept her eyes fixed on the yard while Amber held out the glass of water.

"So, Davis, thanks again for getting Allie and Sammy into the house so quickly." He didn't miss the nudge Amber gave her sister. "And for helping them unpack."

He took another drink. "Happy to help."

"Allie *really* appreciates it. Right, Allie?"

Shy hazel eyes finally met his. "Yes, thank you."

"Sammy," Amber called, coming down the back steps. "Throw the ball like Derek Jeter. Let's see how far Walter can chase it."

"Okay! Who's that?" Sammy stood up with the ball, and Walter started yapping and prancing around his feet.

Davis looked up at Allie, startled. They lived in New York, for crying out loud.

Allie shrugged. "We're not big baseball fans."

"Hey, I only know because I work at a bar," Amber said.

"That's a travesty." He watched as Amber gave a terrible impression of a fastball, fumbling the ball instead. Walter slumped down dejectedly to wait for another try. It was painful to watch. He kept his eye on Amber and Sammy, mentally wincing when she moved the kid's fingers to the wrong position on the ball.

"I think there was a misunderstanding last night," Allie said, giving a little huff-laugh and plopping down on the top step with her knees pulled up to her chest. *Stop looking.*

He took a seat next to her, and they watched Sammy and Amber make pitiful attempts to toss the ball. Walter looked confused but happy to have two new playthings who were as interested in his slimy ball as he was.

"Look, I just want to say I'm sorry for slamming the door on you last night," she finally said, shooting him a level look. "I saw your ring and I... misunderstood."

He couldn't help but be impressed with her directness. Davis looked down at his wedding ring and absentmindedly spun the gold band. The skin under the band was a few shades lighter. "My wife died almost three years ago."

Allie rested her hand on his arm lightly. "I'm sorry."

He was surprised again by her casual touch. She was so open that it felt natural in a way another woman's hands hadn't in years.

He nodded, never completely at ease talking about Mel's death. "Thank you."

"Cheating spouses are kind of a sore spot for me right now." She looked away from him, back to her son and sister. "That's why I moved back here."

He schooled his face, but the shock that someone would be stupid enough to cheat on this woman must have shown because she smiled a little and shrugged. "It's okay."

"I'm sorry that happened to you," he said.

"It sucked, but I'm happy to be back here with our family." She leaned back on her hands, lifting her face toward the sun, and he caught sight of the sprinkling of freckles on her nose. Cute as hell. "I think Sammy will be happier here. At least, I hope so."

He dragged his eyes away. "Are you getting settled in?"

"We're getting there. Still waiting on the moving truck to come later today. But we have beds. Well, one bed. Sammy slept with me." She rubbed her ribs and laughed. "He sleeps like a starfish."

"My son sleeps like that. He wakes up with his head down at the end of the bed."

"You have a son?" She opened one eye and squinted at him through the sun.

"Two kids. Ben's seven and Claire's almost nine."

"Sammy's seven too. He's starting second grade."

"Ben's starting second grade too. Claire's in fourth grade. We live a few streets down that way." He pointed away from the village. "It's a great neighborhood for kids."

"I know. I grew up here." Something in her voice made him glance over at her. "Not in the village. We lived a little further out," she added vaguely.

"Where?"

She hesitated. "Cedarwood."

Davis carefully schooled his features. He didn't know much about the track of housing on the other side of the river except that it was subsidized by the government and not too pretty to look at. The craftsman in him flinched whenever he drove by and saw how beat-up the complex looked. No one should have to live in a place that looked as sad and neglected as Cedarwood.

Sammy skidded to a stop in front of them with Walter on his heels. "I'm playing fetch with Walter, Mom. We're best friends. Watch!"

Sammy rolled the ball underhand a few feet away, and Walter looked at it, confused. Was the kid playing fetch or bowling?

Davis leaned down and picked up the tennis ball. He turned it around until he found the two seams. "See those lines? On a baseball, you make sure your two fingers line up with the seams before you throw the ball." He put the ball in the boy's hand and moved his fingers to the right spot. "And your thumb goes here." He got up and lifted Sammy's arm in an overhand position. "Then you come down like this, with your shoulder pointed where you want the ball to go."

Sammy's nose wrinkled in concentration as he stood in position. "Cool. Like this?" He stood awkwardly and threw the ball far right instead of straight. Walter wasn't picky about direction as long as he had some distance. The boy and the dog took off racing to get the ball first.

Davis winced. "We'll work on it."

Allie leaned forward and cheered. "Great throw, Sammy!" Sammy wrestled the ball away from Walter and threw it again. "His dad and I are not sporty people. I need to get him a bike now that we have all this space."

It occurred to him that what came out of his mouth next could make his life increasingly difficult in keeping his distance from this lady and her kid, but the words were out before he could take them back. "I coach Ben's fall Little League team. If Sammy's interested, our first practice is next Thursday at six."

"Yeah, Mom!" Sammy shouted as he ran toward them. "I wanna play baseball! I'm a baseball player! So awesome!" He lunged for Allie and hugged her hard around the waist. When he pulled back, a shock of hair fell into his eyes. He looked over at Davis with a worried look. "But I don't know how to throw a baseball real good like Peter."

Allie leaned close and brushed Sammy's hair back from his forehead. Her scent drifted toward Davis, warm and sweet. "Who's Peter, honey bear?"

"Peter from the Hankies," Sammy said patiently. "Aunt Amber said he has a good arm."

"From the Hank—" Allie repeated as she met Davis's eyes. She grinned, and his lips twitched. "Derek Jeter from the New York Yankees?"

"Yep, but I'm gonna have two good arms, not just one!" He raised both in the air as he ran off again. "Aunt Amber, I'm gonna play baseball like the Hankies!"

Allie stood next to Davis for a minute, and they both watched Sammy awkwardly throw the ball. Davis was drawn to her profile as she soaked in the sun, a content smile still lingering on her lips. Her face was tilted up, exposing her neck and delicate collarbone. How the hell she managed to look that relaxed with a son with a serious medical condition baffled him. Just the thought of that made his breakfast threaten to come up.

"Better get this lawn done," he said, backing away before he did something else really stupid.

Chapter Six

ON THE WAY home from Allie's later that morning, Davis stopped at the light on Main Street and waited as people crossed over to the village green. Walter's massive head hung over his shoulder as he looked out the window at the families sitting on the benches in front of the Northfield Dairy.

A young mom held a toddler on her lap, and they were laughing as she shared a lick of her ice cream cone. The dad stood nearby with another kid sitting on his shoulders. A drip of ice cream landed on the dad's nose, and the family all laughed together.

Davis flinched.

A few streets over from Allie's, he pulled his truck into his driveway and stared at the house he and Mel had purchased together. A fresh coat of white paint gleamed on the tall colonial, and the lawn was neatly trimmed.

He loved this house. When he and Melody had first bought it, they planned to fix it up together while raising their family. But Mel had gotten pregnant with Claire right away, and Henderson Construction got busier as Davis took over. Renovations were put on the back burner, thinking they had the rest of their lives to make the house theirs. Then Ben was born, and things just got busier. Mel died before they could even get started.

Now, every room in the house had been updated. He had the time and the skills to fix up the house himself, and it had become a lifeline after Melody died to work on the house when the kids had gone to bed. He had hours to fill before he could call it a night. Well-meaning friends always commented on how busy he must be raising the kids on his own, but Davis was surprised how much time he spent alone. Too much, especially now that Ben and Claire were getting older and had their own interests. It made for plenty of long, lonely nights.

Davis tossed his keys down on a pile of mail on the entryway table and made his way to the kitchen. A faint hint of coconut sunscreen scented the house. Claire's shriek, followed by the sounds of splashing drifted in through the open windows. The kids' leftover cereal bowls were still on the table from breakfast, along with Ben's baseball mitt. He cleared the kitchen table and started loading the dishwasher while the kids swam, his mind wandering to Allie and Sammy.

What were they doing the rest of the weekend? Had Allie found a bike for Sammy yet? Every kid should have a bike. That big maple tree out back of their house would fit a tree swing perfectly. What had their life been like in the city? How the hell did someone cheat on a woman like that?

Not his concern, he reminded himself sternly. Even if he was still thinking what a pretty picture she made sitting on the steps this morning, her face turned up to the sun like one of those daisies she'd picked. He scraped a bowl into the sink and shook his head in disgust. He sounded ridiculous comparing her to flowers, for Christ's sake. But the image of Allie on the steps in the morning light, her nose scrunched, a smile on her face lingered and made his chest feel strange as he set the kitchen back to rights.

When the kitchen was clean, he went out back to the pool. "Hey, kids. Hey, boy." Claire and Ben waved and went back to playing Marco Polo, but Walter leaned his massive wet-dog-smelling bulk against him and closed his eyes blissfully. Davis scratched his head.

"Walter, you stink." Walter gave a massive shake of his body, and water spattered him. "Thanks for that. Hey, Lanie," he said, taking a seat next to her at the table. "How was the morning?"

Layne pushed her oversized glasses on top of her head and peered over her magazine at him. "Successful, although we barely made it out alive. Shopping for school supplies was dicey." She grimaced. "Some lady tried to grab the last composition notebook right out of my hand."

Layne had become indispensable since Melody died. The kids adored her, and she loved them too. As a photographer, her schedule was flexible enough to help watch the kids whenever Davis needed her.

"I talked to Shep last night." She was still paging through the magazine, but he wasn't fooled. He kept silent.

"He said your new tenants moved in."

He nodded.

"I also heard you had a door slammed in your pretty face." She was full-out grinning now.

He kept his eyes trained on the kids in the pool. "It was a misunderstanding."

"I think I need to meet this woman."

"It's not like that."

"Ah, what's wrong, big brother? Not used to having to work a little for it?" She punched him in the arm as she used to when they were little. He grunted but didn't move.

"Is she cute?"

"Are we in fifth grade?" he asked irritably. "What's with you and Shep anyway, trying to set me up? I'm not interested in a relationship."

Layne's usually smiling face went serious. "We just want to see you happy, Davis. It's been a long time. You deserve to be happy." Her face cleared. "Besides, it feels right that the first woman to make you look all bent out of shape like that shut you down. It's good for men to work for it. It stimulates your prey drive or something." She waved a hand. "I read that in a column once. Or maybe I made it up?"

Davis ignored her, squinting to inspect the kids for any hint of sunburn. "When's the last time they had sunblock?" he asked, eyeing the sun suspiciously.

Layne checked her watch. "About an hour ago. They're fine."

"Kids, time for more sunblock!"

Layne sighed but didn't say anything more. Davis was grateful.

Davis knew he was overprotective, but sometimes it took his breath away how delicate life was. How one day you could wake up next to the love of your life, perfectly secure in the knowledge of your future together, and then not even twelve hours later, have that dream shatter. It made it hard to look around and enjoy life when you could see disaster lurking around every corner.

"Hey, Daddy." Claire took a seat next to him and Ben. She had grown so tall. She looked like Melody more and more each day. They shared the same smile and the same blue eyes, so much so that Davis sometimes had to look away. Ben was grumbling, but he got out of the pool, shook himself much like Walter had just done, and dutifully presented his back to Davis.

"Hey, Ben. Hi, Claire Bear," he said, gently tugging a waterlogged hunk of her hair. His daughter had not only inherited her mother's smile but also her creativity. Claire saw the world differently than Davis and Ben. She was sensitive, so much so that she cried at commercials, roadkill she was convinced was Bambi's mom, and even when Ben's baseball team lost a game. More times than not, Davis felt way out of his league with Claire, and it worried him. When Ben felt sad or anxious, he wanted to get physical. Davis could relate. Toss a ball, tackle someone, or shoot some hoops, and he could get Ben talking and feeling better, but his little girl was more of a mystery. "You ready for school?"

"Yep." She swung her knobby knees back and forth and sat on her hands. "I got my backpack ready." Claire and Layne exchanged a look.

"What? What's that look for?" he asked warily, looking between the two of them.

"Claire said Carly Lewis told all the girls to wear their hair in a French braid for the first day of school," Layne began.

"Okay, sure," he said with relief. He didn't care how Claire wore her hair.

"But I can't be here in the morning to do it."

He gave one last swipe of lotion to Ben's shoulders. "Okay, done. No pool for fifteen minutes."

Ben grabbed a wedge of watermelon and Walter's ball and headed to the grassy area. A boy and his dog, perfectly content to inspect under rocks for bugs or throw a slimy ball over and over again.

"I'm going out of town for a shoot next week," Layne continued. She had moved into the old Phoenix Hotel building in the village shortly after Melody died to be closer to the kids. She often took them to school in the morning. "So, it's up to you." Two sets of eyes looked at him expectantly.

He looked back and forth between them blankly. "To French braid?"

Layne broke into a broad grin. "Yep, you're going to learn how. Right now." With a flourish, she pulled out a Target bag and lined up mysterious products while he watched with growing trepidation. He recognized a water bottle and tiny plastic hairbands easily enough, but the rest was foreign.

Give him a power saw. A belt sander. A nail gun. He could teach classes all day long on the tools of his trade, but big, purple bows with rhinestones and strange-looking clips gave him anxiety. This was way out of his league.

He'd just mastered the damn gymnastic bun not too long ago, and that one was harder than hell. One of the moms from Claire's class had kindly taken him aside and explained how to spray the hair, then use a tiny comb to pull everything smooth, then spray it again, and wrap it into a bun. He could never get that sucker smooth. Claire was a good sport about it, but he knew she was self-conscious around the other girls' perfect hairdos.

Slowly, Claire pulled out the iPad she had been hiding. With an encouraging nod from her aunt, she slid it over to her dad shyly. "Do you want to watch some hair tutorials I found, Daddy?"

There was only one answer a self-respecting father could give. "Of course I do."

AND SO IT went for the next hour. Davis sweated and tussled with Claire's superfine hair, gracelessly trying to finesse one strand over another with his big, calloused fingers, bobby pins stuffed in his mouth until, by the grace of God, all the pieces stayed where he put them, albeit a little lopsided.

Claire inspected the final result in the mirror doubtfully, tugging the lopsided braid toward the center. "Thanks, Daddy."

Dammit. She didn't like it. "I'll work on it, honey," he said gruffly.

Layne left shortly after, and Davis spent the rest of the day swimming with the kids and doing yard work. Around six, he made one of the five dinners he rotated between, and the three of them ate dinner around the kitchen island. He threw in a load of laundry and cleaned up the dinner dishes. Just like every night, he checked the clock when all the chores were done. Not quite eight o'clock. Soon, the kids would go to bed, and it would just be him and Walter.

The nights were long.

He sat with Ben in his bed, and they read two books together, both about baseball. Ben lived and breathed the sport, and he was a natural at it. He gave him a kiss and a noogie for good measure before turning out the light.

"Night, Ben. Don't let the bedbugs bite." He had been saying that since Ben was a baby, and it never failed to elicit a laugh.

"I'm not afraid of no bugs, Dad," he said indignantly. "That's Claire." He wrinkled his nose in disgust. "Why are girls afraid of stuff like that?"

"*Any* bugs." Davis held up a stern finger. "And not all girls are, bud, but don't put any more stink bugs in your sister's hair. That's not cool."

Ben smiled angelically and closed his eyes. "Okay, Dad." Davis wasn't fooled for a minute. Ben was the spitting image of him and Shep, and they had teased Layne the same way until one day she put Icy Hot in their jockstraps. That had stopped their pranks for good. He winced, remembering the burn.

Ben was snoring before the door closed. He headed down the hall to Claire's room and knocked.

"Hey, Claire."

"Hi, Daddy." She was sitting up in bed with her light-up pen and her diary, a pink-and-purple faux-fur-covered notebook. She had taken to carrying it everywhere this summer. Ben kept asking her what she was writing in it until she put her hands on her skinny hips and yelled, "My feelings!"

She kept it under strict lock and key from her brother, but after hearing that, Ben wouldn't go near it with a ten-foot pole. Davis didn't blame him. Somehow his little girl was growing up, and he had no idea what to do about it.

"Did you brush your teeth?" He sat on the edge of the bed and tried not to notice when she hid the pages.

"Yes." She set aside the diary and looked up at him, all fresh-scrubbed and pink-cheeked, looking more grown up than he liked to admit. He threw a leg up on the bed and settled in next to her against the headboard.

"How are you feeling about the first day of school?" *See, feelings.* He could do this. He was a patient, sensitive dad.

"Good." She worried the edge of the blanket. "Carly Lewis's mom lets her walk to school by herself."

He shot up. "Absolutely not!" He snapped before he remembered to be sensitive. "I will walk you and Ben, or Aunt Lanie will, if I'm working early." Just the thought of what could happen to her made his heart lodge in his throat. Memories of another accident played in his head before he could stop them. What if a car ran off the road and hit her? People were always checking their phones while they were driving. A cold sweat broke out on the back of his neck, and his stomach turned at the thought of what could happen.

She patted his hand. "It's okay, Daddy. I knew you were going to say that. I like when you guys walk us anyway."

Davis settled back warily. "Different families have different rules. One of ours is that we walk you to school."

Natalie and Carly Lewis had moved into the neighborhood at the beginning of the summer. When they first moved in, Davis had initially taken Natalie on a few dates before deciding that dating someone from Northfield was a bad idea. The town was too small to date anyone without gossip, and that was not something he wanted in his kids' lives. Claire and Carly had turned out to be thick as thieves, and he didn't want to make things awkward for Claire if she heard anything. He had explained all that to Natalie, and they agreed to keep it just friendly between them.

Unfortunately, Natalie had found out about the casserole brigade when she moved in, and she sometimes still dropped off food for them. Davis didn't mind it much coming from her. He got the feeling she was lonely. He could understand that better than most.

Claire shrugged. "Okay. But Carly Lewis also has a boyfriend."

"What!" He sat up so suddenly the fluffy notebook fell off the bed. "Absolutely not, Claire. You are not allowed to have a boyfriend." He scowled. "You're eight! Don't even look at boys. Not until you're thirty."

Claire giggled and snuggled into his side. "I'm nine, but I know, Daddy. I don't want one anyway. Boys are gross, except for you and Uncle Shep."

Davis sat back again, still disconcerted and vaguely irritated. Nine. Nine! Thank God, his little Claire wasn't interested in any of that stuff.

"Carly's mom just got divorced from her dad," she went on. Davis listened with half an ear as his blood pressure came down slowly.

"I know that," Davis said cautiously. Indeed, their spouses were something he and Natalie had talked about when they went out. Natalie's ex had been a real asshole and left them for his secretary.

"And Carly said I need a mom too."

"You have a mom," he said sharply.

"I know. I told her that." She smoothed the blanket. "It's just that... sometimes I wish I had a mom so I could talk to her about stuff. Girl stuff."

There went his heart. Cracked right open.

"I wish that, too, honey. You know you can talk to me about anything, right?"

"Well, yeah, Daddy, but you don't get stuff the way that girls do."

"Hey, I can learn. There are tutorials for everything." He now knew more than he ever wanted about hair and beauty. "What about Grandma or Aunt Layne? They're girls, and they would be happy to talk to you about anything."

"I know, but it's not the same. Grandma still buys me baby dolls, and Aunt Layne isn't a mom."

She looked up at him, and he remembered the first time the doctor handed her to him. He had felt weak in the knees at the magnitude of raising a little girl. That had been with an incredible wife by his side. Not in a million years had he thought he'd be raising her alone.

She looked at him solemnly now. "I'm growing up, Daddy."

"Yeah, you are, honey," he said through the lump in his throat. Whether or not he liked it. "I love you."

"I love you too," she said sleepily, snuggling down into the pile of stuffed animals. She lifted one arm to accept Guinevere the Bunny, which she still slept with every night. *Not grown yet, little one.* He tucked the silky rabbit under her chin as she closed her eyes.

"Do you think we'll ever have another mom?" Claire asked with a yawn.

Davis froze on his way down to kiss her cheek. Even on the very few dates he'd been on, he couldn't bring himself to think about beginning a relationship again, not that he had been even remotely tempted. He still couldn't, but when he shut off the light Allie's teasing hazel eyes and freckled nose flashed in his mind. He blinked away the image.

"Good night, honey," he said instead and closed the door, grateful that Claire had already drifted off.

He grabbed a beer from the fridge and settled on the couch. The longest part of the night began now. Closing his eyes, he tipped his head back against the couch. Walter jumped up beside him and slumped his enormous bulk down with a great big sigh, his silent partner on the loneliest nights. He gave him a good ear rubbing, the kind that made Walter almost cross-eyed from doggie bliss.

The house was quiet except for the hum of the dishwasher. Someone closed their garage door in the distance. The light over the stove buzzed faintly. He looked at his watch. At least two more hours stretched before him before he could call it a night. He grabbed Ben's discarded iPad and clicked a new tab.

"Want to learn how to French braid, Walter?"

Chapter Seven

"MIMI LIVES IN A GINGERBREAD HOUSE," Sammy announced.

"Sure looks like it, buddy," Allie agreed.

They stood on the sidewalk in front of a regal yellow Victorian. Two pointed gables set with ornate windows reflected the sun, and crisp-white scalloped trim framed the steeply pointed roofline. The house rose majestically between two towering maple trees, the leaves just turning red on the ends from the cooler nights.

Pretty nice digs, considering where they grew up.

Allie's mother, Annette, had done more than well for herself since those early days after her husband left. Her interior design firm, Hart Home Designs, had grown from their tiny dining room table in Cedarwood into a nationally accredited design firm with eight full-time employees in an office on Main Street. Annette's impeccable taste and eye for design were highly sought after locally, and even nationally.

Their dad's name wasn't mentioned often, but Allie knew the basics. None of the sisters asked about him much because when they did, Annette's beautiful face tightened, and her answers grew clipped.

He was a musician, she said.

Too handsome for his own good, the aunts added.

Too selfish to stick around for his wife and four daughters, Allie realized.

But Annette wasn't one to dwell on hardship. She had no money, no education, and no support other than her sisters after her parents passed away. So, she'd moved herself and her girls into the only apartment she could afford, Cedarwood Village. Somewhat of an ironic name considering it was neither made of cedar nor was it a village, but low-income housing loved a good euphemism.

If Annette had cared, she didn't let it show. She didn't have that luxury. She waitressed at a diner during the day and enrolled in interior design classes at the community college at night.

Those early years had been hard. The aunts watched Allie and her sisters until Allie, as the oldest, could take over the babysitting. Determination eventually paid off, and Annette graduated with a degree and a single-minded desire to have a successful career. As her business grew, she moved the girls to increasingly nicer rentals closer and closer to the village. She had finally bought the Victorian four years ago.

It was intimidating how easy Annette made it all look. If Allie could do half as much as Annette had done as a single mom, she'd consider herself successful.

The familiar trifecta of oregano, basil, and tomato drifted out of the house. Sunday Dinner. Every week, the aunts, and whichever family members were available, converged to eat at Annette's house. They used to take turns at each other's houses, but once Annette bought the gingerbread house, they agreed she had to host since her kitchen was the nicest. Everyone in the family knew it was the best eating of the week.

"Bah! Too much! Too much oregano." Aunt Giulia, her dark

bob swinging forward, barked as Allie and Sammy stepped into the kitchen.

"Hi, everyone!" Allie greeted the original Hart sisters, Rosa, the eldest, twins Sophia and Giulia, and finally, she greeted her mother, Annette.

"They're here!" Rosa clapped her hands in delight as the women moved in for hugs and kisses.

"Finally." Sophia pressed Allie's head into her shoulder and then grabbed Sammy for his kisses but kept a tight grip on the wooden spoon in her hand. As soon as she turned her back, Giulia's own wooden spoon made for the pot of bubbling sauce. Sophia smacked it away deftly. "Get that out of here. You'll ruin it."

"Whoa." Allie dipped down to dodge their spoons then dropped a kiss on Giulia and Rosa's cheeks. "Smells delicious, aunties."

"What did I tell you? Everyone loves my gravy," Giulia crowed. She wore an apron tied around her waist that read, *Kiss me, I'm Italian.* Gravy, as they called it, was serious business. Each week they took turns making the huge pot of tangy sauce filled with short ribs, meatballs, and sausage. Everyone in the family had the same recipe passed down from Nanny Hart, but each woman made it a little differently and would go to her grave swearing hers was the best.

Giulia moved closer to the pot, defensively holding out her spoon. "Everyone knows the secret to the best gravy is the sugar. It balances out the acid from the tomato."

Sophia sniffed. "Allie's been away for too long. She doesn't know what good gravy tastes like anymore."

Ah, the guilt. The aunts were so very good at it.

"Well," Allie said brightly. "We're home now. Right, Sammy? He's missed you guys!" She gave Sammy a little push in front of her to deflect. Hey, there was no shame. Sammy would learn soon enough how to evade the aunts' attention when he needed to. Allie was equal parts awed and terrified of them.

"Ah, you have brought my grandson." Annette Hart's cool hand rested gently on Allie's cheek before ruffling Sammy's hair and pulling him into a hug.

At forty-five, Annette was often mistaken for Allie's sister. Each of Allie's aunts was attractive and generously endowed with curves. Aunt Sophia and Giulia bore a striking resemblance to Sophia Loren, but Annette had something mysterious and elegant about her that Allie had admired all her life. She was like a piece of crystal: delicately beautiful, with sharp edges that could cut if you weren't careful. For Sammy, her only grandchild, her edges softened.

"Mimi! We live here now!" Sammy said, his voice muffled by the hug. The two of them had been close since Sammy was born. Annette never failed to impose a little guilt of her own that Allie had been depriving her of a relationship with her grandson by living in the city.

"You just saw him when we came to visit in June, remember, Mom?" Allie said patiently.

Annette's perfectly sculpted eyebrow rose. "I remember clearly, Allison. My grandson's visits are the highlight of my life."

She held his cheeks and kissed him on his cute little nose. The aunts crowded around the boy and fussed over him. He soaked up the attention and worked his little-boy charm with each of them.

"Mimi, I missed you so much! I have the coolest bedroom and guess what? I start school tomorrow!"

"Try this, Sammy. I made you your favorite almond cake." Giulia cut off a piece of the dense almond cake and held it out.

Feeding people was as natural as breathing in her family, but Allie intercepted it and put it back on the plate.

"No sugar until I check his blood, auntie," Allie said automatically.

Clearly unfazed, Giulia pinched and kissed Sammy's cheeks. "You are so tall, my little prince! Such a handsome young man."

"Come, I have something for you." Annette set him down and led him by the hand to the kitchen table where a small pile of toys was waiting. Sammy climbed up on the chair and held court like a king, even if his throne was stacked with phone books.

"Good to know you're still the second fiddle around here," Amber taunted as she walked into the kitchen. She swiped a hunk of Italian bread off the counter, swirled it around in the sauce pot, and sat next to Allie. "Ow!"

As quick as a striking snake, Sophia slapped the bread out of her hand. "Whatsa matter with you? Were you raised in a barn? Now, go put your breasts away. There's no one here to see them." She winked at Allie as she put the lid back on the pot.

Amber tugged her low-cut halter up a smidge then sat next to Allie on the island, away from the threat of wooden spoons.

"Yeah, how could you not miss this?" she said sarcastically, waving her hand toward the chaos around them.

"I did miss it," Allie answered. "Sammy loves it here. It's loud and fun. All his cousins are here. The aunts are still crazy." She grinned. "But I missed them too."

"Mom's new house is pretty sweet, though." Amber ran a hand along with the veiny marble countertop. "Too bad we didn't get to enjoy it."

"Yeah, Cedarwood didn't have quite the same aesthetic," Allie said dryly.

Amber shrugged. "That always bothered you more than it bothered me."

She was right. Allie had always been painfully aware of the differences, always hesitant to tell anyone where they lived and see the judgment in their eyes, while Amber had brazened it out. Guess she was missing whatever gene that was because growing up in Northfield had always made her feel like an outsider.

Amber popped the last bite of bread in her mouth and studied Allie. "You look different."

Allie smoothed a hand over the buttons on her boho blouse. It was a cheerful blue with tiny flowers, feminine and flowy. She had loved it as soon as she saw it. "I went shopping."

"Good." Amber nodded approvingly. "This is more you. You look gorgeous in that color."

When Allie moved to New York City with Corbin, her wardrobe consisted of what she wore in high school: jean cutoffs and old band tees. Corbin never made it a secret he wanted her to fit in with his friends and coworkers in the city, so when he told her he was taking her shopping, she didn't think much of it. She was already self-conscious about her pregnancy, and she felt like a gauche schoolgirl around his sophisticated friends.

It had started with little changes to her wardrobe, a blouse here and there, dresses to wear to Corbin's business dinners, purses, and shoes that cost more than her old car. One day, a few years after Sammy was born, she had walked by the mirror in their entryway and stopped.

She hadn't recognized herself.

The woman staring back at her was cool and refined. Her hair was slicked back, her clothing tasteful and understated. She matched the decor in the apartment behind her.

One of the most liberating things Allie had done in the four months since her divorce was donate her wardrobe. Little by little, she was replacing her old things with what made her feel like herself.

Thundering footsteps sounded down Annette's stairs. Allie's youngest sister, Lily, came racing into the kitchen with her twin, Evie, trailing a few sedate steps behind her.

"Sammy's here!" Lily shouted gleefully, pulling him from his greedy grandma's clutches and spinning him around.

Allie always thought of them as being young girls still, but at almost twenty-two, they were about to begin their senior year of college. While each of the sisters was only two years apart, Allie had a special soft spot for the twins, even if she didn't see them as much.

Growing up in a family filled with women could have been a nightmare, but it wasn't anywhere close to that. Allie had known only unconditional love, with a healthy dose of humility from the women who helped raise her. Truthfully, most times Allie didn't even miss having a father around as she grew up.

Yet a part of her had always watched other families and wondered what she was missing. She wondered what it must feel like to see a handsome father sitting down for dinner with the family or to snuggle up between a warm mom and dad in bed on the weekend to watch cartoons. She had always been fascinated when a man came up behind his wife at the mall and placed an affectionate arm around her waist or spun their kids around onto his strong shoulders.

Those glimpses of traditional families had pushed her to make the best of her marriage for Sammy's sake for many years, hoping that things would get better. Now, as she looked around the kitchen filled with teasing women and good food and laughter, she smiled.

We're pretty damn happy too.

∼

"I'm so full," Allie groaned, settling back in her chair and patting her stomach. They were still seated around the dining table, which had all the leaves in to fit everyone. More cousins had trailed in and out throughout the afternoon. Various children were either still seated at the kids' table or running around the house playing tag. Annette's little French bulldog, Hugo, snorted in his sleep under her chair.

The table had been cleared from dinner, and tiny cups of steaming espresso and biscotti were set out. Giulia made the Italian specialty the way she liked, studded with toasted almonds and dried cranberries. Allie dipped the cookie in her coffee to soften it, lulled by the easy conversation around the table.

Lily sat on Sammy's left side, dutifully squeezing his tiny bicep while he showed off. "Oh, you been working out, little man?"

"Yup." He nodded happily. "I played catch with Walter. He's a dog," he said, clarifying for his audience's puzzled faces. "Walter's the coolest. We raced and I got to pet him, and Mr. Henderson was petting Mama too."

If there was a record to scratch, the sound effect would have been appropriate for the abrupt silence in the dining room. The aunts' eyes turned simultaneously to Allie, burning into her like a laser. Painful. Allie groaned inwardly. So much for a peaceful food coma.

"Right, Mama? It was so fun! Mr. Henderson's the best. He has a son named Ben, and we're gonna be baseball players together." Sammy went on, oblivious to the looks being exchanged around the room.

Amber gave Allie a side-eye and murmured, "Mm. Snack time?"

"Well, that was a great dinner," Allie said brightly. She gave her best effort at a graceful escape before they closed ranks and attacked. "Excuse me. I'm just going to start cleaning up." She edged her chair back.

"Sit." Annette's voice was cool and authoritative and still made her quake a little. Okay, a lot. Annette was intimidating.

"Missed your chance," Amber taunted under her breath. Allie kicked her leg under the table.

The aunts were doing their silent talking thing where they all looked at each other and had a conversation that no one else could hear. Allie knew the line of fire was near. Taking a deep breath, she decided to charge. "So. Ha. Sammy, Mr. Henderson wasn't petting me. I almost fell. He caught me. That's all." She looked around at the varying levels of scrutiny.

"Oh, that's why you were hugging! Cool. Mimi, can I watch *Dino Dan* on TV?" Sammy wasn't interested in the particulars like his aunts.

"Come on, Sammy, I'll go with you." Evie edged away from the table. Smart girl.

"Of course, my darling. The remote's on the coffee table." Annette helped him scoot his chair back, and he raced from the room along with a few of his younger cousins.

"Tell us everything," Sophia demanded as soon as Sammy had cleared the doorway.

"It was nothing. I was reaching for a glass, and I lost my balance. Davis saw me and caught me before I fell. That's all. Can you pass the cookies, please? Mmmmph." She shoved two in her mouth desperately. "These are delicious," she mumbled around a mouthful.

"Davis Henderson, hmm. Your landlord?" Annette fixed Allie with a look.

"Hugging and petting," Rosa sounded wistful. "I used to love when Peter would do that to me. That man could kiss like nobody's business." Sophia patted her hand comfortingly. Of all the aunts, Rosa's was the only love story that hadn't ended in disgrace. Uncle Peter had passed six years ago from a heart attack.

"John too," Sophia said. "He was good-for-nothing everywhere else, but the man knew his way around the bedroom." She raised her eyebrows suggestively and shimmied her massive bosom in a move that would have put a stripper to shame. Fitting, since Uncle John had had a fondness for strippers, which was why Sophia had divorced him.

Lily whooped and high-fived her. "Get it, Aunt Soph!"

"So, not exactly the same," Allie mumbled around the cookies. "Davis was just friendly and helping is all. Nothing going on there."

Rosa glanced at Annette and spoke up. "Allie, it might be a good idea for you to meet some new *friends*."

"I have loss of fwends. So many." She muttered around the cookie in her mouth.

Amber pointedly moved the plate of cookies away from her.

"I know who Davis Henderson is. We've designed some of his company's new builds. He's a widower, isn't he?" Annette asked.

Allie was surprised she knew anything about him. After Allie's father had bailed, Annette had let very few men into her life. A trail of men looked longingly after Annette Hart, while she made it a point to never, ever look back. Probably where Amber learned it.

"Yes, his wife died three years ago." Amber propped her chin on her hand. "He's a stone-cold fox. All the girls at the pub try to pick him up."

Amber offered this bit of information helpfully while Allie glared at her. Why did it suddenly feel like she had heartburn? The reaction to her grumpy landlord was unsettling. Since when had a pair of broad shoulders and a sexy, square jaw ever affected her like this?

Lily nodded. "Yeah, for an older guy, he's pretty hot."

"Old? How old is he, dear? We'd like more grandbabies out of you, Allie, before you get too much older." Giulia patted Allie's hand comfortingly.

"We are not dating or making grandbabies, thanks, Aunt Giulia. He's my landlord. That's all. He's finishing up the house and agreed to let Sammy and me move in early. I hardly know him."

But that wasn't entirely true, her brain unhelpfully reminded her. She knew he was kind. He had stuck around to help and ended up unpacking her entire car, and then he had rescued her when she almost fell off the counter. He had that kind of capable, bossy energy she normally chafed at, but from Davis, it came across as being rock solid, dependable.

"He's got that sexy older-man thing going, you know what I mean?" Amber waggled her eyebrows suggestively. "Old enough to know what he's doing and patient enough to make it worth your while."

"He's not old," Allie said defensively, and then shut up when Amber winked at her.

Sophia poured herself another glass of Asti Spumante from the jug that had been full at the beginning of dinner, and then looked around slyly. "John was a big man, in more ways than one."

Oh boy. Aunt Sophia's favorite subject. Allie knew that look. Things always got wild when the aunts poured more wine after dinner.

"Oh, you mean his thunder sword?" Giulia giggled girlishly and slugged her Asti like it was a frat party on a Saturday night. The table full of women leaned forward in anticipation, wineglasses at the ready. It was on now.

"Are you talking about the trouser snake?" Rosa, not to be

outdone by her younger sister, piped up mischievously. The women howled with laughter.

"The old one-eyed monster did the j-j-ob?" Rosa couldn't even get the words out.

"Yes, tell us, was his quiver bone big, Sophia?" Giulia snorted and collapsed against Lily as the rest of the women hooted.

"Quiver bone!" Rosa shrieked with laughter, pounding the table and spilling wine on the tablecloth. Even Annette couldn't help herself, wiping her eyes delicately with a tissue as she laughed.

Around the howling, Rosa leaned over and patted Allie's hand with her own. "Are you doing okay, honey?"

Her sweet face was worried, and Allie's heart tugged in response. She had a special soft spot for Aunt Rosa. They were both softer than the other women in the family, both tender-hearted, and perhaps more sensitive than was good for them. Annette always said that she wore her heart on her sleeve, but Allie couldn't see any other way to live.

Loving someone was like a gift. You give it willingly, without demand, and just hoped that your heart was treated just as tenderly.

"Yeah, Auntie, I'm fine. You know how it was with Corbin. We were together for Sammy in the end."

"I know, dear, but was love there once?"

"In the beginning, there was, at least for me. We tried to do the right thing by Sammy, but it was time for both of us to let it go. Corbin just sped the process up. We'll be okay." Allie looked at Annette for a minute. "I just hope I can do this single mom thing half as well as my mom," she said softly.

"You've got more of your mother in you than you know." Rosa patted Allie's hand comfortingly. "But your heart is tender, and that's a gift I like to think I gave you, honey. You're a smart girl, Allie. You know I'd give my life for your mom and Giulia and Sophia, but don't go putting too much stock into what they say about love. There is no curse in our family, just some mixed signals. There's someone out there for everyone, if they want to find them. You just have to have your sign turned on." She nodded sagely.

"My sign?"

"Yes, the one that lets people know if you're interested or not. Think of it flashing above your head. Yours has been off. It's time to turn it back on and meet someone as wonderful as you are."

Allie leaned over and kissed her aunt's velvet-soft cheek. "Thanks, Auntie. But I'm not sure I want to turn it on. Sammy and I are happy on our own."

"Well, you know yourself best, honey, but I think there is the perfect person out there for you."

Turn your sign on.

Later that night, after she bathed Sammy and they said prayers, Allie set her alarm and got into bed. The first day of school loomed tomorrow, and she was feeling nostalgic thinking about how big Sammy was getting. Milestones were hard. She had always wanted a big family, but Corbin hadn't wanted any more kids. He traveled so much for work that Allie hadn't protested. Those early days with Sammy had been spent mostly alone, juggling a newborn and college classes, and they hadn't been easy.

Sometimes, like now, when the house was quiet and dark and Sammy was asleep, she let her fingers drift over the marks on her belly left behind by her pregnancy and let herself think about families. Growing another sweet-smelling baby in her belly to rock and sing to, knowing Sammy would love on him or her and take them under his wing.

She shushed the tiny voice telling her she didn't know what

that kind of love even looked like and just let herself dream about being loved by a man with somber brown eyes that crinkled when he smiled. She didn't let herself feel it often, but when it was just her and an empty bedroom, she thought about what that might look like, and she let the tears come.

Then she dried her tears and channeled her inner Annette because tomorrow was the first day of school for Sammy.

She was going to rock this single mom thing.

Chapter Eight

She was failing already.

"Goddam—" Allie bit off her words, hopping around the next morning, frantically pulling on a boot while trying to close the front door.

Today of all days, her alarm had decided not to work. She woke up in a panic, all thoughts of a peaceful morning long gone out the window. She threw on a bra under the ribbed white tank top she had slept in and grabbed a pair of cutoffs on the wrong side of too short and too tight. She barely had time to brush her teeth before waking Sammy up and getting them out the door.

"You owe the swear jar!" Sammy shouted gleefully, heading to their car. He was unfazed and enjoying draining her wallet as usual.

"I do not, Samuel Elliot Hoffman. I caught myself." She puffed, yanking on the other boot. Awesome. She had grabbed her brand new, fire-engine red rain boots instead of her sandals, but it was too late to change.

She had gone to bed with visions of their morning going a lot smoother than this. They were going to have a nice hot breakfast, and then they would chat as they got ready to walk to the school only a block away. Instead, she had tossed him a hard-boiled egg and a cheese stick and got them out the door with zero extra time.

Winning at single mom-hood already.

"Remember that I'm meeting you at the nurse's office before lunch today, right, Sammy? We'll show her how to check your blood sugar and check your pump." Allie put the car in reverse, but then had to skid to a stop at the end of the driveway. An elderly couple walking their dog waved. Allie gave them a frazzled wave back. She always forgot how friendly people were in Northfield.

Sammy met her eyes in the rearview mirror and saluted. "Aye, aye, Captain."

He was on a pirate kick lately. She had barely managed to wrestle his Captain Hook eye patch off him before they left the house. They had compromised, putting it in his backpack instead. For recess, he told her with an impish grin.

"And you won't forget to go to the nurse to get checked before snack and lunch?"

"I will, Mama. I'm big now. I got this." He did look older. With his hair combed neatly and his little backpack and sneakers with real laces, he didn't look like a little boy anymore. Jeez, she better pull it together or she was going to cry at drop-off and really mortify him.

It felt like she was letting a piece of her heart out into the world, all unprotected and raw. Like much of life, it was terrifying and beautiful at the same time.

"I packed peanut butter crackers for your snack in the little compartment in the front of your lunchbox, okay? Ask your teacher if you can't open it, and she'll help you." She tried to think of anything else he could need her for.

"I can do it," he said patiently. His small face split into a grin when she pulled into the drop-off lane of the school. "Look at that playground!"

The fenced-in playground next to the school was one of those fancy new ones with a huge rope climber and plenty of space for kids to run around.

She carefully pulled the car past a line of safety cones and got in line behind the other expensive cars in front of the main school entrance. The drop-off line was long, and most of the parents looked impatient as they waited their turn. She looked down at her skimpy outfit and slunk lower into her seat, thankful she didn't have to get out.

"Look! There's Mr. Henderson!" Sammy rolled his window down and waved. "And Walter's with him. Hi, Walter!"

"Sammy, stop!" She hissed. Great. Another run-in with the new landlord on an already crappy day. She pulled up a little as another car behind her honked, glancing at the crowd of parents chatting in front of the building.

Davis was easy to spot. He stood at least a head taller than everyone else and wore neither suit nor tie. He was in work clothes, the navy Henderson Construction T-shirt contouring his broad shoulders and strong arms, and a well-worn pair of jeans with work boots. He looked rougher around the edges and larger than the other dads around him. He caught her eye and gave a small, unsmiling nod while he continued talking to a group of people.

Next to Davis stood a tall, thin girl. Her dark hair was loosely braided and listing to the left, and she had her nose buried in a notebook.

The car line inched forward again until it was their turn. "You can unbuckle now, buddy. Have a good day. I'll see you at the nurse's office before lunch."

"Ow. It pinched me. I can't get it. I need help, please."

"Okay, can you—no? Sammy, I'm really not dressed..." She sighed, seeing no hope for it. "Okay, I'll be right there."

She put the car in park, saying a little prayer no one would recognize her from high school.

"And who do we have here?" Allie looked up to see Mrs. Gayle, her former principal, marching over with a clipboard against her barrel chest. She had her usual pursed-lip expression, but it softened in surprise when she saw Allie. "Hello, Allie," she boomed.

People looked over curiously, and Allie's cheeks flamed. Awesome. So much for blending in.

The older woman stuck her hand out formally to Sammy, who shook it properly. Now, where had he learned that?

"Welcome to Northfield. I'm Mrs. Gayle."

"Nice to meet you," Sammy said. He was trying his best to be brave, but Allie felt his body tremble.

"We're glad to have you," Mrs. Gayle boomed. They eyed each other, Sammy with his solemn eyes, and Mrs. Gayle, who knew a thing or two about being the new kid. "Would you like to check out the playground before the bell rings?" Mrs. Gayle asked.

Sammy looked at the playground longingly. "Yes, please."

"The playground it is. Claire?" The girl next to Davis looked up from her book. "Claire Henderson, would you please come here for a minute?" The girl looked up at Davis, who hesitated before nodding. Claire walked over.

"Claire, this is Sammy and his mom, Mrs. Hoffman. Today's his first day at Northfield. Would you be a good friend and show him around?" Mrs. Gayle handled the introduction with the ease of a longtime teacher used to easing social situations.

Claire Henderson had a lovely, delicate face with huge blue

eyes. Allie didn't see much of a resemblance to her father except for her dark hair and long legs. She had a long-limbed grace that reminded Allie of a ballerina.

"Hi." Claire waved shyly. "Would you like to meet my brother, Ben? He's in second grade."

Sammy lifted to his toes against Allie for a quick kiss. "Yes! Bye, Mama! Love you!" He grabbed Claire's hand and raced away without a backward look.

"Bye, Sammy!" Allie called after him, slightly shocked at how well that went.

"He's going to do just fine here," Mrs. Gayle said warmly. "Welcome back, Allie."

"Thanks. I'm back to Allie Hart now."

"Well, we've missed you, Allie Hart." Mrs. Gayle's strong arms suddenly encircled Allie and pulled her in for a hug. Allie froze for a second before tentatively returning the embrace. The woman smelled like Jovan White Musk. A car horn beeped impatiently, reminding Allie she was holding up the line of cars.

"Everybody will get where they need to go, people!" Mrs. Gayle barked before releasing her with a sturdy thump on her back. "Try not to worry about Sammy. He's going to do just fine if he's anything like his mother."

"Thanks, Mrs. Gayle." Allie stepped back toward the curb. "I'll try not to."

A thump and sudden resistance met her tires when she eased her car away from the curb. For one horrifying second, she thought she had hit someone before she noticed a few people in the crowd pointing at her tire. She pushed the gas tentatively, and the engine revved, but the tires didn't move.

Allie groaned and looked around for Mrs. Gayle, but she was at the end of the drop-off line with her walkie-talkie out. *Dammit.* She pounded the steering wheel once before opening the door and sliding out to see the problem. As soon as she rounded the front end of the car, she saw the oversize orange traffic cone twisted inside her wheel well.

Of course, she would run over a traffic cone in the parent drop-off line.

On the first day of school.

In front of a line of cars waiting to drop their kids off. Of course.

She paced back and forth for a minute looking for a place to grab hold of the cone. Finally, she bent over, grabbed the cone with both hands and pulled.

Not an inch of movement.

She tugged down her shorts and tried again. She pulled again, wriggling and jerking her arms back and forth, painfully aware of just how ridiculous she looked in her outfit, wrestling an oversized traffic cone.

Truly frustrated now, she braced her feet on the side of the tire and yanked with her body weight on the cone. "Urrrrrgumpfhhhh."

A horn honked. "That's very helpful. Thank you," she called through gritted teeth, yanking again.

Nothing. Nada. Zip.

She took a deep breath and tried again.

"I DON'T KNOW what's going on over there," Ford Clairmont said appreciatively, looking over toward the drop-off line, "but I think she needs a hand."

Davis nodded at his friends, Toby and Keri Richardson, as they joined the two of them in front of the school.

"Oh no," Keri murmured. "Toby, go help her." She pushed

her husband Toby's arm, and they all followed her eyes to the scene unfolding.

The reason for the honking finally became clear. There, bending and wriggling around in front of the entire parent drop-off line, was Allie.

Davis swore softly. What the hell had she gotten herself into now? She was wrestling with something and, from where he stood, losing. What the hell was she wearing? The bright-red boots and tiny shorts stuck out like a sore thumb in this crowd.

Ah, hell. It crossed his mind he should let Ford help her out, but his feet were moving almost before the thought was finished.

"Stay." He pointed and Walter collapsed in an enormous heap of golden fur while he jogged over to the curb where Allie was parked. A line of cars idled behind her, waiting impatiently, and a crowd of parents and kids watched the spectacle.

He took in the problem— an orange traffic cone she had run over was jammed in the wheel well of her car. She was now bouncing her considerable assets around to pull it out.

It was a gorgeous sight, he had to admit. Even the most stoic of dads and grandpas were grinning appreciatively as Davis walked by.

Allie braced one shapely leg on the tire and pulled with all her weight on the cone.

"Try twisting it more," one of the spectators helpfully yelled.

"Yeah, ya gotta really bend your knees, missy!" This from old Mr. Donahue, who didn't even have a grandkid in the school. He lived in the neighborhood and had his little yappy dog next to him.

Davis turned around and gave them the take-no-shit glare he saved for his crew when they slacked off. "Keep it moving," he barked. He planted himself behind Allie to block as much of her as he could.

"Need some help?" he asked gruffly.

"All set. Thanks," she said through her teeth without looking at him, yanking the orange rubber harder.

The cone loosened a few inches, and she suddenly lost her grip, knocking back into him. The cone remained wedged in the wheel well.

She glanced over her shoulder and closed her eyes briefly. "Oh. You. Figures."

Her honey-blond hair in a loose ponytail had come loose, falling around her face.

"Uh-huh. Need some help?" The dejection on her face made the corner of his mouth tug up slightly in amusement.

"I think I got—son of a b—" She turned back and braced both of her feet on the tire this time and yanked as hard as she could. "—iscuit!" she finished just as the extra leverage caused the cone to slip free suddenly. Her boots slid out from under her, and her body shot backward. *Oof.*

Her back slammed into his chest instead of the road, and they both grunted from the impact. Instinctively, Davis locked his arms tight under her breasts to keep her from falling. He held her there against his chest for a few seconds while she steadied herself. *Soft.* Her scent filled his senses again, something sweet, like cinnamon sugar or vanilla cake.

"Biscuit? Such language." He couldn't help but tease her as he set her down. "This is an elementary school, you know." He loosened his grip on her ribs, his hands falling to her waist to steady her as she turned around.

"Shut up," she muttered. "I'm trying not to owe the swear jar."

He didn't think she realized she was holding onto his arms and rubbing her fingers lightly back and forth over his arms like she had that day in the kitchen.

"This is turning into a habit," he said.

"A habit?" she said breathlessly, still standing close enough that he could feel her body heat.

"Catching you. Again," he said dryly.

"It was an accident."

"You didn't see the bright-orange cones?" He couldn't seem to resist teasing her. Her nose got all scrunched up and a splotch of dark pink spread up from her chest when she got riled. He had caught that same hint of teasing laughter in her eyes the first night he met her. Aware of the eyes on them, Davis stepped back. "You should be more careful," he warned grimly.

She twisted to look around him. He knew the moment she spotted the people left milling around, watching them curiously. "Oh my God," she whispered, closing her eyes. "Everybody's watching."

He dragged his eyes away from her to confirm a line of cars waiting and parents lingering around. "Yup."

"Hey," Ford walked up with his hand outstretched. "I'm Ford Clairmont. I was going to ask if you needed any help. That was, uh, something, huh?" He nodded toward the cone.

"Glad I could be your entertainment this morning," Allie said wryly.

Ford gave her his biggest grin, showing all his teeth. Davis gritted his own. "Oh, me too," he said earnestly, the little shit. "You must be new to Northfield?"

"No," she sighed. "I'm not."

"Oh, nice. I'm from here too. Must have just missed you in school. I've met your sister at the pub, though." He pointed. "The kid running around with the stick, terrorizing everyone on the playground is mine. Landon. He's in second grade."

"I have a son in second grade too. Sammy."

"You do? Well, we should get them together sometime."

Davis stiffened and glared at his friend. Ford grinned back unrepentantly. Ford was a good guy, successful with women, and he was closer to Allie's age than Davis was, with a ton less baggage. Still, something prickled in him unpleasantly while Ford flirted with Allie.

A heavy hand on the horn made them all jump. "Well, welcome back, Allie." Ford grinned down at her as he walked backward. "Maybe I'll see you around sometime."

Davis couldn't tear his eyes away from her face, which pissed him off, and he scowled down at her.

She glared right back.

His lips twitched. She was a firecracker.

"You're an accident waiting to happen," he growled.

"Accident—!" she sputtered. "Good thing I'm not your concern then, Davis Henderson. I can take care of myself."

With that, she bent down and snatched the cone off the ground, set it back up on the curb, a safe distance away from her tires, huffed around to the driver's side of her car, and got in without once looking back.

Davis couldn't take his eyes off her.

"So, who was that?" Keri asked, nudging his side as he returned. "You two looked pretty friendly."

The front loop was empty after the last bell rang and the kids cleared out, but Toby, Keri, and Ford were waiting for him.

Davis looked down at her and raised an eyebrow. "She's renting out the Lincoln Street house."

Keri looked speculative. "Maybe you could invite her out to happy hour sometime. You know, to be neighborly."

"I wish she was my neighbor," Ford said wistfully.

Keri snorted. "Ford, you have plenty of lady friends." She gave him an affectionate pat on the arm to soften her words.

Ford grinned, not the least bit offended. "I've got to run too.

I have a trial starting this week." Ford slugged back the last sip of coffee from his travel mug and headed toward the parking lot. "See you guys for happy hour."

"We'll be there. Gimme a smooch, baby." Keri pursed her lips and tugged Toby's head down for a kiss, which he gave her soundly. "Ooh!" She rubbed her hand over her very pregnant belly. "Baby boy says 'bye,' Daddy."

"Have a good day, Keri. Don't stand too long on your feet." Davis hugged her gently.

Toby and Keri had been good friends with him and Melody. It was an easy friendship because they had been on a similar timeline, married within a month of each other, getting pregnant, and then having their babies at the same time. Melody and Keri had even been in rooms next to each other in the hospital when Ben and their son Max were born. He loved Toby like a brother, and Keri just the same. Watching their happily ever after, once so closely paralleled with his, would never be completely painless, but it didn't stab at him anymore either.

"I won't, honey." She patted his arm. "Have a good day, boys."

Davis whistled to Walter, who had been sleeping after his exciting morning being adored. They made their way through the crosswalk and nodded to Natalie and Carly Lewis as they passed.

"Hi, Davis." Natalie smiled as they passed each other. "Hope you enjoyed that tuna noodle casserole I dropped off last week," she said, wriggling her fingers and walking backward.

He hated tuna noodle casserole, but it didn't matter. He had given it to his crew.

"Morning." He nodded politely at them both. "Actually, about the dinners—"

"Oh, it's no trouble at all, Davis!" she interrupted gaily. "Just a little something."

"Appreciate that, but we don't need—"

"Tater tot hot dish next time! It's my grandma's secret recipe! Come on, Carly, we're late!" She tugged on the little girl's hand and ran so quickly on her pointy heels Davis was honestly concerned she might break her neck.

Toby was almost choking on his laughter. "Man, I love tuna noodle casserole. Who'd you give that one to?"

"It's in the freezer at work," he bit out. They walked together toward the pickle factory. The last of the stragglers walking to school had thinned out, and the neighborhood was quiet and peaceful in the early-morning sun.

"I don't know why you don't just eat that food. It would save you a night of cooking, and Natalie's food is good." Toby would know. He'd eaten enough of it.

"You know why," Davis grunted.

"Suit yourself. Saw the project list for Lincoln Street," Toby began placidly.

Davis kept walking. They were coming up to the four corners of Main Street, and they waved to a group of elderly gentlemen sitting outside the coffee shop. He loved the feeling of community in Northfield, and how people were so willing to help each other out. He didn't like how everyone knew his business, but it was a small price to pay to raise a family with such strong support.

Toby eyed him slyly. "Looks like you'll be over there for a while."

"Yup."

"I could always send over another crew. I bet Donovan won't mind helping Allie out. That is, if you're too busy?"

He hesitated. He could assign someone else to finish the updates on Allie's house. His crew wouldn't even notice. He should do that. It was a smart decision. "I've got it," he muttered instead.

"Okay, if you're sure. It's just that when I saw you two just now, it seemed like there was some tension there." Toby was all but rubbing his hands together in glee.

"Toby," Davis said with his teeth clenched.

"What's up, boss?"

"Fuck off," Davis said succinctly as he pulled the door open to their building and let it slam closed behind him.

Chapter Nine

THE SCHOOL still smelled the same. Pencil shavings and tater tots from the cafeteria, and a little chalk dust mixed in, though Allie didn't see any blackboards as she walked down the school's halls a little later that morning. She peeked into the classrooms on her way to the nurse's office. Smartboards had replaced the blackboards of her schooldays.

She had run home to shower and change after the cone incident. Wearing a pair of shorts and a T-shirt, she headed back to meet Sammy in the nurse's office for their meeting. Thankfully, she hadn't run into Davis at the house when she went home. She needed a little time before seeing his scowl again.

She pushed open the door to the nurse's office and looked around. Plants in stands were bathed in light from a big, bright window behind the desk that sat to her right. Three curtained-off bays each had a blue faux-leather bed.

Allie remembered many a lunch hour sitting cross-legged on those cots to avoid the cafeteria. While no one else paid much attention to which side of the canal she lived, Allie had never felt comfortable in school. She spent her time hiding in the nurse's office or trying her best to blend in when that wasn't an option. Thankfully, Mrs. Wagner seemed to sense this and gave her refuge whenever she could.

Mrs. Wagner held out her hands to grasp Allie's. The silver jewelry on the woman's wrists tinkled merrily as she pulled Allie into her arms. "Allie, welcome back!"

"Hi, Mrs. Wagner." Sylvia Wagner was older and plumper, but Allie would never forget the wild tangle of curly hair, now thoroughly silver. She had taken care of bumps, scrapes, fevers, menstrual cramps, and everything in between with the warm affection of a grandmother. Allie hugged her tightly in return.

The woman's eyes twinkled when she pulled back. "Pish. Call me Sylvia, dear. You're not in school anymore. So, you're back with that cute little rascal, Sammy, are you? I checked on him this morning, and he looked happy as a clam in Sadie's classroom. He looks like you with his freckles on his nose."

"Yes, that's my boy," Allie said proudly. "We just moved back last Friday into a house on Lincoln Street. A few streets down from my mom."

"I know," Sylvia confessed. "Your aunt Rosa told me when we played rummy last week, and then I heard all about the cone this morning."

Allie grimaced. "I'll never live that down."

"I imagine not, but what a comeback," Sylvia said merrily. "I saw that nice Mr. Henderson helping you out, and Ford Clairmont was quick to help too. What I wouldn't give to have the two of them rushing to help me, eh?"

"Yes, they were very helpful," she mumbled.

"You're red as an apple! I'm just teasin' ya, darlin'." Sylvia laughed. "Tell me to zip it, okay? You'll find every single woman in this school has their eyes glued to those two, even some of the married ones." She leaned closer. "Just don't go making him any casseroles. Believe me, I live across the street, and I see enough of them with my own eyes."

Allie looked at her in surprise. "Casseroles?"

"Yes," she said emphatically. "He used to have them coming out of his ears! After his poor Melody died, it was genuine enough to want to help the family out with dinners and the like. I even made a few for them myself, for him and the kids."

She leaned in toward Allie and added conspiratorially, "He said they liked my chicken spaghetti better than anyone else. I use that Pioneer Woman's recipe, you know? With the cream of mushroom soup?" She leaned in closer. "But some of the ladies around here have ulterior motives. They still show up at his door, looking like they're headed on a date."

So, Davis had a fan club. Allie filed that bit of information away for later. She wasn't surprised, seeing as how she had come dangerously close to applying for membership. Despite his scowl, Davis Henderson was hot. Like, scary hot. Yes, he was growly and looked irritated with life in general, but she had already seen moments where he was protective and bossy, and it did something to her. Best not to focus on that.

"Hi, Mama!" Sammy shot through the door like a pistol and bulldozed her with a hug. His head was sweaty, and he had a red smudge of paint on his cheek. He looked happy and relaxed, and Allie let go of the last bit of tension she had been holding.

"Hi, Sammy." She leaned down to plant a kiss on his rosy cheek. "It looks like you're having a fun day."

"I'm having a great day! We have a class pet. His name is Buster the Hamster, and Ben's in my class!" He was nearly hopping up and down in his excitement. "And this is my teacher!" He pointed to the woman who walked in behind him.

"Hi, Ms. Hart. I'm Sadie Nichols, Sammy's teacher." She smiled and Allie could see why Sammy was so enchanted with her. She was Snow White's doppelganger with her big blue eyes and black hair. She half expected a trio of bluebirds to fly around her head. "I'd say Sammy is having a great first day."

She gave Sammy a warm smile. Even her voice was soft and lilting.

"Call me Allie, please." She shook Sadie's hand warmly, and the three women looked down at Sammy.

"So, Sammy," Sylvia said. "I hear you and I will be hanging out here a few times a day to check your blood sugar and give you some medicine."

"Yup, I gotta bum pancreas," Sammy said out of the corner of his mouth like an old-timey gangster, making the women laugh.

"Do you now? And how do you take care of that?" Sylvia said gamely, settling back in her chair and giving him her full attention.

"I poke my finger before I eat to check my blood sugar. Doesn't even hurt," Sammy boasted, holding up his hands with his fingers spread wide. He pricked his fingers anywhere from four to eight times each day. "When I'm a little older, I'm going to get another robot button that stays in my skin like my insulin pump." He pointed to the small black device that he wore on his hip that delivered insulin to his body through a tiny tube that stayed under his skin. "That'll check my sugar for me. No more pokes." He grinned up at the women.

Allie had always been impressed with Sammy's bravery, but she felt an extra bit of pride when she looked at her son now. What kid wouldn't be sad to learn they were going to be pricking their finger multiple times a day for the rest of their life? Even the continuous glucose monitor device—the robot button—Sammy was talking about wasn't foolproof. It was a lot for a kid to deal with, but Sammy had taken the news like a champ. He was all the best parts of her and Corbin.

"Your Aunt Rosa said your mom's a nurse, huh? We're going to need a new nurse here pretty soon," Sylvia said, looking at Allie speculatively over her candy-red eyeglasses. "My husband retired this year, and he's been bugging me to move up to our lake house before winter sets in. What do you think of applying for my job?"

"I think that would be amazing," Allie said with surprise.

"Okay." She clapped her hands together. "Send over your information, and I'll give it to Eileen Gayle. I know she always had a soft spot for you. You'd be perfect for the job."

She looked at Sammy as she settled herself into a swivel chair at the table.

"Now, let's talk about you, dear. It sounds like you know how your body works. I'm here to help you with anything you need. Can you tell us what it looks like when your blood sugar gets low?"

"Oh yeah. I get wobbly and sweaty." Sammy's nose crinkled. "It's scary, but I'm real brave." He was so endearing, clearly enjoying the attention of yet another group of adoring women. Being raised in a family of women had certainly given him an abundance of confidence.

It was somewhat of a delicate balance to keep Sammy's blood sugar levels as close to normal as possible. If they got too high and stayed there consistently, he risked damage to his organs. If his blood sugar was too low, it could be very dangerous, even deadly.

Sometimes, Sammy noticed when he was feeling low and they could correct it by getting sugar into his body quickly with a juice box or another fast-acting sugar, but most times he wasn't aware.

"You're such a brave boy, Sammy." Sadie gave him another of her sweet smiles that made Sammy glow. Someone had a crush on his pretty teacher.

"You sure are, little man. We'll take excellent care of you," Sylvia added. "And, hey, I have a couple of other kids here at Northfield that have diabetes that I'd like to introduce you to. I think you could all help each other out. What do you think?" Sylvia asked, and Sammy's face lit up.

"Cool!"

"All right, that's settled then. How about you show me how I can help take care of you, buddy?" Sylvia took out the small bag of supplies. "Allie, don't forget to send me that email."

"I won't. Thank you."

"He's a wonderful boy. You must be so proud," Sadie said quietly while Sammy got the checker ready, and Sylvia and Sammy bent over his finger to get a reading.

"He's pretty special."

"I don't have any kids yet. My husband, Rob, and I just got married." She smiled shyly. "But I can imagine how hard it must be to let somebody that precious"—she nodded to Sammy—"out of your sight. I promise we'll treat him like our own."

When Allie walked out of the school a while later, she was humming. It wasn't easy to have your heart living outside your body, but it was doable with people like that around.

WALTER'S TAIL thunked excitedly when Allie walked up the front steps to her house a few hours later with her arms full of groceries. The big golden dog was stretched out on the front porch like an oversized furry welcome mat.

After her meeting at the nurse's office, Allie had gone shopping at the boutiques on Main Street for some pillows and throw blankets and stopped by the grocery store before heading home.

Davis's truck was in the driveway, sparking more irritation from his parting shot about her being an accident waiting to happen. He was ornery and just plain wrong. Though she knew she should just ignore him, he had gotten under her skin with that comment.

Corbin would have said something like that to her. He had always been judging her clothes, where she grew up, and her friends. The last thing she wanted or needed was another man in her life looking down his nose at her.

Go fuc—stuff yourself, Davis Henderson.

"Hey, Walter," she greeted the dog and set the bags down next to the door to give him pets. The big furry beast looked at her adoringly. "Who's a good boy? You are, aren't you, you handsome boy? You like that, huh? Come in, then," she invited, standing and unlocking the door.

Walter paused at the threshold, his soft ears perked up and head tilted to the side as if he was making sure it was okay. "Such nice manners you have, Walter."

Better than your owner.

"Sweet Home Alabama" was playing through the house when she walked in. She liked Lynyrd Skynyrd just fine, actually a lot, but she was pissed enough at the radio's owner that she went to the kitchen speaker, queued up Beyoncé, and turned it up.

She took her time putting away the groceries, stopping to tell Bey who ran the world while she arranged the ridiculous assortment of cheeses she picked up in the fridge. A lovely brie, a sharp bleu, and an earthy goat cheese. After all, no one was around to complain about how much she bought or how much space it took up in the fridge. She bumped her hip against the fridge to close it then shook her hips to the beat.

Feelin' herself.

She shimmied into the living room and admired each new pillow she took out of the store bags before tossing them on the couch. Bright pinks and corals and a velvety green, all oversized and perfect for cuddling up with when she watched movies.

She turned the speaker up a titch more and headed onto the front porch to water the ferns she had picked up.

The porch swing got its own treatment, more cozy pillows, and a soft faux-fur blanket. She intended to wake up and bring her coffee out to the porch every morning and end the night in the same spot. Already it was her favorite part of the house, filled with the sun the morning and the moonlight in the evening. She set out a little wicker garden stool she found on clearance next to the swing and arranged candles and matches on it.

It was perfect. Perfectly hers.

Only one thing would make this moment better.

She got up and went to the kitchen and took out the fresh pint of Ben and Jerry's Chocolate Fudge Brownie ice cream and a spoon.

Walking back out to the porch and stretching out on the swing, she rested her head on a pillow, one foot bent at the knee, and with one bare foot on the floor, she gave a push.

She rocked, ate ice cream, listened to Beyoncé, and just... enjoyed it.

For the first time in her life, she had her own place.

The potential new job of her dreams with Sammy right down the hall. It was a heady feeling to be making the choices in her life for once.

She was contemplating that with a mouthful of chocolate fudge ice cream when Davis walked through the front door and stopped short beside the swing.

High on sugar and freedom, she grinned at him lazily. For the briefest moment, she thought he was going to smile back. His stern face softened, the corners of his mouth curved, and she waited, a shiver of anticipation traveling through her body.

"Are we at a concert?" he barked instead.

His T-shirt clung in damp patches on his flat stomach and

wide chest. He looked grumpy and sexy, and all too distracting standing there glaring at her with his gloved hands hitched on his narrow hips. It was the same disapproving look that Corbin used to have when he came home and saw something he didn't like.

Corbin was a neat freak by nature, and, well, she wasn't. She wasn't a slob by any means, but she didn't mind a little mess, especially living with a kid. It was one of the reasons she had been so glad to move out. No more men glaring at her like Davis was right now. Anger pricked the back of her neck even as she slowly, deliberately loaded more ice cream onto her spoon.

His eyes raked over her bare legs, sprawled out on the swing. A muscle in his jaw tightened and released. Only her music was playing now. "Do you mind turning that down?" he finally gritted out.

She thought about it, looked him dead in the eye, and then deliberately spread her bare thigh further to rock the swing again with one foot, not missing the way Davis's eyes followed the movement.

"Yup," she said, deliberately popping the P. Annoying, she knew, but something about Davis Henderson made her want to get a rise out of him. She didn't care to look too closely at why.

He stared at her. "Yup?"

"Yes, I mind."

His eyebrows shot up nearly to his hairline. "What does that mean?"

"It means," she said evenly, holding his stare, "exactly what I said. It's my house, and I want to listen to Bey." She slowly licked the last of the chocolate off the spoon. Davis's eyes followed her tongue. She took her time, enjoying the flush darkening his cheeks.

Finally, he met her eyes. "I'm done for the day." His eyes were shuttered now, but the color was still high on his cheeks.

He stripped off his gloves and slapped them into his palm hard enough to make a sound. "Next time, if you don't like my music, just say so like a goddamned grown-up." He turned on his heel and stomped back into the house.

Touché.

But she had won too. She had seen the attraction in his eyes before he could hide it. It really was too bad her landlord was so ornery. He had moments where that hard stare cracked, and she thought he might be softening to her. Then he ruined it by being an asshole.

"Later, sunshine," she yelled to no one because Davis was already back inside.

She shoveled a spoonful of chocolate fudge brownie into her mouth and closed her eyes to enjoy it, blocking out everything but the taste of chocolate and freedom.

Chapter Ten

"Good job, Sammy! Pedal, bud, pedal!"

The bottoms of Sammy's feet circled furiously on the bike pedals. He looked like a little cartoon character with his feet going a mile a minute on the sidewalk outside their house.

Someone had left a bike for Sammy on the front porch when he got home from school. She suspected Davis, although he'd probably never admit it now after their little standoff that afternoon. As soon as Sammy saw the bike, he had begged to ride it up and down the sidewalk before and after dinner.

"Faster, buddy! If you go too slow, you'll stop moving!"

Sammy's freckled face beamed as he looked back. "I'm riding a bike!" he shouted from a few houses away. He was, kind of. Sammy was marginally better at riding the bicycle than he had been throwing a baseball.

He wobbled back and forth precariously, his little arms turning the handlebars whichever way his head swiveled. His butt would be sore tomorrow, but he got back on every time he fell off.

"You sure are, buddy!"

"That son of yours, he's a handsome one." The elderly

woman next door walked down her porch steps to watch Sammy. Allie had caught glimpses of her watering her potted tomatoes and basil. She was tiny and slightly stooped over with an apron tied around her neck and thick-soled Velcro shoes on her feet. Her home was an older-style Craftsman like Allie's, although not updated.

"That's my son, Sammy. I'm Allie Hart."

"Josephine Autovino. I made you this." The woman thrust a Corelle dish into Allie's arms. "It's my grandson's favorite—rigatoni alla carbonara." She said it with the hard vowels of a native Italian.

The savory, silky scents of cheese, eggs, pasta, and bacon wafted up, and Allie's stomach growled. "Thank you. It smells amazing."

"Bah." She waved away the thanks with a gnarled hand. "My husband loved my dinners when he was alive. I don't make them anymore just for me. You and your boy can eat this."

"I'm sorry for your loss," Allie said gently.

Mrs. Autovino shrugged nonchalantly, but not before Allie saw a shadow cross her face. "We had a good life, my Marco and I. Married sixty-seven years, and all of them here in this house." She pulled a cherry tomato off one of the potted plants on either side of her porch and held it out to Allie. "You will like it here in Northfield. It's a good place for families."

Allie didn't mention she grew up here. The appeal of small-town living wasn't lost on her, especially now she had lived somewhere else. She would probably always roll her eyes at some of the more pretentious Northfield quirks, but it made more sense now why Annette had stayed here. She popped the tomato into her mouth and enjoyed the flavor. It was warm from the sun and delicately sweet.

"I'm still mad at him for leaving me," Mrs. Autovino grumbled, but there was no anger in her voice. "You are not married?" she asked abruptly.

"Divorced. You were married for sixty-seven years? Wow. That's a wonderful life together. That's far enough, Sammy," Allie called out. "Come back this way now."

Sixty-seven years of marriage. It seemed impossible when she couldn't even manage eight. She didn't know a single couple married that long. Even her Nanny and Grandpa, Annette's parents, who had more luck in love than anyone else in the family, hadn't been married that long. She surreptitiously studied her tiny neighbor. What secrets about love did this woman have that none of the Hart women seemed to possess?

"That Davis Henderson, he is a good one, you know. I make him my Bolognese," Mrs. Autovino said casually. "It will make you cry when you taste it." She touched her fingers to her mouth and kissed them. "That little boy of his, he's like his daddy. Eats it all up. Whatever I give him—all gone. His little Claire, she eats like a bird. I tell her, eat! Eat! You will not grow if you don't eat!"

Allie, well aware of most Italian women's obsession with feeding people, just nodded. "You know Davis?" she asked hesitantly. Truthfully, she was feeling a little embarrassed about baiting him earlier with the music. It hadn't been as satisfying as she thought it might be.

The older woman nodded sagely. "Davis is a good one. He takes care of my yard work sometimes. He put in my clothesline. I try to pay him, but he won't take my money. He has good kids too. They don't sit in front of the idiot box all day." She sniffed. "Kids these days." She put her hands up to her face to mimic scrolling a phone. "Do this all day long 'till their eyes fall out of their head. Bah!"

"The idiot box... ah, the TV." Allie stifled a laugh. Mrs. Autovino was a hoot. "Yes, he's been great so far. He's still working on the house, but he let us move in early." A twinge of guilt made her shift uneasily. He had been very generous with her and Sammy, more than necessary, really.

"He's just like my Marco. A hard worker. A family man. He would make a good husband," she added, and Allie caught the twinkle in her faded blue eyes. Someone was matchmaking.

"He's my landlord," she said firmly. "That's all."

"Eh," she shrugged that away. "He lost his wife, you know that?"

"I did," Allie murmured.

The old woman's eyes shadowed. "He's been raising those two babies on his own since."

The tinge of guilt from earlier turned into full-blown shame. To lose a young wife and mother... it was unimaginable. An image of Davis twisting the gold band on his finger on the porch filled her head, reluctantly softening her heart toward him.

Mrs. Autovino nodded. "His heart was broken, but he is ready now, I think."

"Ready?" Allie asked warily.

"A man like Davis needs a good woman to love and take care of. That's what makes him happy. I think he's ready now to find that." She smiled slyly. "Then I see you slam the door in his face."

"That was just a misunderstanding."

The older woman nodded knowingly. "My Marco and I met like that. Sparks right off the bat. He couldn't keep his hands off me." She smiled and for a second Allie caught a glimpse of the vivacious young woman she must have once been. "You don't stop giving him hell. A man like that, he needs someone to make him smile after what he's been through."

"Look, Mama, no hands!" Sammy careened toward them with his arms held up like he was at the top of a roller coaster.

The bike wobbled to the right, and Allie leaped out to steady it before it crashed.

"Whoa. Hands on the bars, buddy." She led him back toward the porch. "Sammy, this is Mrs. Autovino, our neighbor."

"Hi, Mrs. Autovino. Nice to meet you." Sammy took her frail hand and shook it gently.

The elderly woman pinched his cheek and dug around in her apron pocket. "Aren't you a handsome boy? Here, want chocolate?" She handed him a linty-looking Hershey Kiss.

Sammy took it and gave her his biggest smile, the one he reserved for his Mimi and all his aunts. He knew a soft touch when he saw one. "Thanks! I love Kisses. Want a kiss for a kiss?" He pursed his sweet little lips, and Allie saw the moment Josephine Autovino's heart wrapped firmly around Sammy's little finger.

"Oh, come here, you darling boy." She pursed her lips and laid a gentle kiss on his cheek.

"It was nice visiting with you, Mrs. Autovino. Sammy, say good night. It's bath time."

"Good night, you two. You'll let me know if you need any recipes," she said placidly. "For you, I give them."

"Let's try to keep the water in the tub, okay, honey?" Allie knelt on the tile next to the bathtub and mopped up the puddles Sammy was making. He had been in the bath for a half hour now, and his fingers looked like prunes.

"Rawr, my dinosaur will eat you." Two plastic dinosaurs clashed in the tub, making the water surge onto the penny-tile floor. Allie mopped it up and looked around at the bathroom. Like the rest of the house, Davis had kept as close to the original appliances and materials as possible. The tub in her en suite was a heavenly porcelain claw-foot tub that she had used every night since they moved in.

Sammy grabbed the bar of soap from the tray and dropped it into the water with a thunk. He chased it, splashing more water over the tub, before sitting up abruptly. "Mama, what do you think Mr. Henderson is doing right now?"

"I don't know, honey." She had been thinking almost the same thing since Mrs. Autovino dropped her bomb. She had so many emotions swirling through her, she needed some time to process them.

"I bet he's playing catch with Ben and Walter."

"He might be."

Sammy put his lips to the water and made raspberries while she sat back on the toilet and waited for him to work out what was going on in his head. Finally, he straightened up and slicked his wet hair back. It left a spiky furrow straight down the middle of his head.

"I miss Dad."

Her heart cracked right open in the face of those three little words. The nights she had spent agonizing over her decision to leave Corbin were still fresh in her mind. Despite being smacked in the face with infidelity, leaving had been one of the most difficult decisions of her life.

It had felt selfish to choose herself over Sammy's relationship with his father. The uncertainty of moving back home had loomed ahead and, of course, becoming another Hart woman with a failed relationship. In the end, she had done what she thought was right for them both. With Sammy's heartache facing her, she wasn't sure if she made the right decision.

She held out a green terrycloth bath towel to him to give herself a few minutes to collect herself. "Come on, let's dry you off." The towel, with orange spikes on the hood, was one he had used since he was a toddler. *It barely fits him now.* He looked so big all of a sudden. Allie pulled him closer and held him under her chin like she used to when he was a baby. Droplets of water seeped into her T-shirt, but she didn't mind. She sat back and held the corners of the towel closed against his chest.

"Sammy, your dad and I love you very much," she said, kissing his damp head. "I know our family doesn't look like some other families do, but you are so loved by so many people. You're the kindest, smartest, and sweetest"—she nuzzled his neck playfully until he squealed—"boy I've ever seen."

"I love you, too, Mama," he said. Then he looked up with big, earnest eyes. "Don't be sad. I like living here, too. Mimi is here, and Ben is my new best friend. He's so lucky to have his dad live with them all the time."

"Oh, honey bear," she said tenderly. Stroking his hair back from his forehead, her heart ached for Davis and Ben and Claire all over again. That whole family had been through so much grief.

"Ben said he plays with them and takes them camping and everything."

"He is a good daddy, isn't he? Claire and Ben's mommy is in heaven. Did you know that?"

"Like with God?"

"Yes," she said softly. "She died when Ben was little. I don't think they feel very lucky, honey. I think they miss her very much."

"Oh." He thought about that for a minute before his eyes widened. "You mean they'll never see their mommy again?"

"She's an angel now. She takes care of them from heaven, but they won't see her again until they're very old and they go to heaven themselves." Her heart ached fiercely at the finality.

"I just miss Dad. I wish he could come here to live with us." He looked so miserable that Allie gave him a swift kiss on the forehead. There was no chance of that ever happening, but maybe she would call Corbin again to nail down a date for him to visit Sammy. Sammy deserved every effort from them both.

"I'm sorry, baby. It's okay to feel angry. It's okay to feel whatever you need to."

Sammy threw his arms around Allie's neck, and she hugged his wet, warm body close to her, keeping his heat-flushed cheek against her own. With his little arms around her neck and his sweet breath on her cheek, she closed her eyes with fierce gratitude.

"I'm so glad you're my mommy," he whispered in her ear. She hugged him tighter.

"I'm so glad you're my son," she whispered back.

While he brushed his teeth, she went next door to his bedroom and pulled out a pair of undies, then a pair of jammies with superheroes on them, and laid them on his bed. When she turned around, she caught sight of the shelf in the corner. Assembled. "Sammy, did you see your dinosaur shelf?"

He wandered into the bedroom still wrapped in his towel and dripping water on the carpet. "Yeah," he said, "isn't it so cool how Mr. Henderson set it up?" He went over to the shelf and poked around. "The G.I. Joes and the dinosaurs are trying to save the eggs from the bad guys."

"How do you know it was Mr. Henderson?"

"I saw him today when I got home from school," he said. "He showed me how to use the drill, and we did it together."

A warm little glow spread around Allie's heart while Sammy got dried off and put on his jammies.

Stop. It's just a shelf, dummy. And a bike. Two considerate, thoughtful things from a man with a broken heart.

She pulled down Sammy's comforter, and he burrowed into the sheets while she stretched out beside him. He reached out to grab his stuffed puppy and tucked it next to his chin before snuggling under Allie's arm. Corbin had brought the stuffed toy to Sammy after he was born, and it was one of Sammy's most prized possessions. He still slept with it every night.

"Mama?" Sammy asked, low and sleepy.

"Yes, baby?"

"You should be Claire and Ben's mommy on earth until they can see their mommy in heaven."

Sammy drifted off to sleep with the sweet, selfless thought of sharing his mom with two motherless children.

Allie didn't have the heart to tell him that wasn't in the cards, at least not with Davis Henderson. The man was beautiful, generous, and could fix just about anything, but the next time she fell in love—and there would be a next time because she really, truly believed there was someone for everyone out there—she wouldn't fall in love with someone with a broken heart.

In the meantime, she had a feeling they both could use a friend.

Chapter Eleven

On Wednesday morning, Davis was finishing the trim paint in Allie's bedroom when the front door slammed closed hard enough to shake the doorframe. He winced. The woman was hard on doors. If she wasn't slamming them, she was leaving them unlocked for anyone to come in and do God knows what.

He had walked right in this morning after dropping the kids off at school and swore a blue streak when he realized it was unlocked. Allie Hart was too naïve. He was pissed all over again thinking about what could have happened.

Pissed off and turned on.

The sight of her long, tanned legs sprawled out on the porch swing had been seared on his brain since yesterday. She had been playing with him, teasing him with ice cream and her tongue. Then she had spread her thighs and tortured him with glimpses of her yellow panties under her tiny shorts. He was old enough to know that had been deliberate, and he sure as hell wasn't immune. He had gone home and jerked off while thinking about kneeling in front of her on the swing, pushing her shorts aside, and tasting what she was offering.

That made him even angrier.

Because she was off-limits for so many reasons.

He was her landlord, for Christ's sake. Imagine what a shit show that would be when things ended? Now that Ben and Claire were friends with Sammy, there was another, deeper layer of hell no. He had regretted dating Natalie as soon as he saw the potential complications it could cause between Carly and Claire. When and if he dated again, it wouldn't be anything other than two people connecting and sharing their bodies when they had a need. It wasn't much to offer, but it was all he would do, and at least he was honest about it.

So he painted and stewed in his frustration over Allie's carelessness because it was safer.

He made a mental list of the things he needed to tell her to look out for now that she was living on her own. Did she know how to double-check the fire alarms? Where the circuit breaker was? In an old house like this, if the power went out and she had to go downstairs to flip the switch, she could get hurt on the steep stairs.

He was making a note to install a flashlight next to the basement door when Walter's collar jingled, announcing his arrival before he bounded into the room and flopped down next to him in a golden plume of fur. Allie stuck her head in the doorway a second later.

"There you are," she said, all pink-cheeked and breathless. "I was hoping you'd be here." She entered the room and folded her bare legs to sit beside him.

He kept his eyes squarely on the paint can he was tapping closed with a screwdriver.

"Okay," she said after it was clear he wasn't going to say anything. "So I wanted to apologize for yesterday. I was out of line, and I'm sorry. I think we need a do-over."

He raised a brow.

"Yes, like I tell Sammy, sometimes you just need a reset.

We've had a rocky start." She held out her hand to shake his. "Let's start fresh. Come on, give it to me."

He was still looking at her like she lost her mind, so she grabbed his big hand and pumped it up and down once. Her hand was smooth and soft in his. "I'm Allie. Now it's your turn." She looked at him expectantly.

"Allie..."

"No, you're Davis. Nice to meet you. Your house is beautiful, and we can't wait to live here." She beamed at him, so dazzlingly pretty that he couldn't help but stare for a moment. "See, this is how we should have started. I would like us to be friends, Davis," she told him, sounding more serious. "Sammy and Ben are in the same class, and I could use a friend in Northfield."

Davis gave his head a little shake. She could be damn mesmerizing. "Friends I can do," he said eventually, wondering how smart an idea that was.

Allie beamed at him and leaned over to pet Walter.

"You okay with Walter in the house?"

"I don't mind at all. We love this boy, don't we?" Walter rolled over on his back for belly rubs. "So, what are you doing?" Allie looked around the room expectantly, blowing a piece of hair out of her eyes. She looked fresh and young this morning, reminding him once again of just how old and jaded he felt. His mood soured.

"Painting the trim."

She tilted her head up to look at the windows, exposing the slim column of her neck where his eyes lingered. "Oh, pretty. You know, I've been taking care of people my entire life. I think you might have the wrong impression of me."

His lips compressed into a grim line. *Taking care of people by leaving the front door unlocked?*

The silence stretched out until Allie looked at him. "Is everything okay?"

Tap. Tap. Tap. Each sharp rap on the paint lid mirrored his anger until, with a rough breath, he pushed it away and sat back on his heels, his hands on his thighs. "The door was unlocked when I got here."

"Oh, yeah," she nodded, unaware of the frustration burning under his skin. "I didn't know if you had a key, so I left it open for you."

"You can't just leave doors unlocked, Allie," he barked. "Anyone could have come inside."

Allie stopped petting Walter and stared at him like he was growing a second head. "It was only for a few minutes. I knew you were coming here to work after dropping the kids off."

He knew he was being irrational. He knew it the same way he knew when he was being overprotective with his kids, but he couldn't stop worrying then and, for some reason, this woman in front of him inspired the same response. He wanted to shout, *Don't you know bad things can happen? People can be taken away from you, leaving you with a hole where your heart is supposed to be.*

Instead, he took a deep breath and blew it out slowly. Of course she didn't know that.

He hoped she never did.

"It's not safe to leave doors unlocked," he said stiffly. He had started wrapping the paintbrushes in plastic when Allie leaned over and put her hand on his arm. Her light touch stilled him instantly and sent a rush of heat through his body.

She was looking at him with so much soft understanding in her eyes that he pulled his arm back rougher than he meant to. She must have found out about Mel. Everyone looked at him and the kids like that after they found out she died. He didn't think he could handle Allie's pity too.

"I'm sorry, Davis," she said. "I don't always think about that kind of thing, but I'll try to be more careful now that we're living here on our own."

It was an olive branch, sweetly offered.

Allie scooted back until they were shoulder to shoulder. If he hadn't been watching her as carefully as he was, he wouldn't have noticed her nose twitching as she leaned closer, closer. Then she did the strangest thing. She inhaled.

"Are you smelling me?"

"What? No. Gosh, no! That's so weird." She jumped back guiltily. "Hey," she said after a while, nudging his shoulder with hers until he looked at her. "I think I got a job as the nurse at the kids' school."

She fairly vibrated with energy. He was having a hard time not staring at her face, the way it glowed with excitement. He couldn't remember ever being that excited.

"Sylvia Wagner is retiring, and she said she'd take a look at my resume, but that the position is mine if I want it. I'm shadowing her on Friday."

"That's got to make you happy, being around Sammy while he's at school." How she dealt with all that she did, he didn't know, but he found himself admiring her even more.

"It really does. He's going to have to manage his diabetes on his own one day, but for now, I'm happy to be with him at school to take care of him. Hey, I never did say thanks for your help yesterday with the cone of shame."

Cone of shame. Unwillingly, his lips twitched. "You got it unstuck yourself."

"I know, but you saved me from falling and making an even bigger fool of myself."

"There was a line of people ready to help you if I wasn't there," he said dryly. Ford being number one.

"I can only imagine what people must have thought

watching that spectacle," she said. Pink delicately stained her cheeks and the top of her chest. His eyes followed the pink to the neckline of her shirt before he jerked them back to safety. "Not exactly the first impression I wanted to make after moving back home."

"I don't know about that. I bet anyone would think twice about tussling with you both," he said, absently rubbing the bump on his forehead.

She grinned up at him impishly. "We did come back into town with a bang, huh? Does it still hurt?"

"It's fine," Davis said dismissively.

"I'd ask to look at it, but something tells me you'd say no."

"Yep."

She sighed. "Well, on the bright side, it's like ripping off a Band-Aid. The first day is over, and there's no hiding that we're back now."

Davis cocked his head. "Did you want to hide?"

"No," she said slowly, looking thoughtful. "Not hide. But I wasn't exactly relishing anyone knowing my business right away. It doesn't feel great to announce you're divorced, especially in my family."

"Why's that?"

"I forget that you're not from around here. It's well-known that the women in my family don't have the best of luck with love. My aunts tell everyone we're cursed."

He raised a skeptical brow.

"I know, I know. Maybe not cursed." She rolled her eyes. "But none of us have a good track record. My aunts are all divorced except for one, and my dad left when we were little." She shrugged, twirling the strings on her jean shorts around her long fingers. Her nails were short and painted pink. "That's why we lived in Cedarwood. It was what my mom could afford at the time, but I grew up hating where we lived. I was embarrassed, and I couldn't wait to go away to college."

Something in her voice made him look at her more closely. "What happened then?"

She settled back more comfortably. "I met Corbin two weeks after I graduated high school. We spent the summer together, and then I found out I was pregnant right before I was supposed to leave for college. We actually broke up, but I think his parents talked him into coming back and proposing. They didn't want anything to do with being grandparents, but they didn't want any secret baby scandals coming up later."

She said it ruefully, but Davis pictured an eighteen-year-old girl, pregnant with a baby and a boyfriend who should have known better and found himself getting pissed on her behalf. What kind of asshole knocked up a teenager and then left?

"What made you decide to get married?" he asked bluntly.

Her smile wobbled, and for the first time, Davis saw a glimpse of the vulnerability that her easy smiles hid. The rest of his anger drained away.

The house was quiet, with no radio or other noise from the neighborhood to distract from the increasingly intimate feel of the conversation. A tiny voice warned him it was too intimate in her bedroom, too easy to get comfortable when Allie looked at him like that, her head only inches from his.

"I wanted Sammy to have the family I never did," she said simply.

He was torn between wanting to know more and shutting down this talk before it got any more personal. He knew what he should do. "Where's Sammy's dad now?"

Guess he wasn't done making stupid decisions today.

"Corbin stayed in our apartment in the city," she said. "He travels so much for work that he didn't mind when I told him I wanted to move back home to be near my family."

Davis scowled, shocked anew by a man who would willingly give up his family.

"Corbin's not a bad guy. We didn't even really fight. He loves Sammy. Things were mostly normal until Sammy—" She stopped abruptly.

"Until Sammy what?"

"Until Sammy was diagnosed with diabetes, then things changed. Corbin couldn't deal with it. It was too heavy, too awful to see your kid sick, and he just... checked out. He started traveling even more until, eventually, he was gone more than he was home."

"Did you love him?" It was out before he could stop it. He found himself holding his breath while he waited for her answer.

"I think I convinced myself I did." She pulled her knees up to her chest and wrapped her arms around them tightly.

"He sounds like a fucking idiot," Davis said gruffly. "Any man that would give up his wife and son for sex doesn't deserve you."

Allie looked over at him, and they stayed that way, eyes locked, shoulders touching, as the silence moved past a friendly pause and into something heavier.

He sensed the subtle shift over the last half hour taking them from a simple chemical attraction into more dangerous territory. Her cheeks were pinker than normal, her breathing faster, and her eyes dropped to his mouth.

Davis looked away. "Do you regret getting married?" he asked after clearing his throat.

"I regret disappointing my mom mostly. She's the strongest, hardest-working woman I know. It killed her to see me pregnant at eighteen." She shot him a self-conscious smile that made his chest tighten.

"Sounds like you're a lot more like your mom than you think," he said quietly.

She's the strongest, hardest-working woman I know.

Her eyes shot back to his. "Well, anyway," she said awkwardly. "That's why I'm home again. Fresh starts and all that."

"There are plenty of good men, Allie," he said seriously. "Men who will deserve you and Sammy, that will respect you."

She smiled crookedly and nudged his shoulder. "You volunteering for the job, big guy?"

He stiffened so suddenly Walter cracked an eye open to glare at him.

"Kidding, kidding!" Allie teased, her playfulness back. "You should have seen your face." Her soft, pink lips were turned up so invitingly that he found himself grinning back. She gasped, slapping a hand over her mouth.

"What's wrong?" he demanded, sitting up and scanning her face urgently.

She shot up to her knees and leaned toward him, a hand on his shoulder as she inspected his face. "Oh my God."

"What? What's wrong?"

"Davis... you... you smiled." Her face was inches away from his, close enough he could see the amusement in her eyes.

He scowled. "I smile."

She sat back on her heels, her bare knees touching his thigh. "You might not be aware of this, but your permanent expression is a cross between Oscar the Grouch and the Grumpy dwarf. I was beginning to think someone peed in your Cheerios every day." Her teasing laughter filled the room and his head, as tangible as her knees pressing into him.

His lips curved again. It did feel rusty, and he felt more than a little ridiculous sitting on the floor, the two of them grinning at each other, but dammed if he didn't do it anyway.

DAVIS STRAIGHTENED out the wires on the outlet he was replacing and tried again to block out the fact Allie was downstairs. He was aware of her in a way that made it hard to concentrate. He found himself turning down his radio today to listen to her sing. She did that a lot, either humming or singing, as she kept busy unpacking.

Each time he walked by a room, something new and colorful caught his eye. She had about ten of those pillows whose only purpose was to get knocked off the couch. He had never understood why people bought them. He supposed Mel used them, too, but it was hard to remember now. Yet every time he walked by a room, the bright colors drew him in inexplicably. Kind of like Allie herself.

She had been in the kitchen all afternoon, and the whole house smelled like cinnamon and vanilla, which was fine until he was surprised to hear his stomach growling. When was the last time he had felt hungry?

Don't even get him started on what she wore to bake in. The ridiculous flowered apron around her waist and covering her breasts had distracted him all day with wicked thoughts of her wearing it and nothing else. Maybe just undies. Allie's ass was perfect, and he wanted to see it framed in a tiny pair of undies. Yellow, like the ones she had on earlier in the week.

Yeah, he was distracted.

He was in Sammy's room now working on replacing the electrical outlets. They had spent some time in there fixing up the space over the weekend. A basket of stuffed animals stood in the corner, and a small track had been set up for Sammy's race cars. In the corner was the bookshelf he and Sammy had put together.

The door slammed downstairs, and someone thundered up

the stairs and then slid across the landing. He caught a glimpse of a red T-shirt flying past the room and then coming back to a jerky stop in the doorway. The kid was all uncoordinated floppy elbows and knees.

"Hi, Mr. Henderson! Whatcha doin'?" Sammy asked. He was in the habit of coming home from school and finding him.

"Hey, Sammy." He nodded to the exposed wires inside the box. "Replacing these old electrical boxes. How was school?"

"It was fun! We played zombies on the playground. I got tagged and had to get dead." He staggered around, arms out zombie-style, and plopped back onto the bed.

"Sounds like a good day."

Sammy rolled over onto his stomach and propped his head in his hands. Big hazel eyes peered up at him curiously through his mop of hair. Darker than Allie's honey color, but with the same slight curl. "Didja know zombies are dead?"

Davis nodded. "So they say."

"Ben's in my class, and we're best friends now." Sammy picked at the quilt. "He's really good at baseball." His small face, usually so mischievous, looked dejected. Davis couldn't help but reach out to ruffle his hair.

"Hey, you're gonna do great. Your mom said you're going to be at practice next week. I bet Ben would love to play catch with you during recess."

"Yeah." He kept his eyes on the dinosaur quilt, tracing his finger over the outline of a brontosaurus over and over.

Davis cleared his throat, which suddenly felt like he'd swallowed rocks. A surge of anger speared him at the thought of Sammy's dad. Selfish, cheating asshole. He had a little boy and a beautiful wife that loved him, and he had wasted it.

Sammy turned onto his back and scooted to the edge of the bed to look at Davis upside down. "Will all the other kids know how to play?"

Understanding dawned on Davis. "Some. Is that what's got you worried?"

"Yeah," Sammy said dejectedly. "I can't throw the ball far 'nough."

Davis hesitated. "I can help you with that if you want," he offered.

"You can?" Sammy flopped onto his stomach, and the sheer happiness on his face made Davis's heart clench.

"Yeah," he said. "How about on Saturday I'll show you a few things after I do the yard work?"

Sammy's eyes lit up, and he held two fingers up like he was gripping a baseball. "I promise I'll do it right. Two seams, like this?"

"Just like that."

Allie poked her head into the room with Walter nosing in beside her.

"Walter! Come see my room! Come here, boy!" Sammy called, patting the bed. When the dog cleared the doorway, he made an ungraceful leap toward the end of the bed and planted himself happily next to the boy. The two melted into each other like it had been months instead of a day since they last saw each other.

"Walter, off," Davis said sternly. The damn dog knew he wasn't allowed on the furniture. Walter pretended he was hard of hearing and sighed happily as Sammy gave his ears a good rub.

"It's fine. Sammy's in heaven," Allie said softly, leaning on the doorjamb with her arms crossed. Her face was relaxed and soft as she watched her son roll around with Walter. Her feet were bare, and she had on the little ruffly apron. Davis couldn't resist stealing another glance.

"Know what, Mama?" Sammy asked, sprawled under the dog, laughing and dodging Walter's tongue.

"What, honey bear?"

"I'm gonna play catch with Mr. Henderson."

"Is that right?"

"Yep, he promised, and you know what else?"

"No, what?" Allie asked patiently.

"He could teach you, too, so you don't feel sad."

"That's very thoughtful of you, Sammy, but I'm not sad."

Sammy gave Walter's belly another scratch. "Then why were you crying?"

Allie's face reddened. "I wasn't crying."

"I heard you after you put me to bed."

"It was a happy leak, Sammy. We've talked about those."

"Oh, yeah, like when you watch your movies." Sammy nodded sagely. "She likes the end of those movies when they kiss," he confided to Davis, wrinkling his nose in clear disgust.

"Anyway," Allie spoke hurriedly, avoiding looking at Davis. "Why don't you and Walter come downstairs and let Mr. Henderson finish his work? I made you a snack."

"Can Walter have a snack too?" Sammy asked hopefully from under a pile of fur and dog limbs. "Tell her you're hungry, too, Walter." He held up one big paw and waved it back and forth at Allie. "Need food," he growled a la Scooby-Doo. Allie laughed.

Davis didn't feel like laughing. He wanted to pull Allie aside and demand to know who made her cry and then tear apart whoever was responsible.

"Walter's on a diet," he said abruptly. "He's been eating too many cookies."

"Cookies!" Sammy shrieked, making Walter perk up his ears and tilt his head. The dog was very familiar with cookies, thanks to his humans. "I love cookies!"

Allie's eyes met his, and that same half smile stayed on her face. "Walter can have a carrot stick, if it's okay with Mr. Henderson?"

"It's fine." Davis knew his tone was shorter than necessary, but he needed to put some distance between himself and these two. He was uncomfortably aware he was teetering a line he wouldn't allow himself to cross.

"I'll meet you downstairs." It came out more curtly than he intended as he brushed past her, close enough to feel the warmth of her body without touching it.

Without touching was the key. Jesus, what red-blooded male with a heartbeat wouldn't want to touch her? She was a fantasy come to life. That didn't scare Davis nearly as much. Lust was normal. He was a grown man. He could handle that.

It was all the other feelings knifing his gut he didn't want to deal with.

So he did what he'd been doing for the better part of two years. He walked down the stairs and grabbed his hammer. He'd find some demo to keep him away from Allie Hart and her son, who looked at him with his heart in his eyes.

Chapter Twelve

On Friday morning, Allie and Sammy walked to school, but this time Allie had her bag and lunch packed too. Her stomach fluttered with nerves as she adjusted her peacock-green blouse. Automatically, she started to lead them around the crowd of parents at the entrance as inconspicuously as possible, but Sammy made a beeline directly through the middle.

"Mama, I see Ben and Claire! Come on!" He pulled her along until they reached the tall woman Allie had seen dropping off Davis's kids earlier in the week.

"Hi, Ben! Hi, Claire!" Sammy and Ben did a complicated fist bump-twist-high-five greeting. "Ha! We remembered!" Sammy crowed, looking pleased. "Me and Ben made up a special way to say hi."

"Very impressive. Hi, Ben, and Claire, it's so nice to see you again," Allie greeted them.

"Have a good day, kids." Layne gave them both a kiss. "I'll see you in the morning."

The three of them went running off to join the kids on the playground, and Allie rose to her feet to meet Davis's sister.

"Hi, I'm Layne, those two minions' aunt." Layne smiled. She was tall and lovely, with velvety, expressive eyes and the same rich-brown hair as Davis, although hers was streaked with highlights. Layne's smile was wide open and friendly as they shook hands.

"I was hoping to meet you." Her eyes twinkled.

"You were?" Allie asked, surprised.

"Oh, yes. I wanted to meet the woman everyone's talking about," she said.

"Great," Allie groaned. The cone story was going to follow her to her grave.

"Oh, not the cone story," Layne said, beaming. "Although it's definitely something I would do," she added confidentially. "I meant I've been hearing a lot about you and Sammy from Ben and Claire."

"You have?" Allie asked uneasily.

"Yes, all good things. I told the kids I couldn't wait to get to know you too. They made me promise to invite you to our Labor Day barbecue at Davis's house on Monday. Davis grills and we all get together with some family and friends. It's fun."

"Ah... I... thank you, but—" Allie stumbled for an excuse.

The five-minute bell rang, and Layne jumped. Mrs. Gayle began shepherding kids into the building.

"Oops, gotta go. I have a shoot in the city this morning." Layne started to back away. "No need to bring anything—just yourselves. Oh, and don't forget your swimsuits." She waved and headed off toward the parking lot.

After Allie dropped Sammy off at Mrs. Nichols's classroom, she made her way to the nurse's office. Sylvia was busy handing out medications to a line of students, and she barely looked up when Allie came in.

"Oh, good! You're here. Fridays are nuts around here. Here." She tossed a box of freezer bags to Allie while expertly dispensing pills into little white cups. "Can you fill these bags with ice? We have some playground casualties." She nodded to the two middle-school-aged kids sitting on the cots. They were playing rock paper scissors. "The ice is more for street cred," she said with a wink.

An hour later, a steady stream of kids came into the office for anything from a Band-Aid—one for a hangnail, another for a staple that got stuck in a third grader's thumb—to a sniffly nose from allergies, and a senior who came in begging to lie down and sleep for an hour during their study hall. Sylvia knew each student and spent time with them the way Allie remembered from her school days.

Finally, during a lull in the traffic, Sylvia sat down at her desk with a sigh. "I'm gonna miss this place, but my feet are not." She leaned back and took a sip from her travel mug before looking at Allie purposefully. "We got all your paperwork. We can do a formal interview after lunch, but Eileen and I know you're qualified. If you want the job, it's yours."

Allie looked around and thought about the differences in her former job as a nurse at a busy pediatric doctor's office in the city. She had loved working with the patients there, but school nursing was different. She would have more of a relationship with the kids, for one. Sylvia knew each one of the kids and many times their parents and siblings too. She had the extra time to talk with them and catch up, which made the kids relax. For another, there was a level of trust formed when the kids could come down without their parents. Some of them looked scared until Sylvia made them laugh and put them to ease. Allie had known within ten minutes this was the perfect job for her.

She grinned. "It's perfect. I want it."

The door burst open, and Sadie Nichols barged in with a hand on a young boy's shoulder whose face was an unnatural shade of green. "Into the basket, honey. If you have to throw up, use the bas—" She didn't get to finish her sentence.

Maybe not a perfect job, but as Allie stood to help clean up the mess, she was still excited.

❧

"Shit. I mean, shoot!" Allie looked around guiltily for Sammy, but he was still outside playing catch with Davis. Davis had shown up that Saturday morning bright and early to do the yard work. Then he made Sammy's day by offering to play catch. Actually, he had made both of their days. She knew just from the short time she had known Davis that he was a man of his word. After being married to someone who routinely canceled their plans, or just didn't make them in the first place, it was a shockingly nice change.

She dipped the spoon back into the big pot of ribollita she made for lunch, added a few cranks of black pepper, then turned off the heat. She placed a hunk of crusty Italian bread on the bottom of a bowl, ladled the soup on top, grated more fresh Parmesan, and sat down at the kitchen table with her grocery list and her bowl of soup. It was eighty-five degrees in September, but she could happily eat soup year-round, especially this one. Just as she lifted the spoon to her lips, her phone buzzed.

Corbin. She sighed and regretfully pushed the bowl away. They had been playing phone tag since she called him earlier in the week. She wanted to nail down a date for him to see Sammy.

"Hello, Corbin." She tried for upbeat, but it landed more on the resigned side.

"Hello, Allison." The smooth tone of her ex-husband's voice came through the phone. "I was glad to see you called." No one but her mother called her by her full name. She had told Corbin that a hundred times, but he insisted it sounded more sophisticated than Allie.

"Yes, I wanted to talk to you about—"

"I wanted to talk to you too, Allison," he interrupted.

"Allie," she murmured. It never did any good to correct him. Like her clothing, Corbin saw her the way he wanted her to be. She had once seen herself like that too.

"What? What's that?"

Allie looked at her soup. The Parmesan was perfect, all melty and delicious on top, the way she liked it. She needed to speed this conversation up. "Nothing. What did you want to talk to me about?"

"This isn't working, Allison."

"What isn't?"

"Being divorced," he said irritably.

"I'm sorry to hear that." Then, because she wasn't a saint, she asked with only the faintest hint of snark, "How's Dahlia?"

"I don't know. We're not together anymore," he said. "I think we need to talk," he said.

"Corbin, we're divorced, so we don't have to keep rehashing this. I need to set up a time for you to visit Sammy. He misses you. That's why I called."

"Great. I miss him too," Corbin said, the relief evident in his voice. "I miss both of you. I'll come to stay with you for a week, and it can be like it used to be with all three of us. We can take this slower if you want, Allison, but I know how important it is for a kid to have his father around," he said.

Ah, there it was, his ace in the hole. It had been only a matter of time before he played it. Even though she had been waiting for Corbin to drop that familiar emotional bomb he liked to detonate when they argued, it always hit her like dynamite.

She took a breath. Took inventory. Took another breath.

Nope. She was still intact. Guilt was there. Maybe there would always be, but not like before.

"You're welcome to visit," she said firmly, "but you can't stay with us. And Sammy is doing just fine here. He's thriving. He misses you, and he'd like to see you, but we're happy here." She took a breath. "Corbin, we're over," she said more calmly. "The papers are signed. I've moved on. I like living in Northfield. I'm starting over here."

"Allie, do you know where Sammy's mitt is?" Davis stepped into the kitchen doorway. She motioned him in.

"Who was that, Allison? Who's there?" Corbin asked sharply.

"It's my landlord," Allie said distractedly. Davis's T-shirt clung to his chest, outlining the interesting lines and ridges covered by the thin fabric. Very distracting, that.

"Why is he there on a Saturday?" Corbin asked suspiciously.

"To take care of the lawn. Why?"

"Never mind," Corbin said, his interest gone at any hint of a blue collar.

"Hold on one second, Corbin. I'll go get Sammy."

"No, no, I have another call coming in. Tell Sammy I'll try to call him later, and think about what I said, Allison."

She hung up and eyed Davis. "I made soup for lunch. Would you like a bowl?"

Davis hesitated. "No, thanks. I'll take a cup of coffee, if you have some left."

"Sure. Where's Sammy?"

"He's playing with Walter." Davis nodded toward the back window where Sammy and Walter chased each other in circles.

She poured him a cup and set it opposite her at the table. "Oh, sit down," she said when he still stood. "I promise not to fall off a counter or run anything over."

His lips twitched. She tried not to take that as a challenge, but it was hard. Davis was a hard nut to crack, but she had an insane urge to make him laugh as often as possible, even if it meant making a fool out of herself. The man needed a little laughter in his life.

He sat down across from her, leaned his forearms on the table, and cupped the mug in his hands. His hair was damp around the edges, making the ends curl up around the baseball cap he wore. There were pieces of grass clinging to his forearms from the Weedwacker. Davis took a sip of coffee, his eyes steady and calm above the rim.

She liked that about him. He felt sturdy, not just in his size, but in his presence. Solid. Like he wasn't going anywhere.

"That your ex?"

"The one and only. Apparently, he broke it off with the babysitter and wants to get back together." She crossed her eyes. "What an offer, right?"

Davis grunted. "Asshole."

"I said that, too, although a little differently." She propped her elbow on the table and rested her chin on her hand. "I know it's crazy, but there's still this little part of me that's not sure I made the right decision to leave."

Davis sat back in his chair and held the coffee cup on his belly comfortably. "Why's that?"

She sighed. "Because Corbin was a good dad, and Sammy is hurting now. That kills me."

"Were you happy?"

"No," she said immediately. "But I pretended to be for Sammy."

"Then you made the right decision," he said. "Kids know when you're putting on a face. Sammy's a smart kid. Maybe not right away, but he'll see that this was the right move."

She let herself picture what Davis must have been like as a

husband. Even in the short time she had known him, she knew he was dependable. Like the calm, confident way he interacted with Sammy and how he didn't think twice before stepping in to help. An ache of longing for that kind of unconditional love filled her.

"You must have been a great husband, huh?" she said wistfully.

"I tried to be," he said after so long she had begun to think he wouldn't answer. His eyes were unfocused, and Allie knew he was seeing another time. "Mel and I fought about the usual things. But the things that mattered, that we were crystal clear on. I'm older than you," he said gruffly. "It took us a while to get it right, but that came with time."

"She was a lucky woman."

"I was the lucky one," he said simply.

"Where did you meet?"

"We met when I left the Navy. Got married soon after that."

The finality in his voice warned her he wasn't up for any more discussion, so she changed the subject. "Is the Navy where you got your tattoo?" she asked, pointing to his bicep.

He looked surprised. Oh, she had noticed. That dark shadow peeking out from under his T-shirt had intrigued her for days. She wanted to inspect it. For scientific reasons, obviously.

"The requisite mark of the military," he finally said dryly.

"How old are you, anyway?"

"A lot older than you," he said curtly.

She looked up at him in surprise. "I'm twenty-six. You can't be that much older than me." She took in his handsome face and his dark hair with few strands of silver at his temples. Age was being very kind to Davis.

He drained the rest of his cup and stood up. "I've got to get home. I'll say goodbye to Sammy on the way out."

Just as he would have cleared the kitchen door, she remembered. "Oh, I almost forgot. I met your sister yesterday at drop-off. She invited us to your house on Monday for a barbecue." Until that moment, Allie hadn't been sure she was going to go.

Davis paused but didn't turn around. "If you come, come hungry. There'll be plenty of food," he finally said evenly. He stepped outside and whistled to Walter.

Chapter Thirteen

ON LABOR DAY, Allie carefully packed up Sammy, a bouquet she picked up from Aunt Rosa's shop, and the still warm peach-raspberry crisp she had made and headed a few blocks over to Davis's house.

Her nerves were thrumming as she pulled into the driveway of a tidy colonial. From the look of it, Davis took the same meticulous care of his house that he did hers. The house was painted a fresh white, and the lawn had been cut with military precision.

She weaved her way with Sammy through a driveway full of cars, following the scent of barbecue wafting over the tall wood privacy fence around the backyard. Every few seconds, a piercing scream split the air, followed by a splash. Sammy was bouncing, clearly wanting to head to the back, but she tugged him toward the front door.

"Remember to check in on your body, right, bud?" she murmured as he rang the bell for them. "Pay attention, in case you feel low." She had given him a bolus dose of insulin after lunch because his blood sugar was on the high side.

"I will, Mama." He hopped up and down from one foot to

the other. She licked her finger to rub away a smudge of something on his cheek but missed the mark as he squirmed away.

"Ew, gross." He ducked his head just as Layne opened the door.

"He was saving that for later." Layne grinned and held the door wider. "Come on in. We're all out back in the pool." She surprised Allie with a quick hug. "I love the color of your dress," she said admiringly.

Allie smiled, pleased that she had chosen the red-and-purple off-the-shoulder sundress.

"I'm so glad you guys came," Layne whispered, just as Walter bounded toward them. Wet and ecstatic, he gave a massive shake just as he stopped in front of them, sprinkling them with water.

"Hi, Walter." Sammy hugged him. "He's all wet. Was he in the pool?"

"He sure was. All the kids are in the back. Come on, I'll show you."

Allie followed, taking in her first look at Davis's house. It wasn't surprising the old home was beautifully restored. The wide pine hardwoods gleamed, the stain matching the thick trim around the windows in the living room. The fireplace had a built-in bookcase on either side with pretty trim details she would bet money Davis had built himself. The wood and natural light gave the house warmth, but it didn't hide the sparseness.

She saw none of the homey touches that made a house look cozy and feel lived in. No plants, no throw pillows, nothing but the essentials. The furniture looked expensive, and a gigantic TV hung on the wall, but other than a few toys in a basket, and a stack of books on the coffee table, Davis's house didn't have any of the extras that hers did.

"Ben and Claire have been checking for your car every few

minutes, but I finally made them get in the pool to cool off. Here, give me that and I'll put it in the fridge."

Layne took the dessert and led them through a spacious kitchen to sliding glass doors leading out to a stone patio. Allie stopped to set the flowers on the kitchen table and peeked out at the people in the backyard. So much for a small barbecue. The yard was packed. She tried to find Davis in the crowd but gave up when Walter ran over and shook the water out of his fur and all over her.

"Hey, boy." She petted his sleek ears while he looked adoringly at her. "Thanks for sharing the pool water."

Someone called out to Layne about needing more ice. She turned to Allie and Sammy. "I'll be right back. Davis is on the grill." She turned around, and they were alone. Allie looked around uneasily.

"Whoa! Look at that! Can we swim? Right now? Please, Mama?" Sammy begged, pointing to the in-ground pool.

One of the best parts of motherhood was when your kid was too young to swim by himself and you had to go in with him in front of a crowd of people at a party, said no parent ever. "Let's say hello first," Allie murmured, hoping to distract him just as an older woman approached them.

"You must be Allie and Sammy." The woman took Allie's hands in both of her own and led her over to a silver-haired man with Davis's large build and brown eyes. "I'm Margie, and this is Robert. We're Davis's parents. We've heard so much about you two."

Margie Henderson's smile was so wide her eyes crinkled until they almost disappeared. She wore her gray hair in a no-fuss, shoulder-length bob. Her hands where she held Allie's were warm and calloused.

Allie wondered briefly what exactly the Hendersons had

heard about them, but before she could think too much, Margie asked rapid-fire questions. "Do you like potato salad? My sister made it, and it's divine, but don't tell her I said that. Here, I made chocolate cupcakes. Try one. How about a drink? Did Lanie get you two something? Sammy, how do you like living in Northfield?" She finally paused to draw in a deep breath and tuck a wiry piece of hair behind her ear.

Allie took a bite of the cupcake to give herself a minute to process the rapid-fire questions, then nearly moaned. It was divine.

Margie patted Allie's hand in delight. "Better than sex, right?" she whispered in Allie's ear. "You enjoy that cupcake, honey. I'm just so happy to meet you two. I know you just moved into that new house that Davis is fixing up. If you need anything at all, just let me know."

"That's so nice of you. Thank you."

Ben came running over to Sammy, and they did an elaborate fist bump, chest-thumping thing. "Come on. I'll show you my fort. It's boys only," Ben said.

"Can I? Please!" Sammy begged her.

"Sure. But don't go in the pool without me," she called after him as Ben dragged him away. Allie was left on her own. The traitor.

"Come with me, honey. I'll introduce you to everyone." Margie was both mother hen and drill sergeant, Allie thought dazedly a few minutes later. She stopped every few steps to pat a child or pick up a toy and give orders about the food and drinks all with a gentle efficiency that made people hustle in her wake. Margie introduced her to everyone and kept her laughing with funny stories and tidbits of information about them. Finally, they stopped in front of the grill, and Allie realized Margie had led them over to Davis.

"Allie." Davis nodded, his eyes hidden behind aviators. Her mind registered his navy-blue board shorts but then short-circuited because his short-sleeved gray shirt was unbuttoned, and a wedge of his broad, beautiful *naked* chest peeked out.

She knew she was staring, but holy Moses. Davis's chest was a work of art. Her eyes followed the swirl of hair spread over his defined chest, which stopped at his rippled abs and then led her straight, like an arrow, down to the waistband of his trunks. She swallowed wrong and started choking.

Davis thumped her on the back. "You okay?"

"Great." She gasped and people turned to stare. She waved and wiped a few tears from her eyes and tried to look normal.

"Hi, there! Perfect day for a cookout, isn't it?" The *click-clack* of high heels stopped next to her, and she looked up to find a willowy, very attractive blonde looking down at her. At five-foot-five, Allie wasn't exactly short, but she unconsciously stretched to give herself a little more in that department.

"Natalie," Davis greeted her. "Have you met Allie Hart?"

"Hi," Natalie said with a faint smile, but quickly turned back to Davis. She placed her hand on his arm and leaned in for a hug. From the way she was standing, closer than normal, and the familiar way she held Davis's bicep, Allie had the unsettling impression they were more than friends.

Allie couldn't even blame her. Davis was a smoke show, but it still gave her indigestion to think there might be something going on between them.

"I brought my special brownies that you like. I heard you brought them into the shop for the guys to eat." Natalie swatted his chest playfully. "You're so sweet to do that for them, but don't go giving away my chicken spaghetti casserole."

Jeez. Natalie managed to make casserole sound like an illicit sex act. She put Allie's sister, Amber, to shame with the amount of sex appeal dripping off her. Allie peeked to see if Davis was affected.

"Thanks," Davis said. His voice was even, his eyes not wavering past the woman's nose. "But we're all set on food."

"Hello, Natalie, it's nice to see you again," Margie said. "Did you and Carly get something to eat? Let's go make you a plate."

"No, thank you. I can't even think about food when it's so hot." Natalie laughed. Allie remembered the cupcake still in her hand and took another big bite, tasting the silky dark-chocolate buttercream. Bummer for her.

Natalie turned back to Davis, but Margie beat her to it. "Oh, look. The Richardsons just got here, and Keri looks like she could use a cold drink. Can I ask you to help me for a minute?" She put an arm around Natalie's waist and spirited her away. The taller woman looked back with a frown, but there was no escaping Margie. Allie could sympathize. Margie was like a people-mover at a theme park. She put that sturdy arm around your waist and brought you where she wanted you.

"Hello, gorgeous." A tall man behind Davis shouldered him aside and held out his hand to Allie. "I'm the younger, more handsome, and definitely friendlier brother, that he doesn't want you to meet. Shep." He held out his hand with a mischievous smile that she couldn't help but return.

"I'm Allie." She shook his hand and let go, but he held on.

"Shep, it's your turn to watch the pool. The kids want to get in," Margie yelled out from across the yard. She was still holding Natalie's arm, but her sharp eyes had clearly missed nothing. "Davis, take Allie inside and show her where to get changed."

"You got it, Ma," Shep yelled back. "Mom's a good wingman for you, brother. I'll see you later, Allie. Hopefully in the pool?"

He waggled his eyebrows and sauntered away. He was certainly handsome. The Henderson clan all had strapping builds and striking features.

"Wow," Allie said, watching Margie steer Natalie away to the furthest corner of the patio. "She's efficient."

"That's one word for it," Davis said dryly.

She smiled up at him and tried not to look at the wide golden-brown chest in front of her. He was so... muscly. *Come to mama.*

"I'll take you to get changed."

"Your house is very nice," she said as they headed inside and up the stairs to a second story. "Did you do all these renovations yourself?"

"Yes," he said. Talkative as ever. Allie winced.

They passed a pale-pink room first, clearly the bedroom of his daughter, Claire. The bed was a frothy mass of pink and purple ruffles, and a journal lay on the bedside table. She peeked in the next bedroom quickly as Davis led her down the hall and spotted a giant baseball mitt chair in the corner. Davis came to a stop in front of a closed door, and he knocked.

"Someone's in here."

"You can use my bathroom," Davis said tersely. He looked about as happy as a hornet, stalking to the end of the landing and holding open the door for her. She had an impression of navy and gray and quickly swept past an enormous bed before she walked into the en suite bathroom, Davis on her heels.

Her eyes went directly to his shower. The large glass stall took up the entire back wall of the bathroom, and she thought of one thing. "You don't like baths?"

He raised one eyebrow. "I don't take baths."

"I love my bathtub," she said reverently. "I take a bath every night in it."

Okay, that was an unnecessary bit of information based on the look he gave her, but she was flustered. Being in Davis's bedroom was intimate enough, but images of a half-naked Davis in the bathroom was giving her ideas. Steamy, slippery, hot ideas of things that could happen in that big shower. He had a *bench* in there. A visual of Davis on his knees in front of her while she sat on that bench flashed like an X-rated movie. Liquid heat stole through her body, hot and slow, pooling between her legs.

She stepped toward the marble double vanity to give herself some breathing room. His shaving cream and razor were on the counter, still wet from the morning. Apparently, cheap soap and laundry detergent really, really did it for her because she had to stifle the urge to sniff them.

"Your tub is original to the house. I had it reglazed."

Allie looked over her shoulder and came face-to-face with his bare chest. "Oh!"

"Excuse me." He handed her the towel he had reached for around her. The crisp dark curls on his chest brushed against her bare arm, and she nearly jumped out of her skin at the sizzle of electricity that went through her. His clean scent filled her senses, and a tight, needy ache swirled in her belly. The urge to lean her body into his and rub that delicious chest against her breasts made her breath catch.

Davis froze. "There are more towels in the closet, if you need them," he said, backing away slowly.

"Thanks." *For the love, Allie. It's only a chest. You've seen them before.* Her brain reminded her she had only ever been this close to one other, actually, and it looked nothing like Davis's. She couldn't even remember what Corbin's chest looked like now. It certainly wasn't the muscular perfection in front of her.

Davis nodded, his dark eyes just as serious as ever. "See you downstairs."

Allie closed the door behind him and took a deep breath. What was her problem? She looked at herself in the vanity mirror. Cheeks flushed, lips parted, she didn't recognize herself. It was being here, around his family, his house, his bedroom. Seeing where he slept and showered. Being here gave her a glimpse into his private life that felt too personal. The images played in her head the entire time she was pulling her dress over her head and changing into her swimsuit.

The suit was a darling red-and-white smocked gingham two-piece with a vintage flair. The high waist gave her enough coverage that she felt comfortable among so many strangers, and the bandeau top kept the girls contained. She smoothed her hands down her hips, over the silvery lines of her stretch marks and her softly curved belly. She kept active and tried to eat healthy as a good role model for Sammy, especially after his diagnosis, and she was proud of what her body had accomplished. Pregnancy had made her hips and butt rounder, and her breasts would never be the same after nursing Sammy. She wasn't an eighteen-year-old girl anymore, and she didn't want to be. Her body had grown with her, and looking critically, she was content with what she saw. She wrapped a towel around her waist and headed back out to his bedroom.

Her gaze caught on his massive bed again. Each nightstand held a matching lamp. One stand held a book opened, face down, where he must have left off reading. She tilted her head sideways to read the spine. It was an old Sherlock Holmes, the spine creased all over, as if it had been reread many times. A pair of black reading glasses sat next to it. Picturing Davis reading in bed with his bare chest and those glasses on made her insides turn molten hot. Forget the porno arms. She had a new fantasy now.

His dresser held a handmade clay bowl painted like a rainbow with a few pieces of loose change and a screw. A small clay sculpture of what looked like an animal—Walter?—sat next to the bowl. Allie smiled, thinking about Claire making them for Davis, who displayed them proudly. She ran her fingertips down the length of the dresser until they came to rest on a photo.

Melody.

So this was the woman Davis had loved. Still loved.

She was beautiful. Dark hair braided on the side, delicate features with a warm, inviting smile on her face. She held Ben on her knees, and one arm looped around Claire as they smiled softly down at him. Whoever took the photo had captured an intensely happy family moment. A knot formed in her throat. She thought about Davis getting ready for bed at night and waking up in the morning, seeing this picture of his beautiful wife. How did one move on from a love like that? *How do you find love like that?*

Sammy's shriek pulled her over to the window where she pushed aside the curtains and looked out over the backyard. Ford was there now, talking to Keri and Toby. Margie was greeting them, sans Natalie now. Sammy and Ben were tossing around a football with Shepherd and Davis.

She let her eyes linger on Davis. The aviators shielded his eyes again, but she could picture their warm color and how they crinkled at the corners when he was amused. Suddenly, as if she had tapped on the glass, he looked up and met her gaze. The kids, the crowd, the splashing—all of it fell away, and she felt something that could only be described as an ache deep in her chest.

They stood that way, eyes unerringly locked on each other until someone tossed the football to Davis and the connection was broken. Only then did he look away, and Allie slowly let out her breath.

SHE WAS TRYING to kill him.

That was the only explanation he had for the tiny swimsuit Allie came out of the house wearing. Every unattached male, and some women, too, stared as she took the towel off her hips and slid herself into the pool. She was built like a fifties pin-up model, all curves and slopes and soft flesh that made him want to throw her over his shoulder and bring her back to his bed and dive in. The thought tantalized him, but the image of her standing in the window next to his bed had captivated him as much as her body sliding into his pool. He couldn't understand this visceral reaction he had every time he was around her.

He ignored that thought and concentrated on his dad and Toby, pretending to listen to Toby's story about their newest build's shipping delays. Allie's water-slicked head popped up over the side of the pool. He stopped pretending not to stare when Ford jumped in the water after Allie. That little shit. He knew it shouldn't matter that his friend, who happened to be a stand-up guy, was interested in Allie. But it did.

"Just go get in the pool with her," Toby said smugly.

"I'm grilling," he gritted out, glaring as Ford splashed Allie and she laughed then splashed him back.

"You're burning the chicken. Give me those." Toby yanked the tongs from his hands and gave him a push toward the cooler next to the pool. "Tell your son to go get us drinks, would ya, Robert?"

"Son, if you don't keep her away from Ford, you're a fool," Robert said.

Davis was not jealous. He was attracted, that was all. It happened to people every minute of every day, and he was a grown man who could handle it. Instead, he decided to talk to his mom because if there was ever a way to get rid of a hard-on, that was it.

Margie sat under the umbrella at the table with Keri, talking and shucking corn into a paper bag. He sat down next to her. "Hey, Mom, Keri. Need any help?"

"Sure. Here, break these in half. They hurt my hands." She

handed him a bowl of cleaned corn. They all worked in silence for a few minutes while Davis tried not to look at the pool every time he heard a splash.

"Why are you sitting here with me instead of with that lovely woman?" his mom asked, her tone deceptively casual.

"Who?" He concentrated on the corn instead of a red-and-white bikini.

"You know who."

"Let it go, Ma. We're just friends."

"She reminds me a little of Mel, don't you think?" Margie said, her eyes on the corn.

"What? Hell, no." Allie was nothing like Mel. She was blond for one and shorter and curvier.

"Not their looks, son," Margie said, her tone now gentle. Davis firmed his jaw against giving any sort of response and continued to shuck corn. But his mom didn't stop. "It's how she looks at you. She's sweet and a little shy. Layne told me how much the kids like her and Sammy."

"I see it too," Keri said. "She's genuine, and I can see how much she loves that boy of hers."

"She's a good mother," Davis agreed. "But we're still just friends."

"Keri, do you know how to tell when Davis is lying?"

"Oh, this will be good," Keri said, rubbing her hands together. He glared at her too.

"His ears get red," Margie said. "Ever since you were a little boy getting into mischief, your ears gave you away. Remember that time Shep broke the back window on your dad's work truck with a baseball?"

"He didn't break it. I did."

She patted his shoulder. "No, you didn't. You lied for Shep because he was already grounded and wasn't supposed to be outside, but your ears gave you away."

"Hey, I was grounded for a week for that," he said dryly.

"You were being honorable. I didn't want to ruin it." Margie looked at him and then out at the pool. "But now you're just being stubborn."

"Okay, we're done here, then?" He tossed the last of the corn into a bowl and made to get up. Jesus. He was getting it from every angle today.

"Why don't you go join them? Every time you look away, she looks back at you." Margie's eyebrows drew down as she stared him down.

"We're not having this discussion," Davis said stiffly.

Margie patted his arm. "I just hate to see you so lonely, honey."

"She's my tenant, Ma. And I'm not lonely. I'm fine."

Margie patted his cheek with one plump hand. "Your ears are red, dear."

In the end, it wasn't Allie that got him in the pool. It was Walter. Maybe the only golden retriever alive that didn't know how to swim, Walter forgot that fact at the sight of the football flying over the water and leaped straight into the deep end of the pool. He didn't even try to swim. He simply began to sink. Davis was out of his seat and into the pool in seconds.

He cut through the water, wrapped his arms around the dog's massive belly, and swam to the side. Walter sneezed wetly and licked Davis's face in appreciation.

"Oh, poor Walter," Allie said, just as her head emerged next to him. Her eyelashes were spiked with water and her hair slicked back. "I thought goldens could swim." She wrapped one arm around Walter's bottom half and held onto the side of the pool with the other. "Oof, he's heavy."

She grunted as they hefted him over the side. Close together now, they were both treading water. Her smooth legs brushed between his hairy ones, and she shot him a quick look from under her eyelashes.

"Walter, you beast," Shep said from above. "You push. I'll pull."

They heaved at the same time, and Walter finally flopped onto the concrete with a wet splash. He gave himself a massive shake and then looked around for another way to kill himself.

"Put him inside, will you?" Davis asked Shep as he led him away.

Then it was just the two of them. The diving board made a shadow over them as they hung with one hand gripping the side, legs lazily kicking in the cool water. The brush of her legs between his was making him crazy. Was she doing that on purpose? The kids were in the shallow end, unaware of Walter's accident. Shep was back in the lifeguard chair, and Davis was dangerously close to Allie's almost-naked body.

"Cannonball!" Ford's yell had barely finished when he landed in the water, making a massive tidal wave. The force lifted and pushed her flush against him. Instinct had him wrapping his arm around her protectively, caging her between him and the side of the pool.

For the briefest of seconds, her body fit squarely into his. Allie froze, her breasts pressed against his bare chest, and then her arms slid up around his neck to hold on. He let himself hold her, feeling her shiver and press closer. Lust rolled through him, hot and heavy. She was looking up at him with soft eyes, her pink mouth slightly parted. He wanted to lean in and lick the water from her lips.

How long had it been since he'd felt desire like this? Years, and even then, he couldn't remember a time when his control had been so thoroughly tested. The more he was surrounded by Allie's intriguing mix of sweetness and innocent sensuality, the more he wanted to explore each facet.

The thought made him stiffen, all too aware of the pain that went with those feelings. Every cell in his body ached to press closer and taste her, but an equal force whispered just as insistently to protect himself from feeling the devastation of loss again. Then the water receded, and Davis pushed her gently but firmly away.

Chapter Fourteen

STOMACH FLU, *pink eye, and lice...* "Oh my," Allie said as she typed out the list of ailments they were seeing for the What's Going Around column the nurse's office sent out to parents each month. Between taking care of a few minor scrapes from the playground and one case of potential pink eye, Allie had spent the morning checking heads for a gnarly case of lice being passed around the fourth-grade students.

She took another bite of the roasted vegetable salad with maple balsamic vinaigrette she had packed for lunch and saved the document, glad it was a fairly slow morning in the nurse's office. They hadn't gotten home from Davis's barbecue until after eight o'clock the night before, and the alarm had not been a welcome sound at six o'clock this morning. Even Sammy, who usually woke up raring to go, had a hard time getting out of bed.

The hand holding her fork bobbled, and a gob of dressing splatted on her new mint-green blouse, directly on her boob. "Shoot," Allie muttered. She was dabbing at it ineffectively, making the wet spot even bigger, when Sylvia walked in.

"Oops, that's gonna leave a stain. I just caught Lucia and Loretta on the playground rubbing their heads together. Lucia told her she didn't want to go through head lice alone." Sylvia rolled her eyes and laughed her big, warm laugh that comforted even the sickest kids that came to their office.

"Oh no." Allie laughed. She gave up on the shirt. "I think their parents might feel differently."

When the door opened, Allie turned to see Claire Henderson and Carly Lewis in the doorway. "Hi, girls. Come on in."

"Hi, gals." Sylvia waved. "I have to run to the lav, ladies, before the fifth graders get back from recess. They always need Band-Aids." She gave Claire's shoulder a quick squeeze on her way out.

"What brings you two into the nurse's office today?" Allie asked.

The girls sat down side by side on the cot. Immediately, Claire poked a finger into her hair. She had lovely clear blue eyes, and her hair was twisted in a riotous braid, more hair tumbling out than in. She looked a little wild in general. Not neglected, just slightly disheveled. Details that a dad on his own would glance over, see all the moving pieces, and call it good, whereas a mom would whip out a tissue, wipe smudges, and smooth hair.

"Is your head itchy, honey?"

"Yes," she said. "It itches so bad!" She hopped up on the cot and swung her legs while Allie grabbed a comb, doing a quick search through the top part of her braid. Allie moved on to Carly's hair next. Carly looked like her mother with her gorgeous hair and long legs. She would be a beauty like her mother one day too. She had a faint dusting of eye shadow and lip gloss on. Allie had to admit it was tastefully done.

"Your makeup is very pretty, Carly," she murmured, moving the comb through her hair. "Okay, do you girls want the good news or the bad news first?"

"My dad always says bad news first, to get it over with," Claire said.

Allie ignored the little thrill that went through her at the mention of her dad. "The bad news is that you have lice, which is going through your class right now. The good news is that you both get to go home and have a spa day today to wash them all out."

The girls' eyes went round. "Will I have to cut it off?" Carly asked, both hands going to her head as if Allie were going to come after her with scissors.

"Nope, no cutting. Just washing and combing." She set down the comb and sat on a stool next to the bed. "I wanted to thank you both for being such a good friend to Sammy this week."

"You're welcome," Claire said shyly. "Ben says Sammy's his new best friend."

"I'm so glad to hear that. It can be hard to move to a new school and meet friends. I'm glad Sammy has you three. Let's call your parents and get your spa day started, okay?" She sat down at the desk to look up Davis and Natalie's phone numbers.

"Henderson," Davis answered curtly.

"Hi, Davis. This is Allie. I'm calling from the nurse's office."

The silence held for a beat. Then, his voice tight, he asked, "What's wrong?" Allie was reminded yet again of the fear Davis lived with daily. Her heart twisted in sympathy even as she rushed to reassure him.

"Everyone's okay," she said quickly. "Claire is here with me. She's fine," she added, "but she does have a case of lice that's going around."

"Shit."

"Yep," she said cheerfully. "She's waiting here for you to

pick her up for her spa day." She winked at Claire, who was looking happy as a clam.

"I'm at your house. I'll be there in five."

She ignored the thrill that gave her. Yesterday in the pool, even the water hadn't worked to cool down the heat between them. She also knew Davis would rather pretend there was nothing happening, which sobered her quickly.

Davis was not on the list of "snacks" Amber had suggested. He had made it clear he thought he was too old, for one, and two, he was still in love with his late wife. Yeah, they were going to stay friends.

Landlord. Pals. Buddies. Compadres.

Her phone call to Natalie was much cooler, but then again, she did have a whole lot of debugging ahead of her this weekend, so Allie cut her some slack.

Natalie walked in first. Her hair was pulled back in a high pony, and her face had that beautiful glow that only good genes and excellent highlighter can achieve. She was wearing spandex tights and a tight tank with sneakers. She was probably one of those lucky people who actually enjoyed running.

Davis followed her. Standing next to each other, they made quite a pair. Like two puzzle pieces with the same colors that just needed to be fit together to make whole. Davis looked a little grumpier than usual and altogether too handsome in his T-shirt and jeans that hugged his muscular body. Allie's stomach betrayed her with that fluttery feeling in the face of all that raw masculinity.

"Hi, guys," Allie said cheerfully. It came out awkwardly loud. Natalie glanced at her then stared at the huge wet spot on her blouse. *Awesome.*

"Looks like our girls got into some trouble again," Natalie murmured, reaching up to brush something off Davis's shirt and lingering there. Allie froze.

Our girls.

Natalie was touching him again. *And he let her.* What else did he let her do? Allie would bet her fancy car Natalie wanted to do a whole lot more than just touch. But did Davis? She shot him a glance from under her lashes. He was as impassive as ever.

"So," Allie announced awkwardly, feeling like a third wheel. "Thank you both for coming. It's nice to see you again, Natalie," she added.

Natalie glanced her way as if just now placing her from the barbecue. "Thank you for calling." She glanced at Davis with a tiny wrinkle between her eyes as if sensing the undercurrents in the room for the first time.

Before it could get awkward, Allie gave them both her most professional look and handed over a piece of paper listing the supplies they needed. "You'll need to stop at the store for this."

Maybe they would shop together on their way home?

"You ready to be debugged, Claire?" Davis patted her shoulder gently and looked around the office gingerly. "It's busy in here."

"Oh, yeah, lots of lice today. And pink eye. And puke." At their alarmed faces, Allie forced herself to stop rambling. "Nothing for you two to worry about." *You two. Like a couple. How cute. Blech.*

She pasted on a smile. Davis's eyes slid down to her blouse and stopped. And stayed there for a few long, burning-hot seconds.

"You have something..." He finally looked up and pointed at her chest.

"Oh, yeah," she said, her cheeks flaming. "I spilled something."

She snapped out of her daze at Natalie's dainty cough. "Oh!

Yes. Yes. Great. Good luck with the hair. Thanks again for letting us crash your barbecue yesterday."

He met her eyes, and she thought, for only the hundredth time since meeting him, he had the most beautiful eyes. Easy to get lost in.

"See you at home," he said, rapping his knuckles on her desk on his way out. Allie caught the look of surprise on Natalie's face.

"Wait for us, Davis. We're parked right next to you," Natalie said, and just like that, the office was empty again.

Allie waited until the door closed before putting her head down on the desk and thumping once. Twice. Three times.

Yup. She had it bad for Davis Henderson. And she wasn't the only one.

~

DAVIS SWORE SOFTLY as he carried another load of lumber from his truck to Allie's backyard the next day. This project, replacing the rotted deck boards, was the last one on the list, and he was glad to get it started because it meant he was almost done seeing her every day.

Hell, with her now working at the school, he was surrounded by everything Allie. When he had woken up this morning and poured his coffee, a jar of flowers sat on his kitchen table. He knew Allie had put it there. She had a thing for flowers and plants. They were everywhere at her place. He had gotten stuck in one the other day she had hung up in the bathroom, of all places. That wasn't the only thing that had messed with him in there.

Dammit. Don't even think about that.

It was too late. Allie's tiny, pink, sexy-as-hell nightgown had burned itself into his brain the first time he saw it hanging on the back of her bathroom door. Thanks to that image, he'd spent a sleepless night thinking about all the ways he could take it off her body.

Finish the deck and get the hell out of here.

He worked tirelessly until early afternoon before taking a break under the big maple tree to eat. He had packed leftovers in a plastic container and was looking at the contents with distaste when Allie's car pulled into the driveway. A minute later, the front door opened and closed. He put a wilted green bean in his mouth, determined to eat quickly and get back to work.

The kitchen door slammed open and closed again, and he winced. He'd need to check the doorstops sooner rather than later. A minute later, Allie came around the back of the house looking like sunshine and holding out a glass of lemonade.

"Yoo-hoo," she called playfully, holding out the glass as she walked across the yard. "You look like a tall drink of water. Oops, I mean, you look like you could *use* a tall drink of water." She handed it to him and sat down next to him with her back against the wide tree. Her eyes sparkled with mischief. He couldn't look away. "Somehow Amber managed to make that sound less corny."

Her honey-colored hair was up on top of her head again in that little bun thing she put it up in as soon as she came home after work. She drew her knees up and hugged them to her chest, looking vibrant and so damn beautiful. He took a long swallow of the tart liquid and leaned his head back against the bark. "How was work?"

"Great. It's busy, which is nice. I love having Sammy right down the hall. How's the deck coming?"

"Fine. Should be done by the end of the week, early next week at the latest." He finished the rest of the lemonade.

"How did it go with Claire?"

"Fine. It took two hours, but I think we got them all."

"Good. And Natalie and Carly? Did you see them?"

"No," he said, glancing up at her tone. "We didn't see them after we left. Why?"

Allie picked up a leaf and studied it closely. "Just curious. I got a feeling you two were close or maybe had been."

It wasn't a direct question, but Davis knew what she was asking. He also knew he didn't have to answer. He didn't owe her anything, but he did anyway.

"When she first moved to Northfield, we dated," he said honestly enough.

Allie's soft lips were compressed in a way he didn't like, but he went on anyway. It was best she knew the whole story from him rather than anyone else. "She's a nice woman, but I'm not interested in anything more than casual, and it doesn't get any less casual than our kids becoming best friends. I'm not looking for anything like that."

"Are you looking?" She cocked her head.

"I've dated a few times this last year, but nothing serious, and definitely no one my kids know here in Northfield. That's not something I'm ready for." He raked his hand through his hair restlessly. Then she said the damnedest thing.

"Yeah, your sign is definitely not on." Before he could ask her what the hell that meant, she noticed his arm. "Hey, what happened here?" She gently pulled his arm over to look at a long scratch the wood left earlier. She was bent over his arm, close enough that her vanilla sugar scent filled his nose. The urge to bury his face against her neck to see if she tasted like sugar made him grit his teeth. What was with this woman and food?

"It's nothing," he said tightly, pulling his arm back. Allie held on to look at it until she was leaning across his chest, trying to examine it. The press of her body against his felt so good that he leaned back a fraction more, taking her with him.

She took care of people so naturally, it was hard not to let her. He held still while she looked. She reached her hand up to push back the hair that had fallen over his forehead. They stared at each other in charged silence, the weight of arousal surrounding them as heavily as a cloak.

"Davis, do you feel that between us?" she asked suddenly, looking up at him appealingly. Wisps of golden hair fell softly around her face when she leaned over him, pressing her hand flat against his chest. He knew she would feel his heart thudding crazily fast.

With a sigh, he gave in and let himself stroke the silky-soft hair back from her face. Just once. It was a simple, innocent gesture. One he had done a thousand times for Claire, but Allie turned her cheek into his hand and nuzzled into his palm. It turned into a lingering caress. He cupped her delicate jaw, running his thumb over her cheekbone.

"Yes," he said quietly, unable to lie. He was sure she would feel it if he did. His body was strung taut as a bow with an overwhelming need to kiss her.

"Is it usually like this?" She hesitated. "Because this is new for me."

A possessive, feral jolt went through him. "Not all the time," he said gruffly. He wanted to tell her—*show* her—with his mouth and tongue, and more, exactly why they were so drawn to each other, but the words lodged in his throat.

Because she's the furthest thing from casual I could think of.

"Why do you think that is?" she asked softly. Her head was tilted up, her soft lips parted as if waiting for his mouth to cover hers.

"It's attraction," he said stonily. "We've been together in the same house every day since we met. It was bound to happen."

That was exactly why he needed to finish the deck and get

the hell out of there. He couldn't trust himself around her, and it scared the hell out of him. He sat up straighter.

A glint of hurt flashed in her eyes, but she sat up, too, with her familiar, easy smile. "Good thing it's not Mrs. Autovino's house you're working on then. Besides, who says I'm attracted to you anyway, old man, even if I do keep ending up in your arms," she added, giving him a crooked smile.

He let her go reluctantly. "Old man?"

"You said it yourself. 'I'm old enough'," she repeated his words back to him, mocking his deep voice.

"Old enough to know better."

"Know better about what? Retirement? What the blue light specials are?"

He eased his arms back gently and stuffed his lunch back in the paper bag.

"Is that your lunch?" She sounded horrified.

He looked down at the container in question. A few straggly green beans, cold rice, and a chicken bone were left. It had looked more appetizing last night when he served it.

"Davis, I can do better than that. Come into the house and I'll—" She stopped abruptly. "Never mind."

"You'll what?" He couldn't help asking. She looked embarrassed and, for the life of him, he didn't know why.

"Nothing." She blinked.

"What were you going to say?"

"I'm not feeding you."

He shrugged. "I just ate."

"I mean that I've heard all about the casserole brigade and how women like to feed you." She poked one long finger into his chest, which he grabbed reflexively and pressed against his shirt. "You're a grown man. If you want to eat lunches that look like that"—she wrinkled her nose— "... it's not my concern."

He wiped the smile off his face and sighed. Loudly. "Allie." He waited until she met his eyes. "I don't eat that food."

"What kind of monster doesn't like brownies?" she asked with a frown. He knew she was thinking about Natalie's comment at the barbeque and hid a smile.

He looked at her steadily. "I like brownies."

"Then why not eat them?"

"I can't. It doesn't feel right when I know there might be expectations."

"None of it?" she asked skeptically. "Not even Natalie's?"

Slowly he shook his head. "No."

Her face broke out into a smile that rivaled the sun.

"What do you do with it all then?"

"Give it to my crew."

He knew she wanted to ask more questions, but she left it at that. "Oh, okay."

He found he liked when she looked at him like that, all soft and happy. He liked a lot of things about her. *Too many*, his brain unhelpfully reminded him.

"Allie."

She looked up expectantly. "Hmm?"

"Are you going to let go of me?" She looked at her hand still pressed tightly against his chest.

"Oh," she said. Bright color flooded her cheeks. "I just didn't want you to lose your balance, old man." She jerked back her hand and gave him a healthy shove backward as she walked away.

Chapter Fifteen

WATCHING little boys learn how to play baseball was like watching someone herd earthworms. Allie leaned back on the bleachers to stretch her back while she watched Sammy's first Little League practice.

As the sun soaked into her bones, she realized she hadn't felt this sense of peace and contentment since before leaving home. Yes, there were some nights after she put Sammy to bed that seemed to stretch out before her, but it was different than when she lived with Corbin.

Not one part of her missed her old life in the city. Working at the school kept her mind busy. The kids were funny. They came down to the nurse's office many times under the guise of needing a Band-Aid, but they just needed a little reassurance. Providing that was her favorite part of the job by far. Yeah, she was doing just fine on her own, she thought with more than a little pride.

Of course, it also helped to see Sammy thriving here. He loved being near their family, and he and Ben were thick as thieves at school. Aside from Ben, baseball was his favorite thing right now. She thought it might have to do with his hero worship of Davis because every day Sammy followed her around the house in his new baseball cap telling her 'Davis said to hold the ball like this' and 'Davis can hit further than anyone.' He had been so excited about the first practice tonight he barely ate dinner.

She shielded her eyes and watched Ben and Landon, Ford's son, take turns batting. Where was Sammy? Ah. There he was. Bounding over to get the ball he had thrown enthusiastically in the opposite direction from the kid he was paired with. His hair flopped in his eyes as he ran, and his eyes sparkled with laughter.

She kept her eyes trained on Sammy and avoided where Davis and Ford were coaching a group of kids. If she had been looking at him, which she wasn't, she would have noticed the sinful things Davis did to a pair of gym shorts. His muscular legs were on display, and the material clung to his thighs. Put a baseball cap on and a patient look on his face while he taught a bunch of kids, and it did something warm and melty to her insides.

But she wasn't looking.

"Hi. Allie, right?" A very pregnant woman sat next to her. "I'm Keri Richardson, Max's mom. We met at Davis's barbecue." She sat down with a groan on the bottom bleacher and put a hand under her belly. "This is Rachel Steiner. Her son, Julien, is out there." She pointed at the field while Rachel took a seat. "God, these bleachers are horrible."

The two women had a classic Northfield look to them. In their ears were tasteful, sparkling diamond studs, and each had an expensive bag on her shoulder. Allie felt the old twinge of self-consciousness flare up but shrugged it off.

"Hi," she said. "Congratulations." She gestured to the other woman's massive belly.

"Thanks. I feel like I'm going to pop." Keri grinned, showing her perfectly straight teeth. Teeth like that cost money too. Allie had always paid careful attention to people's teeth. Her incisor had grown in crooked, and when she hit middle school, it felt like every kid had a mouthful of metal except her. Annette didn't have money for vanity when the girls were younger, but Allie had always noticed beautiful teeth.

"I was barely showing by six months with the first two, but this third one is like a wrecking ball," Keri said, fondly rubbing her belly. She did look like someone had inflated a beach ball under her shirt, Allie thought a little longingly. She had loved being pregnant with Sammy.

Rachel leaned across and whispered toward Keri's belly. "Don't listen to your mommy. Aunt Rachel thinks you're perfect."

Sammy was up next, trying to hit the soft pitches Ford was throwing. He missed every single one by a mile, her boy. Even without any baseball knowledge, Allie could see he was awkwardly holding the bat. Davis crouched down and talked to him before clapping him on the back, nearly sending him flying, and pointed him to first base.

"So, Allie, I heard you took over for Sylvia Wagner?" Keri said.

Small towns. Gotta love 'em. "I started this week."

They chatted easily during the rest of the practice, and Allie's tension gradually drifted away. Keri was a social worker, and Rachel was an attorney in downtown Rochester. They were both funny and down-to-earth, and she didn't feel awkward or out of place at all even when a few other parents joined them. The group had an easy way about them that put her to ease, and she was actually enjoying herself.

A loud cheer erupted from the field, and the women turned to watch the dirt-streaked boys come running toward them.

Sammy's entire face split into a grin as he ran toward her. He had grass stains on his new baseball pants, and his hat was crooked. He had never looked happier.

"Mom, that was awesome!" *Mom.* Not mama anymore. Man, that happened quickly.

She kissed his dirt-streaked forehead. "It was fun to watch you, bud."

Ford came over with Landon next to him. "Hey, Allie," he said, giving her a flirty smile that Allie couldn't help but return. "Sammy, my man, you are going to crush that ball soon. Don't give up, yeah?" He held out his knuckles to Sammy, who pounded them.

"Yeah, I really am! Come on, guys, let's go find Ben," he said. "Be right back, Mom!" The group of boys took off with a whoop.

Keri gave Ford a look before turning back to Allie. "Did you meet my husband?" She thumped the good-looking Black man next to her who was talking to Davis. They both turned to Allie. "Honey, this is Allie. Allie, this is my husband, Toby." Toby stuck out his hand with a friendly smile.

"Very nice to meet you," Allie said.

"Hi, Davis," she greeted next.

"Allie." *So many words.*

"So, Allie, are you all moved in? Need any help?" Ford asked, nudging her shoulder playfully. Davis's jaw started ticking. Interesting.

"We're all set," she said, "but thanks."

"Sammy had fun today," Ford went on. "We'll work on the hitting."

"I've been playing catch with him. Not sure if that's helping or hurting," she added ruefully.

"I'd be happy to come over and give him some pointers

before practice. Maybe I could show you both." He grinned down at her.

Allie blinked. He was smooth. Since he really was so kind and genuine, she offered him a small smile back. With Davis glowering beside her, and the way he ran so hot and cold, it was refreshing to talk to Ford. He was handsome, even if he didn't give her that top-of-the-roller-coaster feeling. That was a good thing. Maybe just a fun little flirtation, a safe one where she could have fun and dip a toe back into the dating world. What did Amber call it? A snack. Ford was certainly snackable. Davis felt more like a Thanksgiving feast.

Ford tilted his dark-blond head toward hers, "Listen, a bunch of us head to the pub most Fridays if you want to stop by."

Someone's voice rang from the dugout. "Landon, don't climb on that!"

Ford looked over with a pained expression on his face. "That's my cue. Hope to see you, Allie. Later, everyone."

"Yeah, we're heading out too. Gotta feed these animals before they turn feral. Nice meeting you, Allie." Keri grabbed Toby. Suddenly, it was just her and Davis.

"So," she said bemusedly. "They seemed nice."

Davis nodded, his usual scowl in place. "They're good people."

"And Ford?" she asked innocently, testing a theory. "Is he good people?"

He gave her a long look. "He is."

"Hmm. Interesting."

His face looked stony now. "Allie."

"Yes, Davis?"

He turned fully toward her, brows drawn together, his jaw ticking, but that scowl didn't fool her anymore. If actions spoke louder than words, Davis had a lot more under his exterior than he wanted her to know.

"Go home."

She couldn't help the grin that took over her face.

Chapter Sixteen

On Friday, Allie ran out on her lunch to Annette's design studio to drop off the keys to the Mercedes. One of Annette's clients was purchasing it for their newly licensed son. Only in Northfield would a luxury car be a suitable present for a sixteen-year-old, but just like that, another weight was shed from her old life.

Annette's studio sat between the yoga studio and an attorney's office. The entryway was covered with a rounded black-and-white striped awning that had become her calling card. Black and white details filled the entryway, from the glossy black planters filled with an assortment of white flowers on each side of the doorway to the striped welcome mat in the doorway. Annette always paid attention to the details.

"Hey, Mom," she called as she walked into the reception area. Comfortable vintage rugs were scattered around the front sitting area, which featured a tasteful gray settee in front of a concrete coffee table. Old and new. Annette's specialty.

Annette's office, along with other offices for her employees, one of them Amber's, was down the brick hallway. Allie tapped on the first door. "I've got the keys for you." She swung the key fob back and forth.

Her mother sat behind an oversized oak table in front of a large Mac desktop. Her tortoiseshell glasses were perched on her nose as she squinted at the screen and muttered to herself. "Allison. Come in. I'm working on inventory. Amber usually comes in and does it, but she's on another one of her new business side gigs. She started a dog-walking business. Can you believe that?"

Allie took a seat in front of the desk and admired her mother. Annette was in her prime. Her pale skin was smooth thanks to an expensive regimen of lotions and regular facials, and her figure was slim and toned from a dedicated mix of barre and yoga classes at the studio next door.

Any traces of the poverty Annette and the girls had lived through were absent, at least from the outside. She spared no expense in pampering herself now, but she balanced it with giving generously to the women's shelter and several other not-for-profits that had helped her and the girls during their toughest years. Growing up poor gave one an empathy that growing up rich didn't always afford. Annette never forgot who helped her when she needed it most.

"I paid for that girl to go to a private college, and she dropped out to walk dogs."

Annette's aggrieved voice brought Allie back to the present. "Yes, she did mention it. You know Amber, Mom. She's happiest when she's got a million things going on at once."

Amber was always starting new businesses and then either selling them or morphing them into others. It killed Annette to watch because from the outside it looked like Amber was scattered and irresponsible, but Allie knew for a fact Amber had paid for her car with cash.

Annette pinched the bridge of her nose with two perfectly

manicured fingers. "I don't understand her. She could work here with me full-time or go back to school. Honestly…" She sighed. "I think she does it to spite me. All I've ever wanted for you girls was to get a good education and support yourselves."

Allie could never fault Annette for wanting an easier life for her girls than she'd had. "Amber supports herself. She's just always done it her way." She took a seat in one of the emerald-green velvet chairs facing the desk and turned around a fabric swatch book.

"You girls are all so smart. I just want what's best for you. Did you see Lily and Evie are on the dean's list again this semester?" The pride in her voice was unmistakable. "Although, when Lily came home last week, she said she thought Tucker was going to propose." Lily had been dating the same boy since they were in high school, but Annette didn't look happy about the news. "Why would she want to get married? Why ruin a good thing?"

"Some people *are* happily married, you know?" she said.

"Allison, haven't you learned this lesson?"

"Relax, Mom," Allie said dryly. "I know the aunts all believe we're destined to be unlucky in love, but I'm not superstitious. I know you don't believe in that either."

Annette coolly assessed her as she sat back in the chair. "No, I don't believe that nonsense about a curse. But I do think that most of the time, women are better off alone. Desire?" She shrugged. "Indulge it. It's natural. But don't let yourself get swept away. Feelings can change in a heartbeat."

A small bouquet of wildflowers in black-and-white craft paper sat on her desk. Rosa often supplied Annette's office with flowers that Annette delivered to her newly designed space, another of her signature touches. It was a simple, cheerful arrangement amid the rich decor. Allie plucked a daisy from the water and twirled it in her fingers.

"Did Dad ever explain why he left?"

Annette's smooth forehead gave the tiniest twitch before she smoothed it out again and shrugged. "The past is the past. What good would it do to spend time there?"

"No, I know. I'm just curious." Allie hesitated. "Did he?" She remembered cards showing up for a few years on her birthday, and a few awkward phone calls on the holidays, but even those eventually trailed off, and they hadn't heard from him in years.

When she was fourteen and Amber twelve, they had attempted to get their father's information from Annette. She gave it reluctantly, and they spent a weekend unearthing Nathan Powell's new life. They had been surprised to learn he had married again and had two other kids, a boy and a little girl. His new family even lived in New York, only thirty minutes away. He had given up the entertainment industry and was now a manager of a local car dealership.

Allie flinched every time she heard their ad on the radio. She had no desire to see him ever again, but she did hope he was a better father to his new family than he had been to hers.

"When your father left, I had just come home from the hospital with the twins." Annette stood up and walked to the window where a console table stood with an assortment of plants and decor on it.

She picked up a small golden pothos in a chic planter and moved it to the right and looked around the room again, her practiced eye discerning, her motions restless. She strode over to Allie and reached next to her for a decorative wooden bowl on the side table between the chairs. "Perfect," she murmured.

"How did you do it on your own?" She looked at her mother with renewed respect. She thought about how hard it was to parent Sammy, and her mother had raised four while going to school and working.

"I didn't." She looked surprised. "I had my family." She reached out and put a warm, long-fingered hand on top of Allie's. "And so do you."

Allie turned her hand over and clasped her mother's gently. Her nails were painted a subtle pink. She wore no expensive jewelry, only a simple gold ring on her right hand from her own mother's wedding set, inherited when she passed away. Long, faint pink scars on the skin above her thumb lingered where she had burned it on a toaster oven when she was waitressing.

Annette gently pulled her hand away. Allie knew she was always a little self-conscious of her hands. "It is not easy to raise a child by yourself, but it is better to do it alone than to depend on someone and be disappointed again."

"Did you ever have feelings for anyone after Dad left, Mom?" As Allie asked the question, she was suddenly surprised she didn't know the answer. Much like any child or teenager, she had simply looked at her mom as an extension of herself. She never really had given any consideration to whether Annette was lonely.

Now, as she looked at her mother's face, she wondered. Annette's love life, if she had ever had one, was not something she had ever discussed. She never brought anyone home. Annette's entire life consisted of her beloved business, her daughters, and her sisters. Family was everything to Annette.

"Please. Give me some credit. I have needs. Needing a man and wanting a man are two different things." She snorted.

Allie laughed suddenly and waved the daisy like a white flag of surrender. "Stop, Mom. I love you, but I don't want to hear about your sexual needs."

"I wasn't planning on telling you about them, Allison," she said tartly. "I'm just letting you know that it's perfectly fine for a woman to exist, satisfied, without a ring on her finger. Everything a husband could do, I did myself. Have a career? I own my own business." She spread her hands wide to encase the office. "Buy a house? I bought the biggest one," she said with a little un-Annette-like smirk. "Raise my children? My girls are the best thing that ever happened to me. Your father had nothing to do with that."

Allie idly plucked off another one of the white petals and rubbed it lightly between her fingers. "Don't you ever get lonely?" she asked softly. She was honestly curious. Annette was so competent and independent, but did she ever feel the loneliness Allie did? Feeling like other married couples had gotten it right, and maybe Allie had just chosen the wrong man?

"Pish. Never. I have my sisters and my business. I have you girls and my friends. I have all I need." Annette sat down abruptly on the edge of the desk. "Tell me about Davis. He's helping you with the house?" Annette's tone was casual, but Allie wasn't fooled.

"Yes, he's working on a few things."

She paused. "Be careful, Allison." Annette's quiet voice brought Allie's eyes up from the mangled flower. Her dark eyes were serious.

"I'm not planning on doing anything risky, Mom."

She leveled a cool look at her. "No one ever is. That's when things happen."

"One failed relationship was enough for me," Allie said quietly. "I couldn't do that to Sammy again." Another daisy petal floated to the floor.

Annette looked at her shrewdly. "It's easy to play house when he's there every day and you can see all the spaces in your life filled. But you're enough for Sammy. You fill all the spaces on your own, as I did." She pushed off the desk and held out her arms. "Now, I have work to do. When can I have my little prince for a sleepover?"

Allie went into her arms and hugged her. Annette's

perfume rose from her blouse, reminding Allie of other times in her life she had gone to her mom for comfort, and she held on tighter. They had always been close. Her drive to go to school and then start a successful career had sometimes made her distant, but when it came down to the wire, Allie respected her mother. Annette would do anything for her girls. Hopefully, Sammy would feel the same about her someday.

She let go of her mom's slim body and went to find a broom for the mangled petals on the floor.

ALLIE STOOD on the shovel with both feet and jumped up and down. A trickle of sweat beaded down her temple, and she stopped to wipe it away, taking care not to turn toward the house. Davis was working on the deck when she had gotten home from work. Other than a cool nod, he was keeping his distance, which was just fine.

She had changed into an old pair of shorts and a tank top and got to work digging up the old roots in the backyard garden beds. She hopped on the shovel again. It was easier to think when she was using her body, and she had a lot to consider.

Annette's words drifted in and out of her head as she bounced again on the shovel, but the pointed end didn't sink any further into the late summer-baked ground.

... you can see all the spaces in your life filled when he's there. You fill all the spaces on your own...

Needing a man and wanting a man are two different things.

Be careful, Allison...

Annette's words repeated in her head, at war with another part of her brain that slyly whispered not all men were like Corbin. What was so wrong with wanting a happy marriage? Someone who adored her and Sammy, who wanted to be home on the weekends, who would look at her the way she had seen other husbands look at their wives. Was that so wrong?

Do not fall for Davis Henderson. Don't you dare. He is not for you.

She swiped a trickle of sweat off her neck and looked up when she heard Walter's collar jingle. The big dog bounded over for a pet as her eyes searched involuntarily for his owner.

"Hi, Walter, you big lug! Of course, I missed you." She rubbed his ears the way he liked, then she caught sight of Davis, and her mouth went dry.

Covertly, she watched the play of muscles in his back as he carried wood over to the new deck. His wide shoulders strained under the weight, but he never changed his stride. No matter the job, Davis worked hard and rarely took breaks.

Even with Sammy home asking him millions of questions and generally getting in his way, Davis worked patiently while they talked. Many times, he stopped to show Sammy how to use a tool. When he left, Sammy would proudly report back to her that he could fix anything she needed around the house now.

The new deck boards stood out in stark contrast to the older ones, reminding her this was the last project for the house. Soon, he wouldn't be there at the house when she got home from work. She ignored the pang that gave her and hopped on the shovel again. The shovel finally broke through the ground, and she wiped her arm across her forehead. It must be close to ninety degrees, and she was in the generous shade of the maple tree.

She glanced over at Davis working in the full sun and stopped, her eyes as wide as dinner plates. He was using the bottom of his T-shirt to mop the sweat off his forehead, exposing a strip of the tanned abs that drew her eyes like a magnet. His tool belt hung low on his hips, dragging down the waistband of his jeans and exposing a thin line where the sun didn't reach.

He seemed to hesitate a few seconds before peeling off the shirt and, oh my. She gave up all pretense of gardening and just stared.

It wasn't even her first time seeing his bare chest, but the sight would never get old. Davis was tanned to a golden brown all over, his chest broad and lightly covered in dark hair that led to a narrow trail down a ridged abdomen and disappeared into his waistband. Her palms itched to feel the texture, and a tingly heat spread through her body that had nothing to do with the sun. Reluctantly, she dragged her eyes up to find his on her.

They stood still, something hot and primal throbbing between them that she felt echoing in all the pulse points of her body. She shivered when his eyes darkened, the attraction between them as tangible as if he had laid his hands on her body.

A stinging, burning pain pricked her legs, and Allie screamed, dropping the shovel. Tiny bees stung her ankles and legs as she slapped her hands frantically and tried to escape the swarm. Before she realized what was happening, she was picked up bridal style against a bare chest. *Davis.* Her head swirled with aftershocks of pain as he ran with her toward the house.

He set her down gently on the grass and slid his hands up and down her legs, swatting away bees while she sat there in a daze. "Hang tight. You stepped in a ground bees' nest."

"Davis, you need to get a baking soda paste on her," Mrs. Autovino called from over the fence.

"Are you allergic to bees?" Davis looked down at her, and she found herself less than a foot away from his dark scowl. He had thick, dark lashes that were quite unfair for a man, she thought dazedly.

"What?"

"Are you allergic to bees?" Wow. Bare-chested Davis was

something close up. Who had abs like that in real life? Certainly not her. She licked her lips.

"Allie," he barked, shaking her gently.

Good feeling gone. Her legs *were* starting to sting, and she felt rather silly now as she looked around. Walter ran in circles around her, stopping every few seconds to nose her and make sure she was okay.

"I'm fine, Walter," she reassured him when he nudged her. "I'm not allergic," she answered Davis.

They were in the middle of her backyard. Thank God, it wasn't the front yard. She could just imagine what people would say seeing them together like this. Davis had his bare arm curled around her back as she sat in the circle of his arms. He was still running his hands over the angry red bumps on her calves that were swelling and starting to itch.

Heat crawled up her chest and into her cheeks. Why does this keep happening to her? She had lived twenty-six years of her life without any accidents, and yet here she was again being rescued by Davis Henderson.

"I'm a competent woman, dammit."

"You're what?" he asked, scowling and running his hand roughly over her, checking for more bees.

"I'm—never mind." She sighed. "I'm fine now. You can let me up."

"Do you have baking soda, dear?" Mrs. Autovino called.

"Yes, I do." She had picked some up on her first grocery run. It was an essential ingredient in making chocolate chip cookies. "Thank you, Mrs. Autovino," she called over the fence and shifted a little, conscious of the way her bare arm was pressed into the side of the muscled chest she was not going to ogle again.

"You're welcome, dear. Davis, better get her inside and put

something on those," she called, her screen door banging as she went inside.

"I'm, okay, Davis. Really." She started to stand and felt a rush of air as he scooped her up instead.

"Oof!" The earth shifted as he swung her up again in his arms. He didn't even flinch, which was impressive. She knew she weighed more than she looked. She squirmed. "You don't have to carry me. I can walk."

"Stay still," he ordered. His bossy nature should have irritated her, but instead, her stomach filled with tiny flutters. She wrapped an arm around his neck and settled against him instead.

Davis carried her into the kitchen where he snagged a chair with his foot and pulled it out. Gently, he set her down on it and pulled open the pantry door. He found the baking soda, added some to a bowl, then made a thick paste with water before returning to her. He pulled another chair close to hers. His hands closed gently around her ankles as he drew them up and set her legs on the firm muscles of his thighs. That felt...

"... nice," she said. Davis squinted at her. "Not nice," she said hurriedly. "I mean nice that you know what to do. Were you a Boy Scout?"

He snorted and continued dabbing the paste on her legs.

"This should feel better in a minute," he murmured, scooping up the mixture and patting it lightly on a bee sting. He took care of the bites one by one, gently piling the mixture on each red bump. The cold paste soon soothed the burning. It did feel nice, she thought in surprise.

When was the last time someone had taken care of her like this? Certainly not Corbin. She was the one who took care of everyone else, but now, with Davis's competent hands on her, it struck her that it had been a long, long time. Her family was affectionate, and Sammy was always up for a snuggle, but

Davis's hands on her made her aware of how long it had been since she'd been touched by a lover. The tension from the yard hummed to life again.

"You're the most accident-prone woman I know," he was grumbling, although his hands were gentle as they spread the paste on her.

"Hey, accidents happen," she said. "I just happen to have had more than a few since meeting you. It feels better already," she finally said, relaxing back against the chair to let him work his magic. His dark head was bent over her legs. He wore it longer on the top, swept over his broad forehead in a slight wave. Allie idly wondered what he would do if she ran her fingers through it.

"I'm sorry about the nest. I'll take care of it today, so you and Sammy don't have to worry about getting hurt again."

Something in his voice made Allie look at him closely, but he kept his eyes down, shuttered by his lashes. She reached out to rub the stiff muscles in his shoulder soothingly. They weren't talking about bee stings anymore.

"Hey, this isn't your fault, Davis. Accidents happen. No one can protect us from everything."

"I can damn well try," he said fiercely. Stubborn man.

"You can, but it'll make you crazy. Sometimes you just have to live." She wanted to shake him and kiss him at the same time. "If you don't, you could miss the best moments," she said huskily. *Like this one.*

Davis slowly raised his gaze, which caught on her shoulders and lingered on her breasts for a long, hot moment before sliding down her body. He leisurely skimmed her spread thighs and finally, her legs sprawled over his. His jaw tightened.

Suddenly, the cups of Allie's bra felt too tight. Too tight and too hot and not enough at the same time. She squirmed in her seat, shifting her thighs, feeling the muscles of his legs tighten under her.

She lifted a finger and traced the dark lines on his bare upper arm. His skin was warm to the touch, and the muscles bunched when she drew her finger over the tattoo there. "It's an anchor."

An eagle and the American flag wove around the anchor in shades of black and white, a reminder of his time in the Navy. A younger version of Davis flashed in her head, a tall, broad-shouldered sailor who probably made more than a few knees weak at every port.

"What?"

"I've wondered what your tattoo was," she said breathlessly. *Move your hand, Allie.* But she couldn't. She had been staring at these arms for too long, and her hand lingered over the smooth skin and hard muscle, tracing the lines of the tattoo. *Damn. Damn. Damn.*

It was really hot in here.

"Allie..."

She suddenly realized he was done taking care of her bee stings and was now holding each of her ankles loosely in his hands, running the pads of his thumbs lightly back and forth over the bones. *Could you orgasm from ankle bone fondling?* When was the last time she'd even had an orgasm? Months? A year?

His fingers tightened around her ankles, encircling them. "Yes?"

Her voice only wobbled a little as he slid his hands to the back of her knees and gently tugged her closer to the edge of the seat. She bent her legs, feeling his hand glide down the outside of her thighs and settle on her hips, fingers flexing possessively. He gripped the flesh firmly, stroking his thumbs over the bare skin of her belly, and she shuddered.

It was the most erotic touch of her life so far, and it was only her hips. God, she wanted to crawl onto his lap and have dirty, filthy, raunchy sex like she had only ever read about in her romance books. She always wondered if those scenes were exaggerated, but looking at Davis's sexy eyes, she was sure he would deliver.

She was almost to the edge of the chair, practically on his lap with her legs loosely draped around him. It was hard to draw a deep breath, and her hands shook ever so slightly when she stroked her fingers over his bare arms.

They were face-to-face, so close she could see the gold flecks in his brown eyes. Her breasts were inches away from feeling his bare chest against her own. She swayed forward, the sound of her ragged breathing filling her ears. The air was thick and heavy, pulsing with the tension she felt deep inside.

She wanted him. She wanted to slide on him fully, wind her arms around his big body, and find the friction she desperately needed.

Oh, please deliver.

Suddenly, the tension holding him back gave way. With a rough "fuck," he wrapped his hand along the side of her neck, threaded his fingers into her hair, and tipped up her face. The rough pad of his thumb slipped over her bottom lip. She darted her tongue out to taste him, and he growled when it slid over him. He tasted like salt and summer. She let out a whimper. It would have been embarrassing if she hadn't seen Davis's eyes go even darker. Even hotter.

"You're so fucking beautiful." It sounded more like a curse than a compliment, his eyes unsmiling as he leaned in.

Kiss me.

His mouth slanted over hers, finally giving her what she needed, and she opened eagerly. His lips firmly covered hers, tasting her and nipping, his mouth tender and utterly sensual as he tugged her bottom lip between his teeth. Her heart stuttered. He shifted under her legs, parting them, and tugging her closer to his heat. Oh, God, it was so much heat and want. Her body strained closer to his chest, wanting more wet, stroking kisses.

"More," she whispered. She didn't recognize the tremble in her voice. Davis's long fingers tangled in her hair, cupping her head with both hands, tilting it so she could accept his mouth more deeply. She hung on to his neck and let him take control.

His kiss was everything she had fantasized about since that first night in this kitchen. Firm and possessive and sensual. He growled deep in his throat, sliding his tongue over the ridges of her teeth to taste her fully.

"Knew you'd taste like cake," he muttered, swooping back to suck her lower lip. He nibbled kisses down her throat, licking and kissing his way back to her lips. "Want to taste you all over."

"Mom! Hey, Mama! Have you seen my mitt? I wanna practice my catching."

Sammy's voice at the top of the stairs was as effective as a polar plunge. They leaped apart and sat staring, mouths damp and parted, panting like they had just run a marathon. Davis swore softly.

"It's in your closet, buddy," she called up shakily. Footsteps slid across the landing and thumped down the stairs. Davis quickly pushed back the chair and adjusted himself before stalking to the back door just as Sammy appeared in the living room doorway.

"Mom—oh, hi, Mr. Henderson. I didn't know you were still here. Are you staying for dinner?" he asked hopefully.

"Hi, Sammy. No, I have to get home to Ben and Claire," he said gruffly. He kept his body angled toward the door.

"Oh. Do you wanna play catch for a little bit before you have to go?" he asked hopefully.

On the rare times Corbin had been home, Sammy had never failed to ask a similar question. *Do you want to play cars, Dad? Do you want to go to the park?* The answer was always no. Gradually, Sammy stopped asking. Allie couldn't bear to see it happen again. She opened her mouth to give him an easy out. "Sammy, he can't—"

"Sure, bud. Let me finish up out here, and we can throw the ball around for a while before I go."

Sammy's eyes lit up. "You can?" He didn't waste a minute before letting out a whoop. "All right! I'll go find my mitt!" He raced past then turned around and raced back for a quick press of his skinny arms around her middle. "Hi, Mom!"

"Hi, honey," Allie said to the empty doorway because Sammy had disappeared up the stairs.

"You don't have to do that," she said quietly.

Davis finally turned. "I know that. He's a good kid."

"The best," she said simply.

"I'm sorry, Allie," he finally said quietly. "I shouldn't have let that happen."

Her heart paused one long, slow beat as if to give him time to take it back. He didn't.

"Oh. Well." She waved a hand vaguely after a moment. "It's... fine. No big deal." She smiled brightly around the hurt and turned around to the living room. "I'm going to shower now. Have a good day."

She didn't turn back until she heard the screen door slam against the frame. Against her better judgment, she stopped on the stairs and bent her head to watch Davis walk away.

He didn't turn around.

~

After dinner that night, Allie tugged on her dish gloves

and took out her frustration on the sheet pan she had made dinner on and faced facts.

She had a thing, a major thing, for Davis Henderson.

Oh, hell.

He was the absolute worst candidate. She knew this logically in her mind, but other organs in her body were screaming at her to do nasty, dirty, delicious things to him. The feel of him between her legs on the chair, how hard his body had felt under hers, how she had lost every bit of inhibition when his eyes went darker, and he leaned in with his eyes on her mouth and blew up her world with his kiss—

Then told her he shouldn't have touched her.

Embarrassment burned through her again when she remembered how he pulled away. How grim he had looked.

She scrubbed harder at the pan and reminded herself of all the reasons it would never work.

He thinks he's too old.

Please. That was a flimsy excuse, and they both knew it. She was far past consenting age.

He was her landlord.

A sticking point, although not much of one where she was concerned. She knew with certainty Davis would never do anything to hurt her or Sammy.

Northfield was a small town. It would be impossible for it not to get around that they were dating, and now that Sammy was friends with Ben and Claire, there were some serious things to consider there.

Natalie's hand on Davis's chest flashed in her mind. *What exactly had happened between them?*

He's still in love with Melody.

Her hands fell still in the sink. That was the biggest issue, and she didn't have any answers for it. She just knew the next time she fell in love, she wanted it to be the last. She wanted something real and true. The more time she spent with Davis, the more she thought it might be with him.

Amber hip-bumped her and slid another stack of plates into the sudsy sink. She had stopped by to have dinner with her and Sammy before her shift at the Northfield Pub. "What did that pan ever do to you?" Amber's sharp eyes roved over her face. Allie scrubbed harder.

"Not a thing," she said.

Amber leaned one hip on the counter and studied her nails, which were painted an electric blue. "House looks nice."

"Thanks." Scrub. Scrub.

Amber studied her shrewdly. "What's wrong?"

"Nothing."

Amber sighed loudly. "Are you going to talk about what's going on?"

"No." One stubborn baked-on spot and she suddenly wanted to throw the pan across the room.

Amber hopped up on the counter next to the sink. Her vintage Rolling Stones T-shirt was cut to hang off one shoulder, showing her lacy red crisscross bra straps and her tiny jean shorts that were so ripped she might as well have not put on any. Outrageous as usual. "What's up, Al? Is it Corbin? Is he bothering you? Want me to put a hit on him?" She asked it so seriously Allie looked up at her, startled.

"Kidding, kidding." Amber waved her hand. "I'd just do it myself if he ever hurt you."

"No, it's not him." She flicked a soap bubble at her sister. "But I appreciate the offer, Am." She hesitated, wanting to share, but once she said it out loud, it would be more than just some silly crush. "I kissed someone."

"Get out! You little wench," she said with admiration. "I knew you had it in you to get a little snack. Give me all the details! It was Daddy Davis, wasn't it?"

Allie shot her a look. "How did you know that?"

Amber's eyes widened. "I knew it! The looks he was giving last Saturday could have set the house on fire." She jumped off the counter and grabbed Allie's hand. "Tell me everything." She dragged Allie over to the kitchen table. "Leave out no details. Actually, embellish the details if you have to. Make 'em real dirty."

So Allie told her, and she didn't embellish any details at all. Their encounters were hot enough. Amber started fanning herself when she got to the part where she had nearly fallen off the counter. By the time she ended with the kitchen chair this morning, her cheeks were flushed.

"You little sexpot, you," Amber said. "Hot, *lucky* sexpot."

"Not that hot apparently. He apologized and said it shouldn't have happened," she said miserably.

Amber looked at her like she was crazy. "Was he or was he not turned on?"

Allie thought back, and then she was thoroughly blushing. Oh, he had been turned on. She'd bet on that. The look in his eyes as he looked her up and down and pulled her almost onto his lap... She shivered.

"See?" Amber said. "He wants you. Of course he does. Anyone would. You're simply the best, but he doesn't *want* to want you. He's probably angry that he does."

Allie blew out a breath. "Is this what you meant by having a 'snack'? Because it actually sucks. Zero out of ten, do not recommend."

"Just give him some time. He's working some things out. After losing his wife, I would imagine he's struggling with letting himself get close to someone again."

"Ugh. You're right. I'm probably making this into something bigger than it is, anyway."

"I'm proud of you though, Al. You've finally emerged from

your shell, my little butterfly. I thought Corbin had repressed you to death."

"I didn't know it could be this hot, and I haven't even actually done anything with Davis yet."

"Yet. It gets even better," Amber said with a wink. "Just give it time and enjoy the ride."

It sounded so easy coming from her, but Amber was a born flirt. It was as natural to her as air. She liked men, and they really, *really* liked her. What was not to like? She was sharp as a tack, gorgeous, and confident, and she flaunted it. She went through men like people went through the sampler boxes, taking little bites of whichever ones she felt like and then leaving the rest of it in the box for another time. Or person. She didn't care either way. She never got attached.

She certainly had never had an accidental teen pregnancy, gotten married, and then divorced. Allie winced. Maybe she could use a few lessons from her little sis. Clearly, she had a habit of getting involved with the wrong guys, although it was hard to regret meeting Corbin when she had gotten Sammy out of the deal.

But Amber had a point. At twenty-six, Allie had only been with one man, and it had been lackluster at best. She had forgotten what it felt like to be wanted and to want someone in return. Davis made her feel alive in places she had thought were dead, and dammit, it felt good.

It was embarrassing how she always had the urge to snuggle into his big chest and feel his arms close around her, all protective and secure, just for a minute. She forgot how good it felt to let someone else take over. She was always the efficient one, the big sister, the caretaker. She was always the one who held it all together.

"Do I want that though? I mean, I'm finally happy." She looked around. "I freaking love this house. I love having my own stuff here. I don't have to share it with anyone or feel like I'm constantly doing something wrong. Sammy's happier than I've ever seen him. I love my job." She turned back to Amber. "Do I really need anything else? Especially with a man who still wears his wedding ring?"

Amber looked sad. "Was it that bad with Corbin?"

"It was... lonely," Allie said softly. She felt the whisper of that old, cold draft that had been a constant presence during her marriage. But this time it didn't linger as she sat with her sister in her cheerful, warm kitchen.

Amber reached over and held her hand on the table. "I didn't know."

"I know. I didn't want you to bust into his apartment and go gangbusters to get us home." She grinned. "Now, I want to feel everything I missed out on. I didn't even know how lonely I was until I came home."

"Please tell me you're going to kiss Davis some more."

At his name, Allie stopped smiling. "I don't know, Am. He's almost as emotionally unavailable as Corbin. He's still in love with his wife. He probably will be for the rest of his life. How dumb could I be to let myself get involved with that?" She sighed. "Maybe our family really does suck at relationships."

Amber threw a pillow at her, nearly taking out a wine bottle on the counter. "Stop it, Al. If anyone could fall in love again in our family, it's you. There's no curse. You know that. We just don't know how to pick a good man. We pick the wrong ones because that's what we think we deserve."

Allie's mouth opened, but nothing came out for a full ten seconds.

"What?" Amber rolled her eyes. "I took a psych class in college before I dropped out. This can't be news to you. We have daddy issues."

"No, no. I know. It's just... that was insightful. I'm processing."

We pick the wrong ones because that's what we think we deserve.

"Is that why you've never dated anyone seriously?"

Amber grinned wickedly, but Allie wasn't fooled. Her sister had some fears of her own. Nathan Powell had left his mark on his family in ways they all still felt.

"Why choose, Al? Why choose? Anyway, tell me again exactly what happened this morning?"

So she did, every hot little detail, and when she was done, any hint of coldness from before was long, long gone.

Chapter Seventeen

Davis raised his arm and knocked on Allie's front door again. It was early, but it was Saturday, dammit, and she knew he did the lawn early on Saturdays. He glanced at the trusty little Forrester parked in her driveway where her Mercedes was usually parked and pounded the door harder. *Who the hell was over this early in the morning?*

After their hot and heavy encounter in the kitchen yesterday, Davis had gone home and taken a long, cold shower until he could think straight. Even then he had laid awake most of the night thinking about how her soft, pink lips parted for him, how her full hips had felt in his grip, and how he'd wanted to pull her off the chair and onto his lap more than take his next breath of air. *Shit.* By morning his raging hard-on had transformed into a raging headache, and he had come to his senses.

She was damn complicated.

He raised his hand to knock again just as the door flung open and Allie stood in front of him with her arm shielding her eyes.

"Wha—" she whispered, rubbing her eyes.

He froze, one arm up, his fist poised to knock again, and his other hand balancing a drink caddy with four steaming drinks. His eyes leveled directly on her face, scrubbed free of makeup, and her sleep-mussed swirl of honey hair, and her—oh, shit.

Her round, full, unbound breasts still swayed with the momentum of having opened the door, and his mouth snapped closed with an audible click when he caught sight of her pink nightgown. It was one of those lacy things with little straps that bared her delicate shoulders and collarbone. His eyes trailed down and stopped.

The nightgown dipped in around the full curves of her breasts, and each pointed tip of her nipples stood out clearly against the fine material. The nightie fell to midthigh and her slim legs and feet were bare. *Oh, Jesus.* Did she have anything on under that? The sudden primitive urge to hide her from anyone else's eyes was so strong he was moving before he realized it.

"Come here," he said gruffly. Using his one free arm, he hooked her to the side where she wasn't visible to anyone from the street.

"Davis? What are you doing here?" She still looked sleepy and tousled and too damn appealing in his arms.

"It's Saturday morning."

"It is?" She still looked confused.

"Where's your car?"

She rubbed her eyes with both hands. "I sold it." Her hair fell in a mass of curls over her face, and he fought the urge to push it behind her shoulder. *No. No more touching.*

"You sold your Mercedes for that?" He eyed the car in the driveway in disbelief.

She grinned, all tousled and so damn beautiful "Yeah, isn't it cute? It's more me. What are you doing here?"

"It's Saturday. I'm here to do the yard work." He nudged her gently toward the stairs. "Go back upstairs and get dressed."

She blinked at him and turned to head up the stairs. For once, he was glad she had no smart remark for him; he couldn't have handled standing in front of her one more second without reaching out to touch.

As it was, he couldn't look away because his question was answered. Plump cheeks peeked out beneath the hem of the nightie, and this time he did groan out loud. She had a tiny scrap of light-blue underwear doing nothing to contain her ass. He wanted to drag them off with his teeth and bury his face in all that softness.

He made his way to the kitchen instead.

A few minutes later, looking more awake, she reappeared. "Hey." More of her luscious body was covered in shorts and a T-shirt. *Thank God.*

"Coffee?" He held out the paper cup.

"Yes, please." She took it and sipped, her throat moving as she swallowed. She nodded at the four other cups. "Who are those for?"

"Claire and Ben. Layne's out of town, so I didn't have a sitter. They're next door visiting with Mrs. Autovino. I told Sammy I'd practice batting today after I finish." He shrugged. "I thought Ben could practice too."

Her face lit up. "Sammy will love that! Thank you, Davis." She reached over to where he was leaning against the counter and impulsively squeezed his arm. "He'll be up any minute now."

He cleared his throat. "Before the kids get here, I wanted to apologize again for yesterday. I got carried away. It won't happen again."

"You don't have to apologize. It was just as much me as it was you." She grinned crookedly. "Maybe even a little more me."

A quick knock at the front door announced the arrival of

Ben and Claire. "Dad, Mrs. Autovino said to give you these." Ben came racing into the room with a plate of assorted Italian cookies wrapped in cellophane. She spoiled the kids, but he didn't mind. He never had an appetite for them, but he didn't mind if the kids ate her food.

"Claire already ate the one with the cherry on top." Ben glared at his sister.

"You had too much sugar already today. It's not healthy for you." Claire rolled her eyes and looked curiously between him and Allie.

"Ben, Claire, you remember Ms. Hart, Sammy's mom."

"Oh, yeah, you're real pretty," Ben said around a mouthful of cookie. Davis hid a grin. The little flirt was just like his uncle Shep.

Allie smiled at them. "Thank you, Ben. Nice to see you both again. Please, call me Allie. Your hair looks so pretty in that braid, Claire." Allie's voice was sincere as she took in the lopsided French braid.

"My dad did it. He's learning from YouTube tutorials," Claire said, looking quite proud. Davis felt his face turn red, but he patted his hand awkwardly on Claire's silky hair. He was trying, dammit.

Sammy ran into the kitchen, his hair sticking out from his head very much like his mom's had when she answered the door. "I saw Mr. Henderson's truck. Is he here?" He skidded to a stop. "Whoa!" Sammy tackled them in a hug. "What are you guys doing at my house?"

Allie laughed. "Slow down, Sammy. Mr. Henderson's going to play catch with you guys after he does the lawn."

"You are?" Sammy's face lit up like it was Christmas morning. "This is awesome!" He hugged Allie tightly around the waist and buried his head in her stomach. She bent down to kiss his head.

Davis looked at his kids and caught their wistful expressions. He knew exactly what they were thinking. They were such good kids, but losing their mother had left deep gouges in them. As much as he wanted to be everything his kids needed, he wasn't. Reminders of what they didn't have always felt like a knife in his gut.

Allie leaned against the counter and grabbed the steaming cup of coffee. The silence lengthened as they stood in the kitchen, both avoiding looking at the chair where, just yesterday, she had been poured over him like warm melted chocolate.

"Hey, can Ben and Claire come with us on our picnic today?" Sammy and Ben jumped up in down in excitement while Claire stood behind the boys with a Hello Kitty notebook and pen. She tried to look disinterested, but her excitement shone in her eyes too. "We're gonna fish on the canal!"

"Can we, Dad, please?" Ben begged.

"Please, Mom. If Mr. Henderson comes, he'll hook the worms and everything!" Sammy begged Allie. He turned to Ben. "My mom gets all green when she has to touch them," he told him. The boys laughed uproariously at the idea of something as wonderfully gross as worms making a girl gag.

"Sammy, I'm going to make you hook your own worms just for that," Allie said with mock outrage. She looked at Davis. "But you are all welcome to join us."

Davis shook his head immediately. "We can't." Terrible idea.

He was already feeling a lot more than friendly right now. He wanted to carry her back upstairs and muss her up again until she looked just like she had when she answered the door.

"Please, Daddy," Claire asked, and that was all it took. One day his baby girl was going to realize he'd do damn near anything to see her happy, and then he'd be in trouble.

He hesitated then sighed. "Okay."

"Yesssss!" The two boys pounded their knuckles. "Wanna see my room?" The boys went careening off, their socks slipping on the wooden floor.

Claire smiled shyly. "Thanks, Daddy."

He tapped her nose, Melody's in miniature form. "That's a lot of energy to handle. You sure about this?" he asked Allie.

"It will give me a break to have someone else as a playmate for a while," Allie said and turned to Claire. "I was going to bake cookies for our picnic, Claire. Do you like to bake?"

"I love to bake!" Clear blue eyes lit up with excitement. "Can I, Dad?"

Davis felt his heart soften even more, and he tugged on the end of the braid that had taken him thirty minutes this morning. "Of course."

"I'll go put this away!" She raced off with the notebook.

Allie cleared her throat in the sudden silence as Claire walked back to join the boys. "You're going to join us too?"

"Yeah," he drawled. "Who else is going to hook the worms?"

She punched him in the arm, laughing. "Good. That's what friends are for."

He rubbed the spot as he left the house, feeling a whole helluva lot more than *friendly*.

"THEY SEEM to be hitting it off," Allie said, listening with one ear to the boys playing cars upstairs. Now and then, Sammy would yell out, "Oh no," followed by *screech*, the made-up sounds of tires skidding, and then Ben's voice chimed in after with sounds of a crash.

Davis was outside mowing the lawn with a push mower, the roar of the machine blending in with the other sounds of Saturday morning in the neighborhood. Mrs. Autovino was already out hanging her laundry. The kids across the street, middle schoolers, were bouncing a basketball in their driveway.

Allie found herself idly wondering if this was what a Saturday morning looked like for typical families. A big breakfast together, yard work while the kids played with the dog, maybe a picnic lunch at the park. In her daydreams, she always imagined her husband giving Sammy hugs with his big strong arms and circling them both close to his chest. Davis's chest flashed in her mind. *Nope.*

Friends. Buddies. Pals.

She was still feeling shaken and, yes, more than a little embarrassed by their last encounter, but she shook off the feeling and tied on her grandma's pink-and-green floral apron. Annette's mom, Nanny Hart, had given her the vintage apron as a wedding present, and she put it on every time she baked, along with her playlists.

"Here, Claire, you can wear Sammy's apron if you want. I'll help you tie it." Allie smiled at her and turned to get out the baking sheets. "Now, we can't bake without music. What do you like to listen to?" She opened the music app on her phone and looked up expectantly.

Claire looked surprised. "I don't know. I don't bake a lot." She looked around to make sure no one could hear and lowered her voice. "My daddy's cookies always taste bad." She rushed on as if she wanted to make up for her comment, "But he plays Barbies with me, even though his Barbie voices stink."

A stab of something best left unexamined took her by surprise at that image. Davis, with his huge work-roughened hands, played dolls with his daughter. Her ovaries quivered. She tapped on Dusty Springfield's "Wishin' and Hopin'," and the playful lyrics filled the kitchen.

"I won't say a word, honey," Allie said. "After today, you're going to be an expert cookie maker. Maybe you can teach your daddy. How about that?"

"Yes, please!" she said. "Me and Ben don't want to hurt Daddy's feelings, but all his food tastes terrible. I give mine to Walter a lot," she said very seriously. "But even *he* doesn't always eat it."

Allie cracked up at that, and the last of the ice broke between them. Claire was like a little sponge, soaking up tips and instructions. They quickly became comfortable with each other as they worked. Once, Allie caught her staring. "Do I have cookie dough on my face?" she asked, wiping at her chin.

"No," Claire said. "You smile a lot. It's nice." Then she went back to scooping balls of dough, the tip of her tongue poking out through her teeth as she concentrated.

For the next half hour, they measured and scraped ingredients together in a rhythm Allie had always found comforting. Measure, pour, mix, scoop. The steps were rote now since she couldn't remember a time when she hadn't been in the kitchen baking with someone in her family. Annette, the aunts, and Nanny Hart, all her best memories growing up had something to do with being in the kitchen. The tantalizing scent of fresh-baked cookies soon drew down the boys, noses sniffing the air.

"Something smells good!" Ben declared as he ran in, the only speed little boys were set on.

"We made oatmeal cookies for our picnic," Claire said.

Ben's face fell. "Who made them?" he demanded.

"Me and Allie," she said proudly. "These won't break your teeth like Daddy's."

The kitchen door opened, and Davis stepped inside, his nose twitching like his son's. "Mmm. What's that I smell?"

"Not your cookies, Daddy," Ben informed him merrily. "We can actually eat these!"

Davis lowered his eyebrows, swooped down, grabbed Ben

by his ankle, turned him upside down, and gave him a playful shake.

"What's that you say?" He bounced him, making Ben's laughter turn into squeals of laughter. "You love my cookies?" *Bounce.* "You want to eat more of my famous cookies?" *Bounce. Bounce.* Ben was shrieking with laughter and Claire's hand went over her mouth to hold in her giggles.

Allie met Sammy's delighted eyes again and smiled. Watching Davis's playful side with his kids was almost as tempting as watching him mow the lawn shirtless. Actually, more so. Much more.

Chapter Eighteen

SHE HAD FINALLY FOUND something that made Davis smile easily, and it was making her jealous. Very hot and very jealous.

Of a cookie.

They were spread out on a blanket in the village green, relaxing after their picnic lunch. The Erie Canal sparkled in the sun, making tiny diamond patterns in the water. Allie kept one eye on the kids at the edge of the water with their fishing poles and one eye on the soothing water. Now and then Walter, who was sleeping on the grass beside them, would twitch his paws, chasing bunnies in his sleep.

"God, that's so good." Davis sighed as the last bite of her cookie disappeared into his sensual mouth while she studied him from beneath her lashes. As the afternoon wore on, his jaw had lost that stern set it so often had, and he smiled and joked more than she'd ever thought possible. She was musing over this when she caught sight of a tiny fleck of dark chocolate left on his bottom lip. She fanned herself with a napkin.

"Sea salt," she murmured, fascinated by the look of pleasure on his face.

All three Hendersons ate with pure enjoyment. They had

helped themselves to seconds of the caprese pasta salad Allie had made with balls of mozzarella, sweet cherry tomatoes, and torn basil. They mopped up the last of the sauce with pieces torn off a loaf of crusty Italian bread. Cut vegetables and hummus, a thermos full of lemonade, and the still-warm cookies rounded out their meal. Ben had murmured throughout the meal "This is so good" and asked several times, "Dad, can you make it exactly like this for us? Exactly?"

Davis had pretended to have injured feelings. It was so often just her and Sammy, it felt good to watch this family enjoy her cooking.

"Hmm?" He leaned back on his arms, one knee bent and the other stretched out on the blanket before him, and sighed with satisfaction. He looked like a contented lion stretched out in the sun. She wanted to crawl next to him, slide a leg over his lap, and lick the chocolate off his mouth. She fanned harder.

"That's the secret to the best cookies." She tried to sound casual, but it came out breathless. "A sprinkle of sea salt on them when they come out of the oven."

Davis rolled his head to look at her lazily. His eyes were hidden again by glasses. "You okay? You look a little... overheated?"

"You have a little something..." She pointed vaguely to his face.

Davis's tongue came out and licked the wrong corner. She almost whimpered.

"Did I get it?"

"Mmm," she murmured, eyes following the path of his tongue as she leaned in slightly.

"I don't want to touch it!" Claire's shriek pierced the air. "Daddy, make him stop!"

Ben feinted towards her with the carton of poor slimy

worms about to be fish food, and Claire scrambled to hide behind Allie.

Allie sat up and gingerly took the container from Ben's outstretched hand. Worms were not her favorite thing to handle, but she did have some pride. "Okay, come on, Claire, we're not afraid of a little worm. Let's show the boys how this is done."

Claire looked doubtful. "No, thank you."

Ben and Sammy got a kick out of that, while Allie tried to look fascinated instead of disgusted.

"Mom, you're so silly. You always make me do the worm part."

She frowned at her son, who looked back at her angelically. "Just because I don't want to, doesn't mean I can't, Sammy." She sniffed. The little boys laughed and still, she hesitated to pluck out one of the slimy creatures. Walter got up with a deep sigh and lumbered over to see what the fuss was about. Even he looked like he was laughing at her.

"How come you don't just give it to Davis then?"

Davis sat up and pushed his sunglasses to his forehead. "Yeah, how come you don't just give it to me if you're scared?" he asked wickedly.

"I've got this, boys," she said. With more confidence than she felt, she reached in. "Sorry to do this to you, little guy," she whispered, earning more laughter from the boys. "Walter, what's that?" she asked sharply. He raised his head with an excited yelp to look where she pointed across the grass and took off. The boys raced after him excitedly. Allie quickly tossed the worm into the grass and lowered the line into the water. She looked up to see Claire watching her and winked. Claire's eyes twinkled with their secret.

"It was just a duck," Sammy said as he made his way back. "Hey, you did it." He pointed to the fishing pole she held over the water. "Good job, Mom." He held out his grubby little palm for a high five. "Look, Ben, my mom did it!"

"Thanks, boys. It wasn't so bad, and Claire helped me."

Ben looked suitably impressed. "Very cool!" They turned to bait their hooks while Allie sat back contentedly. Claire put her nose back in her book.

Davis leaned over on his elbow, close enough that she could feel the warmth of his body. He smelled like pure heaven, like sun-warmed skin, and grass, and more dangerously, like picnics and bike rides and dreams. She inhaled as deeply as she could without outing herself but then stiffened when he leaned over. She felt the brush of his lips on her ear. "Allie," he whispered.

"Yes," she said faintly. The tiny whiskers above his lips deliciously abraded her skin. She closed her eyes, her pulse pounding.

"The worm is crawling back onto the blanket."

Still dazed, she looked down to see the little pink thing wiggling its way back onto the corner of the quilt. *What in the—* She mouthed the words as she looked up in time to see Davis's wink.

"Let's check your blood sugar before we ride back, Sammy," Allie called out later that afternoon.

After fishing for a long while, the boys had played catch with Davis, and they were now playing fetch with Walter. Claire and Davis sat nearby, Claire showing Davis how to make a daisy chain with the wildflowers she had picked. Davis was mangling another flower in his large hands.

"Not like that, Daddy. Like this." Claire rescued the last flower from his hands and used her fingernail to slice a neat line through the stem, then she pushed another daisy stem through the hole to connect the chain.

Davis's hands were gentle as he tied the ends of the flower chain and placed it on Claire's head. "A crown for my princess."

He dropped a kiss on her head. Their two heads, one dark, and one lighter, bent over together made Allie's heart feel two sizes too big for her chest, and she looked away from the tender moment. Davis as a red-blooded, physical man was dangerous enough for her body, but watching Davis as a father made him dangerous for her heart. He was so gentle with Claire and mischievous with Ben, and the way he showed his love for them both was beautiful to watch. A wave of longing gripped her until she forced herself to turn away.

She dug through her backpack for the little black pouch with Sammy's glucose meter and testing strips, along with an emergency glucagon pen and a packet of pure sugar frosting. Thankfully, she had never had to use either one on Sammy, but she kept them nearby just in case his blood sugar ever dropped dangerously low. Both would raise his blood sugar quickly in an emergency.

"Mom, we just checked me before lunch," Sammy said, with the tiniest bit of a whine. She scooped him up and sat him next to her before nuzzling his sweaty head.

"I know, baby, but you've been running and playing, and we still have to bike home. We'd better check."

"Okay," he said, mollified. Sammy was typical of any kid, and he didn't love being pulled away from fun things to get a finger prick, but he was such a good, sweet boy, rarely complaining. She gave him a loud, smacking kiss on his neck, and he laughed with Ben at the sound, who settled on her other side.

Ben leaned all his weight into her as he watched, and she smiled, not for the first time thinking little boys were like puppies. They always wanted to be snuggled up next to each other. She shifted to get more comfortable, and Ben wedged himself firmly into the extra space.

Sammy dutifully held out his finger for Allie to swab with the alcohol pad. She had done this so many times she could do it in her sleep. She noticed absently as she prepped the test strip and lancet that Davis and Claire had made their way over and sat quietly watching.

"Does that hurt?" Ben's eyes were wide as he took in the tiny needle Allie lined up on Sammy's finger. He looked nervous.

"It's okay, Ben, it's just a little shot," Claire reassured him.

"Not a shot," Sammy informed them. He held out his finger, and Allie pressed the button for the lancet to prick his finger. Sammy didn't flinch. "It's a poke to check my blood."

"Does it hurt real bad, Sammy?" Ben asked as he watched the blood bead on his fingertip.

"Nope." Sammy shrugged. "I do it all the time." Allie caught the drop of blood on the test strip and fitted it into the meter to read while four sets of eyes watched solemnly.

"His blood sugar is sixty-five," she read out loud. She did a quick mental calculation. "Let's get you some juice before we ride home."

Allie passed out three mini juice boxes and leaned back against the tree while the three kids slurped happily against her. They were in a rare state of calm after their outing, content to snuggle and watch the other families around them fish and play.

"We're so lucky to live here," Sammy said, looking around. She followed his eyes to the people sitting on quilts like theirs, picnicking and fishing by the water on a late summer afternoon.

"It is a nice place to live, isn't it?" she murmured. Sammy's happiness soothed any lingering doubt she had made the right choice moving home.

"Can we come over to your house again this week, Allie?" Ben's big dark eyes looked up at her.

"Yeah, Mom, can they?"

"Of course, as long as you clear it with your dad first," she answered with a quick look at Davis, who was giving Walter a belly scratch.

Allie stroked her fingers through Sammy's golden hair, then she looked over as Ben nudged her other hand with his head. *Puppies.*

"Do me, too, Allie," he asked, eyes drowsy. Sammy's head tipped back against her shoulder, and he let out a snore. She smiled and settled in, running her fingers through their hair. Claire's eyes grew heavy, and she nestled her head onto Allie's lap with a sigh. Allie's own eyes drifted closed as she lost herself in the peace of the late afternoon sun with three warm bodies snuggled up to hers.

Later, though how much time had passed she couldn't guess, Allie opened her eyes with a start. All three children were fast asleep on her. She searched and found Davis next to them. He had stretched out comfortably on his side, elbow crooked to prop his head up, watching them. Allie gave him a sleepy smile, but his face was solemn when he looked back at her.

"Hey," she whispered.

"Hey," he whispered back.

"Everything okay?"

He nodded slowly, never taking his eyes off her. "It's good," he said. "*You're* really good."

The way he was looking at her, with that softness he so rarely showed, made her want to pull him close and hold on tight. "I am pretty amazing, aren't I?" she teased instead.

"I think so," he said. Something in his voice made her sit up straighter, trying not to wake the kids that were still piled on her lap.

"Dad, I have to go to the bathroom," Ben announced sleepily, breaking the strange tension.

"Come on. We'll head home. Do you need any help packing up?" Davis asked her as he gently shook Claire awake.

"No, everything is all packed." She nodded to Sammy's bike. "I'm going to let him sleep a little while longer before we head back."

He nodded, his sunglasses hiding his eyes.

"Can we come over this week?" Ben asked hopefully.

"Ben," Davis said. "That was rude."

"It's okay. We talked about it earlier, and I told them it was okay with me if it was okay with you," Allie said. "Of course, you're welcome too," she said casually.

Davis looked at her for a long second and then seemed to make up his mind. "We'd like that. The first baseball practice is on Thursday."

"How about Friday then? I can bring them home from school with Sammy, and they can play until you're done working?"

"That works. Thanks."

"Wait, Daddy!" Ben tapped his chest and wiggled to get down. "I wanna hug Allie goodbye."

He threw his arms around Allie's neck, and she impulsively put her lips to his hair. Such dear children, so loving despite the heartache they had faced. "Thank you for a wonderful day, Ben," she whispered as she laid her head alongside his.

"Bye, Allie," he whispered, pressing a soft kiss on her cheek.

Claire was watching with a look in her eyes that made Allie hold out her arms in invitation. "Hug?" The tall girl threw herself headlong into Allie's arms. She hugged her back tightly. "Bye, honey. I had a lot of fun with you today."

"Me too," she said as she pulled back. "Tell Sammy we said goodbye."

A stray curl fell forward over Allie's eyes, tickling her nose. "That was fun," she said, shaking the curl back to see Davis more clearly.

Davis reached out his hand as if he were going to touch her hair. He stopped abruptly and let it drop without making contact. "I'll see you Friday," he said quietly.

With that, he turned around, whistled to Walter to hop into the truck, and strode away. It wasn't until Allie was packing up the leftover food, she realized she had fed him. And he had eaten every bite.

As Davis chopped a head of broccoli that night for dinner, he thought about the picnic earlier. It had been a great afternoon by all measures. Allie had a way about her his kids were taken with. He thought about how Ben had wormed his way under her arm and how he fell asleep with her running her fingers through his hair. He had wanted to lay his head on Allie's lap and do the same thing, laying in the grass, the sound of water nearby, the sun on his face.

Even Claire, his sweet, shy girl, had enjoyed herself. That was getting tricky these days, to please both Claire and Ben with the same activities. Allie was so damn appealing, with her little prank with the worm, and how she laughed with the boys and spent time with Claire. She was the kind of person people wanted to be around. Including him.

When he left her house at the end of the workday, he found himself looking forward to his alarm the next morning because he'd get to see her in a couple of hours. Even his weekends were different since he had met her. He used to look forward to the time off, but after he left her and Sammy on Saturdays, the weekend lost some of its shine.

"Ew, not broccoli," Ben whined as he walked into the kitchen. "It stinks."

"Vegetables make us healthy, Ben," Claire said the oft-repeated adage dutifully, but her brow wrinkled as she took in the sad florets on the cutting board. "What else are we having?"

"There's chicken on the grill and rice pilaf," he said. "Is that okay with you, Top Chefs?"

Claire giggled, but Ben still looked sad. "What do you think Allie's making for dinner?"

"Something yummy, I bet." Claire sighed. "Like that pasta salad. Or maybe homemade mac 'n' cheese."

"Yeah," Ben said dreamily. "And more cookies for dessert. I wish we could eat over at their house every night."

"Hey, kids," Davis said. "I'm right here." He placed the broccoli in the steamer basket and checked the time on the rice. He wasn't the most creative of cooks, but he made do. Besides, he kind of wished he was eating dinner at their house, too.

"We love your dinners, Daddy," Claire said. His little peacemaker.

"It's okay, honey. Allie's a good cook, huh?" He bopped her lightly on the nose.

Ben climbed up on the stool at the island and started rolling an apple in the fruit basket back and forth. "You should see Sammy's lunches. He gets the best stuff. And Allie writes him a note every day in his lunch box."

Should I make the kids something different for lunches? Shit. Was he relying too much on PB and J? Davis's head pounded with familiar worry.

"Notes?" That piqued Claire's interest. "What do they say?"

The apple slid too far toward the counter, and Ben dove to catch it. "I dunno. Stuff. And Allie makes these little balls that look like cookies, but Sammy says they are *healthy* cookies, and I want to try them." He wasn't concerned about the content of the notes, but Claire persisted.

"What do the notes look like? What color are they?"

Remember to write them a note for their lunch box on Monday.

Ben frowned. "I dunno, Claire. Did you hear me? Healthy cookies!" He looked puzzled. "Dad, can you make those?"

Healthy cookies. Look up a recipe for healthy cookies.

"Does she write different notes every day? Are they folded? What color are they?" Claire was leaning forward, her eyes boring into her brother's intently.

"Claire! Who cares! It's a note. Gosh! Dad, did you hear me? Can you make healthy cookies? Dad? Dad?"

Davis jerked suddenly, shaken out of his thoughts. "Sorry, Ben. Maybe we can try a recipe this weekend. Claire." He looked over at his daughter. "Ben doesn't remember what the notes look like, but maybe he can pay closer attention this week during lunch, okay?"

Later, after dinner was grudgingly nudged around plates and Davis had cleaned up, he sat down next to Claire on the couch. "What are you looking at, honey?"

She turned a photo album towards him. "Remember this Christmas, Daddy? You made me my dollhouse, and Mom decorated the inside." It was their last photo together before she died. Davis felt the burn in his chest whenever he was reminded of Melody unexpectedly. "Mommy was so pretty."

"Yeah, honey, I remember. Mom loved decorating that house for you." He pulled Claire in close and stroked her hair as she turned the pages. Memories of Mel when the kids were little sifted through his head. One by one, he tucked them away. Those memories were more sweet than bitter lately.

"Ben, here you are." Claire giggled. Ben came over on his other side. "Mommy always said Daddy would gag when he changed your poopy diapers when you were a baby."

In the picture, Ben sat on Melody's lap, a sturdy toddler, looking like a bowling ball with arms and legs. Melody was on the back patio here at their house before Davis had redone it. Claire stood next to Melody, wearing a bubble-gum pink dress and a rhinestone tiara on her head. There were balloons and pink streamers behind her. That's right. It had been Claire's birthday party. He touched the photo gently.

"I don't remember that," Ben said with one eye on the TV.

"Yes, you do, Ben." Claire pointed at another photo. "See this one? Mommy used to put the cookie cutters in a plastic jug and let you shake it to make noise."

Ben looked it over. "Nope. Don't 'member."

Claire looked stricken. "But what about this one? Mommy took us to that store in the mall, and we picked out bears, stuffed them, and put a heart in it that really beat."

Ben looked around Davis and shrugged apologetically. "Don't 'member, Claire."

"You don't remember Mom at all?" Claire asked incredulously.

Davis tightened his hold on her. "Honey, Ben doesn't remember as much as you do because he was so little when Mom died."

"Oh," she said, not looking up. "That's sad."

Ben looked unfazed. "I remember getting Walter. He was the biggest one of the puppies, 'member that? He slept every time we went to see him."

"I remember that." Claire's face brightened. "And he cried the whole way home after we went to get him."

Walter lugged himself over from the window at the sound of his name and she petted his head.

"We love you, Walter." Walter lowered his shaggy head and left a long, wet trail on her cheek as he thanked her. "Ew." She giggled. "Thanks for the sloppy kiss, boy."

It was quiet for a minute as Ben hugged Walter's neck and Claire scratched his ears while he sat patiently.

Ben looked up after a while. "I have an idea," he said excitedly. "We can take new pictures. We can take them with Allie and Sammy."

Davis cleared his throat. "They are friends of ours, so we'll make some more memories with them," he said uneasily.

Ah, hell. He knew it wasn't a good idea to get the kids involved. He felt sick at the thought of any more loss in their lives. He should have said no this afternoon when Allie invited them to the picnic. If he, as a grown man, was having a hard time keeping his distance from Allie, how could he expect his kids not to fall for her and Sammy too? It was impossible not to be around her and not gravitate toward all her laughter and warmth. He pinched the bridge of his nose hard.

Claire looked thoughtful. "But we won't have a picture with them on Christmas morning."

"No, probably not Christmas morning," Davis agreed.

"Why not, Dad?" Ben demanded.

"They'll be with their own family for holidays, just like we'll be with ours."

Ben looked thoughtful as he pointed Walter's ears straight up. He looked like a long-suffering, one-hundred-pound red fox. "Then I think we should make them our family, Dad." He looked at Claire. "Allie can be our mom, and Sammy could be our brother." He looked quickly at Claire. "But Sammy gets to sleep with me," he said, putting dibs on him.

Before Davis could say anything, Claire jumped in. "We

already have a mom, Benjamin," she said sharply, using his full name as Davis sometimes did when Ben was in trouble.

She leaned back under Davis's arm and snuggled closer with a yawn. "But if they did want to be part of our family, I wouldn't mind. Then she could write us all notes in our lunch boxes every day."

Chapter Nineteen

"Something smells good," Shep said, sniffing as he walked up Allie's driveway a week later.

Davis had arranged to meet him at Allie's to bring the last of their tools back to the workshop, but when he saw him, he swore under his breath. He should have just made two trips. Shep was going to ask all kinds of questions bound to piss him off. He climbed down from the ladder against the maple tree.

"Does it? I didn't notice," Davis said dryly.

"What are you doing?" Shep asked. They both looked up at the rope attached to a tire.

"Putting up a swing."

"Naturally." Shep nodded cheerfully. "Very landlord-ly of you. And how are our tenants?"

Davis shot him a look. Now that the renovations were done on Allie's house, Davis hadn't seen Allie or Sammy since the picnic last weekend. As much as she had killed his concentration, he had gotten used to seeing her every day. This week had felt... long. He'd caught himself looking at the calendar more than a few times, counting down the days until their dinner tonight.

A loud crash followed by laughter drew their eyes to the back of Allie's house. Four dancing silhouettes passed by the kitchen window in what looked to be a conga line. The scent of dinner cooking and the muffled sounds of kids laughing escaped the house, making for an undeniably homey moment.

Shep squinted at the window. "Is that Ben and Claire in there?"

"Yep."

Shep straightened up and gave his brother a knowing look. "You and the kids having dinner with them?"

Davis glared at him in warning.

Shep grinned, ignoring it. "I could use some new friends too."

"You're not invited," he said shortly.

Shep lifted his nose and sniffed appreciatively. "I'm inviting myself."

"No, you're not," he snapped. "The kids like her and Sammy, that's all."

"That's good." Shepherd shot him a sly look. "I heard Ford's interested."

"Leave it alone, Shep."

"It'll be three years next month, Davis." Shep's voice was devoid of all teasing.

Davis sighed, the anger leaving him just as suddenly as it had surfaced. "I know." He stared blindly at the house and tried hard to remember Mel's face, but only Allie's teasing smile appeared.

"Mel would have wanted you and the kids to be happy."

"I know she would have," he said quietly.

Mel wasn't what was holding him back. He would always love her, but he had accepted her death a long time ago. It wasn't guilt that kept him tossing and turning at night. It was Allie. She forced him to feel things he had buried deep. She made him laugh with her quirky humor and how she wasn't afraid to call him out for being too quiet or grumpy. She offered up her heart without any fear at all. He admired that about her as much as it scared the hell out of him.

"You can't or you won't?" Shep asked.

"I said, leave it alone."

"What happened with Mel was a horrible accident. No one could have predicted that, and it shouldn't have happened, but you can't stop living either." Shep jerked his chin toward the laughter spilling from the house. "That sounds like a lot of living. Do you really want to miss out on that?"

He clapped his hand on Davis's shoulder as he went by.

"Are you going to invite me in or what?" Shep called back as he opened the screen door.

Swearing softly, Davis walked up the steps of the deck and stepped inside. In the short time Allie had been here, she had put her touch on the house. Little things that made the house feel homey and lived in. White cafe curtains with little flowers hung in the kitchen window, and a framed picture of her and Sammy stood on the window ledge next to a plant. A magnet held a drawing of a dinosaur, and another pinned a school lunch menu to the fridge. A sturdy, scarred kitchen table had been set with five dinner plates and a small vase of flowers in the middle.

Claire saw them first. She was banging a wooden spoon on a frying pan and marching around with a huge grin on her face. His beautiful, sweet, serious girl was laughing, and he soaked it in. Ben was behind her, blowing a kazoo for all he was worth, his face red and sweaty as he heaved into the little noisemaker and jerked his skinny hips back and forth.

He and Shep both laughed when they spotted Sammy. His instrument of choice was the loudest of them all. The kid was holding a clear plastic barrel like the one pretzels or cheese puffs came in at the store, only this was filled with what looked to be cookie cutters. Very loud metal cookie cutters all banged into each other. The harder Sammy shook the barrel, the louder they all laughed.

Davis remembered the first day he had met Allie and Sammy, and he was struck by how quiet and lonely his life had felt the last few years as he listened to the racket now.

That's what Allie did. She filled places with her warmth and kindness. She made everyone around her feel important. Worthy. His eyes caught on her and stayed there for a long appreciative minute. She was last in line, laughing and singing along, using a metal grater box and a kitchen spoon as a noise-maker. She was breathtaking. Wild and sexy with her long, honey hair swinging around over her shoulders and her hips swishing back and forth in time to the music. It felt right, being here in Allie's kitchen, watching their kids laugh together and shake off their sadness.

He wanted to reach out and catch her smiling mouth and taste her laughter for himself.

Davis's stomach growled loudly.

It had taken three years, but he was suddenly starving.

ALLIE SCOOPED Mrs. Autovino's recipe for chicken cacciatore onto the plate, making sure to include a ladle of the rich tomato broth. The fragrant scent of tomatoes, briny olives, peppers, and onions rose as she passed the plate to Claire.

"This one's for your dad," she said, plating another serving. The little boys were already seated at the kitchen table with Shep, all waiting impatiently for everyone to be served. Allie had been surprised to see Davis's brother tonight, but like a true Italian, she just set the table for one more and invited him to dinner.

She turned from the oven and came up against Davis's broad chest. "Sorry," she murmured. "I thought you were Claire."

Davis steadied her with a hand on her arm. His big body carved out a little privacy from the rest of the room. "Thanks for dinner," he murmured.

After not seeing him for a week, Allie was uncomfortably aware of how much she had missed seeing him every day. Each night when she got home and there wasn't a big silver truck in her driveway, she'd had to quell her disappointment.

"You're welcome," she said, a little out of breath from the way his touch made her heart race.

"I didn't think I'd ever get another dinner invitation from you."

"I wasn't sure if you would either," she said archly. "But I took pity on those two." She nodded toward Ben and Claire. "They're rebelling against your dinners."

Davis looked wounded. "Traitors. I was going to make tacos."

"Kids are picky little suckers." She grinned, and they stood a little too close. Davis leaned over the plate she still held and inhaled. She could see those sexy crinkles next to his eyes when he was this close.

"Smells delicious."

"I'm hungry, Mom! Can we eat, please?" Sammy's pleading broke the spell.

She straightened up, and Davis's hand fell away. "Let's eat!"

Her tiny kitchen, so spacious when it was just her and Sammy, was suddenly overfilled with noise and life as they ate dinner, and she loved it. Sammy was snorting he was laughing so hard as he and Ben tried to balance the spoons on their noses. Claire's laughter filled the kitchen. Davis and Shep talked about their projects and helped themselves to seconds.

Allie allowed herself one tiny moment to sit back and savor it all.

So this is what it would be like.

"This is the best meal I've ever had." Shep groaned and sat back, rubbing his flat belly appreciatively. "Maybe I should stop by and check up on you every day around dinnertime."

Davis served himself more pasta and grated a block of fresh Parmesan cheese on top. "Won't be any left," he said shortly as he sat back down.

"You're always welcome, Shep."

"Yeah, Allie makes the best food, Uncle Shep," Ben chimed in around a mouthful of food.

"Oh yeah? Tell me more." Shep was helping himself to another plateful. He and Davis had the same large, muscular frames. They looked like brothers with their dark hair, but while Davis's eyes were a warm brown, Shep's were blue and mischievous. She imagined Davis might have had that same openness before tragedy had struck his family.

"Daddy, Allie said she'd teach me how to bake banana bread next," Claire said. "Can I please come over again next week?" Her sweet face was solemn. When Davis turned to his daughter, his face visibly softened.

"If Allie will have you again, that would be fine with me."

"Claire and I make a good team. I'd love to show you how to bake bread anytime you want."

"Can I come anytime I want too?" Shep leaned around Claire to give Allie a wolfish grin.

Sammy perked up at that. "Yeah, Shep can come, and Ben..." He looked at Davis with hero worship. "... and Davis too."

"Deal," she said and smiled at Claire. All afternoon, Claire had followed Allie around while the boys played zombies. She was sweet and gentle with Sammy and patient with Ben, even when he took his role as little brother seriously and teased her mercilessly. A soft spot was quickly growing for the little girl. She gave her a wink. "We'll bake all you want, but you boys are in charge of cleaning up, right, Claire?"

Davis rose from the table, "We'll take care of the dishes. Ben, you clear the table. Sammy, grab a washcloth to wipe it down." With the efficiency of a man accustomed to giving orders, Davis set about washing the dishes while Shep dried, both shooting the breeze with her and the kids. In all her life, she had never seen a man volunteer to help clean up after dinner. It was hands down the sexiest thing Davis had ever done.

Shep left when the dishes were done, kissing her on the cheek, which made Davis's eyes narrow. Claire organized the little boys into making a pillow fort in front of the TV to watch a movie. The beginning score of a familiar movie drifted into the kitchen as Allie turned the lights down for the night. The soft hum of the dishwasher and Walter's snores gave the room a cozy feeling Allie was loathe to end.

"Can I get you something to drink? I don't have any beer, but I have wine or coffee," she offered, pouring herself a glass of red wine.

Davis glanced into the living room at the three kids. "No, thanks. We have to get going soon."

"Oh, yes, right." Allie quelled the disappointment before it showed on her face. She wasn't ready for the night to end.

"Would you like to sit on the porch for a bit?"

He hesitated, and she thought he was going to turn her down when he finally agreed with a nod.

"Grab a sweater. It's getting chilly at night now," he said.

She hurried into the living room to grab her sweater but grabbed a blanket from the back of the couch instead. With a quick kiss on Sammy's forehead, she double-checked his pump. "I'll be on the front porch if you need me."

The late September evening was clear and cool. The sun was just starting to set, casting the wide front porch in dusky streaks of pink and lavender. The neighborhood was settling in for the night. From Mrs. Autovino's open windows, "Crazy" by Patsy Cline played softly. A movement at the woman's window caught her eye before the blind snapped shut. The old woman was matchmaking again, she thought fondly.

Davis sat on the swing and rested an arm against the back while Allie struck a match and lit the candles on the table next to the swing. A warm glow lit the porch. She tucked the blanket around herself.

"You spend a lot of time out here?" Davis asked, watching her routine.

"As much as I can," she said. "I bring my coffee out every morning and usually after dinner I come out and watch the sunset. It's getting colder at night, but I'll be out here until I can't anymore." The snow and bitter cold would put the porch out of commission for a while, but spring would be here, and summer soon after. She was looking forward to each of the seasons in this house.

"It's peaceful here." With his boot, Davis set the swing to gently sway.

They rocked in silence for a few minutes as the night settled in, enjoying the calm after a busy week. "I wasn't sure if I made the right decision coming back here with Sammy," Allie admitted quietly. "I wasn't sure if I'd blow his life up even more after the divorce by moving. I agonized over it, but sitting out here reassures me that this is the right place for us."

"Why's that?" Davis asked quietly. She couldn't see his face in the shadows of the porch, but his presence beside her was solid and reassuring.

"Because it feels good to be a part of this." She waved toward the street. "People stop and chat when they walk by. Mrs. Autovino brings over dinners and hangs out, and I like to watch the families. I get to peek in on little bits of their life when they walk by. I like to see how they are together, sisters and brothers, moms, dads, even the little old couple that walks their dog three times a day and bicker about whose turn it is to pick up the poop. It feels good to be a part of that."

"When I was little," she said thoughtfully, "I used to think Northfield was like a beautiful snow globe. I'd sit on the bus and look out the window on the way home to Cedarwood and admire how calm and peaceful it was here, and how everyone looked so happy. I felt like I was outside looking in, but I wanted to be on the inside. I used to imagine that there was a code or some secret lock to be invited in." She laughed self-consciously. "My mom and my sisters weren't as sensitive about it, but I still sometimes get that feeling."

She shivered with a chill from the air. Davis stretched his arm along the back of the swing, and Allie settled back into his warmth.

"I'm glad you're here," he said gruffly, squeezing her shoulder.

She shrugged and settled back more comfortably. "Well, in any case, I wanted Sammy to be a part of this community. It was just Sammy and me most of the time in the city. I missed my mom, and my sisters and aunts. I wanted to come back home the day I moved."

"Tell me about Cedarwood."

"It was loud. There was always someone yelling or fighting or playing music. The police were there every night, it felt like. Their lights would keep us girls up. It wasn't anything like here, but we had friends there too. I met my best friend Lucy there. Her mom worked nights, and Lucy spent most nights at our house. That's how it was if you lived in Cedarwood. You stuck together because no one else understood what it was like to live like that. I couldn't wait to move to the city with Corbin, but I didn't feel comfortable there either." She smiled up at him. "I finally figured out that it doesn't matter where I live as much as how I feel about myself, and I'm happy now."

He was studying her face intently. "How do you do it?"

"Do what?"

"Look at things the way you do. I've never seen you get down about anything. Your divorce, Sammy, moving back home. You find something good in everything."

"It's not that hard to find something to be happy about." She shrugged, smiling.

"I think it is. Life is fucking scary," he said quietly.

"That's why I wanted to come home," she said softly. "I knew Sammy and I would be taken care of here."

"When Mel died, Northfield took care of us too. I'll never forget that."

"Was she from around here?"

He nodded. "She loved Northfield, and everyone loved Mel." Davis sat silent, rocking slowly. "That night—it was the worst night of my life," he finally said. "Sometimes I still dream about the accident. I hear the tires squealing. If I'm lucky, it wakes me up."

She didn't ask what happened if he didn't wake up. Instead, she reached out to touch his arm, just a light touch to offer comfort. "I'm so sorry, Davis."

He sighed deeply. "I'm sorry too. It took me a long time to get to where I am now. I'll always love her, but the kids and I are okay now."

Mrs. Autovino's radio was still playing, and Hank Williams' "I'm So Lonesome I Could Cry" came crooning out the window. *Well played, Mrs. Autovino.*

Allie turned to find Davis studying her face. "I don't think I'm imagining things." She met his eyes to make sure they were on the same page. He nodded slowly. "Do you feel it too? Between us?" She stopped and put her head down, briefly closing her eyes as heat warmed her cheeks.

Strong fingers cupped her chin and tilted her face up to his. "You're not imagining anything. I feel it too." His thumb stroked her jaw before he let go.

She wanted to pull his hand back to her face and lean into it.

"I care about you and Sammy enough to know you both deserve more than what I have in me to give," he said. "I live for my kids. I work. I go home, and it's lonely as hell, but when I think about the alternative—" He stopped. "I don't let myself think about the alternative. I don't see things like you do, Allie."

He looked out at the street for a long time, his throat muscles working, before she felt a sigh travel through his big body.

"What Mel and I had was supposed to be forever. That's what I planned for. And when forever didn't happen, I think a part of me shut down too."

She felt the loss in those words as keenly as a wound. She wanted to gather him tight. Not as a lover, but as a human, and comfort him. No one should have to live through what Davis and Ben and Claire did. How did someone live fully after that? She didn't know, but she was certain of one thing.

"What's on the other side of forever, Davis?" she said softly. "Because there is another side. You're proof of that. Your life didn't end up the way you thought it would, but it's not over."

The swing jerked to a stop. Davis leaned forward to rest his elbows on his knees. "I don't know if there is another side. I don't know if I'll ever be ready to find out. But I know it's not fair to ask you to wait if I'm not sure there even is another side."

The weariness in his voice prompted her to lift a hand to his back. She rubbed small circles, feeling the tight muscles relax under her touch. He was so noble her heart ached.

He turned and leaned back, trapping her arm around him and pulling her into his body. "You have no idea how much I admire you," he said roughly. "You're strong, and you're brave." A small smile curved his mouth. "You're sexy as hell. You make me want things that I have no business wanting anymore."

He tightened his arm around her, and she went willingly.

"I'm not brave, Davis. I'm honest. I lived with someone for too long without being honest with myself. You were lucky to have found love like that with Mel," she said softly. "I'm not asking to replace that, but what if you let yourself care about someone differently? Not any less or more, just... differently."

Davis reached out a long finger and lightly touched her jaw. His eyes were cast in the shadows of the porch, their lips close enough to touch if she moved.

"If I could, I'd make damn sure it was you," he finally said huskily.

Her nose stung, and the back of her throat ached until Allie nuzzled her face against his neck to hide. It wasn't easy to be the first one to reach out. It hurt more than she could think about right now that Davis didn't trust this fragile, new thing happening between them. She knew, if he gave it a chance, it could be something beautiful. But she wasn't sorry she had brought it up. She was pretty sure she was already halfway in love with the man sitting beside her. The difference between them was she knew the reward was worth the risk.

She gave his arm a fond squeeze and lifted her head to take a sip of her wine around the tightness in her throat. "Ah, well, like you said, you're too old for me anyway," she said, easing the tension that hung heavily over them.

He chuckled quietly. "I am too old for you."

"Just how old are you?"

"I'll be thirty-eight in December."

"Oh, Davis," she teased. "That isn't old. Haven't you ever heard of a silver fox?"

He rubbed his hand over his whiskered jaw where only a few glints of silver showed. "Is that what they're calling it now?"

"Mm-hmm." She took another sip of wine and let the tart flavors swirl on her tongue. She leaned back into the cove of his body. He settled his arm over her and pulled her close.

"Still friends?" she asked softly. If nothing else, she could do a lot worse than Davis in the friendship department.

"If you'll have me," he said gruffly.

That was enough for now. She wrapped her arm low across his middle and pressed closer to his chest, feeling his stomach muscles clench.

"Allie," he said warningly.

"Shh. Friends cuddle." She laid her head on his shoulder as they sat there swinging, watching the lights go on up and down the street, listening to Johnny Cash drifting over from next door. Like friends. Like friends who wanted to do each other. She surreptitiously inhaled.

"You're smelling me again, aren't you?"

She stopped guiltily. "Just checking. I think my grandpa wore that cologne."

He placed one big, rough hand on the side of her head and squashed her head flat against his chest as she sputtered. "Davis!"

"I can't hear you. My hearing aids aren't turned up."

Chapter Twenty

ANNETTE CALLED one Friday in early October and asked to pick up Sammy after school for a sleepover. Allie helped him into her mom's souped-up Lexus SUV that still had that new car smell and kissed him goodbye.

"Don't give him those in the car, Mom." Allie snatched the baggie Annette had been about to hand to Sammy. "You'll be fishing Goldfish out of the seats for a year."

Annette snatched them right back. "Then I'll buy another car. Here, my little prince," she crooned. "Do you want to go to the toy store?"

Annette zoomed off, and Allie let out a breath. She wasn't overly concerned about her taking care of Sammy's diabetes. Sammy would be just down the street, and she trusted her mom. It was just hard to let anyone else take over.

After their talk on the porch a few weeks ago, she hadn't seen much of Davis other than when they ran into each other at drop-off, or when he dropped the kids off to play. She didn't invite him to dinner, and he didn't ask, despite the kids begging for a repeat with them all. She was glad. It was too hard to pretend being around him didn't wreak havoc on her. Davis's sign wasn't on, as Aunt Rosa would say, and she wasn't a glutton for punishment.

She wandered the house for a while, listening to the TV blaring through the open windows at Mrs. Autovino's house and putting away toys while she thought about what she could do tonight. She could give the house a deep clean. Except it was already pretty clean.

She could review charts for work. She could take a bubble bath and read. That was her usual go-to when she had some free time. Today she had a tingly, restless feeling of anticipation that made her want something else. Something fun. Something she never had the chance to do.

She picked up the phone.

An hour later, Allie walked into the dimly lit interior of the Northfield Pub. A live band was playing something that made her hips start swaying even as she looked around for Amber. The place was busy with the after-dinner crowd, but Allie spotted her sister playing pool and holding court with some men in uniforms.

She knew from waiting tables at the pub in high school that the Northfield police and firefighters liked to walk over after their shifts to grab a beer and indulge in some good-natured ribbing. They could get loud and rowdy with each other, but they were always generous tippers.

"Boys, meet my sister, Allie. Allie, meet Northfield's finest," Amber introduced then leaned over the pool table to eye the balls. She wiggled and squinted, and the cue slid effortlessly through her fingers, knocking the last solid ball neatly into the pocket. She straightened and blew off the chalk on the tip of the stick delicately. "Gee, I won again."

"Damn, Amber, you took all my money." One of the burlier

guys groaned. He had a chest that looked like an actual barrel. His boyish face was creased with a grin from ear to ear as he adoringly gazed at Amber.

Amber patted that broad expanse affectionately. "I did, didn't I, Johnny? But you love it." She reached up to murmur something private in his ear that made his cheeks redden.

"I'll be back, boys. Don't miss me too much." Amber blew the group a kiss, and they headed to the bar.

"Thanks for meeting me. Did I interrupt your plans?" Allie asked. Amber in her natural element was something else. Where had she learned that?

"Nah, they're my regulars. It's good for them to miss me. Aren't they cute? I could hook you up with any of the single ones." She paused. "Except for Johnny. He's the biggest sweetie with the biggest... *hose*." Her eyes danced wickedly.

Allie took off her jean jacket and draped it over the back of the stool.

"Whoa." Amber did a double take. "You look smokin' hot, Al. Mama needed a night out, huh?"

Allie looked down at her dress, a short, flirty little red scoop neck, peasant-style number fitted just right over her curves. It made her feel like a sexpot minus the sex. Although that might be nice too. Images of Davis's brawny arms and chest flashed through her head. Yes, that would have been nice. It had been a long, long time.

She gave her sister a shimmy. "Yeah? You like it?"

"It looks like it came out of my closet," Amber said approvingly.

"Is that you, Allie Hart?" Lucy Merchant, her childhood friend from Cedarwood, squeezed onto the stool next to her.

"Lucy! So great to see you. Come here!" Allie pulled her in for a hug. Lucy still wore her hair long and wavy down her back, and her leggy form was still dressed in black. Unlike her goth looks in high school, Lucy's all-back ensemble had transitioned to chic and sexy. "You remember my sister, Amber, right?"

"Hey! So, what brings you back, Allie? You visiting your mom?" Lucy's pretty face was as kind as ever, and Allie knew she hadn't heard about her divorce. After she left Northfield, Allie lost touch with everyone back home. She didn't have much free time between Sammy, nursing school, and then work, but as she looked at her dear friend, she regretted not staying in contact.

Lucy and her mom had moved into the apartment next door to theirs during middle school. The girls had clicked immediately—both were used to being on their own, although it was just Lucy at home with her mom. Mrs. Merchant was tall and thin and chain-smoked Virginia Slims. She was incredibly glamorous with her high heels and makeup, and her big, easy laugh that made her a popular dancer at the Klassy Kat, which the girls eventually learned, wasn't very classy at all. Lucy spent many nights on the couch at Allie's waiting for her mom to get home from work.

"I'm back for good." Allie smiled at her friend to make it less awkward. "I'm divorced now."

Lucy's face fell, but she didn't look surprised. "I'm sorry to hear that." Lucy and Corbin had only met once, the summer before Allie moved. Corbin had asked disapprovingly how old she was, as if she were too young for him to take seriously. Allie had reminded him Lucy and she were the same age, but Corbin had missed the sarcasm.

"Thanks. It's a good thing, actually. And, hey, I have a little boy now, Sammy." Allie beamed. "He's seven. I can't wait for you to meet him."

"I heard! Your mom comes in to get her hair done at my

salon, and she's obsessed with him. She calls him her little prince. I've never seen Annette so..." Lucy grinned wickedly, "grandmotherly."

"What can I get you to drink, darlin'?"

"A strawberry basil margarita, please." Allie closed the drink menu and looked up at the bartender. And blinked. And stared some more even when Amber started snickering.

The tall, dark man behind the bar looked like he belonged on a billboard for... well, anything. His black hair fell rakishly on his forehead, and the black button-down shirt gave him the look of a slightly dangerous, but devastatingly handsome, mobster. He was grinning at her while he waited for her to stop drooling. "Hello," he said smoothly. "I'm Killian Kennedy, Amber's boss."

"Blink, Allie. Don't let my boss's ego get any bigger," Amber said dryly.

"Oh, uh, sorry. I'm Amber's sister."

"Older sister," Amber chimed in cheerfully, sipping her gin and tonic.

"I've heard all about you, Amber's sister. Do you have a name then?"

Allie flushed bright red. That's how good-looking he was. Women forgot their names. She was only a little disgusted with herself. And still tongue-tied. But those eyes! A dazzling blue that sparkled with humor and maybe something darker too.

"Killian, the one you're slobbering over is my sister, Allie. And this is our friend Lucy Merchant."

"Nice to meet you." Allie made a conscious effort to pull it together.

"We've met," Lucy said, sounding considerably less warm. Allie glanced curiously at her, but Lucy's face was shuttered.

"We have," Killian murmured with only a flicker of a look in her direction. "What brings you ladies in tonight?"

"Drinks, Boss, and plenty of them," Amber said. "But don't get your hopes up. Allie's off-limits to you." She jerked her thumb at a table full of women unabashedly checking him out. "Go back to your entourage. They want your autograph."

Killian's mouth curved sinfully. "You're fired." He pointed to Amber and turned back to Allie. "Can you take your sister's shifts? Her job duties include insulting the boss, hitting on the customers, and helping herself to free drinks all night."

"It's a tough job, but—" Amber started.

"Your sister could do it," Killian finished, and Amber lunged to elbow his side. He held her off with a finger on her forehead.

"You love me," Amber said fondly, then she took the last sip of her drink. Lucy's lips were still pressed together tightly into a thin white line. Interesting.

"Are you ladies hungry? The bleu cheese burger is the special tonight: sharp bleu cheese, Angus beef, and arugula on a brioche bun." Allie nodded hungrily. Her margarita was almost gone, and she felt a little warm and a lot happy.

"I'll put the order in. Lovely to meet you, Allie," Killian murmured before heading through the swinging doors to the back of the house.

"I know, girls. I know." Amber sighed when he walked away. "Try pouring drinks all night while looking at that mug. He's Irish."

"I didn't know the Irish made 'em like that," Allie said.

"Me either. But he doesn't date anyone that works for him. He's also a nice guy, but don't tell him I said that. He's friends with Davis. They hang out sometimes."

Lucy turned toward Allie, picking up what Amber was putting down. "Oh? Are you friends with Davis?"

"He's my landlord."

"But she wants to see him naked."

"Amber!" Allie hissed. She wasn't wrong, but still. "He's been very good to Sammy and me. We're friends." That word was starting to irritate her.

Lucy cupped her chin in her palm. "Okay, so you and Hot Landlord want to get naked together. Tell me more."

"It's complicated." Allie sighed. "Tell us about you, Luce. What have you been up to?"

While they caught up, the front door to the pub opened and closed, letting in more regulars ready for a beer and live music on a Friday night. She wasn't paying much attention until, suddenly, a tingling spread through her body. Weird. Was it the second margarita? They were going down quite nicely.

Then the door opened and in walked Davis, all brawny and lumberjack-looking in a green-and-black plaid. The tingling gave way to a short, sharp burst of yearning at the sight of his handsome, serious face. He held the door for several people behind him, which gave her a minute to compose herself. Toby and Keri, Ford, and... Natalie filed in.

Her heart sank. Were they on a date? Natalie was beautiful and smart and single, and she probably could have anyone she wanted. *Just not Davis,* her heart whispered.

Get it together, Hart.

She slapped a smile on her face. No way was she going to ruin her night out by pining. "Allie, did you hear me? I said—" Amber started. "Oh, Hot Landlord is here," she murmured. Amber knew all the details about that night on the porch. "Quick, start laughing." Amber tossed her head back. *Ha ha ha.* Johnny looked over forlornly. "Look like you're having fun."

"I was laughing. We *are* having a good time," Allie said, frowning.

"Put a smile on your face," Amber hissed. "He's coming over here." She tugged down the neckline of Allie's dress, revealing a serious amount of boobs. "You have to meet Johnny's friends,

Allie," she said loudly. "They really know what to do with their hoses, eh?" she said, adding an exaggerated wink.

Allie stared at her sister. Was she having a seizure? Was this one of those horrible heart attacks where the person spews out nonsense, but they don't know it? She saw a clip once of a newscaster that had happened to. Scary stuff.

Then Davis was standing next to them, all tall and dark, with the usual grumpy look on his face. She stifled the urge to climb up his body and kiss it off. He glanced over at her curiously, lingering for quite a few seconds on her newly exposed cleavage.

"Oh, hi, Davis, we didn't see you there," Amber said. "We're just having a girls' night before we choose one of Northfield's finest to go home with and have sex. Hot sex. So much hot sex, right, girls?"

Davis's lip twitched.

"Amber, you're embarrassin' your sister." Killian dropped off more food and drinks in front of them.

"Who's having hot sex?" Ford appeared next to Davis. "And can I please offer myself up for this important job?"

"Hey, Davis, did you still want to dance?" Natalie slinked up behind Davis. She was as well-dressed and put together as ever and pressed up close enough to Davis's side to get pregnant. A band cinched uncomfortably tight around Allie's throat. Davis had said he could only handle something casual. Did that mean he was finally taking Natalie up on what she was offering?

Allie did want Davis to find someone to love. Someone to wipe the sadness out of his eyes and make him laugh. He deserved that. She wanted that for him. She just wanted it to be her.

She spent about two minutes being the bigger person before deciding, even if Davis had a casual relationship with Natalie, she didn't have to watch it happen in front of her.

Allie slid off the stool and held out her hand to Amber. "I'm ready to dance now."

～

IT WAS CROWDED and hot and loud on the tiny dance floor, but Allie laughed harder than she had in a long time as she spun. It felt so good to let loose a little bit and just allow her body to feel the music. She lifted her hands in the air, swaying as the hem of her skirt danced higher at the tops of her thighs. The music was fast, beating a steady drum in her body, making her hotter and hotter.

She knew there were eyes on her. Davis's eyes. He was still at the bar with a group of friends, but his eyes were locked on her every time she looked over. She ran a hand under the damp hair on the back of her neck, lifting it with one hand and sliding the other down her side, sketching the curve of her waist and the flare of her hips. Even her own hand felt sensuous on her body.

She danced with Lucy and Amber, by herself, and with anyone around who was up for it. She danced with a gangly college student who could get down, a spiffy-looking elderly man in an old-fashioned bow tie who gallantly dipped her, and a woman with spiky pink hair who twirled her over and over until she was too dizzy to do more than laugh.

She did not, however, dance with Davis.

Davis sat at the bar. Staring at her.

Stubborn man.

Breathless and ready for another of those yummy margarita drinks Killian blended up so perfectly, Allie headed back to the table. A warm hand held her shoulder. "Hope you saved a dance for me."

Ford grinned boyishly and, really, who could resist that

smile? Not her. Ford was too cute for his own good, and he knew how to have a good time.

"I sure did," she yelled above the music and let him pull her out onto the dance floor as a fast song came on. He spun her around by the hands until she was laughing and caught up in the fun of dancing with a partner who knew what they were doing.

"You're a good dancer!" she yelled as they came back together in a twirl. He dipped her dramatically over his arm as the music ended.

"Save another one for me," he told her.

Another arm slid around her waist.

Davis. Finally.

But the pair of eyes meeting hers weren't Davis's warm brown ones, they were a deep blue.

Killian smiled wickedly at her and held out his hand.

"Care to dance?"

Allie hid her pang of disappointment. "I don't think I can handle anymore," she said breathlessly.

"Listen." He pointed up toward the stage. Sure enough, the guitarist strummed the first strains of a sexy, slower song. Couples were moving into each other's arms. "I requested this song next." A lazy smile curled the edges of his mouth, and Allie didn't mean to, but she found herself staring.

"Why?" She winced at her starstruck tone.

"So that I could do this," he murmured. Effortlessly, he moved her from Ford's arms into his own. Allie let herself be drawn into the music and the strong arms holding her as they whirled around. Killian danced with a self-assurance that made her look good, too, even when she stumbled over the steps. His strong arms caught her when her feet got tangled. When she looked up, she caught him watching her with a serious expression.

"What?" She smiled up at him. "Am I making you look bad?"

"I think I'm the envy of every man here right now."

"I think it's the opposite," she said dryly.

He had the grace to look embarrassed. But when he pulled her closer, Allie closed her eyes and rested her head on his shoulder. She felt pleasantly floaty, and it felt so nice to be held. Killian was a good egg, as her aunt would say. He made her feel comfortable, if a little tongue-tied.

As the song ended, he drew her to a stop and very gently kissed her on the cheek. Oh, so nice. So gentlemanly. "Thank you for the dance."

He led the way over to a table where Amber, Lucy, and a few more people sat talking. She sank into the chair Ford held out for her. "Would you like a drink?" he shouted over the music.

"Sure!" she shouted back and laughed because the music was so loud, they could hardly hear sitting right next to each other. Ford handed her a glass of what looked like water. Allie made a face just as Davis walked up. His eyes never left hers, and her stomach clenched in a tight, achy ball that radiated heat through her body.

He looked unusually stern tonight, his jaw all tight, his warm brown eyes shooting daggers at his friends.

Don't find that sexy. Don't find that sexy. Two gorgeous, emotionally available men were sitting at this table, and she was not going to pine after the one who was as accessible as a Brink's truck.

"Ford, Killian." Davis nodded to his friends. "Allie." God. That voice. So deep she could feel it down to her toes.

"Hi." She fanned herself and grabbed Amber's drink to slurp the last few inches. "Oops, all gone." She let out an undignified giggle.

"Okay, that's enough for you, Al." Amber deftly slid the water in front of her while Killian pushed a basket of chips toward her. "Eat those. We make them fresh every day."

Allie picked up a chip, nibbled, and looked around her.

Ford and Killian were smiling at her. They really were such nice men. She gave them her best smile back. She wasn't going to be stingy with those like Davis.

"You're looking even more radiant than usual tonight, Allie. What brought you out to the pub?" Ford nudged her shoulder playfully. Allie almost tipped off the barstool. He righted her by the arms.

Allie watched, fascinated, as Davis's jaw grew even stiffer when Ford touched her. "Thanks," she said very casually. As casually as one could with a hiccup in the middle of the word. "I'm celebrating meeting new *friends*." She stared pointedly at Davis, but he was still glaring at Ford. "I have the best *friends*. So many *friends*. Like Lucy. You're such a good pal, Luce." She gave her friend a high five from across the table and missed. "Hey, let's get another one of those frozen drinks!"

"Are either of you driving home?" Davis asked Amber.

"Nope, we walked, big guy." Amber was thoroughly enjoying herself, looking back and forth between Ford and Davis like it was a Ping-Pong match.

"Where's Sammy?" Davis asked.

"Sleepover at the gingerbread house. They're probably getting ready for bed." Allie looked at her watch upside down. She squinted. Still couldn't see it. She thrust her arm out below Davis's nose. "Mmm, it's not on."

Davis held her arm and gently turned it toward him. "It's eight-thirty."

Allie sighed happily. "This is a fun night." She hopped off the stool, gave a regal nod to everyone, and then promptly spoiled the effect with another hiccup.

EVERY UNATTACHED MALE and some women stared as she made her way to the bathroom. A flair of possessiveness gripped Davis's gut. He had wanted to rip Killian and Ford's faces off when they were dancing with her. He had no right to feel that way, and he knew it, but he did anyway.

She was so gorgeous he was afraid to look at her for too long or she'd see the need on his face. If he thought a week was a long time not seeing her smile every day, then the last two weeks with no more than a passing wave was a level of hell he never thought he'd be in.

She was under his skin, dammit. Burning hot, flaming, keep-you-up-all-night thinking-about-her kind of under his skin. The minute he got into bed and closed his eyes, she appeared. Her soft hands touched him like she always did, so easily and freely, making him remember what it was like to feel something good.

He missed her laugh the most. He could almost hear Shep laughing at him for even thinking something like that. He knew it made him sound like a lovesick asshole, but when Allie looked at him, when her eyes lit up with a joke, or even when she teased him for acting like a grumpy old man, he wanted to wrap her up in her arms and hold her so tight nothing bad could ever happen to her.

And he worried about her. Was she remembering to lock the door? Was she being careful? Allie took care of everyone around her, but who was taking care of her?

He had it bad. Real fucking bad.

That little red dress wasn't helping tonight. It clung to her breasts and hips like it was slicked on with glue. Don't even get him started on her legs. They looked about a mile long in those high heels. She was all curves and slopes and soft flesh. It made him want to throw her over his shoulder and bring her back to his bed like a caveman. He sipped the lukewarm beer in front of him grimly.

"Hey, handsome." Natalie slid onto the stool next to him. "How's it going?"

"Can't complain."

"You never do." Her red lips curved up. "How about a dance?"

He considered it for a millisecond. He was just lonely and miserable enough to let his mind work out what that would look like if he said yes. They would dance, and she would be warm and willing. Maybe that would make some of his ache for human companionship go away for a while. But then what? He had never been the kind of man to substitute one woman for another, and a certain hazel-eyed woman possessed all his thoughts these days.

The somberness on his face made her wince, and she leaned up to kiss him softly on the cheek.

"Allie's a lucky lady," she said in his ear.

"It's not like that." He could feel his face heating, but he met her eyes steadily.

"Relax, Davis. Little Miss Mary Poppins is good for you. I bet she could whip you up something to make you smile." A sad look crossed her face. "Lord knows I've tried."

"It's not like that," he said gruffly.

"Would it be so bad if it was?"

He had asked himself that question many times in the last few weeks, but the answer was even less clear now. "I don't know," he finally said because that was the truth.

"If you ever looked at me the way you look at her, I'd consider myself the luckiest woman in the world." She slipped her arms around his waist for a quick hug.

"Hey, what's this about?" he asked softly as his arms came around her.

"Just saying good night."

He pulled back until he could see her eyes. "I'm not leaving."

"Not yet," she said. "But you will soon."

Davis knew she didn't mean leaving the bar.

"Now go on before somebody else decides they'd like a spoonful of sugar too." Natalie leaned close and kissed his cheek before heading to the pool table. Davis watched her thoughtfully.

"You're looking the wrong way, dumbass." Killian yanked the empty beer bottle from his hands and pointed toward the bathroom. "That's where you should be looking."

Ah, hell.

"Damn." Ford whistled next to him. "Looks like you're a popular guy tonight. Maybe I'd better help you out. Is Allie available, man?"

Killian leaned forward to look him in the eye. "I'm asking too."

"She's mine," Davis growled immediately then pinched the bridge of his nose when he realized what he'd said. "Fuck."

Killian was grinning. "Then don't be an asshole."

He glared at his friend. "I'm not an asshole."

"Our girl seemed pissed at you," he said cheerfully. He slapped him on the back before heading back to the kitchen, calling over his shoulder, "Better make her happy, or I will."

"She's not pissed at me."

"Yes, she is," Ford said affably. "So don't fuck it up because I won't if I have the chance." He pounded him on the other shoulder and turned back to the table.

Complicated.

Davis raked a hand through his hair in frustration. Things were getting complicated, which he did not need. He should head home, get a good night's sleep—alone—and *uncomplicate* things. But he didn't want to go home, not yet. Normally, he looked forward to the peace and quiet when the kids were gone. He could have another beer and sleep in for once. But not tonight.

Instead, he found himself heading toward the bathroom because... complicated.

Chapter Twenty-One

ALLIE SQUINTED in the dim bathroom mirror, tugged up the top of the dress, and then tugged down the bottom. She'd give her right arm for a pair of her fleece pajama bottoms right now. And these heels? They might need to be surgically removed from her feet. She'd worry about that later. She was having way too much fun now. She made one last failed attempt to cover her boobs and swung open the bathroom door.

Davis was leaning against the opposite wall. Tiny ripples of sensation skittered down her spine and pooled between her legs at the sight of him waiting for her. She hadn't known, until this very second, how much she had hoped to be alone with Davis tonight. His presence in the dark hall brought back every feeling she had tried so hard to ignore these last few weeks until it was all she could do not to bury her head in his chest. She took a deep breath, prepared herself, and stepped out of the doorway.

Davis's arms were crossed over his chest, his face in the shadows, but she would bet money he wasn't smiling.

"Stingy," she muttered.

"Excuse me?"

"I said, you're stingy." She walked past him almost perfectly in a straight line. She could totally pass a sobriety test. Maybe.

Gentle fingers wrapped around her upper arm and pointed her in the opposite direction. "This way."

Damn, it was hard to stay mad when he held her like this. For such a large man, he handled her like spun glass, like she was precious.

"I know that."

"You do?" Warm brown eyes studied her face, and she forgot what they were talking about.

"I do what?"

"You know that was the wrong way?" he repeated patiently.

"Yes, but thanks anyway." She turned away.

"Allie." He held her chin between two fingers and nudged her face toward him. "You're angry."

"Me? Nope. We're all good."

"Tell me why."

She pulled her chin away. "Why are you waiting for me?"

"I wanted to make sure you were all right."

"Is that all?"

He sighed heavily. "Why won't you look at me?"

She stared at him hard. "Was that the only reason you followed me back here?"

His lips curved up in that lazy half smile of his, showing her a flash of his white teeth. "I also wanted to tell you how beautiful you look tonight," he said gruffly.

Finally, she looked up, and her breath caught at the intensity in his eyes. "I wanted to dance with you tonight," she blurted. She didn't know where it came from, but she was glad it was out there.

"I think you know why we didn't," he said quietly.

"I know." Her shoulders slumped. That warm, fuzzy buzz

from earlier was starting to wear off. "And I have no business even asking you that because I also know we're just friends."

"I hated seeing you dance with Ford and Killian." The possessive growl in his voice did something carnal to her.

She slid her hands up his hard chest and tilted her head back to look at him. "What are we doing, Davis?"

He leaned down and rested his forehead on hers. "Damned if I know," he said with a deep sigh.

She reached up to cup his cheeks. "I've missed you."

"I've missed you too," he said quietly. He eased her into him, spreading his legs and leaning against the wall to settle her comfortably into his body. The rigid evidence of his erection throbbed against her belly. She tilted her head up for his kiss, but he tightened his hands on her hips and buried his face in her neck instead.

She swallowed her disappointment and backed off, but he gripped her hips harder and held on.

He was so confusing.

They stood in the dark hallway for several long minutes, slightly rocking, until her mouth opened on a yawn. Davis squeezed her one last time, a lingering caress of his arms wrapped tightly around her ribs.

"Come on. I'll walk you home." He grabbed her hand, and they walked out into the bar. Allie waved to Amber who was in the lap of Johnny with the big hose.

The cool night air dispelled the last of Allie's pleasant buzz while they walked. At one point, she stumbled over a crack in the sidewalk, and Davis held her hand in his warm and calloused one. She shivered.

"Cold?" he asked her.

She wasn't, not really. The night was mild for October, but she nodded anyway. Davis put an arm around her and drew her into his side. All too soon, they stood in front of her house.

"Do you want to sit on the porch for a while?"

Hesitation flickered briefly in his gaze but to her surprise, he nodded and led them up the steps to the swing.

It was dark on the porch. The only light came from inside the house where she had left a lamp on. Allie struck a match and lit the candles. Mrs. Autovino's windows were open again. The soft tones of a radio announcer faded and Dusty Springfield's "Wishin' and Hopin'" spilled over to the porch.

"I love this song," Allie said, turning around. "What—" She looked down to find Davis with his hand out, palm up.

"Will you dance with me?"

"Here?" She looked up at him in surprise.

"Here." He nodded. "I should have done this earlier. I wanted to," he said. She put her hand in his and he pulled her gently into his arms, swaying with her.

She ran her hands up the soft flannel of his shirt, feeling the muscles in his chest bunch until she reached his neck. She ran her fingers through his hair, lightly playing with the dark strands. "This is nice."

"Yeah," he said gruffly, "it is."

Wishing and hoping.

That wild, edgy feeling was back, enhanced by the heat of his body against hers. He was so solid and warm. Davis's breath hitched when her breasts brushed against his chest. Once. Twice. He gripped her waist and pulled her closer until she felt the unmistakable thick length of him cradled against the softness of her belly. *Oh my.* She let out a soft sigh and cuddled her hips closer, wickedly thrilled to feel what she did to him. She wanted to feel that hard length of him sliding into her heat, into her wetness, hard and fast.

Or maybe slow.

She twined her arms around his neck and lifted her nose, drawing it slowly along the side of his jaw, feeling it clench as she made her way to his neck. His scent, fast having become her favorite, filled her nose with clean, masculine, aroused male. His big hand drew slowly down her body, over her hips, until it gripped her bottom. He pulled her into him, rubbing her ass hard and then soft in his big hands until she wanted to scream. She moaned and bit down gently on the tightly corded muscle in his throat before circling the mark gently with her tongue. "Kiss me, Davis."

Never in her life could anyone say Allie was a sexpot, but the way that request had husked out of her mouth, they would have been dead wrong. Her nipples were tight, and the throb of her pulse beat throughout her body.

Davis abruptly pulled away, holding her by the arms away from him. Her body was cold where it had once been hotly against his. She blinked at him, the shock of his sudden move holding her frozen.

Then she snapped.

"That is the last"—she poked him hard in the middle of his chest—"time you push me away, Davis!" she yelled, poking him again.

He tried to catch her hand, but she whipped it back.

"Don't touch me. Do not touch me anymore until you make up your damn mind. Either we're friends or we're lovers, but I'm not doing this anymore!"

She had shouted the last word. Anger and desire fought in her until she wanted to scream, or tear into his flesh with her teeth.

"You don't get to glare at me for dancing with other men," she hissed. "You don't get to say anything at all when I do anything with them because you're too much of a coward to kiss me." She turned to go inside and end this horrible night. "Maybe I'll kiss Killian or Ford—"

He grabbed her arm and spun her back to face him. His strong arms drew her up to her tiptoes and into his chest, tilting her head back while he towered over her. Allie gasped at the sharpness, her lips parting. His mouth met hers with a fierceness that took her breath away.

As suddenly as her anger appeared, it fled, leaving behind wicked, hot desire. She wrapped her arms around his neck, and when his tongue swept into her mouth, she met it just as forcefully, until their kiss was a battle she was determined to win.

Davis growled low, releasing her arms, then cupping her head and chasing her tongue with his own. In and out. Over and over, he licked into her mouth. He kissed her as if he wanted to devour her whole, as if he couldn't help himself.

She never wanted to be kissed any other way.

The deep, wet, hot kisses made her eyes see stars as she met him stroke for stroke. He tasted like beer, sex, crisp autumn nights, and every fantasy she'd ever had. Davis drew back, looked around wildly, and grabbed her around the waist. Then he sat on the swing, hauling her into his lap.

Moving with the instinctive need to press her softness closer, closer, closer to his hardness, Allie straddled his thighs and looked into the face of a very angry, very aroused man. He gripped her with an arm around her waist and one hand in her hair. "Christ. The things I want to do to you," he whispered against her neck. The rough glide of his tongue there made her whimper.

"What kind of things?" she panted, squirming to press closer. A flush burned her cheeks at the way she was grinding on his lap. She wanted to know. In explicit detail.

"Dirty things. Despicable things. Things that will make your pretty face blush more than it already is."

"Okay," she whispered. She didn't know if she could handle

a dirty-talking Davis, but she was willing to try. He lifted her higher and pressed a hot kiss at the edge of her dress, on the upper curves of her breasts.

"Can I touch you here?" he asked huskily.

"Please, yes," she said, lifting onto her knees to get closer to his sinful mouth.

Davis tugged down the cap sleeves until they caught on the curve of her arm, trapping her arms to her sides. Pure male appreciation lit up his eyes when he pulled back and stared.

She had always had big breasts, just like her mom and sisters. They were perky enough, even though she had nursed for a year, and her nipples were almost unbearably sensitive. Younger, she had been embarrassed by their size, by the attention they got, and how they got in her way when she did anything, but Davis's sharp inhale when they sprang free made her want to do a little shimmy.

So she did.

She reveled in the quiet curse Davis bit out. He hooked his thumbs under her bra straps and pushed them off her shoulders, pulling the cups down with them and exposing her nipples to the cool air. They puckered immediately while he watched. He planted his hands under her arms and lifted her until she hung above him, burying his face in between the scented skin of her breasts. Hot, open-mouthed kisses over and around the heavy swells turned into deep, sucking pulls on her nipple while she held his head.

She buried her nose in his hair and inhaled. *So good, so, so good.* She dragged her fingernails through his thick hair. God, she loved his hair. Her hips rolled sensually against his belly, seeking friction.

Davis let go of one deep-pink tip and turned to give the other the same attention. He alternated teeth and tongue and then pulled back to look at her hungrily. Her body slid down his until she was seated firmly in his lap again. Rough hands caressed the outsides of her bare thighs where her dress hiked up.

"I knew you'd be like this," he growled in her ear. "So soft. So fucking delicious."

Davis kneaded and plumped her bare flesh possessively, and Allie's breath caught when his long fingers grazed the edges of her panties then under the seams, sliding against her wetness. He growled, and she held onto his shoulders for dear life.

"Tell me what you want, Allie," he said huskily, his fingers stroking, teasing lightly. His voice was deeper than she'd ever heard it, his chest rising and falling fast and hard. She had caused that. This stoic, reserved man burned for her, coming dangerously close to losing his precious control. It made her almost giddy with need.

Davis planted his feet on the porch and pulled her hips down, firmly grinding her against his cock. Again and again, until the lace of her panties grew damp and rode up, he caused delicious friction against her clit. She moaned into his mouth and reached impatiently for his belt. His stomach muscles flexed against the back of her hands.

"I want..." She nibbled on his square jaw "... you..." A soft, sucking kiss on those beautiful, masculine lips, she finished with her mouth at his ear, "... inside me." She was nearly panting with desire. Never in her life had she ached with wanting more than at this moment.

She sat back to undo his belt, and the shock of cold air hit her damp nipples painfully.

Oh my God.

The sound of their breathing echoed around them in the quiet. Mrs. Autovino's music wasn't playing anymore. Her fingertips were tucked just inside the waistband of Davis's belt as she looked around in a daze. Did she just come dangerously close to having sex with Davis Henderson on her front porch?

Davis's cheeks were flushed, his hair mussed from her fingers. He looked wild and deeply, darkly aroused. The intensity in his eyes made her voice shake, and she was suddenly inexplicably shy.

"Hey," she said shakily.

Davis unclenched his hands from her hips one finger at a time. "Hey yourself," he said, blowing out a deep breath.

"Did we just almost hit third base on my front porch?"

"Yeah." He let out a pained laugh. "We almost did."

She rested her forehead against his, and they sat there panting slightly, mouths damp and sore from use, drawing in ragged breaths until she shivered. He laid two gentle kisses on the top of each breast, gently pulled up the cups of her bra, then her dress, until she was covered again.

That was...was... She had no words.

Apparently, she did, because she had spoken out loud. Davis swooped down to give her another deep kiss before he pulled away with a sweet sucking sound. His hands lingered on her ass, lightly now, but comfortably, as if they had a right to be there.

"Come here," he ordered, pulling her toward him.

Her eyes closed, and she filled her senses with him and let herself be held in the security of his body. He was warm and solid as he slid his hands up and down her back, soothing and stroking now instead of inciting.

"I'm sorry for earlier," he murmured in her ear.

"I'm sorry too. I shouldn't have said that about Ford and Killian."

His eyebrows drew down sharply, and he gripped her bottom hard. "No, you shouldn't have." He relaxed his hands. "But I probably deserved it."

"You definitely deserved it."

"You make me fucking crazy." He brushed a kiss on her temple. "I can't think straight when I'm around you."

His wonderful, warm eyes crinkled at the corners while he studied her, and she thought with startling clarity, *this man could break my heart.*

"I don't have any answers either, Davis," she whispered back, looking down. "There's no guarantee for either of us. You're my landlord, which is risky, but more importantly, our kids are involved. That's scary for us both."

He cupped her jaw, bringing her eyes back to his. "I would never do anything to hurt either of you," he said forcefully.

"I know you wouldn't." She reached out to kiss the corner of his mouth.

"I need you to trust me," he said. "Can you do that for me, sweetheart?"

She nodded, and he pulled her to him tightly. So tight she buried her face in his neck and just held on. They sat there rocking, sharing heat, until her bladder screamed loud enough to wake Mrs. Autovino's little matchmaking heart. *Dusty Springfield. How did she know?*

"I have to pee, big guy." She patted his shoulder to get up.

Davis let her go, but as she turned to go inside, he grabbed her arm and hauled her back into his arms.

"I have to go, but I'll be back in the morning," he whispered, low and fierce. She tried to read the meaning of that in his eyes, but the shadows were too deep.

She nodded, wondering which version of this man would show up at her door tomorrow morning.

"Goodbye, Allie," he said. Then he kissed her forehead before striding down the steps without looking back.

He dreamed about Mel that night.

He didn't often dream about her now. When she first died, he had nightmares for months about the scene of her accident. Accident. It always pissed him off when he heard that. She didn't have an accident. Someone else had. Some drunk shit, middle-aged man on his way home from the airport had one too many cocktails on the plane then got into his car to drive home. Only he couldn't see straight, and he drove his car into Melody.

She had been on a run that night. She liked to run a few nights a week with Keri or Rachel when he got home. They did the baby hand-off, and then she went out with her girlfriends, chatting about their day and catching up. That night, she went by herself. It had been a beautiful early-spring evening. When Davis got home from work, she had kissed him, a loud, smacking kiss with a little tongue, then she handed him the baby with a smile.

"I'm going for a run. Dinner's in the oven. Make sure Claire gets a bath before bed. I'll be back soon, handsome."

She had headed out the door still putting her earbuds in. She wore a bright-fuchsia warm-up to ward off the chilly evening breeze. He loved when she wore that thing. He had teased her when she bought it and told her no one would ever overlook the loud color when she wore it. She had run her fingers through his hair and told him, "Just as long as you never do." They had made love right there on the living room floor, on top of the shirt.

That night, she paused to give him an exaggerated wink before walking out the door. "Don't fall asleep on me. I have plans for you later."

She was like that—playful and fun, even after being home with kids all day. He felt so goddamned lucky. She had a temper, he was well aware of that, but it took a lot to rile his Mel. That's how he thought of her: his Mel.

Less than an hour later, when Davis was sitting down after putting the kids to bed, he heard the sickening sound of tires screeching. He still didn't know what prompted him to leave the house. The kids were in bed, and he wouldn't normally ever leave them alone, but something had made him walk down to the sidewalk and look up the street. Neighbors were just starting to come out after they, too, heard the horrific noise.

Bob Bishop, their neighbor, met him in the middle of the street with his wife, Cindy, behind him. "That doesn't sound good," he had said.

They all looked toward the intersection they could see from where they stood. Tires squealing like that were as out of place in their residential neighborhood as the rip of a revving motorcycle.

Davis had picked up his pace and began to run. As he got closer to the wreck, he realized it was just one car involved. The car was just past the crosswalk, a line of black tracks still smoked faintly behind it, a visual of what had happened. Davis spotted a man leaning against the side of the car, groaning and holding his head. But what had the car crashed into?

A bright-fuchsia piece of clothing stuck out awkwardly from underneath the front of the car. Davis had kept running, but his brain had slowed down as he looked at the pink fabric. Someone else had a warm-up shirt like his Mel's?

The man was yelling now, on his knees in front of the pink fabric that Davis could now see was attached to a hand. His footsteps slowed. Everything was in slow motion now. The weeping man. Bob taking his arm and yelling something. Cindy screaming.

A family was out for a walk, the Williamsons. He and Mel had had them over for dinner a few weeks earlier. They stood on the sidewalk behind the car, but they weren't watching the car. Their horrified eyes were watching him. *What a shitty thing for your kids to witness,* he had thought sadly. He had been suddenly glad his kids were safely asleep in their beds.

His last few footsteps brought him to the hood of the car, to a splatter of blood on the front bumper. Silently, he followed the trail down to the pavement and, finally, his eyes widened at what his heart hadn't been yet able to comprehend. Mel's hand under the car, attached to that silly pink sweater they had once made love on.

Her dark hair, still in the ponytail she had twisted it into so deftly as she left the house not even sixty minutes ago, was covered in red blood. A pool of it spread around her, dark and ominous, reaching out to touch his knees when he knelt in front of the car his wife's body had been crushed under.

Suddenly, the slow-motion that had held him in suspense drop-kicked him back into reality. The scream of a fire engine as it raced down the street. The roar of blood in his ears as he push, push, pushed the goddamn car that wouldn't move off his Mel. The strange, inhumane sounds he heard coming out of him. Grant Clairmont, Ford's oldest brother, and a Northfield deputy had held him around his waist and pulled him away as he let out another sound, a roar.

Waddell's triad of trauma. He had never heard that before, but that night a surgeon with sad eyes explained it to him at the hospital. It was common in high-velocity accidents, such as a car hitting a pedestrian. A combination of blunt force trauma to the femur, abdomen, and head. Mel had been dead within seconds from a significant internal hemorrhage, the doctor said. Davis heard the words, the explanation, but it didn't make sense. Mel was out for a walk. She was coming right back. Long after he left the hospital, he heard her last words to him.

Don't fall asleep on me. I have plans for you later.

In his dream, Mel sat on the back patio of their house with Ben on her lap and Claire in her party dress next to her, like the photo he kept on his dresser. She looked utterly peaceful as she held their babies and, as he watched, she reached toward a platter and picked up a chocolate chip cookie. It was still warm. He could smell the vanilla and brown sugar in his dream as she opened her mouth and took a bite. She smiled and offered a bite to Ben, then Claire, before looking back up at him and smiling serenely.

And that was it.

He woke up with the smell of Allie's cookies in his nose and tear tracks on his face. He rubbed the worn gold band he hadn't taken off his finger since their wedding day.

I love you, Mel.

I miss you.

The kids miss you.

He sat up with his elbows on his knees and let his head drop between his knees.

Claire talks about you all the time. She tells Ben about you.

He's too little to remember much.

I met someone. She's got a son, Sammy. He's on Ben's base-ball team. He's a great kid.

Allie. She makes me laugh. She makes me feel like living again.

And it scares the shit out of me.

Then he was quiet for a long time.

He hadn't even noticed until Allie fell into his arms the night he met her how dull his world had become. Her smile had made things bright again. Her laughter lit him up. His world had color again, and he didn't want to let that go.

It was terrifying.

It was more terrifying to think he'd never see that sunshine smile aimed at him again.

His thumb passed lovingly over the band one last time before he got out of bed. His knees creaked as he walked to the dresser. He twisted off the wedding band and rubbed his thumb over the indent the band had made. Then, carefully, he set the ring in the lopsided clay bowl Claire had made him for Father's Day.

I'll see you when I see you.

Chapter Twenty-Two

THE NEXT MORNING, Allie woke up early and stared up at the ceiling for a long time, and thought about the night before.

Davis Henderson knew how to make out.

Dirty, wet, throbbing, eat-you-up-and-come-back-for-more kissing and touching. She shivered, thinking about how hot and firm his mouth had felt on hers. He kissed like he couldn't get enough. And his hands. Oh, lord, his bossy hands on her. It had been so long since she was touched like that. Had she ever been?

God, it had felt so good.

She compared her other kissing experiences, a grand total of two. No competition there. Ivan Szymanski kissed her after their tenth-grade prom. She hadn't liked that much at all, considering he had been drinking from a flask all night and kissed her with enough sloppy tongue to make her never want to kiss anyone again. She had slipped inside the house and ignored his calls after that.

Then there was Corbin, of course. She had been attracted to him when they first met, but their sex life after they got married had been more of the lights off, missionary position, garden-variety sex after Sammy had been born. To say she hadn't missed that was an understatement.

With Davis, she finally understood why Amber had come in so often after a late night out with her high school boyfriends, dark-red lipstick worn off and a dreamy look on her face. It really was that good.

And yet, it might never happen again with him.

She was surprisingly peaceful about the way things had ended last night. Maybe Davis would show up this morning wanting more. Maybe not. Only time would tell. The only thing she knew for certain was the sobering truth in Amber's words: *you get what you think you deserve.*

Maybe it was time to ask for more.

She had seen glimpses of what more looked like. Aunt Rosa and Uncle Peter, Mrs. Autovino and her late husband, and Sadie, Sammy's teacher, and her husband Rob. Sylvia and her husband. Davis and Mel. Love was all around her. No one knew what the end would look like, but she had a feeling if she asked any of the couples, not a single one would regret spending the time they did have here on earth with their loves.

Knowing who the right person is was the hardest part. Because her heart was screaming for Davis while her head whispered that he wasn't ready.

She sighed, tossed the pillow away, and headed to the bathroom.

An hour later, Allie pulled up her baking playlist and tied on Nanny Hart's apron, prepared to take her frustration out on a batch of lemon ricotta pancakes for Annette and Sammy when they got here. She had perfected a high-protein version with Greek yogurt that didn't spike Sammy's blood sugar and was just stirring together the batter when her favorite Temptations song popped up in her playlist. She turned it up and began washing the berries, melting butter, and mixing the batter as she sang.

"More than any—" She spun around with the spatula as her mike and stopped short.

"Please, go on," Davis drawled. Leaning one broad shoulder against the doorframe, he looked entirely too sexy for nine o'clock in the morning. His face was scruffy with a day-old beard, and he looked rugged and sleepy. She thought he was the most handsome man she had ever seen.

"Must you do that?" She sagged weakly against the counter, telling herself it was just surprise that made her legs tremble.

"Sorry," he said, not looking sorry at all.

She turned back to the stove. "How are you doing after that late night? Your old bones must be feeling it today."

He raised an eyebrow. "I didn't hear you complaining about my old bones last night."

She ignored him and rose on tiptoe, opening the cabinet for a mug. She hopped a few times to reach them before the heat of his body was at her back. A big arm reached up and took out the mug. "This what you need?"

Did she ever. Lust shot through her, magnified a million times now that she knew exactly what that hard body felt like between her legs, and she controlled a shiver. "Mm-hmm." She nodded and felt the bun on top of her head tease the whiskers on his chin.

He turned her around gently by the shoulders. "Can we talk?"

He looked so serious, so somber that she had a sinking feeling she knew what he was going to say.

"How about later? Sammy will be home soon—"

The front door burst open and slammed into the wall. Davis winced.

"Mommy, I'm home!" Sammy raced toward her in a blur of limbs and wrapped her in a hug before turning and spotting Davis. "Davis!" he shouted excitedly. "You're here too!"

"Hi, Sammy, how was your sleepover?" Davis asked as Sammy bounded over to give him the same big hug.

"We had a wonderful time, didn't we, darling boy?" Annette said from the doorway, flanked by all the aunts. The four of them looked at the scene before them with varying expressions of delight and surprise. Except for Annette. Her face was impassive. Allie knew how cozy the scene looked, however incorrect. Both up early in the kitchen, cooking together, drinking coffee after a night spent together.

"Hi, Mom. Hi, aunties." She went over to kiss each of them on their perfumed cheeks. "You're here early." She turned with a sigh and introduced Davis. "Mom, I think you've met Davis Henderson, and Davis, these are my aunts, Sophia, Rosa, and Giulia."

She had no idea how Davis would respond to her family. Corbin had tried his best to ignore them as if her humble roots would rub off on him. But she wasn't making that mistake twice. Her family could be a little much, true, but they came with her and Sammy.

At least it was too early for drinking.

"We brought mimosas!" Sophia said, her eyes twinkling.

Alcohol. Yay.

"Hello, dear. I hope we're not interrupting anything." Aunt Rosa kissed her cheek.

"Nope, not at all. Zero interrupting. Not a thing going on here." Allie waved a hand breezily. "Davis was just heading outside to mow. Don't let us hold you up, Davis," she said pointedly.

Here's your chance to escape. Better take it.

He settled more comfortably next to her against the counter and raised his eyebrows like a challenge. "No hurry. Pancakes smell pretty good," he said, sniffing appreciatively.

He took the spatula out of her hand.

She snatched it back. "I'm sure you have to get back home soon," she said, budging him out of the way with her hip. He didn't move.

"Don't be silly. Please stay and eat, Davis. We've heard so much about you." Rosa tittered and hustled over to the counter to wrestle the spatula out of Allie's hand. What was up with women wanting to feed him, Allie thought, exasperated.

Sophia and Giulia swooped in and started taking out plates and silverware, blatantly eyeing Davis while Annette and Sammy sat down with a coloring book and colored pencils.

"Plenty of food for a big man like yourself," said Giulia, looking him over appreciatively as she poured orange juice and a generous amount of champagne into glasses. He grinned at her, and Allie's eyebrows shot up. That was easy.

"Don't flirt with Allie's man, Giulia. It's rude," Sophia chastised. "But you do look like a man that enjoys a meal. You remind me of my boyfriend," she said admiringly.

Allie choked back a laugh. Sophia's boyfriend was the sixty-five-old captain of the Northfield Fire Department. They had met at singles night at the bingo hall, and Sophia liked to over-share about his sexual prowess.

"Here, come sit down and let me get you a coffee. Allie, get the man a mug!" she barked, leading Davis to the table.

"He can get his own mug, Auntie," Allie called, getting more plates from the cupboard. She snuck little glances at Davis whenever she could. Something was different about him this morning, but she couldn't put her finger on what.

"Is that any way to take care of your man, Allie?" Giulia

tutted, taking the seat next to Davis and leaning over to reveal an impressive amount of cleavage. Feminists the aunts were not.

"Cheers." Sophia held up a glass and took a long drink. "Tell us all about yourself, Davis," she said, stopping just short of stroking his arm.

"I'd rather hear about you," Davis said, meeting Allie at the cupboard. "Allie speaks so highly of you all," he said over his shoulder, taking the stack of dishes out of her hands.

"You had your chance to leave," Allie muttered under her breath.

He winked at her.

"Oh, he even knows his way around the kitchen!" Giulia clasped her hands together under her chin and blinked her eyes as if Davis had solved world hunger. Allie crossed her eyes at him and turned around to cut a cantaloupe as she listened to the aunts fawn over Davis.

"Sammy just thinks the world of you, and of course, our Allie told us how helpful you've been around the house," Rosa said from the stove.

"He's the landlord, Auntie," Allie called, exasperated. "It's his job. Let's not hand out medals quite yet."

"John never did anything around the house," Giulia said, pouring another shot into her glass. "Davis is much more helpful, isn't he, Annette?" she asked pointedly. Annette didn't look up from the coloring book.

"It's good to see you again, Annette." Davis set a plate in front of her.

"Mmm," Annette murmured. "Did you want to show me your new bike, Sammy?"

"Yesth, Mimi," he mumbled around a piece of fruit. "Come outside, and I'll show you." He led her out the back door toward the garage.

So, that went well.

"Well," Giulia said brightly, "breakfast looks like it will be a few more minutes, right, Allie?" Without waiting for an answer, she turned to Davis. "Davis, Allie tells me you can fix *anything*. My car started making a noise on the way over here. Would you mind taking a look?" she asked, blinking her eyelashes so rapidly Allie wondered if something was stuck in her eye.

"I could do that," he said easily.

"Oh, would you?" She grabbed his arm delightedly.

Sophia jumped up. "Cars have always fascinated me." Allie knew she was lying through her teeth. Sophia was just determined not to let her twin get prime alone time with Davis. "I get so dizzy sometimes. My vertigo, you know? Mind if I hold your arm?" She wrapped her hand around the thickest part of Davis's other arm, nestling it into her boobs.

"Breakfast will be ready in ten minutes," Allie called to their backs.

Davis looked back with wide eyes. She grinned and waved. He was in for a wild ride with Sophia and Giulia.

"If you don't want him, I'm sure they would take him off your hands," Rosa said, wiping her hands on a dishtowel and coming to stand next to her at the stove. The aunts' voices rose and fell from the driveway: *You make it look* so *easy, Davis! Oh, my, you must be so* strong *to lift that.*

"I think they've already started," Allie said dryly, watching through the window as Davis leaned over the hood to look at the engine while the aunts leaned over and looked at something else appreciatively.

"Are you upset about your mother?" Rosa asked more seriously.

"No, I'm not upset. I know she's just worried about me." Allie paused. "He didn't spend the night, you know."

Rosa shrugged. "You're a grown woman capable of making your own decisions."

"I don't feel very capable. I'm falling in love with him, but I'm not sure he's on the same page," she said glumly.

"He will be," Rosa murmured knowingly. "He's scared."

"Probably." Allie poked at the bubbles in the pancake.

"He must have loved his wife very much. He doesn't want to get close to anyone and risk losing them again."

"I know." Allie sighed.

"I can't blame him for that. But the heart is a funny thing. The more you deny it, the more of a fuss it makes." Her aunt patted her hand. "Don't give up on him. He just needs a little time to wrap his head around it."

"Around what?"

Rosa poked her in the forehead. "Turning his sign on again."

Later that morning as she listened to the aunts flirt with Davis, she realized what was different about Davis.

He wasn't wearing his wedding ring.

Davis handed Sophia into her car a little later, absently rubbing at the lipstick on his cheek where she had kissed him goodbye. He had a sneaking suspicion he had a matching one on the other cheek from Giulia.

Aunt Rosa hugged him tightly when she left. He saw immediately where Allie's tender heart came from. They both smiled with their whole heart right in their eyes. People like that were rare. At that instant, even more than last night, he knew he was making the right decision. A feeling of peace settled over him, quieting the fear.

He wanted her to smile at him like that again.

Allie had been wary this morning when he got there. He didn't blame her. Last night had set them on fire in a way they could either grab onto with both hands or begin separating their lives. There would be no in-between with them. Not with the way he felt.

He had received no warm goodbye from Annette. She was as coolly polite as ever when they ran into each other on work-sites. Her company came in to measure and consult while Davis and his work crew were building. Davis had always admired her professionalism. She wasn't exactly a warm bundle of sunshine like her eldest daughter, but she hadn't run him off from her daughter and grandson with a pitchfork either.

To his utter surprise, Davis had felt surprisingly... at home around Allie's family. Had it been even six months ago, he would have probably left as soon as he saw the speculating looks the aunts were giving them, but he hadn't felt anxious at all. It was hard to feel anything other than comfortable with the amount of life in Allie's house. He'd watched the way she brought the house to life after she moved in. How she was with Sammy and how she brought out the laughter so easily from Ben and Claire. He wanted to absorb all that, so he pulled up a chair to the table with her family. That choice felt like the easiest one he'd made in a long, long time.

"Hey." He took a seat next to Allie on the porch steps. She had her hands behind her, her face tilted toward the sun. For all her relaxed pose, he saw a tension in her body that he wanted to soothe. He hadn't exactly left them in the best spot last night, but he was ready to fix that now.

"Hey," she replied. "Sammy, knock first!" she called over to Sammy, who was walking up Mrs. Autovino's driveway.

"He's grown so much since you moved here," Davis observed.

"I know. Corbin's coming to town this weekend. He's going to be shocked at how big he is."

An unpleasant jab shot through Davis at her ex-husband's name. He would never understand how a man could let go of his wife and kid for another woman, but he was happy for Sammy's sake that his father was in his life. The kid had a special place in his heart.

"So, you survived meeting the aunts." Allie rolled her head to look at him. "Aunt Sophia might ask you out. She thinks you look like a Viking."

He smiled crookedly, and Allie's gaze lingered at his mouth then lifted to his face where he met her gaze steadily. All the unsatisfied desire from last night flared hotly between them. Feeling her last night, touching her body in ways he had been thinking about since he met her, flooded him. Now he knew what her skin tasted like. He knew how slick and wet she got under his hands and the little whimper she made when he used his teeth and tongue on her neck.

"I like your family. I can see where you get it from," he said.

"Get what?"

He leaned over, close enough that Allie had to tilt her head back to see him. "Your feistiness," he said. "Your independence" —he grinned wickedly—"and... other attributes." His eyes made a lazy trail up and down her body and stopped on her chest.

She blinked at him for a full ten seconds. "Are you flirting with me?"

He nodded slowly, holding her eyes.

"Oh."

"That okay with you?"

"Mm-hmm," she whispered. Then the brightest, warmest grin spread over her face.

There's my sunshine girl.

"Good." He reached up and tucked a strand of hair behind her ear. It fell out again immediately. This time when he pushed it back, he let his fingers linger on her satin skin before cupping her chin and turning her face up to him. "Allie, I need to tell you something."

She swallowed hard, the sweet look in her eyes dimming, and he couldn't have that. He leaned over and looked her hard in the eyes. "I went home last night and thought about what we have."

"You did?" she whispered. He couldn't resist brushing a quick kiss on her mouth. Her lips were pink and parted, and he wanted to stay there for the afternoon, but he knew he didn't have much time before Sammy came back.

"Yeah, sweetheart, I did. I thought about how lucky I am that a woman like you came into my life when it felt like it would be dark forever."

"Davis," she whispered, but he kept going.

"Let me just get this out, honey, because when you look at me like that, all I can think about is kissing you."

"Go on," she said then, laughing softly and turning pink. He leaned over and pressed another kiss to her nose. God, he loved when she turned pink.

"I can't promise I won't be a cranky son of a bitch, and I'm never gonna be okay with you leaving the doors unlocked or doing shit that could get you hurt, but I'd be the biggest idiot around if I didn't do my best to try to make you happy. You're like the sunshine, Allie. You make things brighter, and when you're gone, I can't stop thinking about when I can see you shining again."

He had more to say, but he didn't get a chance because Allie threw herself into his arms. She dropped kisses on his jaw and cheeks and finally, finally, his mouth. He closed his hungrily over hers, yanking her closer until she poked him in the forehead with a finger. Hard. "Shit. What was that?"

She poked him again, but softer this time, and followed it up with a kiss on his hard jaw. "You turned your sign on."

He caught her finger and held on, looking at her suspiciously. "What?"

"Never mind. Kiss me again before Sammy comes back." She laughed.

"Thank God." He let out a whoosh of air, pulled her into his arms, and then lowered his mouth to hers, kissing her until they both couldn't breathe.

Chapter Twenty-Three

Sunday

UNKNOWN NUMBER

I hate tExting. Thumbs are too bIG for this
keyboard.

ALLIE

Davis? Is that you?

DAVIS

YeS.

ALLIE

Is everything okay?

DAVIS

YeS.

ALLIE

Okay…

DAVIS

DiD u lock the door?

ALLIE

Come over and find out...

DAVIS

Kids h0mE

ALLIE

Send me a nude so I know it's you.

DAVIS

Hanging up Now.

ALLIE

It's a text, old man. You can't hang up.

Tuesday

DAVIS

U look PreTty 2day

ALLIE

Are you stalking me?

DAVIS

Saw u @ drop off. Luv when you wear yellow.

ALLIE

Why didn't you come into the nurse's office?

DAVIS

Had Walter with me. Got 2 go to WorK. Claire
taught me 2 text. :)

Wednesday

DAVIS

At Claire's gymnastics thing. Layne said she
would take all 3 kids Friday. Can I take u to
dinner?

> **ALLIE**
>
> Yes! What time?

DAVIS

6

> **ALLIE**
>
> I'll be ready. What should I wear?

DAVIS

The red dress if you want to kill me.

> **ALLIE**
>
> RIP xoxo

"Stop, look, and listen," Allie called out to Sammy on Thursday night before they crossed the street to the baseball field. They were early for practice tonight, but Davis and Ben were already climbing out of their truck. Cars pulled into the parking lot, spilling out boys in baseball uniforms with their bats and gloves ready.

She spotted Keri and Rachel spreading out a blanket next to second base and waved. She had been hesitant at first, but Keri and Rachel would have none of that. They were wickedly funny and completely happy to open their circle to her, which Allie was settling into nicely.

Tomorrow night was her first date with Davis, and she planned to ask him about how open they were going to be with... well, whatever they were working on. She knew Davis avoided dating people in Northfield, and while she wasn't going to be anyone's secret, she could understand if he wanted to take this slow, especially around his friends. They had all loved Mel.

Ben raced over and threw his arms around Allie's waist, nearly knocking her over. She hugged him back. "Hi, Allie!"

"Hiya, Ben."

"Hi!" Exact replicas of Davis's warm eyes looked up at her adoringly. What a charmer. "Me and my dad and my sister are going camping next weekend, and we want you and Ben to come." He had said it so fast the words ran together. Allie had to take a minute to process it while Davis walked up.

"Hi, Davis," she said, studying him from under her lashes greedily. His dark hair under the baseball cap was longer than it had been when they met, and his face was darkened with a five-o'clock shadow. He looked edible, entirely too sexy for a Thursday night.

"Yeah, Mom, can we? Please?" Sammy latched onto her other side and begged. "They're going to fish and have a fire and do fun stuff. You said we could go camping, and if we go with them, you won't have to put the tent up by yourself." The boys looked at each other, and a mental high five was exchanged.

"Hey, I know how to put a tent up." Okay, so she had never put one up before, but Sammy didn't know that. It couldn't be that hard. And starting a fire? Pssh. She could figure it out.

"Okay," Sammy said, sounding doubtful. "But when you tried to put my bookcase back together you said the really bad word when you couldn't do it. The *really* bad one. The one that costs a dollar."

Ben looked interested. "Which one? My dad hit his thumb with a hammer once and yelled fuc—"

Davis clamped his hand down on his son's mouth firmly.

"Take your bags to the dugout, boys, and then start running the bases to warm up." The boys took off, laughing like the little menaces they were. Allie looked up to see Davis looking at her teasingly.

"The F word, huh?" he asked with one eyebrow raised. "I've heard your bad words before. Son of a *biscuit*, I believe you shouted at that cone. What's your big, bad F word? Fudge?"

"It slipped," she said, continuing to walk.

"What did? Which word? Whisper it in my ear. Was it frick? Funk? Freak?" A wolfish grin spread across his face, making her belly do that flip-flop thing again. "You can't even say it without blushing."

She shoved him, which felt much like hitting a giant rock. "Moving on. I don't want to crash your camping trip. I'm perfectly capable of putting up a tent." She would be having a discussion with Sammy later about telling all her secrets.

"You should come."

She stopped walking. He continued. "Seriously?" she half yelled. "You want this worm pacifist and her oversharing son to join you guys for a fishing trip?"

"Yup," he said. *So many words with this man.*

"I'm so proud of you, by the way. Text messaging is so twenty-first century."

"I don't know how people type on those little things," Davis said with a frown.

"It's called communication, you Neanderthal." She snickered.

He stopped so abruptly, she walked right into his chest. She stayed there for one blissful minute when his arms came around her. His arms tightened, and she gave in to the urge, nuzzling her face in his chest. "You smell so good," she whispered into his warm chest.

"Look! They're K-I-S-S-I-N-G," a chorus of little boys sang. Allie jumped and dropped her arms guiltily. A sea of boys' faces were pressed against the chain-link fence watching them.

"Nope, no kissing here, boys," she said firmly. "Coach Henderson had a boo-boo that I was fixing. Remember? I'm a nurse." She thumped Davis' rock-hard chest. "Yep, right here, but I fixed it." She nodded.

"Doesn't look like there's a boo-boo there," Ben said doubtfully.

"Yeah, I don't see nuthin'," echoed a few more voices.

"You can kiss my mom," Sammy announced. "That always makes me feel better," he added seriously.

"Do you need another hug, Coach?" Toby called out, grinning as he walked over with Ford. All eyes were on them now. Allie tried to slink away. So much for being discreet.

A heavy arm settled over her shoulders and dragged her back against a solid chest. "Yup," Davis drawled. "I think I do." He wrapped his big arms around her and lifted her off her feet in a massive, theatrical squeeze. Her Converses swung merrily as the boys let out whoops. Davis set her down slowly and gave her one hell of a smokin' hot grin.

"Well..." She patted her hair. "Okay. Well. I'll let you boys get to practice." She gave him one last bemused look before edging out of the dugout and heading toward Keri and Rachel, who were not even pretending not to have seen every moment of their interaction.

"Just practicing first aid," she said as nonchalantly as she could, dropping down on the blanket beside Kari and fanning her flaming face discreetly.

"Mm-hmm," Keri said with a knowing smile. "It saves lives."

Chapter Twenty-Four

DAVIS ARRIVED at her door promptly at six for their dinner date, dressed in dark slacks and a crisp button-down, his thick hair combed, and no trace of a tool belt or hat in sight. Her mouth did that funny thing where it moved, and no sound came out when she answered the door. It would have been funny except that Davis was staring at her just as hungrily.

Davis picked her favorite Greek place that overlooked the canal, but when he opened the door of the truck to hand her out, she paused with her hand in his.

"You know what people are going to say when we go in there together for dinner, right?" she asked carefully. If he wanted to keep this under wraps for now, this wasn't the place to do it.

"Do you want to go somewhere else?" he asked, studying her face.

"No," she said quietly. "Do you?"

He handed her out of the truck and squeezed her waist. "This is where I want to be."

He meant it too. He walked into the restaurant with his arm tight around her, making a point to stop and chat with people he knew, which were quite a few. Northfield, Allie could see, thought as highly of Davis as she did. People asked his opinion about matters or asked about his kids and siblings, and seemed to genuinely care about him. Not hard to do, she knew from experience.

At first, Allie hung back, watching to see if anyone that knew Mel would look at them with disapproval, but all she saw were people that genuinely respected and cared about Davis. When Davis noticed her hesitance, he slid his warm hand into hers and squeezed reassuringly. He made sure there was no mistaking that they were on a date. He held out her chair, brushing a kiss on her temple when she sat.

Her heart was near to bursting with how perfect the night was.

As perfect as it was, there was another place she really wanted to be. Her dress felt too tight on her skin, the satin fabric of her bra like sandpaper on her nipples, which were pebbled and aching.

When the waiter came with the dessert menu, she set it down impatiently. Davis glanced at his menu then raised an eyebrow at her.

"If we leave right now," she said evenly, looking at her watch, "we'd have thirty-seven minutes alone before your sister drops the kids off at my house."

Davis dropped a handful of cash on the table and pulled her through the restaurant fast enough to make her dizzy.

～

She was on his lap again.

This time it was her living room couch, and it was quickly turning into her favorite place. From the look on Davis's face, it was also his.

"Oh, fuck." Davis gasped as she ground down harder on his cock. As soon as they had walked in the door, they landed on her couch. His eyes were darker than she had ever seen them, narrowed on her face as she looked down at him. She gripped his wide shoulders and rocked harder while Davis gritted his teeth. Hot honey slid through her body, warm and slow, when he looked at her like that. She leaned over and nipped his ear.

"I knew we should have stayed in for dinner," she teased. Then she gasped when Davis sat up abruptly and tossed her onto her back on the couch. She bounced on the stack of pillows and almost tipped over, but Davis grabbed her while tossing the pillows to the floor.

"How many of these are there?" he muttered, tossing another one behind him.

She started to laugh, but it caught in her throat. He rose over her, shoulders wide enough that he blocked out the light coming from the lamp by the couch. He gripped her knees, spreading them open until her dress was bunched around her hips. *Oh, my.* His expression was feral, his hard jaw taut while he took her in, lingering for long, intense seconds at the scrap of black silk between her thighs while she tried not to pant. Then the weight of his body settled into her hips, hot and solid between her thighs. He leaned down, braced his forearms on either side of her head, and nuzzled her neck with his nose.

"This okay?" he murmured.

"More than okay," she whispered back, testing the weight of him with a swivel of her hips. He followed her hips with a thrust that left no mistake that he was as aroused as she. She wrapped her legs around his and took hold of his wrists as he lowered his head to hers. His mouth was gentle this time, pressing kisses to the sides of her mouth, moving down her chin, nipping there, and sucking gently. The rasp of his stubble was a delicious contrast to the silky slide of his tongue on her throat.

Her breath came fast between them, and she let out a whimper. "Davis..." she cried when he tilted her chin up to taste her. He didn't stop, laving and taking tiny nibbles of her collarbone and moving back up to her mouth until she was writhing beneath him. Finally, he cupped her face and looked her hard in the eyes before settling his mouth on hers again. His tongue swept inside her mouth, silky and hot, playing with hers until she was gasping, undulating underneath him.

"Sweetheart," he growled. "We've got to stop. The kids will be here in fifteen minutes."

"We can make it quick," she husked, pulling him back down. He resisted, sitting back on the couch and tugging her up next to him. Allie closed her eyes and blew out a deep breath, willing her body to cool down.

"I don't want quick," he said roughly, but the side of his mouth was crooked up. "I want to take my time with you." Her breathing quickened as she thought about where else she wanted Davis wanted to kiss her.

"Love when you pink up like that, sweetheart," he murmured, pulling her against him for another hard, fast kiss that left her fighting to catch her breath.

"I've never been kissed like this before," she mused, staring at his mouth.

He drew away with an eyebrow raised. "Never?"

"Actually, I'm not positive. Can we try again, so I can be sure?"

Davis laughed, the sound strained. "This is new for me too."

"Did you and Natalie ever...?" She held her breath.

He opened his eyes and pierced her with a look. "We never had sex. It wasn't like that between us," he said firmly.

"I know you think that, but Natalie cares about you." She twisted until she faced him and rested her palms on his face. "You're an easy man to care about," she said quietly, and then because it was very close to revealing how much she felt, she added lightly, "and an absolute rock star at making out."

Davis caught her wrist in one hand. "I haven't had sex with anyone since Mel."

Her heart stuttered. "No one?"

He shook his head slowly. "No one I wanted to do this with," he said, brushing the hair off her face and tucking it behind her ear.

"I haven't been with anyone either, in over a year," she told him. A possessive look swept Davis's face. He grasped her chin and brought his face up to hers.

"Good," he murmured, covering her mouth with his just as a car door slammed outside. Davis got up and held out his hand. "Come on, let's go get our kids."

Our kids. Her heart absolutely trembled.

Layne, Sammy, Ben, and Claire were getting out of the car when another car parked on the curb in front of her house. They all turned to see who it was, but Allie knew. The sleek, back sports car matched her old one. She sighed. "It's Corbin," she said to Davis.

"Dad?" Sammy called out when the tall blond man got out and walked toward them. "Dad, you're here?" Davis stiffened next to her.

"Of course, I'm here. I had to see my boy's last game of the season." Corbin held out his arms to Sammy. Corbin's smile was frosty above Sammy while he eyed Davis.

She might as well get this over with. "Hello, Corbin." Allie made her way down the steps. "I wasn't expecting you until Sunday."

"I have a meeting tomorrow, so I thought I'd drive down early," Corbin said, his eyes missing nothing. "I hope I'm not interrupting your plans. Is this the baseball coach you've been telling me about, son?" he asked, eyeing Davis.

Allie froze, not knowing what to say, but Davis thrust out his hand. The two of them shook hard, eyes locked on each other.

"Davis Henderson," Davis said coolly. "Sammy's a great player. We're lucky to have him on the team."

Sammy gave Davis a quick grin before turning back to Corbin. "This is Layne, and these are my best friends, Ben and Claire." Sammy introduced them all proudly.

"Pleasure to meet you. I'll take these two home, Davis," Layne said. "See you in a while." She hugged Allie and Sammy then rounded up Ben and Claire to the car.

"How long are you here for, Dad?"

"That depends on your mother, son. I've missed you both." Corbin smiled blandly and settled one hand on Allie's shoulder and one on Sammy's. Davis stiffened.

Allie managed to keep a civil face. "Sammy, why don't you show your dad inside while I say goodbye to Davis?"

"Yeah, Dad, come see our new house!" Sammy said, racing inside the house ahead of Corbin. He was so happy to see his dad that some of her irritation eased. No matter what, she needed to remember they loved each other, and she wanted Sammy to have his dad around.

"Wouldn't miss it," Corbin said on his way up the stairs. He stopped when he was at the top and looked down at Davis. "Thanks for keeping an eye on my wife and son. We've had some rough patches, but I intend to be around more. A lot more." Corbin gave Davis a thin-lipped smile, and Allie was back to irritated. Blazing angry.

"I'd say that's up to Allie," Davis said easily enough, but the muscle in his jaw flexed.

"We're a family," Corbin said. "I'm sure you understand this will take some time."

"Your idea of family and my idea of family must be different. Mine doesn't include fucking the babysitter," Davis said evenly.

"Okay, inside you go." She all but shoved Corbin through the front door and turned back down the stairs to Davis.

His jaw was ticking. She reached up and rubbed it. "Are you okay?" he asked.

"Yeah, I'll text you later. Still on for the Apple Festival tomorrow?"

Davis studied her silently, his dark eyes roving her face before he finally nodded, as if satisfied she could do this on her own. "Wouldn't miss it," he murmured. He kissed her temple and turned to go.

ONE HOUR and two Advil later, Allie was not convinced she could handle anything at all. Her head ached from tension, and she was acutely aware of Sammy and Corbin's soft laughter coming from upstairs where Corbin was reading to him in bed. Each one of Sammy's giggles felt like it was tearing her heart in half with the old, heavy weight of guilt.

Had she made the right decision?

Should she have tried harder to mend things with Corbin for Sammy's sake?

Had she been selfish by leaving her son's father?

Self-flagellation was fun.

She picked up the pillows Davis had tossed off the couch, remembering the look on his face. Guilt swamped her again. She had been so happy tonight. The happiest she had been in a long time, but seeing Sammy with Corbin made that hint of guilt grow. That old chill, the one she hadn't felt in months, blew through her, and she shivered.

She was surprised to see Corbin show up tonight, but not

shocked. Corbin liked to do things in his own way. She knew he had arrived late on purpose so she would have to invite him to stay over with them. All the feelings she had spent months working through had flooded her when she saw his car pull up.

Shock. Anger. Sadness.

Yes, even after a failed marriage, a part of her would always care about him. She had tried so damn hard to make their marriage work. For Sammy's sake. And for hers, too, if she was being honest. He was her first love and the father of her only child. Even his sleeping with Dahlia wouldn't change that.

Ah, so complicated. Her head throbbed again.

Their marriage hadn't been anywhere close to perfect. That was laughable, especially as she pictured how it had ended, but she didn't hate Corbin either. It was more complex than that.

"He's out like a light," Corbin said.

She turned and saw him leaning against the doorway. He held a bottle of expensive red wine. Her favorite.

"I brought this from home. I'll get us some glasses."

Allie sat still and, for a minute, remembered many nights just like this one. Corbin putting Sammy to bed and coming down the hall with a bottle of wine to share. She remembered quiet nights on the couch. Sometimes Corbin would lay his head in her lap while they watched a show together. It hadn't all been bad.

"So, this is your new place," Corbin said, taking a seat next to her on the couch. He looked around curiously. "It's very... colorful."

He wore his usual weekend outfit, expensive, perfectly pressed jeans and a camel-colored cashmere sweater she had bought him last Christmas. She hadn't given it to him until the following week because he had been out of town. Actually, she had never seen him wear it. She hadn't even thought he liked it, but he had it on today. His dark-blond hair was cut stylishly, and the same swoop Sammy had was gelled back from his high forehead, making his blue eyes stand out. Objectively speaking, Corbin was a very handsome man.

He turned to her and gave her dress a slow once-over. "You look beautiful, Allison. I've never seen you wear anything like this before."

It didn't fit his image of her. Her earlier nostalgia gave way, and she remembered the many more nights she had been home alone. The wine stayed corked in the fridge, the monitor sat next to her as she sat by herself in their cold apartment while he worked late, and she kept her unhappiness quiet until she felt like she'd shatter from the loneliness. Anger replaced nostalgia.

Divorce was confusing.

"My name is Allie," she said quietly.

"What?"

"My name is Allie, not Allison," she said more firmly.

Corbin started to say something and stopped. Took a deep breath and started again. "I get it. Allie. I think we've both changed over the last six months," he said. "I want my family back together."

She almost looked behind her. Surely she was being punked? "I'm sorry. Have you been drinking? I'm not the one that gave up our family."

His lips tightened, but he reached for her hand. Corbin's hands were beautiful. Long fingers, neatly trimmed nails, not a callus to be seen.

"I've been doing a lot of thinking since you left, and I want to try again."

Dimly, she heard a dog barking on the sidewalk across the street, but his words didn't make sense. "Why? Why now?" she finally asked.

"Because I miss my family," he said, gripping her hand tighter. "I'm sorry," his voice was faster now, more urgent. "I'm so sorry I did that to you. I don't know what I was thinking. You and I were on different islands for so long, and I was numb. I just wanted to feel something, but I ended up making the biggest mistake of my life. It was you and Sammy that I needed. I'll spend the rest of my life making it up to you both. We can start over. You and me and Sammy. We can have another baby. I know you want more babies. We can be a family again."

More babies. She would have given her eyetooth to hear that a year ago. Now, it filled her with sadness.

He had moved closer on the couch until his thigh touched hers. His cologne was the same as when she first met him, heavy, expensive, and seductive. Suddenly, he leaned over and cupped her face with two hands, rubbing his thumbs over her cheekbones. "I miss you, Allie. Everything is wrong with you gone, and I didn't realize it until it was too late. I know I've been a shit husband. I want a chance to make up for it," he whispered.

She reached up and gently tugged his wrists until he let her go. "You left us. Everything changed after Sammy was diagnosed." A wave of grief unexpectedly rushed over her. The night Sammy was admitted to the hospital, Corbin had been away on a business trip. She had tried to contact him for hours while sitting next to Sammy's hospital bed.

He took a breath. "After Sammy came home, I could feel you pulling away from me, so I left. I started taking longer trips and volunteering to go overseas. I knew you could handle everything. You're just like your mother. You didn't need me. I know it was wrong, but I thought if I could just focus on being a good provider for you both, that was enough."

"We needed you with us."

Corbin's eyes softened. "I'm here now. I can make it up to you. We were good together until I fucked it all up."

"It wasn't all your fault. I did pull away, and you left and then had an affair, and now it's too late," she finished sadly.

"It's not too late. I still love you, baby." For the first time since she had met him, his blue eyes filled with tears when he looked at her.

"I'm not in love with you anymore. I'm sorry," she said gently. She looked at his handsome face and regret washed over her, but she let the old hurt and their old life go. She could say so much more. But what good would it do? The time for that was past.

Corbin sighed heavily and dropped his head into his hands. "Shit. Are you in love with Davis? Sammy talks about him all the time," he added bitterly.

"It's not about Davis," she said simply. "I'm a different person now. I'm not the girl you married anymore. I'm not afraid to ask for what I need. Corbin, Sammy still needs you in his life. You're his father. That will never change."

He lifted his head. "I love him to death," he said fiercely. "I'm going to be in his life. I can promise you that."

"I'm glad," she whispered, tears in her own eyes now. "I want that too."

He dropped his head into his hands, his elbows on his knees. "I'm sorry," he said finally, tipping his head to look at her. "For everything." It was the first apology from him that felt real.

"I'm sorry too."

She walked him to the door, and they stood on the front porch. "You'll be there for Sammy's game on Sunday?"

"Yes, I'll be there," Corbin said, and she could see how it would go, or at least how she hoped it would go in the future. Corbin visiting more, maybe even eventually Sammy spending a weekend with him in the city. Still so much love between them all. She wanted that, for Sammy and herself, and Corbin. It would be a gift for them all.

"You sure I can't stay here with you two?" he asked. "We could have pancakes in the mornings if I can find anything in that fridge. How much cheese can one person eat?" he asked with a frown.

She smiled. "Not a chance."

He sighed, leaned down, and brushed her cheek with a kiss. "See you on Sunday."

He headed down the stairs and paused at the old Forester in disgust. "Really? You traded in the Benz for this?"

Chapter Twenty-Five

"Want a bite, Mom?" Sammy held out the apple-cider doughnut. Allie took a bite, brushing cinnamon sugar off her fingers and looking around. Every year, the village blocked off Main Street for the Harvest Festival. The fire station and the shops handed out cider and doughnuts, and Main Street was packed with face painting and games and tents filled with local food and crafts. A cover band played oldies in the gazebo where couples danced and watched from hay bales. It was the best part of living in a small town, and one of Allie's favorite memories of living in Northfield.

"Hey, guys." Amber handed her a Styrofoam cup of hot cider then licked a drop from her cup. Her tiny blue-checkered baby-doll shirt and painted-on jeans stood out like a strobe light among all the flannel. A group of teen boys tripped over each other as they walked past. Amber gave them a saucy wink before turning back to Sammy. "Mimi's over there by the game booths with tickets." Sammy took off without a backward glance.

Amber sat on a hay bale and patted the seat next to her. A

sly grin spread on her sister's cherry-red-painted mouth. "You finally got some, didn't you?"

Allie looked around furtively. "Shhh, Mom's around here somewhere."

"Mom and the aunts," Amber agreed. "What happened to Hot Landlord's cold feet?"

"They're hot now. Very hot. Sizzling hot. He took off his ring," Allie said in a low voice.

"Good for you, Al," Amber said sincerely. "You deserve the best, and Davis is one of the best around."

"Who deserves the best?" Annette asked as she walked over. She held a plastic bag with a live goldfish in it. Oh no. She was not getting suckered into a fish.

"Mom, that better not be for us. Sammy would love to have a pet fish at *your* house," Allie said firmly. The thing looked half-dead already, which meant there would be a frantic trip to the pet store to replace it before Sammy realized the fish kicked the bucket.

"Sammy said he will take good care of it, won't you, my love?" She pinched Sammy's cheek.

"Here, Goldie. Here." Sammy tapped on the bag. *Shoot.* He'd already named it. Now she'd never get rid of it. She glared at Annette who just smiled placidly. "Mom, can I sleep over at Mimi's tonight? Mimi said it was okay."

"If it's okay with Mimi, it's okay with me," she said, waving at the aunts as they weaved through the crowd.

"Hello, Allie, you're looking very well." Rosa kissed her on the cheek, and Allie returned it, then did the same for Sophia and Giulia.

"Oh, yes, very, *very* well, Allie." Sophia winked at her, and Allie sighed. The three aunts looked like they would burst, while Annette watched Allie, a shrewd look in her eye. So the news hadn't made it to her mom yet.

"Yes, you looked so *satisfied*, my dear," Giulia twittered. "I love when I look that *satisfied*."

"Yes, well, life is good, aunties. Anyway, we'll see you guys for Sunday dinner, right?" She reached for Sammy's hand, and her sweet little obedient son shook her off and headed toward a target game where the prize was a stuffed bear the size of a twin bed. No way was she going home with a sickly fish *and* a creepy man-sized bear.

"Why are you so red right now, Allison?" Annette looked back and forth between her sisters and her daughters suspiciously. "What's going on?"

"How come no one thinks I look satisfied?" Amber sniffed. "I'm always satisfied. I make sure I'm always satisfied. It's a winning trait of mine."

"Because, dear, it's your sister's turn." Rosa patted her arm. "I can't wait to hear the details."

"What did you name it, Allie?" Sophia waggled her brows as she tore off a bite of her funnel cake and handed it to Allie.

"Name what?" Allie popped the cinnamon sugar confection into her mouth. Mmm. So good.

"His pork sword," Sophia said matter-of-factly. "Did you name it?"

She choked, and Giulia pounded on her back.

"Something with a Viking ring to it," Giulia said thoughtfully. "The berserker? Thor's hammer?"

Allie wiped the tears from her eyes and wheezed. "This is a family event."

"What's going on? Somebody fill me in." Annette looked suspiciously around the group.

A muscular arm slid around Allie's waist. "Hi, ladies." Davis leaned in and kissed her temple casually. "Hi, Allie."

"Hi," she said shyly. His warm hand squeezed her waist and tugged her closer.

"We knew you two would end up together," Rosa said. "They're so perfect for each other, aren't they, Annette?"

Allie held her breath and looked at her mom. Annette wasn't glaring. That was the first thing she noticed. Her lips were pursed though. Allie held her breath while she waited for her reaction. She was with Davis with or without Annette's approval, but she wanted the support of the woman she respected and loved most of all.

Annette's aquiline nose lifted, and for one horrible second, Allie thought she was going to turn around and walk away. Instead, she stepped forward and handed the bag with the goldfish to Davis. "Take this, and be careful with it," she said looking him in the eyes. *You'll answer to me if you don't.*

"I will," Davis said gravely, a message passing between them. *I'll take care of them.*

Annette lifted her chin. *You'd better. That's my little girl and my grandson's heart you have in your hands.*

"This is getting a little too Hallmark Channel for me," Amber cut in. She held up a red Solo cup. "I brought a flask to spike these babies. Who's in?"

An hour and a couple of hundred dollars later, Davis guided Allie towards a hay bale with the goldfish still cradled protectively in his big hand. The feel of his hand on her lower back, possessive and firm, made her shiver.

All afternoon his little teasing touches had been driving her crazy, keeping her on edge, driving her pulse to pound and her body to jolt with tiny sparks of electricity. The brush of his rough hand on hers as they walked, pulling her close to his solidness and stroking her hips while they stood in line to order funnel cakes was making her feel dizzy. Tense. Good, old-fashioned hot and bothered.

He knew exactly what he was doing to her.

Davis took a seat next to her, handing her a cup of hot cider. "I like your sweater."

She looked down at her newest purchase, a fitted, soft yellow V-neck sweater, and grinned. "Because of the cleavage?"

Davis didn't smile. "No."

"You like yellow?" she asked in confusion.

He shook his head slowly, studying her face. "Never did before."

"You do now?"

"I love it."

"Why?" She was suddenly having a hard time drawing in a full breath.

"Because it reminds me of you. You can't help but be happy when you're around it."

Oh. And there went her heart.

"I'm happy too," she finally whispered around the lump in her throat.

"I'm glad," he said gruffly. He nudged closer until their thighs pressed against each other, a slight secret touch in the middle of a crowd of people.

She cleared her throat. "Did you get my text last night?" She sent him one to let him know Corbin left for a hotel and she was going to bed.

Davis nodded. "How did it go?"

Allie took a sip of the tart drink and licked the sweetness off her lips while she thought about her answer. "Sammy was disappointed that Corbin's not staying with us, but he understands that things are different now, I think."

She smiled, watching Sammy, Ben, and Claire play charades while they waited in line at the ring toss. Maybe her heart would always hurt a little bit that it didn't work out the way she thought it would with Corbin, for Sammy's sake more than her own, but she had peace about it now. They were doing okay. *Better than okay*, she thought, watching Sammy puffing up his cheeks like a squirrel and pretending to look for nuts. "We're where we belong now."

"Yeah, you are," Davis said quietly, and a jolt of sheer happiness made her heart skip.

"Is that so?" she asked, leaning into his side.

He nodded. "Yes. That okay with you?"

She reached over to touch the hand that still curved carefully over the goldfish bag. "It's more than okay, Davis," she said softly. "It's exactly what I want."

His eyes were warm and steady on her face, and she suddenly wished they were alone so that she could show him exactly what she wanted. The message must have registered because Davis stood up abruptly, pulling her up after him.

"Let's get out of here."

"Okay, but I think he should sleep at your house." She nodded toward the bear. "Your house is bigger, and his eyes creep me out."

"I think I should sleep at your house," he said, watching her intently. Her lips parted in surprise. He leaned in quickly and swiped her bottom lip with his tongue. Quick. Hot. Burning.

"You do?" Her voice was uneven and breathy and entirely too sexy for a family festival. Well, that was his fault.

"Tonight." His voice was low and sexy, so close to her ear she felt his lips move on the sensitive area. "My parents are taking the kids."

He leaned back and raised one eyebrow. *Your move.*

She had never been more certain of anything in her life.

"I'll be ready."

Chapter Twenty-Six

WAITING for Davis to come and ravish her sounded a lot sexier than it actually was. In reality, Allie was a mess. Stomach knots, clammy hands, restless—she felt more like she was getting ready for a high-stakes interview than sexy time. Davis, for all she teased him, was older and more experienced while she was... not.

She wanted him to do all the things to her she had been imagining, but at this very moment, her lady parts were more terrified than turned on, which was really irritating. She'd just have to brazen it out because they had a whole night without kids. Who knew when that would happen again?

Nope, she was just going to have to fake confidence and hope he didn't catch on. Because this was happening. She had her best panties on and everything.

She had taken a shower when she got home, taking extra time to use lotion. She had put on a pretty matching panty-and-bra set with shaking hands, fixed her hair and makeup, and then sat down on the bed in her wrapper to wait. It felt dumb, and not like her at all. So she got dressed again and headed for the kitchen, where she tied on her apron. Baking was always calming. Besides, she had brought home a thirty-pound crate of New York's finest Empire apples.

She queued up Dusty Springfield's "Son of a Preacher Man" and soon the kitchen filled with Dusty singing while she peeled and sliced apples and mused about the sensuality of music and food. Her hips swayed softly, and she got lost in the lyrics as she thought about what was going to happen.

Her hands slid into the flour and let the softness sift through her fingers. The butter warmed and molded to her fingers as she worked it into the dough and thought about gripping strong shoulders, kneading the muscle and bone that had tempted her for so long. She was licking her thumb, tasting the sweet sugar and cinnamon and the bite of fresh lemon juice just as the kitchen door opened.

Davis walked in on a rush of crisp air, a few stray leaves fluttering in with him, and stood looking at her. His eyes were watchful and, if she didn't know him so well, she would have turned around and run at what she saw there. She took in his tall form. His gray thermal clung to every solid muscle of his chest. It was his eyes, though, that made her belly clench hard. Turned on Davis was direct, hungry, almost predatory. She swallowed hard.

"I... I'm making an apple pie," she said, and her voice came out exactly how she felt inside. Hot and quivery.

He held her eyes steadily as he walked toward her.

She backed up a step.

He followed.

She backed up again, her spine pressed tight against the counter, and her breath caught in her throat.

"Wa-want a taste?" She held out a sugared apple from the bowl. There was no help for it. The man had her so worked up she couldn't think straight. She was dizzy and hot and kind of needed to sit down.

Their entire relationship had been one deliciously long bout of foreplay, and it was finally coming to an end. The entire afternoon he had teased her, handling her waist, stroking her neck, and running his thumb down her palm. All so innocent in public, but he had known exactly what he was doing to her.

Allie's breath hitched when his arms caged her in against the counter, and his big body pushed into hers until she felt his heat surround her. She filled her lungs. Soap and pure aroused male. He filled her senses now just like the first time they had stood together like this, in her kitchen months ago.

"I do want a taste," he murmured, catching her hand in his. Instead of taking the apple she held, he licked a hot line down her palm, licking the sweet juices from the apples and sugar. She felt every single one of the sugar crystals press into her skin as his tongue rubbed lazily against her, sucking, licking, and tasting as he held her gaze. It was the single most erotic thing Allie had ever experienced in her life. Apple pie would never have the same meaning again, she thought faintly.

"Oh," she whispered as his tongue did something particularly filthy. She wanted to feel him do that again. Everywhere. She arched her back, lifting her breasts toward him, begging for attention. Her nipples were aching points pressed against her bra.

Large hands gripped her waist and lifted her onto the kitchen table. Blindly, she reached for his neck and twined her arms around him as he settled between her spread thighs and pressed the full, hot length of him against her belly. The seam of her jeans rubbed against her panties unbearably until she wanted to rip them both off.

"You...." He moved closer and swept aside her hair, finding her neck with that sinful tongue. "... taste..." He gave her a tender kiss on her jaw. "... so..." Following a sharp nip, sharp enough to feel down to her toes. His tongue soothed the tiny mark. "... fucking delicious."

At last, his mouth settled on hers. Softly at first, he tasted her. Deeper and wetter, he stroked into her as the kiss turned biting and demanding. His hands kneaded her hips, pressing her tightly against the thick bulge in his jeans until she rocked softly against him, thankful for the sturdy table beneath her.

"Allie," he whispered in her ear.

"Hmm?"

"Lift your arms, sweetheart." He yanked her sweater over her head in one quick pull, and the cool air touched her bare shoulders. He growled when she leaned back, his eyes devouring her breasts offered up to him so innocently in the pink satin-and-lace set.

She felt the barest second of shyness while he studied her, but when he dragged his hands up and stopped at the sides of her breasts, it floated away at the pure lust on his face.

"So beautiful," he murmured, his thumbs stroking the tender undersides, feeling their weight, plumping them together until she felt crazy with need.

"Davis, let me..." She started to put her arms behind her back to undo her bra when he caught them behind her, arching her back and keeping her chest up and offered to him.

"Let me," he said roughly. He dipped his face into the deep cleavage of her bra and then backed off to nuzzle one eager nipple as she felt the clasp on her bra open. He pulled back and watched as her breasts released from the cups and fell free.

She leaned up and placed soft kisses at the corners of his mouth. "Touch me."

"Like this?" he drawled, bringing her hand with the sugared apple slice still in it to her nipple. She gasped and looked down, her mouth parted at the sensation of cold fruit meeting her hot skin. He used her hand to draw a circle around the straining tip, leaving sugar and cinnamon in his wake. Her nipple drew up tight, sending shivers skittering up and down her spine. Just when she wanted to scream, he closed his mouth tightly over the peak and sucked it into his mouth.

Holy mother of—The air whooshed out of her lungs, and her hands instinctively held onto the sides of his head while he sucked the sugar off her. She drew her knees up on either side of his body, clinging to him, as he licked and sucked a leisurely path from one breast to another.

She let out another whimper when his mouth left her and a hand cupped the back of her head, guiding her back down to the table.

"Wait," she said, coming up on her elbows and plucking at his shirt. There was no way she was missing a second of the Davis Henderson show. "Take this off."

He reached back with one hand and hauled the thermal over his head, tossing it aside. Her eyes didn't know where to settle as each new inch of skin was exposed.

Davis's body was a study of hard work. Small scars and nicks dotted his hands and forearms, which were corded with muscle. An image of him slowly rolling his sleeves up over his forearms while she watched flashed through her mind, and suddenly she had a new fantasy. They were that good.

His chest was wide and powerful, still lightly bronzed from the summer, narrowing down to his waist and hard stomach. The hair around his nipples was coarser than the hair on his head, and it got lighter as it disappeared into his waistband. She wanted in there too.

When she reached out, he grasped her hips and hauled her to the edge of the table. Then he settled on the chair in front of her.

"What are you doing?" she asked nervously, but she knew. She absolutely knew.

"Tasting you," he growled. Then he slid his hands under her bottom, pushed up her apron, and tugged down her jeans. He lifted her easily, which gave her a secret thrill. She liked—no, she *loved*—rough Davis. He looked dangerous, with his eyes bright and his cheeks flushed, as he moved her where he wanted with a casual dominance that made every part of her body light up like a carnival ride.

Oh, my.

Davis had two thumbs hooked under her panties when she stopped him. "You don't have to do that," she whispered, trailing her hands along his shoulders.

His hands paused, and he sat back. "Do you want me to stop?"

"No." Nope, definitely not. "It's just that you don't have to do that." She waved vaguely between them and pressed another kiss to his lips. She would never get tired of kissing his lips. His five-o'clock shadow was dark on his jaw, and she gave in to the impulse to run her tongue along the rough surface.

He considered her for a second then tucked his thumbs back under the elastic on either side of her hips and tugged. "Sweetheart, I can't think of anything I want more right now than to taste your pussy."

Dead. She was dead. Her heart stopped and she was dead because no one in her life had ever spoken like that to her before, and the absolute thrill of it made her heart stop.

"Oh," she said faintly as he smiled his slow, sexy smile. The one she wanted to lick right off his face. "By all means."

He gripped her knees, spread her thighs wide, and then paused. He took her in hungrily, her smoothness hiding nothing. She had never felt so open and exposed in her life. Instinctively, she closed her legs with a snap and sat up on the table. Oh my God. "It's a Brazilian. Amber made me do it. She said it was a postdivorce thing. I don't normally do this. I mean *look* like this, not *do* this. I've done this before. Lots of times. I do it all the time." She babbled nervously, edging back from the table.

Davis sat back slowly and looked her dead in the eye. "No, you don't."

"I know." She sighed. "Ignore that last part. I haven't done this in a long time. I'm a little nervous. Do you like it like... that?" she asked.

He flashed her that devastating smile again. "Sweetheart, everything about you is desirable." He wrapped each arm around her thighs from underneath and bent over her bare mound, using his thumbs to hold her open.

"Sweet," he murmured then licked a straight line of fire directly from the bottom up, and she felt her heart start beating again. It was... the hottest thing she had ever felt in her life. She wanted more, and it appeared Davis was going to give it to her because he dragged her even closer. He lapped again and again, murmuring praise in between until she was a puddle spread out wantonly on the table before him.

He was soft and gentle at first, nibbling and licking, while she got used to the sensation, then when her hips were jerking and she was pulling his hair, trying to get him closer to her, he sped up, and oh my God... The things this man could do with his tongue. And his hand. Oh, his talented fingers. He thrust two deep and curved, and the kitchen reverberated with the sound of her cries.

She begged and said nonsense things, pretty sure she would deny them later even with her hand on a Bible, but she didn't care. At one point, he reached up to hold her hands when she had yanked too hard on his hair, but she reached up to pull her own because if she didn't, she might just fall completely over the edge of reason.

She tugged and arched as he pushed her closer and closer to orgasm until, with a sob, she went over.

~

Davis nuzzled Allie while she lay on the table and watched her come back to life slowly. Tasting her, giving her pleasure with his mouth, had put his restraint to the test in a way he hadn't felt since he was a damn teenager. He'd had a picture of her sprawled out in front of him, bare and soft and open, while he did absolutely filthy things to her for so long, it almost didn't feel real to see her here now. The painful throbbing in his jeans told him differently, but he didn't rush her.

Eventually, she opened her gorgeous eyes and gave him a slow, satisfied smile that made him feel like he could move a mountain.

"Wow."

He grinned at her and nipped her thigh. "I like that look on your face."

She sat up, and he draped his arms over her thighs, looking up at her.

She ran her fingernails through his hair. "Do you remember that first time we were in this kitchen?" Her voice was husky.

He nodded, remembering how much he'd wanted to kiss her then, how hard it had been to walk away. "I've had visions of stripping you naked and fucking you on this chair for months."

Her sharp inhale let him know the impact of his words, and he pulled her down onto his lap to straddle him. Her eyes went wide as she settled on him, naked and wet. He slid his hands around her plump ass, tugging her harder over his erection. She gave a sexy little gasp that made him want to eat her up all over again.

"Do you have any idea what I want to do to this ass?" He grabbed handfuls of the tempting flesh and rubbed her back and forth across the fly of his jeans as she let out another moan.

She leaned into him until her breasts pushed against his

chest and her lips touched his ear, tracing the edge. "Davis," she whispered, all husky with need.

He went completely still. "Yeah," he said, need making his voice tight.

"I..." She took his earlobe in between her teeth and tugged. "... want..." She nipped and bit delicately, making her way to his jaw. "... you... to..."

"Tell me," he rasped, his hands tightening on her ass.

She leaned down, close enough that he felt her lips moving. "... *fuck* me." She said the word clearly, watching him remember the day at the ball field.

What's your big, bad F word? Fudge? You can't even say it without blushing.

He pounced on her then, growling deep in his throat and gripping her hips as he lifted her. He took the stairs two at a time, holding her tightly to him. The things he had in mind for her required a bed because it was going to be a long, long night.

When they reached her bedroom, he slammed the door closed behind them and pushed her against it. She clung to his neck and kissed him back with soft, delicate kisses that made him feral. For being married, something in the way she responded to him so sweetly made him think Allie was more innocent than she let on.

It made him want to dirty her up. He pinned her arms against the wall on either side of her head and slid his tongue along hers until the taste of apples and cinnamon would never conjure up innocent things again.

Her tongue shyly teased his, and she sucked on his bottom lip while sheer lust slammed into his body. He let go of her wrists to hold her head and slanted their mouths together in a deep, hungry kiss. He leaned back to catch his breath and growled at the look on her face. Her eyes were half-closed, lips wet from their kisses. She lifted on her tiptoes like she wanted more.

He snapped, swirled her around, and backed her up until her knees touched the bed. She trailed soft kisses down his throat, using the tip of her tongue in a way that made him shudder while he got rid of his boots and undid his jeans.

"Let me do that," she whispered and sat down on the bed in front of him. She looked up and moved his hands away from his belt, placing tiny kisses on his stomach.

Off came his belt, and his button was undone by her busy fingers. Finally, she tugged down the zipper so slowly that his teeth ached from clenching his jaw. Then she slid her hot little hands into his briefs.

"I knew it." Her eyes rounded when she looked up at him, her hand lightly wrapped around his length. "You're big all over."

Her little gasp was his undoing. He couldn't help it. His restraint was gone. He had held it together for months, but now, seeing her lush, soft body naked on her bed? Done.

Down went one knee by her hip, then his hand, until she had no choice but to lay back against the pillows with his body covering hers.

"Need you now," he said. She opened to him, and he settled between her thighs while she bucked up beneath him.

He kissed and caressed her breasts, cupping them until they spilled out of his hands. He pressed them together until he could reach both flushed nipples. Biting and sucking, he worked his way from one side to the other while she made hot, breathy noises underneath him. His hands slid down her softly rounded stomach, and further until he cupped her slickness and swirled her arousal around in teasing circles.

Her hand reached between them and grasped his taut

length. Despite her bold touch, she looked up at him uncertainly from beneath her lashes. "Do you like that?"

"Love it." He covered her hand with his and showed her what he liked and, together, they watched their hands stroking him. When she pushed lightly on his shoulder, he looked up.

"Can I... do you want me to?" She looked down to where their hands were entwined on him.

"Not now," he said huskily. "I want to feel you now." He nudged her hand away and rubbed his length through the slickness he had spread around. "Are you on something?"

She nodded. "Yes, and I got tested after Corbin..." She waved her hand, and he nearly lost it again because the thought of being inside Allie with nothing between them was almost too much.

"You ready for me, sweetheart?"

"Now, Davis. I want you now," she said breathlessly. She was biting her lip again and giving little gasps of air, pressing her heels into the bed as she lifted to meet him. At her shy nod, he pushed inside her smoothly, stopping halfway to let her adjust. It was a snug fit, making him clench his teeth again. He made small circles with his hips, erotic nudges against her that hit all the sweetest spots.

"Put your legs around me," he ordered, his voice strained. At the feel of her thighs around him, he slid the rest of the way inside her and they stayed like that. Foreheads touching, mouths parted against the other's, not moving, gazes locked.

"You feel so good."

Her surprise made him chuckle. "You're perfect."

He thrust once, then again when she made that sound that was quickly becoming the best thing he'd ever heard. Slowly he withdrew and thrust again, teasing them both until the bed frame rocked and creaked. He lowered his mouth to her rosy nipple and sucked while her hands stroked over his shoulders as they moved together.

He lifted his head and caught sight of her, eyes closed, a languid expression on her face that made him stop to look closer. "Look at me," he ordered roughly.

Her hazel eyes opened wide, and she smiled sweetly up at him. Not burning, not out-of-her-mind, need-to-come-right-now, going-crazy-with-lust like he was feeling. He stopped moving and lifted himself onto his elbows.

"Don't stop, Davis. You feel so good." She tugged him deeper, but he didn't move.

"What do you need?"

A pink flush spread across her cheeks, and she tried to turn her head, but he held her hip to keep her still. She knew what he was asking. "I'm good. So good. I, um, finished downstairs." She stared at his chin.

He nipped her jaw and didn't move despite her pulling his hips back down. "Sweetheart, that's not how this works. Tell me what you need."

"Davis." She groaned and tried to cover her face again, but he pulled her hands away. "I can't finish like this," she finally whispered. "Not during sex. I don't know why. I just can't let go. It still feels good. Please don't stop."

He wanted to laugh because for a minute he thought she wanted to stop, and he wasn't sure he could manfully pull off the tears he would have been sure to shed. Instead, he pulled out of her body with a hiss. The asshole she had been married to went down several more notches in his head. He knew damn well Allie was a passionate, responsive woman. How anyone could stay married for that long and never give her an orgasm during sex was a mystery he didn't want to think about. He had better things to do.

He lowered himself onto his side next to her. When she

made a little moue of disappointment, he couldn't resist nipping her lips. "Tell me what gets you hot," he whispered in her ear. "I know you like this." He cupped her and stroked her slickness, sliding his fingers through her swollen folds and circling. "I can feel it." She arched her back, legs spreading. "Show me what you like," he ordered. Then he took her hand and placed it over her soft, bare pussy.

"Davis," she whimpered. "This is so embarrassing."

"Shh," he whispered into her ear, taking soft nips of her throat and soothing them with his tongue. "Show me what you need."

He twined his fingers through hers and leaned back to watch as she stroked herself. Her fingers were uncertain at first, moving in tiny circles that widened as she grew more comfortable.

He nuzzled her ear, inhaling her sweet vanilla scent, still with a sharp eye on the story her fingers told. "Tell me what else you like."

"This, like this." Her voice was breathy. Her index and middle finger separated to form a vee over her clit as she rubbed up and down more firmly.

"Keep going, sweetheart." Instead of languid, her face was now the same bright, half-wild, utterly desperate look she'd had in the kitchen. Fucking perfect. He slid two fingers deep inside her, and she moaned, clutching him to her with her other hand as her hips began to move against him. "What else?"

"Mmmm." She moaned, low and sexy. "I... I... like it when you talk."

He grinned wickedly and moved his lips to her ear. "That's so good, sweetheart. You're such a good fucking girl, Allie, my good fucking girl." He nuzzled her neck and murmured delicious praise until she was gasping and trembling.

"Please, now, Davis." Her fingers turned frantic, and he knew she was ready.

He shifted onto his back and pulled her over him until her thighs fell on either side of his hips. With her gorgeous breasts heavy on his face, he thrust up into her, feeling the heat from her body and the sweet give as she adjusted. Her head tilted back, eyes half-closed, as she settled on him, opening with a gasp when she felt his fingers in a familiar vee. "Yes, just like that, beautiful. Take what you need," he growled.

"Oh my God!" She gasped. He watched her as she moved against his hand, her eyes half-closed and her hair trailing wildly down her back. She looked like an angel still, but a thoroughly mussed, fully decadent version he couldn't get enough of.

He pulled her close, one hand on her hip guiding, the other hand rubbing exactly the right way, and he whispered every filthy, obscene thought he'd had about her since the day they met until she was grinding and yelling so loudly, he wondered briefly if Mrs. Autovino's windows were open.

He decided it was worth it if they had to look her in the eye after this because when he looked up, he saw the most beautiful thing in the world: Allie falling apart.

Chapter Twenty-Seven

Later, much later, Allie opened her eyes and tried to figure out what was different. One heavy, hairy leg was draped over hers, and a forearm held her close against a chest that radiated heat. Her lips curved in a satisfied smile.

Her body felt achy and sore in places that she didn't ever pay attention to. After the first orgasm, she had been insatiable, as if now that she had found a man who knew what he was doing, she needed to make up for the lost time.

Davis had been only too happy to oblige, and they had gone at it another two times until she was a limp noodle when he finally carried her into the shower and soaped her up.

They went downstairs long after dinnertime where she put away the pie. Then Davis made them veggie-and-cheese omelets that they ate together on the couch, still touching each other just because they could.

"Jesus, are your feet always this cold?" Grumpy Davis was back. His voice was muffled by the pillow.

She wriggled backward against his chest and tucked her feet tighter along his calves. "Shush, you." They were, and he'd best get used to it. "You have heat to spare."

He tightened his arm around her waist and pulled her closer, cupping her breast and rolling her nipple into a tight bud. Her breasts were pink from his scruff, her nipples swollen from his lavish attention through the night. She laughed softly. "You're a boob guy, huh?"

"I'm a *you* guy," he said, leaning up to press his hot erection against her cleft insistently. She wriggled her bottom and let the silky-smooth skin slide hotly between her thighs.

She sighed happily.

One hand moved to her hip to guide her, and they rocked together, feeling her turn slick and hot until she slid against him, and her breathing shifted to gasps. Davis lowered his head and kissed the spot on her neck that made her absolutely crazy with lust at the same time he thrust up, pulling her back onto him in one steady, hot-as-hell, stroke. Her body gave way to his familiar intrusion as if they were made for each other.

Unlike last night, they were silent now, moving lazily against each other, content to let the pleasure build slowly and enjoy each other. Davis's rough hands stroked over her smooth thigh and hip and tenderly plucked at her nipples until she no longer felt lazy at all. Her body was on fire, heated and languid, almost scaring her with how much she wanted this man.

Davis was larger than Corbin, rougher and more demanding, and she lost herself in him. She had no time to be self-conscious, or worry if she was doing this right, or if she was making too much noise. The rawer and more natural she was, the more Davis praised her. The sweet, scary, darkness was closing in on her again, starting low in her back and spreading in tighter, harder circles until the edges of her vision started to gray.

He was behind her, his big body pressing hers into the bed with his thrusts, making the glide of the sheets against her nipples an unbearable tease. She moved her arm back to twine around his neck and tug his hair. Davis gripped her thigh to pull it up and back, giving her more of him. He pushed deeper into her, eyes locked on hers until she pulled him down closer with her lips parted, begging to taste. Gaze hot, Davis watched her breasts bounce with each thrust before he groaned and took her mouth again in a hard kiss.

She had no time to worry about how she looked, or what he felt because he was licking into her mouth, sliding his tongue over hers, and thrusting deeper inside of her. The restless, edgy darkness pulled at her, and he pushed her closer and closer to a ledge she wholly wanted to go over.

"You take it so good," he murmured into her neck, nipping the tender skin, burying his face in her neck. "So good, sweetheart."

She whimpered. *That mouth.*

Suddenly, one big hand splayed on her back, pushing her firmly forward into the pillow, gripping her by the hips, hiking them up, and thrusting into her hard and fast. She was head down, ass up on her lovely little pure white bed, and it was Davis behind her, holding her, pushing into her hard, and *oh my God*, she was going to come again.

"Come, sweetheart," he demanded roughly. "Let go for me." His thrusts came shorter and faster, and one blunt-tipped hand reached around between her legs, parting her and rubbing in the way he knew intimately by now. Her vision went dark around the edges, and fire licked through her as she bucked and ground back on him until she felt herself... untether.

"You're going to kill me," he groaned eventually, pulling out and falling back on the pillow with one arm dangling across his forehead.

Allie patted in the general direction of his body, landing somewhere low on his hard belly. "Don't worry, old man. I'll be on top next time." She panted, grinning wickedly over at him.

He gave a half-hearted swat at her, but it only landed on her thigh. "Respect your elders."

They were quiet for a while until Davis rolled toward her and pulled her close. "Are you okay?" he asked gruffly, adjusting her until she was tucked into her favorite spot again. Safe and warm next to his heart.

"So good," she sighed. "For an old man, you're a firecracker in bed."

He barked out a laugh with his eyes closed, the hint of a smile on his lips. Impulsively, she leaned up and kissed them, first the top lip, then the bottom one with a little nibble before she let go and settled down on his chest again. It was still wild to her that she could do that now.

She let out a deep, happy sigh and snuggled back down. "You so want me."

"Woman, of course, I want you." His big hand smoothed her hair away from her face. "I've wanted you since the second I laid eyes on you after you made me fall off my ladder," he grumbled, and her heart squeezed until she wasn't sure it could contain this much happiness. "And that damn apron you have was meant to torture me."

She popped up on her elbow. "You like my apron?"

"It's my favorite fantasy," he said dryly, closing his eyes.

She slapped his chest. "I knew you had a thing about women feeding you!"

"Ow." He grunted and caught her hand, kissing her palm before settling it back on his chest. "No food necessary. Just you wearing it and nothing else."

She settled back down on his chest comfortably. "I think I can make that happen," she murmured, a slow smile spreading over her face.

After a while, she said thoughtfully, "I never knew sex could be like this." She hesitated but then admitted, "It never was before."

He squeezed her bottom possessively. "It wasn't, huh?" She grinned at the satisfaction in his voice. *Men.*

"Not at all, and you can gloat all you want about it. I had a hard time letting go with Corbin. I didn't even know what I was missing," she mused. Her fingers idly trailed the ridges on his stomach. "How'd you get these abs, anyway?" she asked, leaning down for a closer look. "When do you have time to work out?"

He shrugged with his eyes closed. "The nights are long after the kids go to bed," he said, a faint hint of color on his cheeks. "Got to keep busy somehow."

She had seen so many facets of Davis's personality, but shy Davis did her in. She let him pull her down and snuggled up next to him with her nose buried in his chest, breathing him in. "Mmm, lucky me."

Chapter Twenty-Eight

"Look, Mom! I finally caught one!" Sammy hopped up and down from one foot to another as Davis helped him reel in a tiny, floppy sunfish onto the dock.

The water rippled on Seneca Lake, and the late-afternoon sun beat down warmly enough that Allie had taken off her sweater, leaving just her plain white tank top and a pair of well-loved jeans on with her Converse.

Davis had taken one look at her when he pulled into her driveway to pick them up for their weekend of camping, frowned, and asked where her hiking boots were. Allie had only laughed. She had no intention of doing anything more strenuous than lounging on the dock or at the campsite this weekend.

It was the perfect fall day, with a bright-blue sky, and the lake was so still it looked like glass. Too cold to swim, but the boys were happy to fish while Allie braided Claire's hair on the dock.

Davis stood between the two boys, keeping a careful eye on them. Occasionally he adjusted the line for them or repositioned their hands. He was infinitely patient, answering question after question the boys threw at him. He crouched down to show Sammy and Ben a lure, and the sight of their heads bent together—two dark and one light—made her chest squeeze, and she had to face facts.

She was in love with Davis Henderson. Head over heels, giddy, the second chance kind of love she had been afraid to let herself hope for.

The kind she knew he was terrified of.

"Mom, look! I caught a big one!" Sammy held up the tiny sunfish proudly while Davis showed him what to do next.

He made it so easy to love him. He was the best man she knew. She swallowed the lump in her throat.

"I see, honey! Throw him back to his family, please," she called. Walter got up from where he was curled up next to her and lumbered over to see if he could eat it.

"Wait! Not yet." Ben scrambled to his feet with the instant camera he brought from home clutched in his hand. "Lemme get a picture first."

"There, honey." She patted Claire's Dutch braid. "All done. You have beautiful hair," she said, twisting the last plait with a rubber band. "When you take it out, your hair will be curly." Claire had packed a big pink Caboodle full of makeup, much to her daddy's dismay, and they sat at the picnic table, playing around with eyeshadow and lip gloss earlier. Allie had shown her how to apply just a little bit to play up her pretty eyes. She heard herself repeating Annette's advice about makeup enhancing rather than detracting from Claire's natural beauty while Davis glowered at them. She would talk to him. He had a lot to learn about girls, just like she had a lot to learn about Sammy in the coming years.

Claire ran her fingers over the braids. "Thanks, Allie. I love them." She gave her a quick hug and held on tightly. "I'm so glad you're here to do this stuff," she said as she pulled back.

"It's usually just me and the boys." Her nose wrinkled to show what she thought about that.

"Hey, I heard that," Davis said, but he looked relaxed when he took a seat on the dock next to Allie. "You look real pretty, Claire."

His gray Henley hugged his chest and stomach and faded Levi's hung low over his hips, making her long for some alone time with him. She sighed. Dating with kids was hard. It had only been a week since the Apple Festival, and her body felt like it was craving him. She tore her gaze away and looked out over the lake.

"Thanks, Daddy, and you were meant to hear," Claire said, hopping up. "I'm going to find some flowers."

They watched the boys sitting side by side, kicking their legs over the edge of the dock and laughing together. Claire sat down by their campsite, looking for flowers. Everything felt so good, so right at that moment, it was hard to believe this was her real life.

"Smile!" Ben bent and snapped a photo of them and ran off after Walter and Sammy.

Davis leaned in and buried his nose in her neck and sighed something.

She laughed and arched her head to give him better access. "Cake? You want cake?"

"Mm-hmm," he rasped, all sexy and growly. "You smell like vanilla cake. Want to eat you up," he murmured, nuzzling her. He was learning all about her spots, each one of them, over and over. She sighed with happiness and closed her eyes.

"Your dad sure gets a lot of boo-boos," Sammy said, very seriously. Allie opened her eyes to see the three kids standing at the end of the dock, staring at her and Davis.

"Dad, do you need another hug?" Ben called out helpfully.

"I think they're kissing," Claire said knowingly.

"Oh, ah," Allie stammered nervously. "Your dad's just got a

splinter I'm helping him with." Davis let out a grunt of laughter. She poked him in the ribs and whispered, "Hush, you. What will they think?"

He shrugged, looking amused. "That I have a lot of boo-boos." He wrapped a piece of Allie's hair around his finger and tugged playfully.

They walked back to camp and, while Davis got the grill going, Allie set the picnic table with a red-and-white gingham tablecloth. She sent Claire to get water for the wildflowers she had picked earlier. She set the mix of daisies, asters, and cone-flowers in the middle of the table before unloading the food she had prepped at home.

From the cooler, she took out the individual foil packets of chicken and potatoes seasoned with lemon and herbs, and a big Greek salad with feta, tomatoes, and cucumbers. The boys started sniffing around as soon as they smelled dinner cooking. She put them to work finding long sticks for s'mores, which turned into a contest for who could find the best one.

They sat at the picnic table and ate dinner like a family, laughing and talking, sharing stories about baseball and school. Once, Claire mentioned Melody, and Allie's eyes sought Davis, but he continued smiling.

After dinner was picked up, Davis started a fire in the firepit, and they bundled up under blankets around it. The stars appeared, along with a brilliant harvest moon, while they roasted marshmallows.

"Not too many, Sammy," Allie reminded him from her spot near the fire. She had checked his blood sugar before dinner and given him insulin, but she still worried when he ate sugar. He had been running around camp nonstop today, but she made a note to check him again before she fell asleep.

After scaring themselves silly by playing Ghosts in the Graveyard, the kids settled down, and eventually, their eyes started to droop. Ben snuggled up close to Allie's side, and Claire tucked in on the other side of her, trying to keep warm under the blanket. Sammy and Davis lay sprawled out on a blanket pointing out stars. Davis's arm, covered in flannel now, traced the Big Dipper as Sammy yawned hugely and rubbed his eyes.

"Best camping trip ever," Ben mumbled, nestling into her. He smelled like woodsmoke and burnt marshmallows, his small body sturdy and warm. "Now we have new pictures for our album."

Claire leaned in on her other side and said sleepily, "Yeah, you always make things nicer, Allie, just like my mom did." Her sharp elbow dug into Allie's hip bone, but Allie wouldn't have moved her for the world. She tried to swallow around the lump in her throat, but she could only nod and press them closer.

After a while, Davis carried a sleeping Sammy to the tent. She waited until he came back for Ben and Claire then followed him to remove the kids' shoes and jackets before zipping each of them into sleeping bags and piling on extra blankets. It was chilly now that the sun was down.

Sammy woke up briefly but didn't open his eyes. "Where's Puppy?"

"Here, buddy." She tucked the worn stuffed animal under his arm and pressed a kiss to his cheek before ducking back out.

Davis was stoking the fire. Walter was already curled into a semicircle next to Davis. The shadows danced across the planes of his face in the firelight. He patted the space in front of him on the blanket.

"Come sit. It's warm here." He tucked a blanket around her when she settled down and leaned back against his chest. Davis wrapped his arms around her, and they sat quietly, watching the logs shift and send embers flaring into the dark.

"Amber said something to me a while ago that I keep

thinking about," Allie said after a while, leaning her head back against Davis's shoulder.

"What's that?"

"She said that we get what we think we deserve in life. I've been thinking about that a lot after talking to Corbin last week."

"Tell me," Davis said simply. He put his hands on her shoulders, kneading her tense muscles, and let her talk.

Allie stared at the fire and tried to put into words what she had been thinking about. "When my dad left us," she said slowly, "there was a part of me that thought that it was my fault. I was so young that I thought if I were only quieter, or picked up my toys, or didn't bicker so much with my sisters, he wouldn't have left."

"Oh, sweetheart," Davis murmured into her neck. She put a hand over his on her shoulder and squeezed reassuringly.

"I know that's not true, but when I was talking to Corbin, I realized that's how I started our marriage. There was a part of me that still believed if I could just fit in a little bit better in his world, act different, or look different, Corbin would never leave us, and Sammy would never grow up feeling the way I did. Corbin never had a chance to know the real me because I never showed it to him."

"It's not your fault that ass—" Davis started to growl, but Allie turned around and laid a palm on his cheek.

"Shh, don't get angry," she said tenderly. "I know it wasn't my fault that he cheated, but I do take responsibility for not asking for what I needed. I settled for what I had because I was afraid of asking for anything different."

"You do deserve more, sweetheart," he said fiercely, pulling her against him.

"I know that now," she said. She scooted to her side and laid her head on his chest. Davis threaded his fingers through her hair, over and over, letting the heavy strands slide through his fingers.

"I still want to throat-punch him for doing that to you," Davis said gravely, startling a laugh out of her.

"That's a no from me, big guy." She kissed his chest right over his heart and patted it. "I wouldn't be sitting here with you, if he hadn't cheated." She was quiet a minute, thinking about what else brought Davis to this night with her. Sadness filled her. She knew he was thinking about the same thing when she heard him clear his throat. "I know it's different for you," she said hesitantly. "You didn't have the choice."

Davis was quiet for a long time. "It's different, but it's not any less or more. Just different." The echo of her words to him on the porch that night hung in the air. "I'm glad I get to be here with you," he said simply.

Allie turned fully against his chest, and he fit his lips over hers softly, at once a balm and a reminder.

That life went on. That pain could sometimes turn into something beautiful.

She returned the sweet press of his mouth until the ever-present undercurrent between them hummed to life. She wound her arms around his neck and threaded her fingers into his thick hair. She channeled all the feelings she had for him, the respect and admiration, into her kiss until they were both panting.

Davis's hands went to her hips, squeezing and stroking under the cover of the jacket she wore. She shifted to give him more space and was rewarded by his firm hands on her breasts. Tiny pinpricks of heat followed his hands until his fingers dipped into the cups of her bra to find her aching nipple. The pad of his thumb ran over the tip, back and forth, making her gasp as it hardened. She dipped her hands under his sweatshirt, exploring, tracing the dips and valleys of his muscular stomach, remembering how powerful he looked hovering over her in bed. She buried her nose in his chest and breathed in.

"When's our next sleepover?" she asked unsteadily. He laughed and kissed her temple, then he tucked her shirt back in and settled them back against the log. Allie's eyes grew heavy, and she drowsed that way, warm and utterly content against him, until the fire was nearly out.

She sat up sleepily. "I have to check Sammy's blood sugar."

"Go on into the tent," he told her. "I'll make sure the fire is out before coming to bed."

Coming to bed. She liked how homey that sounded. All three kids were piled together on the far side of the tent when she crawled inside. Sammy was on the end closest to her, making it easy to reach his finger. She rubbed his middle finger with an alcohol swab and poked him quickly with the needle. He didn't flinch. She checked the number and did a mental calculation. He would be good until morning.

She was so tired she didn't say a word, just slid into her sleeping bag and closed her eyes. Davis unzipped the tent a while later and took off his jacket and boots. Walter's collar jingled as he stepped inside and flopped down at their feet.

An arm landed on her waist, and she turned into his warmth. Davis pulled her closer and tucked her into his side protectively. Just as she fell asleep, she felt the soft brush of his lips against her hair.

THE EARLY PREDAWN light filtered through the tent along with the sound of rain sprinkling the nylon when Allie opened her eyes and squinted to see what woke her up.

"It's too early to go out, Walter," Davis grumbled, his voice rough with sleep. His arm was crooked over his eyes, the edge of the eagle peeking out on the underside of his bicep. His other arm was still curled around her, possessive and warm, keeping her close to his heat. The solid wall of his chest rose and fell, lulling her back to sleep.

Mm, she could get used to this. She wiggled closer and closed her eyes, but Walter yipped again. Sharply. She opened one eye.

Walter sat at the bottom of Sammy's sleeping bag. Did he miss him? So sweet the way those two loved each other. Maybe she would surprise Sammy with a puppy for Christmas. The thought made her smile. Sammy's mouth was open, and the tuft of hair that was always in his eyes blew up and down with each breath.

Except... She sat up quickly and looked closer. Tiny bubbles had formed at the corners of his mouth. Walter barked again and used his long golden nose to nudge Sammy's side.

"Sammy," she said, leaning over and shaking him. His body rocked limply; his eyes didn't open. "Sammy," she said, louder. "Wake up, baby."

She grabbed his shoulders and shook him harder. His eyes flickered open and rolled back as his body began to twitch. *No. No. Oh, shit.*

"Sammy, wake up!" she yelled in his face. Ben and Claire were up now, watching with wide eyes. Her brain felt like it was moving in slow motion. How could this happen? What was she thinking taking him camping, away from a hospital? Panic flooded her as she looked around frantically for the backpack.

Davis knelt beside her. "Allie, what's going on?"

"Backpack," she shouted, tossing pillows and blankets around. Where was it? She had put it right next to her after she checked him. She could feel the hysteria rising, threatening to choke her, but she pushed it away. "I need the backpack!"

"Here." He handed it to her, and she frantically dug into it while he held it open. "What can I do?"

"He needs sugar. Frosting. Glucose," she said, digging through the backpack. *Oh my God, how could this have happened?* She had checked him before dinner, and he was a little low, but she had corrected him with the right amount of insulin after he ate dinner. Then he had s'mores, and she checked him again, thinking his blood sugar might be high, but it had been within normal range. But, her brain reminded her, he had been playing, running around, and burning off the sugar, and she didn't actually watch him eat all of his dinner like she usually did.

There. There it was next to the glucagon pen, the one the diabetes doctor explained how to use the night she first brought Sammy to the hospital. Fear made her hands clumsy when she tried to unzip the pouch. Sammy was making small noises in the back of his throat now, gurgling almost. *Hurry.* She grabbed the small blue tube of frosting and tore off the top with her teeth.

"Sammy, swallow." Frantically she opened his mouth and let the thick frosting pool on his tongue. Davis shifted and put an arm around Sammy's back. His arms hung limply to the side as the frosting softened and ran out of his mouth. "Eat it. Swallow, Sammy!" She tapped his cheeks and closed his mouth, moving her own unconsciously. *Dissolve, dammit!*

"It's not working," she cried, searching for the emergency shot. Ben and Claire had huddled in the corner of the tent, Ben with his thumb in his mouth, and both were crying softly. She registered that this was probably terrifying for the kids, but only distantly.

Sammy's body jerked, sharp motions that made his hands and feet flap involuntarily. His eyes rolled back, and his eyelids fluttered.

Allie's stomach plummeted. Dizziness swirled for a few

seconds as panic turned into terror. She yanked her son's super-hero pajamas down, and in one swift motion, jabbed his thin thigh with the needle. He didn't flinch. The tent was silent except for the rain as they watched him. She turned him onto his side in case he got sick and started praying. *Please, God, let him be okay. Please. Please. Please.*

She registered Davis's hand stroking Sammy's hair back from his forehead. The kids continued softly crying. Walter paced. Davis's voice penetrated her concentration. He was on his phone with 911, his voice calm and steady as he explained what was happening and listened to directions. "Yes, I know where that is."

He ended the call and moved her aside before picking up Sammy. His arms hung like a rag doll as Davis carried him out of the tent. Allie followed numbly.

"Get in the truck. I'll hand him to you." He turned to Claire and Ben. "Get Walter and get in the truck. Leave everything here."

She slid into the front seat and held her arms out for Davis to settle Sammy on her lap. She didn't take her eyes off his sweet face. His lips were pink from the frosting, and he was shivering now from the cold rain, but his eyes were open.

Davis helped the kids in the truck, and Walter jumped into the cab. Everyone was silent as Davis drove the dark, wet road carefully, two hands on the wheel to navigate the twists and turns until they reached the end of the park where an ambulance waited with its lights flashing. When they pulled up next to it, two EMTs met them at the passenger side and reached in for Sammy.

"He's type 1 diabetic," Allie told them. "I gave him frosting and glucagon ten minutes ago."

They asked all the usual questions. When did he last have insulin? How much? Did he have any other medical concerns?

Sammy was awake now. He was spacey, but he could answer their questions. He even smiled when the medic, a young man with the reddest hair Allie had ever seen, told him he was going on an ambulance ride.

The other medic, a stout older woman with short gray hair patted her on the back. "You did good, Mom. He's going to be okay." Allie tried to thank her, but everything felt numb, and she could only nod.

When she stepped up into the ambulance, a warm hand landed on her back, and she looked down at Davis.

"I'll drop the kids off at my mom and dad's and meet you at the hospital," Davis said. She paused as she climbed in and looked at the three of them. Davis held Ben against him with one arm over his chest. Ben was crying softly, big, fat tears rolling down his cheeks as he watched silently. Claire's face was too pale and tight with emotions that children shouldn't have to feel.

They've been here before.

Her heart sank with that terrible thought. She wanted to reach out to comfort them, to pull Ben and Claire into her arms, and reassure them Sammy would be okay. Unlike their mother, Sammy would be coming home.

But the ambulance doors closed, and her attention snapped back to Sammy, where she was needed the most.

Chapter Twenty-Nine

THE EMERGENCY ROOM was eerily quiet in the early morning hours. She'd have to remember that the next time they were admitted, she thought numbly. There probably would be a next time, according to the ER doctor who had just left the triage room. Blood sugar could be hell to manage sometimes. Extreme lows and highs happened, the doctor said kindly. "Don't blame yourself," he told her on his way out.

If only it were that easy.

Sammy was almost back to himself now. The doctor had ordered blood work, and they were monitoring him for a few hours, but his skin was pink and healthy again. Just remembering how lifeless he had been a few hours earlier made her heart plunge to her stomach. *The bubbles coming from his mouth. The convulsions. God, don't think about that now.*

"I'm sorry, Mama," he whispered, giving her a sleepy smile.

Mama. How long had it been since he had called her that? She swallowed the lump in her throat as she reached out to smooth his hair.

"You have nothing to be sorry for, honey bear. You did all the right things."

"I know," he said solemnly. His eyes, so much like her own, looked older than they should. "But I'm sorry I scared you."

"Not your fault, baby." The chair squeaked on the linoleum as she bent over the bedrail and kissed his face. He smelled like campfire and rain and little boy. Once, twice, three times she landed kisses on his nose and cheeks until he laughed softly and pretended to push her face away.

"Mommmmm," he groaned, but only half-heartedly. "I'm big now. Not a baby."

"I know you are."

"Do we have to tell Mimi?" Sammy asked through a yawn. "She's going to freak out, isn't she? She's not going to let me do *anything* fun once she hears about it."

"You know her bark is worse than her bite," Allie agreed. "But you let me worry about that. I can handle Mimi."

As much as Allie dreaded telling Annette, a part of her wished she was here right now. She could use her mother's support, or Amber's. But she didn't call them yet, even though she knew they would come in a heartbeat. For now, it was just the two of them.

A little part of her, the one she was ignoring, hoped Davis would come, but she had taken care of Sammy on her own for most of his life. She did call Corbin about an hour ago. He had already booked a flight for later that day, surprising the hell out of her. Maybe he really had changed.

Sammy's eyes grew heavy, and she sat back in the hard plastic chair to watch him fall asleep. Her own eyes felt gritty, her body so bone-tired even the hard plastic recliner was almost comfortable. Her clothing was damp from the rain, and she shivered in the cool hospital air. The bite of discomfort was welcomed, though. Anything to keep the feelings welling up inside from seeping through the cracks.

"Hi, Allie," their nurse whispered a while later. The older

woman, named Christine, had cartoon frogs on her scrubs. She had been nothing short of an angel since they got there, keeping Sammy smiling and sneaking him a tablet to play on from the child life specialist's office. He barely noticed her taking his blood and checking his vitals.

"We're ready for discharge after you sign these papers." Christine held open the door. "Do you want to sign them out there so he can sleep?"

They settled down the hall in an empty family waiting room. A few Styrofoam coffee cups and a crumpled candy bar wrapper sat on the end table next to the love seat where Allie sat. She stared at the cup and shivered, thinking about the people who left it there, while she signed the packet of papers.

How many other parents had sat in this room before her, waiting for good news? Were they still somewhere in the pediatric wing, sipping yet more coffee and watching their child in a sterile bed, or were they home now? It was naive to think every child went home, but the thought of anything less was too raw to think about now. Her teeth clattered together so hard she clenched her jaw.

Her throat tightened. "Is-is it cold in here?"

Christine looked her over assessingly. "Tonight was scary, but Sammy's going to be okay." She patted Allie's arm. "Why don't I get you some coffee?"

She left the waiting room, and the blood rushed into Allie's head. She bent forward to bury her head on her knees. The whooshing sound in her ears was loud enough to drown out the TV in the corner.

The brick wall was cracking; anxiety, guilt, and fear were clawing at her from the inside, making it hard to breathe. She gasped for air and tried to remember her training. Hyperventilation. Controlled breathing. In through your nose, 1-2-3, out through your mouth, 1-2-3. It wasn't working. She felt the fissures dissolving and breathed harder.

The panic she had held off all night leaked through the cracks faster than she could stop them. She was supposed to be the strong one, the one who held it together. Right now, she felt anything but. She was more alone than ever before, and it terrified her.

Someone settled next to her on the couch. She kept her head down and concentrated on breathing.

"Sweetheart." Davis's deep voice startled her enough that she jerked up her head. When he saw her face, he froze. "Sammy....?" The horror in his eyes devastated her.

"He's okay," she managed to choke out in between gasps for air.

"Thank God," he breathed shakily. "Come here," he said sitting down next to her and gathering her into his chest, and—dammit—she needed it. She didn't want to. She had never needed anyone before, but tonight, just this once, the relief welled up and she buried her face in his chest, taking her first deep breaths in hours. So many nights of doing this by herself. So many hours staring at the ceiling and wishing she had someone to share the worry, someone to share comfort with. Now Davis was here.

The pent-up fear and helplessness finally escaped with a sob, then another until she felt the last bit of control shatter, and she gave in. They sat there for long minutes, her face buried in his solid, warm chest while he stroked his warm hand up and down her back soothingly. Occasionally, he handed her a tissue, and she blew her nose noisily, but he didn't say anything or rush her. At some point, Christine came back and silently left the coffee. She felt Davis nod, but she didn't move.

"I'm sorry." She sniffed, picked up her head, and looked at

the dark splotch on his hoodie. "There's a wet spot on your shirt."

He ignored that. "How's Sammy?"

She wiped her eyes self-consciously and sat up. "They've stabilized him. His blood sugar dropped too low, but he's okay now. We're being discharged."

Davis tugged her back and settled her against him. It felt good. Her body soaked up his heat, his strength, and she felt some of the weight of the night lift. "You came," she said tiredly.

The harsh fluorescent lights revealed the tiny lines beside his dear, calm eyes, the creases from his hard work, and the lines from his pain. His hair was damp and curling. He looked tired and rumpled, but never had he looked more handsome to her.

"Of course, I came."

"Where are Claire and Ben?"

"I took them to my mom and dad's." It hit her then. He had driven an hour home and then turned around and drove back.

She cleared her throat. "You didn't have to do that."

"I wanted to be here," he said simply.

Christine appeared in the doorway and discreetly tapped the doorframe. "Knock knock, folks. You're all set to leave when you're ready. Sammy's still sleeping, so take all the time you need in here."

Allie smiled tiredly at the nurse. "Thank you, Christine, for everything."

"You bet. You take care of yourself now. Keep this big guy close, okay?" She winked and left.

Davis handed her a box of tissue. She blew her nose and wiped her eyes.

They walked silently down the hall. On the way there, her hand found its way into Davis's. She didn't let go even when they walked into Sammy's room.

THE RIDE HOME was silent aside from the radio playing softly and the steady chatter of Allie's teeth. Davis kept his eyes glued to the road, driving carefully in the early Sunday morning traffic. It was still raining. The constant, hard rain beat against the windows and echoed ominously in the truck. He glanced in the rearview at Sammy sleeping. He had only woken up briefly when they were leaving the hospital and given Davis a sleepy grin.

"I'm so sorry you had to see that," Allie said quietly. She was huddled under his jacket, shaking hard enough he could hear it. He turned the heat up higher. "I know that must have brought up some memories for you and the kids."

"We'll be okay," he said tersely. "As long as Sammy is."

"The doctors warned me when he was first diagnosed that episodes like this were a possibility for the rest of his life, especially as he gets older and goes through puberty." Her voice broke on the last word, and he reached over to squeeze her knee. A fresh wave of terror shot through his gut.

He pulled the truck into her driveway and got out to open Sammy's side.

"I can do that," Allie whispered as he unlatched Sammy's belt and picked him up.

"I've got him. Get the door."

She stood aside at the doorway, and Davis walked ahead and up the stairs. He carried Sammy easily up the stairs and laid him on the bed. Allie pulled the curtains closed and put out a fresh pair of his pajamas on the bed. Davis paused awkwardly in the doorway.

"I'll be downstairs," he said finally.

He walked downstairs, pent-up adrenaline from the night still coursing through his veins. Sitting on the couch, he felt every one of his thirty-seven years and then some. He eased his head back on the couch and closed his eyes. Images of the night flashed like a ticker behind his eyes.

The obscene foam bubbles around Sammy's mouth.

The scream of the ambulance's siren.

The devastation on the kids' faces as they watched Sammy being loaded up on the stretcher.

Allie's terrified screaming.

The nightmare of another night, another ambulance ride, and more devastated faces raced one after another until he finally dug his fingers hard into his eyes to erase the images.

Jesus.

The fear he'd been holding off all night crept into the edges of his consciousness. He shot off the couch, driven by a frantic need to block out that emotion with physical labor.

He worked methodically, unloading the truck, bringing in the coolers, and what little camping gear they hadn't left at the site. Allie's house was comfortably tidy already, but he swept and unloaded the dishwasher. He threw in a load of towels, and still, he prowled around looking for more work to do. Finally, when there was nothing left to take care of downstairs, he took the stairs up, two at a time.

Sammy's room was rain-dark despite the early morning hour. Allie and Sammy were asleep in the rocking chair. Davis's knees protested, but he ignored the aches and knelt next to the old wooden rocker. Instead, greedily, like a man presented with one last wish, he took in the details of their faces.

Allie looked like an angel asleep, soft and lush and pink in the dim morning light. He let his eyes travel to the high curve of her cheekbone then down the natural upward tilt of her mouth that gave her such a beautiful, teasing smile. Sammy was curled around her. He was too big to fit, but that would never stop Allie from pulling him onto her lap. They both needed soothing tonight.

The blanket she had wrapped around Sammy had fallen. Davis reached for it and tucked it over Sammy, covering him up carefully. Protectively.

Allie made a soft noise and frowned in her sleep. He reached out and smoothed his thumb over her lips.

"Wake up, sweetheart," Davis murmured in her ear. Her eyes blinked open when Davis lifted Sammy from her lap. She sat quietly and watched him tuck Sammy back into bed. He knew all the nuances of putting a child to bed: how to tuck the stuffed animals around him and pull the blankets over his shoulders just so. He smoothed back Sammy's wild hair, letting his hand rest on the boy's forehead.

Davis bent over the rocking chair next and lifted Allie with an arm under her knees and one around her shoulders. "I can walk," she whispered, but she wrapped her arm around his neck.

"Let me."

Out the door, he carried her, down to her bedroom, and straight to the bathroom where he stood her against the door and turned toward the tub.

"What are you doing?"

"Getting you warm." He straightened up and matter-of-factly began peeling off her wet clothes. He worked quickly, not letting his hands linger anywhere while she shivered in the cool air. His knees creaked when he crouched down in front of her and lifted one leg and then the other, taking off her damp jeans.

He stood, pulling her sweatshirt and T-shirt off. Allie was left bare except for her simple yellow panties and bra. Davis never let his eyes stop or his expression change. He turned around and poured a bit from a bottle of vanilla-scented bubble bath into the steaming tub.

"Come here," he ordered, holding out his hand. She didn't hesitate. His hand swallowed hers as he turned her gently, unhooking her bra. She let out a sigh of relief when the material fell away from her breasts and turned around to face him. His hand settled on her hip; his thumbs hooked under the band. Then he stopped with a question in his eyes. She nodded, and he peeled the panties down her legs and quickly stood up.

Steam rose from the tub when she stepped in. First one foot, then the other, until she sank slowly into the scented water and rested her head against the back of the tub. Davis picked up her clothes and moved to open the door.

"Will you come in?" she asked.

"I don't think that's a good idea."

"Please," she said quietly. She held his eyes, communicating without words something he wasn't ready to acknowledge.

Davis hesitated then reached over his back to tug his hoodie over his head and pushed down his jeans and boxers. He climbed in behind her, settling them both against the back of the tub as the water swathed them. He barely fit, his shoulders touched both sides, and he had to crook his knees, settling his hard thighs around her much softer ones. Water sloshed over the sides when she settled back against him.

"This is nice," she said, sighing deeply.

"Hmm," he rumbled against her back.

She sighed and settled back fully against him. The thick, hard length of his erection pressed insistently against her back.

"Ignore that," he said gruffly, tucking his arms around her to keep her still. "This is me taking care of you."

"Maybe we both need taking care of."

"I want to take care of you," he said, his lips moving against her ear. "You take care of everyone else. Sammy. Your family. The kids at school. Let me do this for you."

She was quiet for a minute as the steam rose around them.

"I didn't take good care of Sammy tonight," she said with a wobble in her voice. Davis's heart ached at the sound. This beautiful, passionate woman loved so openly, with endless grace and determination, that he was in awe of her strength.

"That's not true," he said fiercely, tightening his arms around her.

"He was running and playing all night, and I didn't watch him eat his whole dinner. I never should have—"

"Stop." His arm tightened around her middle, making the tops of her breasts break the surface of the water. "Kids get sick all the time. You did everything right. Everything. Every day you take care of him and keep him safe." He gave her a little shake. "Sometimes shit happens. You can't blame yourself."

"I should have—"

"Don't do that to yourself. You're an incredible mom. Sammy's healthy and strong, and you take excellent care of him, okay?" He nudged her chin with two fingers until she turned and met his eyes. "Do you believe me?"

Allie laid her head against his shoulder. "Yes," she whispered. "I think you're an incredible father too."

He pressed a kiss against her temple. Her skin was warm now, and damp tendrils of hair clung to the side of her face. He nosed them aside and brushed her cheek with another kiss, leaving his lips there as he spoke. "We're both doing the best we can. That's all we can do."

"I'm sorry if we scared Claire and Ben tonight."

"They'll be okay," he said finally, praying he was right.

Allie shifted to lean up into his neck and bury her nose. The low current of attraction become more insistent when she turned fully on her hip, draping more of her softness against his body. The water swirled around them, circling her breasts and turning her nipples into taut points against his chest. Davis's eyes followed the movement. The insistent evidence of his desire bobbed between them against her stomach.

"Kiss me." She breathed against his stubbled jaw. Abruptly, he sat up and threaded his fingers through her hair, cupping her head, and pressed his mouth onto hers hungrily. She whimpered into his mouth, and he was gone, lost in the elemental need to chase the fear away with the pureness of the woman on top of him.

Allie's honey-colored eyes were half closed and hot with need when they broke apart. She lifted her thigh over his to straddle him and caused water to swell over the side of the tub. She balanced her hands on his shoulders and rolled her hips. The tight move stroked her slick heat over the length of him, making him hiss. He startled a cry from her when he stood up, wrapped her legs around his waist, and gripped her bottom, carrying her to the bed.

Carefully, he laid her down and knelt between her thighs to feast on her with his eyes. Allie lay perfectly still, her eyes and her body open. She smiled softly and let him look as if she sensed this was more than just two bodies slaking a need. A surge of emotion overwhelmed him, and he wanted to give back to her what she gave so freely.

He leaned forward and pressed kisses to his favorite places on her body, making his way up the scented path. He worshipped the tender skin on the inside of her knees with his mouth and moved down, lingering on her sleek inner thighs. He spent long, pleasurable moments caressing the faint silvery lines that fanned her stomach with his lips and tongue.

Allie's hands roved through his hair, holding him to her and sifting restlessly while he savored her. The delicate hollow between her ribs tantalized him next. Her heart beat frantically under her breastbone, and he was struck anew by the ferocity of the spirit being held inside such a fragile body.

He let his lips and tongue whisper what his own, much less brave, heart wanted to say.

She was breathing fast when he reached her mouth. He shifted them to their sides facing each other, her legs still wrapped high around his waist. Spread open like this, her wet heat tantalized him, and he gave in, dragging the head of his cock once through her soft folds.

"More." Allie gasped. He gripped her ass with both hands and buried himself inside her. Allie let out a soft sob and clutched his shoulders.

The rain outside beat on the windows, but they were in a cocoon of heat and need, eyes locked on each other. The scent of vanilla rose between them along with the spicier scent of arousal while they rocked together. The intensity of the moment grew and pushed forward into a realm he hadn't crossed with her before. Each of their sexual encounters had a wild, almost uncontrollable feel, like a forest fire burning out of control, but as he held Allie now, rocking slowly, relentlessly into her body, he realized they were making love.

He was loving her.

The thought shook him, and his rhythm jarred. Allie drew back and searched his face, perhaps sensing his inner turmoil, but he pulled her closer and firmly stroked into her again. He lost himself in sensation, taking his time until the pink in Allie's cheeks had deepened, and her beautiful eyes lost focus, telling him she was close. He gripped her hips, pressing down and angling her on every upstroke to give her clit more friction. Her eyes widened, and her legs tensed around his waist.

"So good," he murmured, eyes locked on her face. "You're so good."

"Ohhh." She cried out sharply, closing her eyes. He let go of her hip and clasped her neck, tilting her face up to his. Greedily, he watched her every expression, mesmerized by the way she looked at him. God, he loved how she looked at him.

Her eyes fluttered closed again.

"Look at me," he said roughly, close to his own release. "I want to see you come."

She let out a low, sharp cry and tensed, her mouth falling open, her eyes locked with his while she broke apart. Her eyes glittered with unshed tears.

"Shh," he murmured, gathering her closer, "don't cry." He held still against her trembling body. "Do you want to stop?"

"No, don't stop," she said urgently, her body clenching around him. "I need you."

The tight, scorching grip sent him spiraling into his own climax. He lay there, catching his breath and riding the pleasure until it faded.

Fear curled around the edges of his satisfaction. He closed his eyes to block it out and keep this moment between them. Allie shifted closer, seeking more of him, neither one of them wanting the closeness to end.

Gently, he disconnected their bodies and rolled to his back.

A warm hand settled on his stomach. Her fingers rubbed soothing circles there.

Soothing him. Calming him. Consoling him.

Gradually, he became aware of the rain still coming down outside. The curtains were open enough that he could see the ribbons of water streaming down the window. Davis rolled his head to find Allie looking at him. He didn't know what she saw in his eyes, but the usual upward curve of her lips fell flat. "We need to sleep. We can figure this out after we rest," she said hoarsely.

He pulled her to his chest and settled an arm around her, pulling her closer. He was almost sick with exhaustion, but when her body found his, he gave in to the comfort she offered and let sleep claim him.

Chapter Thirty

ALLIE'S EYES CRACKED OPEN. Her eyes were scratchy, and her head throbbed from lack of sleep. She looked around the room in confusion. The clock on the nightstand said it was early afternoon, but the room was dark. Rain still pounded the windows.

A heavy arm draped over her stomach, and when she moved, the muscles tightened, pulling her closer. Long, rough legs spooned her. One pressed up high between her legs, wedging a promising erection against her back. She closed her eyes happily.

Sammy. The hospital. Davis.

She shot up, heaving the blankets back, and leaped out of bed. She was halfway across the room when Davis caught her arm.

"I have to check on Sammy," she cried, trying to twist her arm free in a blind panic.

"I know," he said. "Put this on." He tossed her the pink nightgown, and she looked down, realizing for the first time she was naked.

"Thanks," she said through the material as she jerked it over her head.

Davis helped her pull it down and followed her out of the room. He stopped in the doorway while she bent over to check Sammy. He was breathing peacefully, almost in the same position Davis had tucked him into only several hours before. She found his finger, swabbed it with the alcohol pad she kept in his bedside drawer, and pricked his finger. She sighed in relief at the number.

She motioned for Davis to follow her back to her bedroom. "He's good," she said in response to the question in his eyes. "He can sleep for another hour or so, then I'll wake him up and have him eat."

"Thank God." Davis let out a thick breath. He sat down heavily on the edge of the bed and rubbed his hands over his face. When he pulled them away, his eyes were bleak, the faint lines around them deeper.

Instinct, the same one that told her when a patient was in pain, made her take a seat next to him on the bed. "I didn't think you'd show up at the hospital."

"I would never have left you there by yourself." Davis blew out a harsh breath, turning to look at her fully.

"I know you wouldn't. You're a good man, Davis. The best," she whispered, laying a palm on his face and stroking his eyebrows, smoothing the deep frown between them. She took a deep breath. "That's why I fell in love with you."

Davis's face froze before he crushed her against him. She cupped his neck, running her fingertips through his hair tenderly. His fear was as palpable as his arms around her.

"I'm giving my love to you because you're the most wonderful man I've ever met, and I think you need to hear it often. You're an incredible father, and you're an honorable man, and I'm in love with you because you've shown me what I was missing."

"Allie..." he whispered.

"Let me finish, okay? I know last night was awful, and it brought back memories and feelings for you and the kids. I get that, and I'm so sorry you had to see Sammy sick. My heart broke seeing the looks on the kids' faces." She looked away then.

"But that's us. That's our reality. Sammy could get sick again, or I could, or you could," she said. "There aren't any guarantees. Accidents happen. Good people like Melody die. But we have to go on loving anyway. We can't shut people out." A flicker of anger sparked in her. "That's what you're doing isn't it, Davis? Pulling away again?"

He closed his eyes briefly, shielding them, but she knew.

"I deserve more than that," she said quietly. "I'm not going to spend another eight years of my life with someone that can't love me better than that." She concentrated on her breathing, on the steady beat of her heart, on anything besides the mean streak of pain splitting her chest open while she watched the struggle on his face. "I'm choosing that."

He studied her face for a moment as if memorizing it. Then he leaned over and gently pressed his lips across her forehead. "I'm sorry. I wish I could give it to you," he finally said hoarsely. It wasn't enough, and they both knew it. He cleared his throat again. "I'm still going to be here for Sammy," he said. "I'm not going to disappear. I'll be here. I care about him—both of you— very much."

"He cares about you too," she said softly, and her mouth trembled slightly before she firmed it up, along with her voice. A tear spilled down Allie's cheek, and Davis reached out a finger to stop it. They sat there in silence, knowing this was the end, yet unable to move from the moment.

Finally, she closed her hand on his. He had such beautiful hands. Long-fingered, work-roughened, and yet tender too. She stroked the inside once, just a light fingertip over his calloused palm, feeling his hand clench in response.

Then she let go.
She deserved someone with a whole heart.

Chapter Thirty-One

"I won! Again. Mom, I'm smokin' you!" Sammy crowed, taking her last checker. He slurped the last of the chocolate milk in his plastic cup, slammed it down like a beer pong cup, and let out a burp.

This kid. He wasn't the same little boy from three months ago, even if he did drive her crazy sometimes with his heathen manners.

"Yeah, yeah, rub it in, kid, and say excuse me when you burp," she said automatically. The coffee table on his side had a pile of red checkers. Not a great showing on her part but, hey, she was trying.

It was Friday after one hell of a long week. A very long, very awful week in which she had learned a few things about herself she never knew. For instance, she cleaned when her heart was broken. Not a single closet or cupboard in her house had been safe from her efforts this week.

Her office at school had undergone the same treatment. Purging, organizing, and then putting it all back together had been intensely satisfying. Also exhausting. It had helped, though, because if she wasn't frantically cleaning the grout in the bathroom with a toothbrush, all those soft little memories of Davis, which now felt like shards of glass, accidentally surfaced and left jagged cuts at the worst times.

She did okay during the day if she kept busy. The nights were harder. The good news: her house was spotless since she didn't seem to sleep anymore. It was strangely therapeutic to scrub the floors with Gwen Stefani circa 1996 blaring "Don't Speak" in her earbuds.

Sammy's week had been long for different reasons. Tomorrow was the Northfield Little League's last game of the season. Allie would have to see Davis again, the first time since she'd told him she deserved something more last Sunday.

Oof. That shard of glass again. She concentrated on wiping the crumbs off the table.

"How are you feeling about the last game this weekend, buddy?"

Sammy's smile slipped. "Okay. One good hit, Mom. I just need one. I can't end my season with zero hits."

Sad, but true. Sammy hadn't had a hit all season. A few fouls, sure. A couple of walks to first base when the opposing team's pitcher stunk. One time he had been hit by a pitch, so he got to take a base. But he'd had no actual hits and definitely no runs scored.

They had spent a lot of time talking about the importance of being a team player and how Sammy was contributing in other ways, but he wanted that hit so badly he could taste it, which meant she could too.

Whoever said it was hard to raise babies was misinformed. Raising older kids was when it felt like your heart was walking outside your body, all tender and vulnerable, waiting for something to bruise it while you could only watch.

Yep, you could say this had been a tough week.

"Mom," Sammy asked a while later, coming downstairs

after his solo shower, another first for him. Her little boy was growing up so much. He crawled onto the couch, all bony elbows and pointy kneecaps threatening to poke her in the eye, and settled down in her lap. He had a smudge of toothpaste on his chin.

"Yes, honey bear?"

"I'm sorry you're sad about Davis."

Oh. Well then.

She swallowed. How did one navigate these conversations? She didn't have a clue, but lying didn't feel right. "Thanks, buddy," she finally said, opting for the truth. "Sometimes grown-ups just don't work out together, but he's still a wonderful person. He still cares about us, and you'll always be friends with Claire and Ben."

He nodded, and a curl of hair flopped into his eyes as he snuggled against her. "Yeah, we will. But he's really missing out on you."

This boy. She loved him so.

"Is this one of your happy or sad leaks?" He wiped a wet spot on her shirt.

"It's a little of both, buddy." She laughed and wiped away more tears. "The Hendersons are the lucky ones because they get to know a special kid like you."

"I know," he said happily. "Can I stay up late and watch TV with you?"

"I love you, kid, but it's bedtime."

She had to start cleaning.

Later, when Sammy was in bed and Allie was elbow-deep in sudsy water in the sink, the doorbell rang. On the porch stood Amber and Lucy.

She held open the door and tugged off her dish gloves as they filed in. "Did I miss a girls' night memo?"

Amber held up a case of wine. "I called an emergency meeting. I know you're planning to clean toilets all night, or something else disgusting, and we couldn't let that happen."

"Ha. I'm not cleaning anything on a Friday night," Allie said trailing after them to the kitchen, kicking the mop bucket further into the pantry.

Lucy eyed the rubber gloves in her hands doubtfully but kept quiet like a good friend, unlike Amber who grabbed the gloves and snapped them against Allie's butt as she reached up to get the wineglasses.

"Ouch!" She grabbed her butt and glared.

"No more cleaning, Al," Amber said severely. "We're going to have one last night of moping, then we're getting you back on the market. I have it all planned out. I'm setting you up with one of the guys from the fire department."

Just the thought of dating again made Allie want to cry. "I'm totally fine," she said, a suspicious wobble in her voice.

Lucy put an arm around her and guided her to the kitchen table. "Come on, let's go sit down and rage eat then. That's more fun."

Amber handed her a glass of red wine. A very full glass. She took a big gulp.

"Okay, let's have it." Amber's jaw was set familiarly. "If he hurt you, I'll spit in his drink the next time he comes into the pub when I'm working."

"That asshole. He's so getting a buzz cut next time he comes into my salon," Lucy vowed, taking a beautiful brie and crackers out of a Whole Foods bag.

Allie looked back and forth between them. "I ended it." She sniffed, tears leaking like traitors. She looked around for something to clean.

"What do you mean?" Amber asked suspiciously. "You love that grumpy asshole. What did he do?"

"I told him what you said," Allie said wetly. "That I

deserved more." Another little sob escaped. It felt good to let it out. Maybe even better than cleaning. She let out another one.

"What the hell kind of advice is that?" Lucy hissed at Amber. She patted Allie's back.

Amber glared back. "It's good advice. I'm tired of seeing my sister give her heart away to people who don't deserve her."

"It's okay. I'm going to be okay, guys. It just sucks right now." She took the tissue Lucy handed her and blew her nose.

"We'll egg his truck, Allie," Lucy said grimly. "You know he loves that thing. No, we'll set up a Tinder profile with his phone number on it."

"Oh, good one." Amber nodded, impressed. "Then we'll send the link to the casserole brigade," she added gleefully.

Amber pulled out her phone, and Allie snatched it.

"He's not bad at all," Allie said quietly. "He's just trying to protect his family, and himself too. Last weekend, when Sammy went to the hospital, it brought back their trauma from losing Melody."

The kitchen was quiet except for the hum of the refrigerator.

"He's afraid to lose someone else. I can understand that." Allie's eyes were dry now. "But I'm not willing to wait around for that to change. I spent eight years waiting for a man to love me the way I needed, and I won't do that again," she finished quietly.

"Well, hell." Amber sighed. "It would have been so much easier if he were an asshole to you."

Lucy propped her legs up on the chair across from her and stared morosely into her glass. "Yeah, that doesn't track for Davis. He's always been one of the good ones."

Allie looked back and forth at both of them. Funny. Two months ago, she had felt more alone than ever before. Now, she was sitting between two women who would commit potentially criminal acts to avenge her broken heart. Life was funny like that. Sometimes you had to lose something to gain something better.

Allie sniffed. "I love you guys so much."

Lucy topped off their glasses. "We love you, too, Allie."

"To us?" Allie raised her glass.

"Yeah," Amber said, her red lips curving. "And to fire-fighters."

HE DIDN'T WANT to be there.

The pub was crowded with happy-hour people laughing and having a good time on a Friday night. Except him. He was having a shitty night. The whole week had been shit.

He stared moodily into his beer and contemplated heading home. When Layne had picked up the kids for a sleepover after school, he couldn't stand the thought of being home alone all night with just his dark thoughts and Walter to keep him company. He'd called Shep and Ford and headed to the pub for a drink. Now, he wished he'd stayed home. He could have been just as miserable there.

Killian set down a fresh beer in front of him. "You look like shit," he said cheerfully, the Irish bastard.

Davis glared. "I'm fine."

"If you say so, man." Killian snorted, heading back to the kitchen with an armful of plates.

He was mostly fine if you didn't count the last few months of his life. Kids. Work. Family. He was content, if not happy, with them all until two months ago when Allie had walked into his house and all hell broke loose. The little part of his brain that pissed him off whispered that surviving and thriving were different, but he shut that down immediately, just as he had all week long.

Ford leaned around the blond he was currently flirting with at the bar. "Happy hour is supposed to be happy, Davis. Stop glaring at everyone and be social. Hey, Stella, do you have any cute friends here that could put a smile on my friend's face?"

The woman turned and blinked her extremely long eyelashes at him.

Wrong eye color.

His favorite eye color was hazel. She gave him a slow, flirtatious once-over that made him strangely queasy.

"Ooh," she cooed, gripping his bicep. "I sure do, handsome, but maybe I'll just keep both of you to myself."

Davis sighed and gently extracted himself from her clutches. He thought about the silence of his house, now only slightly more attractive than the pub, but still better than this. He threw some bills down on the bar.

"You can't go yet," Shep said, sliding onto the stool next to him. "I just got here. I'll have the usual," he told Killian.

Ford extracted himself from the blond and took the stool on the other side of him. "To be twenty-five again," he said wistfully.

Killian set the beer down in front of Shep. "She's twenty-one. I checked her ID."

Ford blew out his beer. "Oh, Jesus," he groaned. "I hate dating."

"Speaking of dating," Killian began, but Davis cut him off with a look.

That he ignored.

"Where's your lovely girlfriend? I'm off at seven, and I feel like dancing."

Davis's teeth clenched.

"She's at home, along with Amber and Lucy," Shep volunteered.

They all turned to look at him with varying degrees of interest. "What? Her house is on the way, and their cars were parked there."

"Now those are some women." Ford sighed, and Davis glared at him. "What? You know it's true. All three of them are out of our league."

"One is anyway," Killian added. "I don't date employees, and Lucy"—a hard light entered his eyes— "she and I seem to knock heads."

"I get along fine with all three," Shep said cheerfully. Davis wanted to punch him. Hard. He settled for glaring.

"What happened between you two?" Killian asked while wiping down liquor bottles. "Didn't you just go camping together?"

"We did," Davis said curtly.

"Ah. It didn't go well." Killian's voice was filled with false sympathy. "Blended families are hard, I hear."

"It went fine," he said tightly. Images from their picnic flashed in his head. The dinners they shared. Camping. They'd gotten along perfectly. Ben and Claire had been sad not to go over to Allie's all week. Almost as sad as he was.

"Oh?" Killian nodded knowingly, "Was she too clingy for you? That can ruin a good thing."

Davis shook his head. If anything, he hadn't had enough of her and how she made everything in his life brighter and happier by being near all that goodness. The nights they spent on the porch swing, rocking and talking, replayed in his mind until the ache for her was a physical wound in his chest.

He found himself looking for her every morning at drop-off like some lovesick asshole. He had lost the best thing to happen to him in a long, long time.

Fuck. Bitterness flooded him. He'd done everything in his power to avoid what happened between them. He'd spent the last three years building a wall around his family to protect them. He'd stared at the ceiling for hours at night because images of accidents, choking, and drowning raced through his head and stole his peace until he felt like he was barely hanging on.

So he'd built a life without any risk.

He carefully controlled everything. He faithfully applied sunblock, cooked green vegetables for dinner, and made damn sure his family was connected to a community that watched out for each other so they would never be torn apart by loss again.

And yet he had been fucking miserable. Until Allie and Sammy came into his life. Never in a million years had he thought he would let himself care about a woman and child that could take all that safety and security he'd surrounded himself with and shatter it.

Ah, hell. What had he done?

Killian took down a bottle of Jameson and poured four shots, a slight smirk on his face. "Did our Allie put you in the friend zone? Is she fair game now?"

Shep winced. He was the only one Davis had talked to this week about what happened, but from the evil look on Killian's face, he suspected.

Ford's eyebrows rose. "What's up? I thought things were good with you two."

"They were good." Davis finally sighed in resignation. "I fucked them up."

"Thought so," Killian murmured, holding up a shot glass and looking Davis in the eye. "To fucking up." He downed his whiskey. "And making up," he added with one brow raised in question. He pushed Davis's shot glass toward him.

Davis stared at it for a long time before nodding once. Then, in one smooth move, he slammed the shot, slid back his chair, and headed to the exit.

"About time, asshole," Killian called from the bar. Davis threw him a rigid middle finger and kept walking.

"Where are you headed, Davis?" Natalie caught his arm when he passed the table where she sat with a few friends. She gave him a friendly smile. "How about a drink?"

"I'm sorry. I can't. I have to do something," he said, already pulling away.

Natalie looked him over carefully. "Oh, I see. Go get her back then."

Davis stopped abruptly. "What?"

She waved her hand around the bar. "You know how it is in this town. Everyone knows everything. Plus, it's written all over your face," she said. "You're in love with her."

He stared at her. Yeah, he really was.

"Go on. Get your lady back. I'm happy for you," she said with a sigh. "Mary Poppins will take good care of you."

"Thanks, Natalie." He paused. "Those dinners..." he started gently.

"I know. They're going to waste on you." She sighed. "I just like to cook, and it's no fun to cook when Carly's with her dad, but I'll find somewhere else to bring them. Now, go get your woman."

Impulsively, Davis leaned down and kissed her cheek. "You're a good friend."

He left the music and noise of the pub behind with determined steps. His car was parked to the left against the curb on Main Street, but a black-and-white awning on the left caught his attention, and he turned that way instead. It was almost seven thirty on a Friday night, but lights glowed softly from the inside.

He tapped lightly on the old-fashioned glass front door and waited.

Annette opened the door and looked at him without any expression on her face. She crossed her arms and leaned against the doorframe. "I can't imagine you having anything to say that I'm interested in hearing."

He almost smiled, before catching himself, seeing Allie in that regal, delicate face. Annette was better at hiding her feelings but, like mother like daughter, they both flushed when they were upset. Or hurt.

"I promise I do," he said gently. "Can I please come in?"

Chapter Thirty-Two

"Do you need a Xanax? How about a mimosa? Now would be the time, Mom."

Amber stage-whispered to Annette then leaned back against the bleachers, thrusting her boobs out even more in her tight sweater. A few of the baseball dads got a hard poke in the ribs from their wives. Allie caught Keri's eye, seeing her seated a few rows over in the bleachers, and they shared a grin.

It was a perfect fall day for a ball game. One of the last dry ones in the forecast, and it looked like most of the village had come out to watch the game and enjoy the fall afternoon. It helped that the concession stand had the grill going and the tantalizing scent of Zweigle's hot dogs lured everyone in the neighborhood to come down and watch.

Lily peered around Evie. "I have some melatonin. Want some? It helps me relax before recitals." They were both in town to watch Sammy's last game. The aunts had come too. Rosa sat with her knitting bag next to her, and Sophia and Giulia arrived with a picnic basket full of food and a thermos of red wine.

No hot dogs or Cracker Jacks for the aunts.

"I took a yoga class this morning and meditated, girls,"

Annette murmured, adjusting her Northfield baseball cap. It looked out of place on her expensive highlights, but Annette was a dedicated Baseball Mimi now.

Allie spotted Mrs. Autovino and waved. Just last week her neighbor had given Allie a pile of her recipe cards to keep. They were stained from years of use, priceless if that kind of thing mattered to you. It mattered to Allie.

Sylvia and her husband looked tanned and relaxed from lake life, and Eileen Gayle and her wife were next to them. All had come to watch the game and cheer on the Northfield boys. She waved to Sadie and Rob, who were feeding each other popcorn when she walked by. Lovebirds.

See? She could be happy for other people in love.

She had been surprised to see so many familiar faces in the crowd, but it made sense the more she thought about it. This was Northfield, no matter which side of the canal you lived on. This group of warm, funny people welcomed her and Sammy back into the community wholeheartedly. That snow globe she had imagined as a child? It took a while, but she had finally figured out that she needed to stop peering in from the outside and allow herself to be seen. With that came belonging.

"Here, honey, have some ravioli." Giulia handed Allie a plastic takeout container that looked like it had been washed and reused about a million times. "I made the gravy just how you like it."

Amber sniffed with interest and reached for the container. "Mm, I'll try one."

Sophia shooed her away. "Let your sister have it. She's got a broken heart."

There it was. The elephant in the room, or the bleachers as it were. The thing they had all been avoiding despite Allie's best efforts to look unaffected. Each of the aunts had called this week, one after another, after they heard the news about her and

Davis. They offered advice for healing a broken heart, which ranged from dating someone else immediately (Sophia went so far as to get a list from the Captain of the eligible bachelors at the firehouse), to potentially criminal revenge tactics (Amber, always Amber). She had politely declined it all.

She was okay on her own. It sucked, but in addition to the suck, she also had a sense of peace that had come with choosing herself, maybe for the first time ever.

"We're still friends," she said, absently rubbing the ache in her chest and forcing her eyes away from the dugout where she had last seen Davis's dark head of hair. She handed Amber the ravioli and dug around in her purse for sunglasses to cover her leaky eyes.

Corbin sat down next to her gingerly holding a bag of caramel corn. "How can you eat this? It's full of preservatives," he muttered.

Allie reached for the bag and stuffed a handful in her mouth. "Mmpfh," she said around the sticky stuff.

"What's a little more after all that Botox in your face, right?" Amber said cheerfully.

"You'd know all about silicone, wouldn't you?" Corbin snarked back.

Allie rubbed her forehead. Oh yeah. She wasn't completely alone. Corbin was in town for the weekend to see Sammy's game. He was surprisingly relaxed—popcorn and Amber aside. Some things never changed. She had to give it to him, he was making more of an effort to be present for Sammy.

"Hey, Allie." She looked up to find Davis standing in the bleachers. He was smiling at her, the dangerous one, the one he really shouldn't use with her anymore because it reminded her of kitchen tables and apple pie, and picnics, and she was suddenly very, very glad for the sunglasses.

"Hi," she said politely. If she could just stay away from those warm brown eyes of his, she might make it through this without embarrassing herself. Besides, it was a beautiful view. Davis's Northfield T-shirt clung to his chest and arms where the muscle curved and hollowed, and the hint of his tattoo peeked out. An image of her tracing those lines with her tongue made her swallow painfully. She looked around the stands.

Everyone was watching them. Annette stared at her, one eyebrow raised.

"What?" Allie blurted. She could feel the flush on her chest from the stares. She started fussing with things in her purse. So many wrappers and receipts. Now was a good time to clean it out. "I think the game is about to start," she mumbled.

"Allison, look up," Annette said firmly, confiscating her purse.

"Allie."

She froze.

Because Davis was standing in front of her now. Her eyes took a long time traveling up, up, up his tall body and finally settled on his eyes. His beautiful eyes, at once hopeful and unsure.

"What?" she squeaked. Amber snorted.

"Hi," he said again.

A lot was packed into that greeting.

What are you doing right now?

I miss you.

You left!

I'm here now.

He crouched until he was eye level, and he was pushing her glasses up until she could see his beautiful eyes with the crinkly corners moving over her face. His wonderful, comforting soap and laundry detergent smell filled her senses. Suddenly, the longing of the last week was too much.

"What are you doing?" she asked shakily.

"I came to give you something," he said, holding out his hand. "If I'm not too late."

In it was a wild, riotous bouquet of colorful wildflowers, and mixed in were several pure white daisies, their centers like little stars. It had all been wrapped in familiar black-and-white craft paper. Annette's signature wrapping. Surely that was a coincidence? She glanced at Annette with her brows raised. She gave her a cool nod.

A blessing, so to speak.

"Oh, for Christ's sake," Corbin said irritably. "Shouldn't you be coaching my kid or something?" The aunts turned simultaneously to hiss at him.

"I love daisies," she finally whispered, meeting Davis's eyes. They were warm and dark as velvet, gentle on her face, and she knew the message in them now.

"I know you do, sweetheart," he said quietly. "And I love you."

"You do?" she whispered. The bleachers were silent, so silent she heard the thwack of the ball on the catcher's mitt while he warmed up.

"I think you're the bravest, most worthy, most beautiful woman in the world, and if you'll give me another chance, I promise you I will work harder than I ever have in my life to be exactly what you deserve."

Tears streamed down her face, but she managed to nod. "Okay." *Okay? That was her answer?* She didn't even know because she was close to ugly crying. Davis didn't seem to care. His hands threaded through her hair, cupping her face gently.

"Thank you, sweetheart," he whispered gravely. Then he kissed her. Softly. Tenderly. His lips just barely settled over hers as the ump yelled out, "Play ball!"

"I have to go," he said louder, grinning because the aunts were cheering now. Cheering and crying.

"I told you he'd get his head out of his ass eventually," Sophia was telling whoever would listen while she dabbed at her eyes with a hankie.

"Go on then," Annette said irritably, "and make sure you win this game."

Davis got to his feet. "I'm on it, ma'am," he said winking at her.

Allie watched in amusement as a slow flush spread across Annette's cheekbones. Nobody could resist Davis when he smiled like that. She settled back with her bouquet to watch the game.

Now, if Sammy could get a hit, today would be perfect.

Davis was sweating bullets.

He didn't usually put too much stock in winning or losing a Little League game. Kids had to do both to grow. It was just part of life, but he'd be lying if he said he didn't want to win this one. The boys were pumped up, the crowd was wild, and they were the underdogs. Even Allie's ex was here to see it. He didn't much care for the guy, but Sammy loved him, and that was enough to make Davis start sweating.

He checked the scoreboard. They were down by two in the last inning, with two outs, and bases loaded. They just needed a solid hit to win. Just one base hit.

It all came down to Sammy.

This was the perfect recipe for a comeback. *Or a disaster.* Davis kept his face perfectly relaxed as he strolled over to where Sammy was taking practice swings at home plate. His face was pinched, his shoulders up around his ears. The poor kid was 0-2 for the game, and now it all came down to him. Didn't that just figure?

"Hey, Sammy."

"Coach." Sammy stopped swinging and looked up at Davis with big hazel eyes. *Ah, hell.*

He was such a good kid. Respectful. Kind. A good teammate, even if he wasn't the most skilled player. Dammit. He wanted this win for Sammy.

"How do you feel right now?"

"Like I want to throw up."

Davis laughed at that then crouched in front of him to look him in the eyes. "Do you like playing baseball?"

"Yeah." He scuffed his cleat in the dirt. "I love it."

"What does it feel like when you and Ben are playing ball in the backyard?"

Sammy's eyes lit up. "It's my favorite thing to do," he said solemnly.

Davis settled his hand on Sammy's shoulder and felt his body shaking. "Then that's what you're going to think about, okay? Just you and Ben, hitting some balls in the backyard, just for fun."

Sammy thought about it. "Okay... but you, too."

"Me too?"

"Yeah, it's the best when you're there with us."

Sammy's heart showed in his eyes, and Davis pulled him in for a quick, fierce hug. Such a good kid. "I feel the same, kid. Now, have fun out there, got it?"

"Got it, Coach." Sammy smiled at him, the tension on his face was replaced by a determined jut of his chin. *Just like his mother's.* His stance was solid, hands choked up on the bat. From the dugout, the team started to chant.

"*We want a single, just a little single. S-I-N-G-L-E, single, single, single.*"

Sammy loaded up. And swung too early.

"Nice and easy, bud. Watch the bat hit the ball," he called out.

Strrrrike one!

Come on, Sammy. His insides were churning. The crowd was silent now, collectively holding their breath.

Strrrrike two!

"You got this, Sammy!" Allie yelled from behind them.

This was it. The last out that would determine the game.

"Sammy," Davis called out, his voice casual. "You know who Peter from the Hankies is?"

Sammy grinned and loaded up, remembering. "No, Coach, but I know who Derek Jeter is!" His knees bent, hips twisted, and he swung the bat with the force of his whole body.

Crack.

The ball rocketed in a line drive over the third baseman's head into the shortened outfield. Sammy stood stock-still for a second, bafflement on his face. Then he took off like a shot, legs pumping, arms swinging as he ran toward first base, caught sight of the ball, and kept going to second as the runners from second and third base slid into home. One run. Two runs.

They were tied now. Sammy slowed down as he rounded third, looking for the ball. The outfielder bobbled the ball, and Sammy ran home with a grin lighting up his whole face.

Home run.

So rare, so coveted by all the boys, and it was all Sammy's. The crowd went wild. Feet stomping on metal, screaming, and cheering like it was the World Series instead of a Little League game. Amid all the noise, the Northfield boys charged the field and surrounded Sammy. Davis hoisted him on his shoulder, and Sammy's face—that was the stuff a kid's dreams are made of. His eyes lit up, his dirt-streaked face beaming as he took it all in from up high.

Davis searched the stands for Allie and laughed out loud in

pure appreciation at the sight. She was jumping up and down on the bleachers with the rest of her family, hands in the air, tears streaming down her beautiful face.

Damn, but he loved that woman.

"You go on in for a minute, kids. I need to talk to your mom," Davis said, holding the door with one hand and not letting go of Allie's with the other. They had been touching in one way or another since after the game, and Allie's heart rate hadn't settled down since.

The team had all gone to the Northfield Dairy for ice cream after the game to celebrate. A wonderful way to end the season, but Allie hadn't had a minute alone with Davis yet.

Claire glanced meaningfully at their hands, which were locked together, and giggled when Allie tugged her ponytail as she walked by. Sammy and Ben were already pulling blankets off the couch to make a fort.

"Come sit down." He led them over to her beloved porch swing and held it steady as she got on. She lit the candles next to her and grabbed the blanket to spread over their laps.

They rocked in silence for a minute. The sun was setting, and it was a brisk night. It would be Halloween next weekend. Allie was excited for Sammy to celebrate his first one in North-field. The whole village got into it with costumes and decorations, and all the businesses on Main Street handed out candy.

"That was some game. I still can't believe Sammy's face when he hit that ball," Allie said as Davis draped an arm over her shoulders and tucked her into his side. That settling, the subtle shift and meld when their bodies fit together, took her breath away for a minute with the rightness of it.

"Hey," he said, his eyes roving her face as if it had been

months instead of a week since they had last been together. She devoured his beautiful features just as hungrily. The sharp planes of his cheekbones, his proud nose. Those beautiful, masculine lips that had touched hers so briefly at the game.

"Hey, yourself," she said.

He brushed his lips across her forehead. "I missed you."

She kept it together, just barely. "I missed you too."

His face was as serious as she'd ever seen it. "I'm sorry for pulling away that night. I wish I could go back and be there for you in the way you needed me that day. I can't promise I won't mess up again, but I can promise that I'll do everything in my power to be the one sitting here on this porch, rocking with you for the rest of our lives."

His first kiss landed on her forehead. "I love the way you make me laugh." A kiss on her cheek. "I love how you take care of the people around you." He slid his lips down, took her jaw between his strong teeth, and nibbled. "I love the way you pretend you don't like feeding me." He soothed the spot with his lips. Her eyes closed, and she tipped her head back.

"Mmm, you do?"

"Yeah, I do. Can I kiss you the way I couldn't earlier?"

Who was she to argue?

"Ew, they're kissing again!" Ben, or maybe Sammy, whispered loudly.

"Scram, kids," Davis ordered gruffly, and Allie peeked around him to see the three of them standing in the light of the doorway watching with big grins.

"We'll be inside in just a minute, kids." She tried to sound normal. The door slammed closed again, and it was quiet and dark except for their breathing.

"I think they're pretty happy about us," she said finally when her breath evened out.

"They've already made it clear that I better not mess this up."

He leaned in and brushed a soft kiss across her mouth. "The day I met you, I knew that you'd give me a run for my money. You were prickly and prone to accidents"—he lifted his head to grin wickedly when she sputtered, but then he got serious—"but I couldn't keep away from you." His eyes were dark and intense as he lifted her hand to his mouth and kissed her palm. "I promise I'll be the man you deserve."

"I love you too." Her eyes welled up, and he used his thumbs to brush away the tears. This was it. The happily ever after, and it was too much to contain. The dream she'd had since she was a little girl watching other families was finally coming true. She was already picturing babies with Davis's dark hair and fine features that Claire and Ben and Sammy would adore. Her heart felt so light she wanted to float except... "Why are you frowning?"

Davis's eyebrows were drawn together, and his lips were pressed into a tight line. He looked more like a man squaring up for bad news than someone who had just confessed his love. "Are you going to want to do the whole dating thing?"

She raised an eyebrow. "You don't want to date me?"

"No, I want to marry you." The exasperation was clear in his voice. "But if you want to date for a while, we can do that too." Davis sighed.

Wait.

"Did you just ask me to marry you?"

He scowled. "Of course, I want to marry you. This is a forever thing for me, sweetheart."

"Oh, well, I might say yes," she managed casually, despite the tears in her eyes because she would never stop trying to tease a smile out of him.

A cheer went up from the house when Davis leaned over, grinning too big to kiss her properly. She didn't mind. Davis's smile was the most beautiful sight in the world.

Epilogue

ONE YEAR LATER...

Allie licked her thumb and tried to smooth the stubborn cowlick on Sammy's hair while he wiggled away to peek out through the double doors of a packed church. The first strains of music filtered out, and she took a deep breath.

"Are you nervous, Mom?" Sammy noticed, taking her hand. "There's a lot of people out there."

There were indeed. The old church was packed full on this beautiful early fall afternoon. It felt like everyone in the village and then some had come out to wish her and Davis well.

Over the last year, their families had met and spent time getting to know each other. Annette invited Shep and Layne, as well as Davis's parents, to a few Sunday dinners. Allie had been worried at first her family would be overwhelming (and she kept a close eye on the wine intake after dinner), but it went beautifully. Davis's family was thrilled to welcome Sammy and her too.

Much like the last year with Davis, things had fallen into place as if they were meant to be. They had found a lovely old Craftsman home near the village that would fit them all comfortably, even in the future. She gently touched her still-flat belly, savoring the news she had yet to tell Davis.

Her favorite part of their new home was the porch swing that Davis put in for her as a surprise before they moved in. She'd cried hard seeing that little detail.

"I'm not nervous at all, honey bear," she answered Sammy truthfully. "I'm so happy."

"Uh-oh, you're happy leaking again," Sammy said with a grin.

Looking handsome and so grown up, Sammy held out his arm. They stepped together over the threshold.

"Hey, Dad," Sammy stage-whispered as they passed the very last pew in the back, waving.

Corbin nodded, a little stiffly, but he smiled and waved at Sammy as they walked by. Talk about a surprise guest, but Sammy had asked if they could invite him. Allie would have bet a million bucks he wouldn't have wanted to come, but it wasn't the first time she was wrong.

Thank goodness for that.

The tears slid down her cheeks as she walked down the aisle past the faces she had come to know and love. Mrs. Autovino and Lucy waved when she walked by. Many of her new friends from school had come to celebrate with them. Sammy's teacher, Sadie, and her hunky police officer husband, Rob, Mrs. Gayle, and Sylvia and her husband had come back from the lake to be there.

She dabbed her eyes when she passed Keri and Toby and Ford and Killian, all looking so sharp in their suits and ties, each one a little part of her and Davis's love story.

The aunts were in the front row, decked out in their finest. A feather bobbed on Sophia's hat, and Giulia batted it away from her face with a scowl. Annette sat regally waiting with Amber, Lily, and Evie.

Amber leaned over the edge of the pew as she passed to blow her a kiss, her slinky red dress standing out in the sea of sedate colors. Allie caught it and blew it back. Her sister might not believe in her own happily ever after, but Allie had enough faith for both of them that Amber was next.

Finally, Davis stood at the end of the aisle waiting patiently. He towered over the priest, looking darkly handsome and slightly intimidating in his suit and tie, yet when their eyes met, his were tender. Ben and Claire, from their positions on either side of him, stood solemnly, and Allie gave them a watery smile. So many blessings.

"Who gives this woman away?" Father O'Connell asked the question they had rehearsed last night.

"We do," the kids said together, and now Davis's eyes were suspiciously wet.

"Thank you," Allie whispered, leaning down to kiss each of their cheeks before putting her hand in Davis's warm one.

"Oh." Sammy popped up in between them. "I forgot to take those." He reached for the bouquet, a mix of wildflowers and daisies of course, but missed. Just when it would have fallen to the floor, Davis bent and rescued it. Their heads cracked against each other's, and Davis let out an *oof*, making the church laugh as he rubbed his head ruefully.

Dark eyes. Square jaw. Broad shoulders.

One completely in-love man looking right at her.

THE END

If you enjoyed this book, please consider leaving a review to help other readers find it. Thank you!

∾

Want more of Allie and Davis? Would you like to read a bonus scene featuring Davis's favorite apron?

Subscribe to my newsletter by tapping the link or use the QR code below to read *THE OTHER SIDE OF FOREVER*'s bonus scene!

Already subscribed? Keep an eye out for the playlist inspired by this book and nab Northfield's most infamous recipes right in your inbox! Norah XX

Continue the Series

Don't miss Amber's story next in *Maybe Someday With You*. A flirty, steamy, enemies-to-lovers, opposites-attract match between the bombshell and the boss, Northfield's straight-laced and sexy mayor, Theo Clairmont.

Read Maybe Someday With You now!

Continue the Series...

Connect with Norah

Northfield Bonus Materials

Want to read a bonus scenes, listen to the playlists inspired by this series, and nab Northfield's most infamous recipes?

Subscribe to <u>my newsletter</u> for all the bonus content!

Join <u>our Facebook reader group</u> for bonus content, sneak peeks, sales, and book news.

<u>Follow me on Amazon</u> for preorder and new release alerts.

For book sales and news,follow me on BookBub!

Or tap the QR code for all the links!

Acknowledgments

While this book is a work of fiction, there are bits and pieces of me sprinkled throughout that made it very special to write.

From Allie's experience growing up, her family of wonderfully loud and inappropriate women, and starting over only to come out stronger, there are themes here that I bet you can relate to as well. Who doesn't love a good comeback story?

I especially want to acknowledge my niece, Lauren Sherman, and the thousands of kids diagnosed with type 1 diabetes every year. You show us all what being brave looks like.

Thank you to Lauren and my sister, Jennifer, for answering my questions while researching this book. Any mistakes are mine.

With that said, this book would still be on my computer if not for a small group of wonderful people.

To my husband, Tom, and our three kids, thank you for being patient with me on the many nights and weekends I disappeared into the office to write "just one more chapter." Your love and support mean everything to me.

My mom, Linda, and my sisters, Melanie and Jennifer, to all of my aunts and cousins, and all the other rabble-rousing women in my life for paving the way.

Amy Gamet, office mate, fellow romance author, and dear friend, thank you for generously sharing your time and knowledge about the writing and publishing industry.

My beta readers for reading Allie and Davis's story and helping shape it in its earliest stages.

Julie Days for her brilliant help on each draft of this story. Your gentle nudges pushed me in the best possible way.

Jessica Romito for reading each draft and responding to my frantic texts with patience and gentle feedback. Everyone needs a hype squad like Jess.

Echo Grayce from Wildheart Graphics for her gorgeous covers.

Lara Zielinsky from LZ Edits for gracefully not mentioning my inability to keep tenses correct.

To my ARC and other early readers, thank you endlessly for your excitement and help in sharing this story. It is not easy to send out a book baby into the world, but you guys made it a lot less intimidating.

Oh, and one more—I have to mention Herself, the inimitable Diana Gabaldon, and her book *I Give You My Body*, which inspired the Sunday dinner scene with the aunts and their naughty synonyms.

And finally, to every reader who took a chance reading a new author, enjoyed the story, and shared it with a friend. I am so grateful to you.

About the Author

Norah Pritchard has been reading romance novels since middle school when she found her mother's gold mine of mass-market paperbacks, and she hasn't looked back since.

She teaches in higher education by day, and by night you can find her writing about swoony, sexy heroes and sassy, independent ladies who aren't afraid to ask for what they want. She lives in New York with her husband and three children.

Find her at norahpritchard.com